WARRIOR'S SONG

Song of Prophecy Series Book 2

P.E. PADILLA

PARTIAL MAP OF DIZHELIM

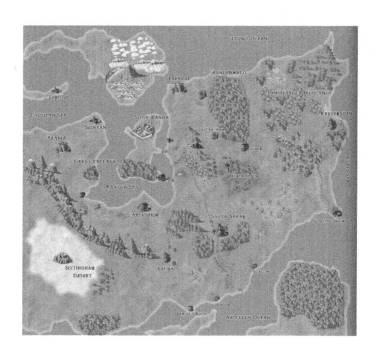

Some of the so-called scholars adhere to the belief that the Prophet's words, and the Prophecy itself, are figurative and do not reflect a literal future. They should be flogged and have their quills taken away.

The History of the War of Magic...and Beyond, by Devis Tousel, Historian, formerly Historian, Second Rank in the Souveni emperor's court, Year 29 AOD.

PROLOGUE

Suuksis, lord among the animaru in their dark world Aruzhelim, watched the creatures he had captured, confused by their shapes, colors, and actions. And, of course, by their weakness. How could the others, in the world called Dizhelim, have sent these as explorers when they were so weak? Before his eyes, they seemed to be withering.

The group had somehow crossed the great expanse between Aruzhelim and Dizhelim, something none of the animaru had ever been able to do. It would have taken tremendous power, or at least vast knowledge, to accomplish it. Suuksis's god S'ru himself could not manage it. The animaru lord would never say that aloud, of course, but he thought it. As long as he was not in his god's presence.

The figures below him, in a pit that served as a prison, moved around, trying to devise an escape. The animaru's mouth twisted into what could be called a smile—though animaru typically did not do such things—showing his pointed teeth as his dark eyes glinted in the near blackness. The expression was a relic from when the animaru themselves were in Dizhelim all those centuries ago, and he had kept the habit, one of the few who did.

Aruzhelim was a world of darkness. Even at the height of the day, the world and all in it was dim. Ancient stories revealed that Dizhelim, from which the animaru had been banished, was bright and had colors. Suuksis couldn't understand why, didn't remember seeing such things. What did colors do? They could not aid one in fighting nor make one stronger. What was the use? It was just another show of weakness from the world his people no longer had need of. They had come to Aruzhelim, and they were more powerful because of it.

Dizhelim had changed. Or the animaru had. He didn't recall the creatures—he remembered they were called *fessani* in the animaru tongue—being so weak, though it had been more than eight thousand years since that time so he might have forgotten some of the details. The things in the pit would never have been able to cast out his people if the war had been in current times.

Suuksis wondered if he could learn any useful magic from his captives. He had been trying to communicate with them, but their language had changed. The groups understood each other, but all nuance was lost. It was like communicating with the forgren, among the lowliest of creatures on Aruzhelim.

As the animaru lord watched, one of the fessani grew closer to another. The smaller one had been leaking some kind of fluid from its eyes and the larger had wrapped its appendages around the other. Now, they were moving, vibrating, and making grunting sounds. It fascinated Suuksis. Were they sharing power or casting magic?

The activity did not last long, and then the creatures settled down to rest. They rested often. It seemed good for little, but it was part of their ritual. Suuksis noted in his mind to ask about it the next time he spoke with the captives. And he would ask about what he had just witnessed.

Unfortunately, his learning was curtailed by the fact that the weak creatures were failing. He had found, through experimentation and crude communication with the creatures, that they needed to put things into their bodies to continue to function. They put some of the succulent plants growing near his compound into their bodies, through their mouths. Something of the magic or darkness in Aruzhelim affected them adversely, it seemed. Two already had succumbed and all of their natural processes had ended. He had given their unmoving bodies to some of his faithful servants for their amusement.

The remaining fessani seemed to have been affected somewhat by their absence. Suuksis wondered why the two did not rise again. If they had the twinkling, then why were their bodies still where they had stopped moving instead of transporting to their home? Asking the remnants did no good. They were too inferior to understand him well. He would have to observe and find out for himself.

Time passed, and more than half of the prisoners succumbed to their new environment. The opportunity to study the creatures would soon be gone. Suuksis had to take advantage of it. It was time to experiment.

He chose one of the smaller creatures and had it brought to him. From its shape, he determined it was a female, somewhat like the animaru females, with their requisite differences in anatomy. He had noted such things on some of the animaru as well, but had never figured out what the differences indicated.

He remembered some of this from before the banishment, but he had never cared much for learning about the others that had shared Dizhelim with his people. Except for how to kill them. They had been at war for almost three hundred years before being sent to Aruzhelim.

Emulating the actions he had witnessed with the two creatures, he found that interesting changes occurred both in his own body and in that of the creature. Their anatomical differences seemed to fit each other well. He had it taken back to the holding pit while he noted the information in his log. After that, he let it slip his mind as one of many thousands of experiences from which he had gained knowledge.

The other fessani died off one by one until there was only the smaller creature he had studied. It seemed to have changed shape, with a large protrusion growing at its middle. Fascinated, he watched the sole remaining creature carefully as it seemed to grow more misshapen every day.

As Suuksis sat going over the reports of his minions some time later, a strange sound reached his ears. It sounded like a wounded aliten and seemed to be coming from the prisoner pit. When he looked down into the area, he was surprised to see not one, but two creatures: the misshapen one and another, much smaller one.

Where had it come from? Why was it so small? How would it survive? Its size was not only negligible, but it did not seem to have full control of its own appendages. Curious.

But he had work to do, so he pushed the creature from his mind and continued with his reports. He would investigate the appearance of the tiny creature soon enough.

It was some time before Suuksis remembered to inspect the new thing that had appeared in his domain. He sent for both his prisoners to be brought to him. To his surprise, the original creature, the one that had come from Dizhelim, had regained its shape. The malformation was gone. But the smaller one, that was the true surprise.

Standing on its own feet, the little creature had grown since he had seen it last. It stood waist-high to the other one and appeared to have gained some semblance of control over its limbs. He drew closer to see it better.

The small one had a darker complexion than the other creature, though not so dark as one of the animaru. It had a color; Suuksis believed it was called blue. Instead of an abundance of the fine fur the other creatures had, the smaller one had a little on the top of its head, and even that was shorter than most of the other creatures that had been captured. It also had something coming out of the top and back of its head. They looked much like tentacles of aceti animaru. Other than that, though, its form resembled the other prisoner.

When Suuksis asked where the smaller creature had come from, the larger creature—which had learned to communicate more effectively—said it had been "born" from itself; that it had come out of the creature. Suuksis laughed at the most ridiculous thing he had ever heard. There were old myths about how the other creatures in Dizhelim made more of their own kind, but it could not be believed.

Suuksis struck the creature, causing it to fly from him and slide across the floor of his chamber. It knew better than to tell false tales. Realizing he would get no other answers, he sent the two back to the pit and promptly forgot about them again. There was war to wage on other factions and S'ru's favor to strive for. Investigating this inferior creature would not gain the dark god's attention.

Some time later, another strange sound came from the prisoner pit. He had almost forgotten he still had any held in that particular place. The noise was not wholly unlike the last one he had heard, when the smaller creature had appeared. Wondering what he would find, Suuksis looked down, but was disappointed. He saw only the smaller creature, though it was bigger than the last time he had seen it, and the other one. The larger's body was splayed out on the pit floor, unmoving.

Realizing it had broken down and stopped functioning, as the others it had come to Aruzhelim with had, he ordered one of his minions to take the body away. As an afterthought, he ordered the other creature to be brought to him.

He was impressed at the rate of growth of the strange creature. He didn't think it was one of the fessani; it had somehow been generated here, within his stronghold.

It was taller now, up to his own waist, and it moved like it knew how to use its limbs. Its color had changed a little, slightly darker than it had been before, and its eyes were unlike a fessani's, large and colored a little lighter than its skin. They almost glowed.

"Can you speak?" Suuksis asked it.

"Yes," it answered in the accent shared by the other prisoners.

"How did you learn to speak?"

"My mother taught me."

Suuksis paused, wondering at this word the creature had spoken.

"What is 'mother'?" he asked.

"The one who bore me, the one who just died, that you had your minion take away."

"I see," Suuksis said. "Mother. What shall I do with you? Have you any use?"

The small creature glared up at him, defiance spelled out in the blaze in her eyes and her proud stance. Suuksis respected the strength it tried to show.

"None?" he said. "Then perhaps I should give you to my underlings for them to do with you as they please. I have no time to study you. There are many things I must do, with war against at least three other decur occupying my time right now."

"I can do whatever I need to do," it said. "Whatever you want me to do."

"Hmm. Well, maybe you can perform menial tasks in the stronghold. You do not look to have any strength, but perhaps there is something suitable. See Arxus and it may be that you will live another day."

The small creature was taken away to live or die. It mattered not to Suuksis. He had S'ru's favor to gain and enemies to defeat.

The blue creature, easily spotted amongst the animaru because they were all darker and without color altogether, performed its tasks as ordered. Suuksis asked about it occasionally, if only because he wondered how long it would survive. He caught sight of it from time to time and it had grown taller every time. More, it had developed the growths on its upper body the other prisoner, its "mother" had possessed. If it was the same as with animaru, that would mean it was female.

A day came when Suuksis was inspecting the animaru under his command. He strolled the practice yard and watched his troops train, all of them, from his high-level fighters down to the nearly useless forgren. A flash of color in one corner of the field caught his eye.

Two of the desid were pressing the creature Suuksis had allowed to live. They looked ready to attack it, but for what reason Suuksis could not determine. He moved closer to get a better look, sure the creature would be torn to pieces. The claws of the desid were sharp, and the other creature was as unarmored as the visitors that had died in his prison pit.

One of the animaru swiped at the blue creature with a razor-sharp claw. The creature shockingly ducked under it and kicked the animaru in the face with a crunch. It turned and, before the other animaru could attack, balled up its fingers and slammed them into the other desid's head, knocking it down. As the two animaru tried to rise, the blue creature stomped down on their faces and necks repeatedly.

One of them had the twinkling and, after several blows, disappeared to respawn elsewhere. The other grew still, so damaged that it would take some time to recuperate enough to move again.

The blue victor spat on the remaining animaru and returned to the work it had been doing.

"What happened there?" Suuksis said, coming up to the creature. It jumped.

"Two of your minions attacked me."

"And?"

"I defended myself. I am no easy prey." The creature's light eyes glowed with its conviction.

"I see. How did you learn to defend yourself?"

The creature ducked its head and looked toward the ground. "I have watched some of your fighters practice. It is a simple thing. They were only desid."

"Indeed," Suuksis said. He considered his servant for a moment. It had learned to speak without the muddy accent of the fessani. Almost like a real animaru. "Would you like to learn more?"

Its eyes grew even brighter, almost painfully so, and its head snapped up. "I would. I am sure I could do well in combat, maybe even join your battle forces."

Suuksis laughed. "Do not get carried away. I meant only that you can train to learn combat and perhaps you can entertain me by fighting with the desid or maybe the forgren. If you become more skilled."

"I will learn, and I will show you that I can be a great warrior."

Chuckling at the audacity of the creature, Suuksis agreed. "Tell Arxus you have my permission to train. In addition to your regular tasks. I will not lose your work simply so I can gain a tiny bit of entertainment."

"As you command." The blue creature ran off to find Suuksis's officer.

Suuksis watched it go with interest. He looked forward to seeing it battle.

"Bring my blue creature to entertain me," Suuksis called out much later as he shared a meal with some of his closest allies.

Within minutes, he saw the color of his pet. It had grown again, nearly tall enough to look most of the animaru in the room in their eyes. At least the ones that stood on two legs and had eyes. It also moved with more grace than previously.

"What has happened to change it so?" Suuksis asked Zhelam, another of his officers.

"My lord, it has been practicing combat every moment it is not performing its assigned tasks," Zhelam answered.

"Has it been shirking responsibilities?"

"No. It does all its tasks with all its faculties. I have found nothing to complain about."

"Interesting," Suuksis said.

The blue creature stepped in front of Suuksis and bowed.

"You will engage in combat to entertain myself and my guests. Defeat your enemies or not. You will make it interesting."

"Yes, my lord." It turned to take its place at the edge of the combat square.

Suuksis waved his hand toward the ring and held up two fingers. Arxus pointed at two of the combatants sitting on the floor with others of their kind. They jumped to their feet and bowed, then turned toward their blue opponent.

"Begin," Arxus said.

The two animaru charged the lone blue creature. Both were seren, bipedal with sharp claws and teeth. The fur covering their bodies was short, not nearly long enough to be grasped, but rigid and coarse enough to cause cuts or abrasions on the delicate skin of their opponent.

The two animaru swiped at their foe at the same time.

And missed completely.

The blue fighter had jumped up and over its foes, flipping to land on its feet. It didn't remain there long. One of its legs shot out, colliding with the knee of one of its opponents. A snapping sound accompanied the leg bending backward in a position it was never meant to hold. The animaru to whom the leg belonged screamed.

Without letting the foot hit the ground, the blue creature swung it back the other way, its heel striking the second animaru in the face with such force the dark fighter's head snapped around and it dropped to the ground, its neck broken. It flashed and disappeared. The twinkling would cause it to reappear at its spawning point.

Before the combatant with the broken leg fell all the way to the ground, another blue limb shot out, grabbing the dark foe's head in a loop. The blue creature threw its leg out to generate momentum and flipped over backward, dragging the captured animaru along for the ride. Mid-flip, the animaru's neck snapped. By the time the blue creature—and its cargo— landed, the second opponent had a broken neck and lay on the floor unmoving. This one did not appear to have the twinkling. It would be several days before it regenerated enough to be ready for minimal labor.

Suuksis stared at the lithe azure combatant. It had incapacitated two mid-level animaru in a handful of seconds. Perhaps it did have some natural skill.

"Come," Suuksis said, waving the victor toward him. It approached him as bidden. "I directed you to make the fight entertaining, yet you ended it too quickly to be interesting. You will be beaten and will not be allowed to train for two days. The next time you have the opportunity to entertain me, you must do a better job of it."

The blue creature gritted its teeth and nodded. "As you command." It turned and walked toward the area set aside for punishment with its head held high.

Suuksis watched it go. This one had fire, he had to admit. And perhaps some skill that could be entertaining.

Gradually, Suuksis allowed his strange fighter to spend more time training and less on menial tasks. It continued to increase its skills and to defeat all the foes put in front of it, either singly or in groups. It was uncanny how skilled it had become in combat. It was time Suuksis learned more of the creature that was fast becoming his favorite combatant.

"You have done well in the contests," he told the creature. "Your skill is becoming impressive, maybe enough to make me think of allowing you to join our forces."

"I would be honored," it said. "I want only to defeat your enemies."

"To do so, you will have to fight me," he said. "To prove your worth."

Its eyes went wider than normal and they lightened, glowing more brightly than he had seen before. Suuksis resisted the urge to squint against the light. "My lord, I could not," it said.

"You will!" he spat. "Do not think that since you are a favorite pet that you can argue with me. Prepare for battle. I will not kill you, but I will not coddle you either."

It swallowed. "Yes. My lord."

Suuksis smiled and rushed at the thing. He was a master of many different weapons, but for this contest, his claws would be sufficient. His dusky grey form blurred as he moved with the speed only a few animaru could match. He struck out at his pet with his right claw.

It blocked his strike and returned one of its own, nearly

hitting him. If he hadn't tilted his head slightly, he would have been struck. How had this thing become so fast?

Suuksis increased his speed, slashing with his claws, sweeping with his legs, even thrusting his hairless round head at his opponent. None of the attacks managed to contact the blue thing, though a few got close.

Back and forth they battled, Suuksis releasing all restraint, trying to hit the elusive creature. Finally, he struck it a glancing blow, but was surprised when his opponent twisted, converting the momentum from the strike into a turn and a counterstrike that landed solidly on the side of his head.

He staggered back, and by reflex he threw a bolt of power at it. Realizing too late that he was probably going to kill his new toy, he despaired of losing it.

But the bolt never struck. Instead, his opponent moved its hands in small circles and intercepted the magic, deflecting it to the ground.

It had the use of magic.

"Stop," he shouted. "Where did you learn that? How did you gain the skill?"

The blue creature's eyes were even wider, but this time in obvious fear. "I—I do not know. I sensed the power coming toward me and I did what I felt to be the correct thing. Have I acted wrongly?"

Suuksis's anger abated. No one had trained it, then. Again, he was impressed with its natural talent. "No, not wrong. It is surprising, though, that you would have the use of magic. Most animaru do not, and you"—he waved his hand as if to display her to others—"are clearly not animaru. I am not really sure what you are."

"I am your servant," it said simply.

"Yes. I suppose you are. We will discuss this later. Perhaps I will test you to discover your affinity to magical forces. Continue training. You have not reached your potential yet."

It wasn't long until the God of Darkness, S'ru himself, heard of the strange blue warrior with some affinity for magic. He commanded his servant Suuksis to bring the creature to him so he could inspect her.

Standing in front of the essence of the god of Aruzhelim, the blue creature found favor in the god's eyes.

"I will take her to complete her training myself," he told Suuksis.

"Yes, my God," Suuksis said, shifting his eyes to the blue fighter that had up until a few minutes ago been his.

"It will not do for a disciple of S'ru to be nameless, however," the god said. Turning to the creature, he told her—for it was obviously female—"Your name will be Khrazhti, and you will be my greatest servant."

1

eden Tannoch inspected the one called Khrazhti, the former leader of the animaru that had come to destroy Dizhelim, from the side of his eye. He wasn't sure about her, or about much else since he had first fled the army of monsters that seemed to be after him.

She was tall, topping him by a couple of inches, and had the form of a human. A very fit and shapely human. Never mind that her body was a light blue-green. She had two shapely legs, two toned arms, all the other parts that would make her appear human as a silhouette, and she moved like a human, too. Like a dangerous, graceful human.

Maybe her head was a bit oddly shaped for a human. It was roundish and her forehead seemed longer than most people's, though that could be because of her hair. She had only short strands on the very top of her head, and she had... things coming out of the back of her skull. They kind of looked like tentacles. He was almost tempted to reach out and touch one. They appeared soft, like elongated earlobes, though she had those, too. They didn't move like tentacles. Maybe enlarged strands of hair?

Her nose wasn't quite human, either, though it wasn't a snout or anything so bestial. It was more like a human nose but pushed flat. It changed her appearance, made the few facial expressions she used look a little bit off. She wasn't hideous or even particularly ugly. Just...different.

The most dramatic thing about her appearance, if you didn't count the strange coloring, was her eyes. They were wide, bigger than a human's—though maybe they only looked that way because of being near her flattish nose—and had no pupils. They were a very pale blue color and they seemed to glow. For an animaru, it seemed strange to Aeden. All the other ones he'd seen were darker colored and shunned the light, but Khrazhti's eyes held a soft radiance. Strange.

The animaru seemed to sense his scrutiny and turned her head to him. He realized he had turned as well, not merely viewing her out of the side of his eye any longer, but standing there staring at her. She blinked once, cocked her head, and stared back, expressionless.

"We should probably go now," Tere Chizzit said, allowing Aeden to break eye contact and look toward the man. The grizzled archer was standing to Aeden's left in the stone audience chamber where they had battled Khrazhti and finally defeated her. It wasn't any easier to look into Tere's eyes. They were the milky white of blindness and they still made Aeden uncomfortable when he had to meet them.

Somehow, the older man could still move around and "see" though he was blind. Even stranger, he was by far the most astounding archer Aeden had ever seen or heard of. He could hit a fly buzzing a hundred feet away. Aeden had seen the man do things with his arrows that should have been impossible for someone with perfect eyesight, let alone a blind man. He still hadn't puzzled out how Tere did it, but he was glad the bald, white-bearded man was on his side.

"Why leave?" Urun Chinowa asked. "We have here the

leader of the animaru. She has made a vow to aid us. She's on our side. When the rest of the animaru get back, she can tell them we're allies now and we'll have an instant army. The war is over, don't you see? We can relax now."

Urun's dark hair was a mess, as always, and he had three day's growth of beard on his face. The nature priest of the goddess Osulin had argued with the party's course of action every step of the way since he joined them, but he was a good ally to have. His healing spells alone made him worth any trouble he caused ten times over. Well, maybe five times.

Aeden hadn't really considered what Urun said, but it seemed logical. Khrazhti was the leader of all the animaru that had been transported from their dark world Aruzhelim to Aeden's world, Dizhelim. She was the top animaru authority on this side of the vast expanse separating the two worlds. Maybe they *were* actually done.

Thinking of Khrazhti made Aeden look back toward the statuesque animaru. She was paying close attention to all of them as they spoke. She understood only her own language, an animaru variation of Alaqotim, the ancient language of magic.

In fact, hers was probably closer to the original language as it had been given by the gods. The animaru culture didn't seem to change as much as humans did. While the languages on Dizhelim had probably morphed over the centuries, Aeden doubted the animaru language had.

"Raki," Aeden said. "Can you please translate for Khrazhti so she understands what's going on?"

"Uh, I can try," the boy said. "My Alaqotim isn't very good. Tere's is better."

Raki was slight and small. At fifteen years old, he probably hadn't reached his full height yet. Aeden hoped not, anyway; he could use a few inches. His mop of brown hair never behaved and his brown eyes never rested. He had been learning how to move silently from Tere, along with other skills Aeden wasn't sure about. The boy seemed to have some kind of magic that allowed him to virtually disappear when he wanted to. It had come in handy in the past few months, and Aeden was sure it would again.

Not only that, though. Raki was a natural with any thrown weapon. He had picked up the ability to strike his target with knives, spikes, anything edged, really, more quickly than should have been possible. Aeden figured that was another magical gift. The Gypta people had more magic in their blood than many other groups of people. At least they got some good from being a generally despised, wandering race.

Raki stepped up to Khrazhti and looked up at the tall animaru. He started to stumble through sentences, doing what Aeden had asked. The blue woman swiveled her head to Aeden and nodded to him, the light in her eyes twinkling. Aeden nodded back, feeling that their new ally knew much more than she should with the limitations of the language. He looked forward to learning to communicate with her.

He also hoped she wouldn't murder them all in their sleep.

The stone walls and the high ceilings around them made spoken words echo slightly before they were captured by the ragged tapestries hanging on the walls. The room was in what used to be the main spire of a fortress long ago. The keep had been abandoned until the animaru had taken up residence to use it as a base.

Outside the windows stretched miles and miles of dusty, desolate land with rocks that looked like they had exploded out of the ground, trying to reach the sky. Watchtowers poked up at odd intervals on the hills surrounding the fortress. Most of the outbuildings were abandoned and crumbling, as the one they were in now was, to a lesser extent.

As Raki continued with his translation, Khrazhti began shaking her head and making comments of her own. Raki seemed to try to explain something to her, but she shook her head more vigorously and spoke again. Raki's look of frustration made Aeden take notice.

"What's wrong, Raki?" he asked.

"I don't really know," the boy said. "I was translating the part about staying put because she can command the animaru and she kept disagreeing. She was speaking too fast for me to understand it all. Something about an 'ardgyptous.'"

"Ardgyptous?" Tere repeated. "Is that what you said? I don't recognize that word." He turned to Khrazhti and spoke with her for a moment. She answered him and he seemed to ask for clarification.

"Ah, she said it means 'disapproved one,' or simply 'disapproved.' It has something to do with their god, this S'ru, rejecting or casting out an animaru."

"So, it's like when the Church of Vanda casts out someone for doing wicked deeds?" Aila Ven asked. She was a devout follower of the god Vanda, after whom the church had been named. They'd had quite an argument a few weeks back about that very subject.

"Not quite," Urun said. "The Vandals cast people out if they don't pay the church enough, or for political reasons, even for personal reasons if someone has angered the high priest. With most gods, a casting out is more of a cutting off. There are tangible effects from it."

Aila Ven's brown eyes flashed and her mouth set.

"Stop," Tere said, listening to Khrazhti continue her explanation. "According to her, one who is ardgyptous will be attacked instantly by any other animaru. The worship of their god is not like it is here on Dizhelim. There is but one god on Aruzhelim, where Khrazhti is from. Everyone is a worshiper, or at least a subject, of S'ru.

"She says that she has observed once in her three thousand years of life an animaru being made ardgyptous. Every other animaru instantly turned on him and tore him to shreds. He did not have the twinkling, so he would have eventually recovered, she says, but then S'ru himself took part. The god is apparently the only one who can destroy an animaru permanently. Only he has the power."

"Wait," Raki said. "We have destroyed plenty of them."

Tere listened to Khrazhti, not even needing to translate. "She apologizes for the incomplete information. Some magic here in Dizhelim can destroy an animaru as well, something we have all discovered just recently."

"Life magic," Aeden said. "Some other types of magic seem to harm them, but only life magic can destroy them."

"Yes," Tere continued. "It fits. Aruzhelim has no life. The animaru are unliving and so can be affected by magic based on this strange power, in her words."

"But," Fahtin broke in. She had been quietly listening up to this point. She shook her long, chestnut hair and pursed her lips. "The animaru can't communicate with S'ru right now, so they don't know that Khrazhti is disapproved. She can pretend she's not and continue commanding them. Since there are no others in the world, she can continue the charade. At least, she can until more come."

Khrazhti shook her head again, chattering at Tere.

"I'm not really sure I understand everything," the archer said. "The dialect may as well be a different language, and I'm not proficient at Alaqotim anyway. I think she's saying that there will be no mistaking that she's ardgyptous. The sign will be there for all to see."

"Sign," Aeden said. "What sign?"

Whoever was going to speak next was interrupted by Aila's gasp. She pointed at Khrazhti. All other eyes went to the animaru as one.

Khrazhti had stopped speaking. Her eyes dropped and her mouth drooped into something very close to a human frown.

Her color was changing.

No, that was incorrect. Her color was lightening, going from a dark blue-green to a lighter color, coming close to a turquoise or teal. Her skin seemed to be dusted with radiance for a moment, and when she raised her eyes to meet Aeden's, the glow in them was more pronounced than before.

Aeden thought it made her look better, more human, more like someone good. He shook his head at his thoughts. Where had those come from?

Khrazhti muttered a few sentences and Tere nodded.

"She says now you understand. She has lost the blessings of S'ru, lost the darkness he had blessed her with. She is now easily recognizable as ardgyptous, but not just because of the color. S'ru has marked her and other animaru can sense her location. Any animaru that catches sight of her while she has the mark will instantly try to destroy her. It doesn't matter that they probably cannot."

"Probably?" Aeden asked.

"Yes," Tere said as the animaru was already explaining to him. "She is only half animaru. Without S'ru's blessing, it may be possible for them—or anyone—to kill her permanently."

2

"Wait," Aila said. "Are you telling me that our new ally is a beacon for all those creatures? They can track us because she's with us?"

Tere continued to translate out of habit, though by the time he finished with what Aila had said, he frowned at the woman. Khrazhti started speaking again and drew his attention back to her.

"She says that the 'mark' will be on her for a time. While it is, the animaru can sense her. When they are far away, they will just have a feeling of which direction she is in. As they become closer, they can pinpoint her location and use it to find her. The mark will fade with time."

"How much time?" Urun asked.

"She doesn't know," Tere said. "The only occasion she saw it in action, the ardgyptous was already surrounded by animaru. He tried to escape but was torn apart in minutes. She has never read or heard of how long it takes for it to fade. With an entire world full of animaru that suddenly turn on you, your lifespan is measured in minutes, not hours or days."

"And once it fades, then she can take command of the troops again?" Raki asked.

Tere shook his head. "No. They will always recognize her as ardgyptous. It's just that they won't be able to sense her presence to hunt her down after the mark has faded. She will still obviously be lacking S'ru's dark blessing. You saw her change. She has too much light in her now—or more correctly, absence of dark—to be accepted by even the most ignorant of animaru that come over from Aruzhelim. Besides, her disapproval is tied to S'ru's power. Every animaru on both worlds knows of her existence."

"Oh, great," Aila said. "As if it wasn't bad enough, now we have a signpost advertising where we are. The entire army will swarm us. She should leave and fend for herself."

"Aila!" Fahtin scowled at the smaller woman. "Look at Khrazhti and think of what you're saying. She has just been abandoned by her god for choosing to keep the laws he himself made, though he did not do so himself. She was his high priestess. Look at her. Can't you see how much it has affected her?"

Aeden looked over at the blue woman. Khrazhti's shoulders were slumped, head hanging down. The regal, confident warrior from earlier had been replaced by someone almost frail, someone who had the weight of the word—two worlds —upon her. Defeated. Abandoned. His heart felt like a lump of lead in his chest. He knew what it felt like to be cast off from everything he knew.

Fahtin went to the animaru and gently put her hand on the woman's shoulder. Khrazhti flinched, and Aeden thought for a moment she would shake the arm off or push it away, but the high priestess sighed and dipped her head again, caught up in her thoughts.

"No," Aeden said abruptly, causing Fahtin to start. "She is our ally. Her dedication to her beliefs, though they were given to her by her god, is so strong she's sacrificing everything to do right. We are not going to cast her off because things might get dangerous. We will let her stay with us for as long as she wants. If the other animaru can track her, then we will have to stay one step ahead of them until the mark fades. If they find us, then we will fight. No one needs to stay if they don't agree, but I am not going to abandon her because things are tough."

Fahtin smiled at Aeden and nodded firmly. Khrazhti lifted her head enough to meet Aeden's eyes. She blinked as if she had just realized he was standing there, and then dropped her gaze to the ground again.

Tere had translated, more out of habit than anything else, but now everyone was silent.

"I'm staying with you," Raki said. "We Gypta don't abandon our friends."

"Raki's right," Fahtin said. "We'll stand by you, Aeden. And Khrazhti."

"We still all have the same goal, as far as I see it," Tere said. "I'm in."

"Against my better judgment, I have to keep going," Urun said. "At least until Osulin tells me to quit." He looked up at the sky as if waiting for just such a communication. When nothing happened, he sighed.

All eyes turned to Aila Ven. She swallowed, eyes darting, avoiding anyone else's. "Oh, I wasn't serious. Of course I'll continue on. Who wants to live forever anyway?"

With that settled, the group began to discuss what they would do next.

"We don't have much choice right now," Tere Chizzit said. "Khrazhti said that they came to Dizhelim through a portal to the east of Broken Reach, where we are now. The other animaru went looking for us to the north and west, so as they come back to try to find the ardgyptous, they'll be coming from those directions. That leaves us only the south to try to escape. South toward Satta Sarak."

Aeden went through his memories of the place. He had traveled through there with his adopted Gypta family at least once, but sometimes his recollections got tangled up. The name Satta Sarak applied to both the city and to the nation for which it was the capitol. It was one of the great cities of Dizhelim. Ah, he remembered now. It was surrounded on three sides by the Mellanor Forest.

"Is it wise to go to where there are large numbers of people?" he asked Tere. "What will the animaru do when they get there, looking for us?"

"I'm not sure they're ready to attack entire cities yet." The archer looked to Khrazhti questioningly, then said something to her in Alaqotim.

Khrazhti's brow crinkled as she listened. It took a lot of effort on both sides to communicate. Tere had admitted his Alaqotim was not the best, and the animaru version of the language seemed to be different even than the one Tere knew.

After the blue woman had spoken, Tere translated. "Normally, they wouldn't attack a city yet. They are too few and are trying to hide their existence until more animaru arrive and they can attack in force. However, when someone with the mark is near, they will do everything and anything to get to her, even if it means their own destruction. The compulsion is too strong to resist."

"Then we will be leading danger and death to the city," Aeden said. "I will not be responsible for an entire city being destroyed. There has to be another direction we can go."

Tere shook his head. "We can go south and east, around the Mellanor Forest toward the coast and the Aesculun Ocean, but then we could be trapped. My plan was to get to Satta Sarak and get passage on a boat to the Kanton Sea. If we can do that, we can outrun the animaru and get to Hero

Academy. I'm assuming our goal is still to go the masters there to inform them of the danger and ask for information. Is that so?"

"Yes," Aeden said. "But I don't want to sacrifice other peoples' lives to do it."

"If we hurry, we should have a few days until we're overtaken. Once we're on the boat, they won't be able to catch us, but they'll know we're gone. There will be no need to attack the city."

While Tere was talking, Raki had taken over trying to translate for Khrazhti. She perked up at the last part and chittered something at the boy.

"She says that the animaru will not follow us onto the liquid that flows through channels," he said. "They don't understand it. It scares them."

"Good," Urun said. "It looks to me that the best and perhaps only choice is to get to Satta Sarak as soon as possible and get on a boat going north. If we have any chance of escaping, we need to get moving. I'm sure the monsters aren't going to wait around before coming after us."

They discussed it for a few more minutes, but there didn't seem to be a better option. The party gathered their gear and headed toward the southwest.

It took almost seven full days to make it to Satta Sarak. They ran for a time, then walked, alternating and sometimes inserting sessions of fast walking. The urgency of their plight kept them from sleeping more than a handful of hours each night, and the constant anticipation of being caught drained their energy.

Khrazhti fared best of all of them, despite the way the light of day seemed to sap her strength. Aeden believed it was because the animaru was accustomed to not sleeping. In any case, she moved through the terrain with the others, never complaining, hardly speaking, glowing eyes observing everything.

The land around them gradually transformed from the dry, fractured land of the waste around Broken Reach to having small patches of vegetation and then to areas that, while not lush, looked that way compared to the land they had passed through. Small, rolling hills with trees and other greenery dotted their path as well, relieving the flat and cracked landscape.

On the sixth day, they spotted a green and brown splotch on the horizon.

"What is that?" Raki asked as the party crested a rise.

"It's the Mellanor Forest," Tere said without looking up. "You'll be able to see Satta Sarak in a few hours, if we continue at this pace."

Aeden wondered if the archer ever needed to point his head in the direction he was looking. How did his strange sight work?

"We're almost there," Fahtin said. She swept her gaze behind them to make sure no one was following them. "We're going to make it."

"Focus on what's ahead," Tere said. "We have a distance to go yet, and we need to be on a boat and away before the animaru get to us. Concentrate on what's important."

The others went silent and lengthened their strides. The trees were sparse and did not impede their travel, but Aeden thought it felt good to have something to hide behind—or in. He would be glad when they were standing on the deck of a boat traveling north.

As the party got closer, the details of the city grew. Aeden and the two Gypta had been through the area before with the family, but Aeden had never seen it from the angle they approached: from the north.

How different the picture before him was from the village

he was born into in the highlands of the Cridheargla. The Croagh aet Brech—it meant Blood Warriors in the Chorain language—lived in small groups according to their clans, not in walled cities. People called them Crows, but it was a mispronunciation of the word Croagh and not because they were like the ebony birds in any way.

Satta Sarak sprawled before them, a series of walls surrounding sections of the city with one large wall encircling the entire thing. There were no main roads near them, so there was only a small gate ahead, and it was closed tight. They would have to travel around the wall toward the south until they got to one of the larger gates.

"*Aruna recipia dui!*" Aeden said under his breath. Khrazhti blinked at him. Twice. "Oh. Sorry." He'd have to remember not to use Alaqotim curses around her.

The city itself looked like chaos incarnate. Because of the hills within the city, they could see parts of it clearly when they were a distance from the wall. Buildings were scattered around in no apparent pattern, built anywhere they could be built, even on the side of a hill. Within and surrounding the sturdy brick structures were trees of all kinds. It did not appear that they were planted around the city; it looked like the city had to cut its way into the area where the trees lived and that it was a constant struggle to keep the vegetation from pushing in on the humans and reclaiming the lost space.

A sound reached Aeden's ears. He didn't recognize it at first. Turning his head toward Khrazhti, he was surprised to find her standing still with her eyes wide and her mouth open. Playing back the sound in his head, Aeden realized it had been a gasp.

His blue companion began chattering in her language. He had learned a few words from her in the days since she had joined them, but they did him no good with her speaking so quickly. He didn't understand any part of it.

"She's surprised," Raki said. "She has never seen trees and bushes like this. She didn't know there were this many in the whole world. Also, the color shocks her. There isn't really any color where she comes from. The green especially impresses her. "As he spoke, she continued to gesture not only at the city, but at the edge of the forest visible off to their left.

Aeden smiled imagining how she would react to flowers of many different colors. The world she came from had no color? How horrible would that be? A dozen things popped into his head, things he wanted to show her. Things that would make her gawk in wonder at how beautiful this world was. She needed to see what she was trying to save.

Khrazhti saw his smile and mirrored it. She still looked awkward when she wore a smile, almost like she put it on to mimic others, but he liked it when she smiled. He wondered if she had a sense of humor.

"Whatchya smiling at?" Fahtin asked, stepping up beside him.

"Khrazhti has never seen trees like this before and the colors are impressing her. It's almost like a child the first time she sees snow. Hey, I wonder if they have snow on her world. If not, it's going to really surprise her."

"Focus on getting to the city. She'll get used to all the sights, just like the rest of us have." Fahtin patted Aeden's arm and continued walking toward the city wall.

Aeden had to tap Khrazhti on the shoulder to get her attention. He pointed toward the wall and how far the others were ahead of them. She smiled at him again—this one a little more natural than the last—and moved ahead to catch up. As she did, Aeden gestured for her to pull the hood down on her cloak to cover her face. It was Fahtin's cloak. They had given it to her so she could keep all her skin out of sight. Even if she didn't cause a panic, people would definitely remember a blue-skinned woman. He felt bad she had to hide, but it was necessary.

Raki and Aeden shared a look and almost identical smirks at Khrazhti's reaction to the city and followed after the blue woman. Aeden told himself again he had to learn to speak with their new ally. She must be a fount of information, living for thousands of years like that. He wanted to talk to her. Besides, he needed to learn more Alaqotim anyway. It would help him with his work in translating the Song of Prophecy. Tere had said all the references to the Song he'd ever seen were in that language.

The wall hugged the hilly surface of the land, conforming to the rises and dips while still building it so that the top of the wall was level, creating the curious effect of the wall being different heights as it encircled the city. It seemed to Aeden that the builders made no effort at all to make the location more suitable for a city. Instead, they conformed their structures to how everything was when they found it. Because of this, the simple walk around the wall to the open gate was an exercise in hill climbing and descent. It took much longer than it should have for the short distance.

When the party did finally make it to the east gate of the main city wall, they were ready to sit down and rest. Tere shook his head and motioned for them to keep going.

"We don't know where our pursuers are," he said. "They could be behind that last hill. We can rest, but only after we check on a boat. We need to get out of this city as soon as possible or the animaru will catch us and probably do a lot of damage to the citizens to get at us."

There were grunts and moans, but no one argued. Khrazhti, only half listening to Raki translating, swiveled her head around as if trying to catch all the sights at once. Aeden chuckled once again. He wasn't sure what kind of cities they had in Aruzhelim, but if they did exist, they were apparently not like Satta Sarak. He'd have to ask her about it sometime.

"Satta Sarak," he said to her, waving his hand to get her attention. "The city is called Satta Sarak. The nation is also called the same thing."

Raki translated.

"Satta Sarak," Khrazhti said, swinging her arm out to encompass everything around them.

"Yes," Aeden said, smiling at her. "City. How do you say city in your language? How do you say nation?"

Raki translated that in Aruzhelim, *clasis* was a community, though they used the same word regardless of size. There was no word for nation, but there were forces and clans that had a single leader. These were called *decur*, though some specialized military groups were called *viris*.

Aeden continued to ask questions through Raki as the three followed Tere through other, smaller gates, and down streets ranging from wide cobbled roads to narrow hard-packed dirt. Aeden didn't pay it much attention. He was focused on his language lessons.

They finally reached the mighty Gwenore River. It spanned from the Kanton Sea in the north all the way to the Aesculun Ocean in the south. It split the city into two parts, but there were a number of high bridges connecting things. He had not seen the bridges when he had been in the city before with the family. They were impressive. There were also docks on either side of the wide waterway.

Khrazhti's head stopped swinging when she caught sight of the river. Her mouth parted as she stared at it.

"Raki," Aeden said. "How do you say river in Alaqotim?"

"Alveus," the boy said.

"Ah. Thanks." Aeden turned to Khrazhti. "Alveus. Alveus?" he repeated when she gave him a blank look.

"She doesn't seem to understand the word," Raki said.

"Maybe it's different in the animaru dialect." He spoke to Khrazhti for a moment, trying out different words. She didn't seem to recognize any of them.

"Aga?" Aeden said, remembering the word for water. The blue woman just shook her head.

Another few sentences from Khrazhti and Raki nodded. "Oh, they don't have water where she's from. None at all. She has seen a few streams since she's been here, but she hasn't seen anything this large."

"No water?" Aeden asked. "Then how do they survive? What do they drink?"

Tere stepped up to the trio. "Remember, Aeden, they're not alive. They are un-alive."

"Oh, right. I forgot about that." He turned to Khrazhti, made eye contact with her, and then pointed toward the Gwenore. "River. River."

"River," she said.

"Good."

"Come on now," Tere said. "We need to find a boat and get out of here as soon as we can. She'll learn all she needs to know about rivers when we're on it."

That sounded much easier than it proved to be. The next riverboat, *Brenain's Tears*, was not leaving to go north for three more days. They had no choice but to wait or to go on foot, a risky notion since the animaru would be coming from the north, the very direction they needed to go. They had plenty of money, taken from what the animaru had gathered at Broken Reach from their raids on towns and villages, so they paid for their passage and decided to settle in and try to lose themselves in the city. They hoped the animaru would not find them in time or that they would be hesitant to attack a large city, despite what Khrazhti said.

"We should find an inn in the middle of the city," Tere said. "We can get supplies, repair any weapons or gear we need to have mended, and be ready as soon as the boat leaves."

On the way toward their inn—Tere had been through the city many years before, he said, and knew where they could stay—Aeden felt as if someone's eyes were on him. He tried to scan the area and spot his hidden observer, but the streets were filled with people and he couldn't see anything out of the ordinary. If it had been a forest, he could have spotted whoever was viewing him, but cities always seemed to dull his senses. Chalking it up to anxiety over the animaru, he continued on, Raki and Khrazhti at his side and the others ahead.

$\mathscr{L}$ 3 $\mathscr{R}$

I zhrod Benzal covered his mouth with his hand, making a show of yawning. The thing in front of him didn't even pause in its speech. It was probably too stupid to understand the underhanded insult. Or it could be that it didn't know what a yawn was. Did the things even breathe? Probably not. The animaru were not alive, after all. They had un-life. He would have to think of another subtle way to insult it.

"Yes, yes," he finally said. "I understand that your god will be thankful for my help. We have an agreement. There is no use in further discussion. I know what I am about."

Benzal was average height, but the dark humanoid creature in front of him was shorter than most humans. The man glanced at himself in the mirror and compared the two of them. He had wavy brown hair—women loved to run their fingers through it—and clear, blue eyes. He was slender, but that was only because his training had formed his body into an efficient frame, wire-thin but strong as steel. He didn't need all those muscles that bulky warriors used to lug around their weapons. He himself was a weapon.

The animaru, on the other hand, was hairless and even thinner than Benzal. Its eyes were dark, as with most of the creatures from that other world, Aruzhelim. The thing's fingers ended in sharp claws, as did its toes. For all that, though, it had the shape of a man. A very dark, hairless, crooked man, but still a man.

These animaru spoke a dialect of the language of power, Alaqotim. Benzal himself was fluent, but not only because he had studied at the famed Academy at Sitor-Kanda, the so-called "Hero Academy." No, he had been fluent in the language before he ever set foot in those hallowed halls of learning. His parents, both high-level priests of Surus, spoke Alaqotim as often as Ruthrin, the common tongue. It was not a stretch for him to consider the language of power as his native tongue.

But the creatures' dialect was a sloppy, dirty form of the ancient language. He often felt as if he needed to wash out his mouth and ears after speaking with one of them. The leaders, such as Khrazhti, the high priestess of the God of Darkness, S'ru, spoke in a most sophisticated manner, but the language was still obviously inferior. It did get the job done, however. He could converse with the animaru. Sometimes with difficulty. That would have to be sufficient.

Benzal sighed again and shifted his gaze from the mirror to the dark creature in front of him.

"It will be soon. You can tell Khrazhti that once I have opened the portal to Aruzhelim, I will ensure that the new arrivals are brought to her. I hope she has listened and knows that we are to keep the secret of the animaru being here from spreading. We must not allow the Hero Academy to know. We must take them unaware."

"Of course, high priest," the loathsome thing drawled. Izhrod had told it many times he was not a high priest, but high ranks were few in animaru culture, apparently. It was either high priest, lord, or general. He would prefer to be called a lord, but the high priest was the most elevated position for the animaru, so it would do. He made a note in his mind to explain the concept of true nobles and royalty to his ignorant allies.

The creature calmly looked Izhrod in the eye and opened its mouth to continue speaking, but its eyes suddenly widened and its head whipped toward the back of the audience room. Toward the west. It started to visibly tremble. No, that word did not describe the intensity accurately. It vibrated.

"What is it?" Benzal said. There was no response. "I said, what is it?" he shouted. The noise drew the animaru's attention.

"Ardgyptous," the creature said.

"What? I know no word in Alaqotim such as that. What is it?"

"Ardgyptous. A disapproved one."

"Disapproved?" Benzal said. "Disapproved for what? By whom?"

"One has lost S'ru's favor, has been declared disapproved. A betrayer. This one must be destroyed. I must leave. Now."

The creature bounded across the chamber, through the open doors, and out into the hall. When Benzal lost sight of it, it was heading for the main doors of his keep. The two human guards standing at the doorway looked up, their eyes asking whether they should pursue the dark shape. Benzal waved their concern away.

"No need. It can run back to Broken Reach, for all I care. I have other things to think about." Surus's eyes, he wished he had one of the animaru lords or generals to deal with instead of the more common animaru.

The last he had heard from his animaru contacts, the party of humans that had been causing problems were heading toward the Academy. Of course, he'd also been told they were tracked going toward the old fortress at Broken Reach. Did they have something to do with this betrayer? He had better find out. Knowledge was as important as power, and he didn't like to be ignorant of anything.

It was time to call in some of his allies. Ones who were *not* from another world.

Izhrod Benzal stepped into another room, a smaller one than the audience chamber he had been in. This one could probably be called his sitting room, but he cared little for labels.

Behind a false stone front, a chest sat in an alcove. Its dark wood was strong, capable of taking damage from blade or hammer, even fire, before giving up its treasure. With a thought and a few arcane words, he opened it and swung the lid up silently.

Within were more than a dozen small tablets. Benzal read the labels and selected the one he had come for. A stylus was ingeniously hidden in the frame of the tablet. The wood of which it was made resembled the chest. The stylus was not strictly necessary. The smooth surface of the tablet, almost like a grey glass, would accept writing by any other implement, even fingers, but Benzal learned penmanship when he was very young. If one were to do something, it should be done correctly. Even flowing script, when written with the fingers, was sloppy and unrefined.

Sliding the stylus from its location, he began to write, each letter perfect. He was from a noble family, after all, and perfection in all things was expected by those who were lesser.

THE ENEMIES ARE AT THE OLD FORTRESS IN BROKEN REACH. GO THERE AND MAKE SURE THEY DO NOT LIVE TO SEE ANOTHER DAY.

Benzal waited for a few moments. He knew his answer

would not be long in coming.

UNDERSTOOD. IN SATTA SARAK. LEAVING TO GO NORTH NOW. WILL REPORT WHEN MISSION IS COMPLETE.

A smile slowly grew on Izhrod Benzal's face. He and his allies had been preparing for this time for many years. Using the assets they had created warmed him inside. Soon, nothing could prevent his plans from coming to fruition. Betrayer or not, things would come to pass just as he planned.

As he went to put the tablet back in its chest, he noticed another of them was glowing faintly, indicating that it held a message for him. He picked it up. It was from another group of operatives he had contacted earlier. He read the latest words.

HAVE DESCRIPTIONS OF HUMANS CAUSING TROUBLE. RED-HAIRED WARRIOR, BALD ARCHER WITH WHITE EYES, TWO BEAUTIFUL DARK-HAIRED WOMEN, BOY WITH CURLY BROWN HAIR, BLACK-HAIRED YOUNG MAN WEARING ROBES. LAST SEEN HEADING TOWARD BROKEN REACH THREE DAYS AGO.

Ah, now that was interesting. He wondered where they had gotten their information. He doubted they interviewed the animaru. Regardless, it was a good thing to have. He acknowledged receipt and used the relay function of the tablets to copy the message to the tablet he had used earlier. They would need a description.

On second thought, he decided to relay the descriptions, with a short introduction, to all the tablets he held. Having several sets of eyes looking for his prey would increase the chances of finding them. The animaru indicated that these humans were clever and difficult to pin down.

With that done, Izhrod closed up the chest and left the room. It was nearly time for the evening meal. What had his chef prepared for him this evening? It was good to have power and wealth. Very good.

❧ 4 ❧

The inn Tere selected was south of the central part of the city. Urun, Aila, and Khrazhti had never been to the city before, and those who had come with their Gypta family hadn't spent a lot of time within the city itself. The Gypta tended to keep to themselves, carrying on their business from the outskirts of a community and then moving on to the next place.

There were lots of things to see. Even the jumble of boxy buildings proved to be mildly fascinating to those who had never seen the style. For Urun and Khrazhti, the number of people was shock enough, but even to those who had spent time in cities, the Sarakians' clothing was something different.

Their wardrobes consisted of long, snug coats, clasped tightly around the neck and extending to the ground. Both women and men wore them, the former wearing their hair in elaborate braids and the men wearing triangular hats that barely covered the tops of their heads. The coats ranged in color from black and dark greys to the brightest yellow that hurt the eyes to look at it for too long. They looked dread-fully uncomfortable to him, but the wearers moved around without apparent discomfort.

As the party traversed the city, they went from relatively well-off areas uphill down toward the moderate housing and finally to crowded buildings that, though high quality and clean, were obviously for the less affluent citizens. Aeden was glad when they stopped at the inn before they reached some of the areas that looked a bit rougher.

Maybe it was the way things were arranged, or it could have been that the streets looked dirtier and more cluttered than the ones they'd been on. Whatever it was, Aeden was satisfied that they didn't continue down the main street they had been traveling. He had no desire to enter into combat with thieves or street toughs. He'd seen plenty of fighting in the last few months, enough to last a while.

He stood with his friends around him and looked up at the wooden sign over the inn. It hung above the double doors proclaiming the building as *The Spotted Frog Inn & Tavern*. It was complete with a picture of a large tree frog, suction cups on its fingers and toes and multi-colored spots painted along its skin.

Shrugging, he followed Tere inside, scanning the street as he did so. He politely allowed the women, including Khrazhti, to enter before him as he took note of a small, thin man leaning against a building on the other side of the street. He had seen the dull grey cloak earlier in the day, or one just like it. He didn't like that another feeling of being watched tickled him between his shoulder blades. He rolled his shoul-ders back, stretched his neck from side to side, and entered the inn's common room.

The inn had enough rooms for the entire party. He would share with Raki, Tere and Urun would be together, and the three women would be in one room. Once they got settled in and dropped their belongings off, they met again in the common room to have their first kitchen-cooked meal in some time.

They took their time eating, drinking wine or ale with spring water that was refreshingly cool. The fire in the room's great hearth cast its flickering light over the other patrons, and Aeden relaxed for the first time in longer than he could recall.

"This is a nice place, Tere," he said. "Thank you for bringing us here."

The tracker took a sip of his ale and nodded. "I've always liked this inn, though the truth is, it's been a long while since I've been here. I'm glad to see it is still the same. Old Master Bartle Stouth used to make the best bread, and did a bit of brewing on the side. I don't see him about, so maybe he's retired now. Hopefully he's well."

"Aye, master." The bar maid, a plump woman with hair shot through with grey and her face wearing what seemed to be a perpetual smile, sidled up to the blind man. Tere had kept his hood drawn since they came into the city. Aeden figured it was because of the shock of people seeing his white eyes. He could tell when someone first got a peek under Tere's hood and saw them. He didn't blame the man for wanting to avoid that reaction. The bar maid didn't seem to notice anything different about him. "Master Bartle has since retired to enjoy his hobbies. He relishes his brews and trying to pull all the fish from the river. His daughter, Maggie there, has taken over running the place. She's kept things as they was with her father."

"Ah, that would explain it then," Tere said. "The bread is as good as ever and the ale even better. Please tell Maggie of our appreciation and ask her to kindly send our well-wishes to her father."

"I will, master, thank you. Your name, sir, if I may ask?"

"Oh, he won't remember me, I'm sure. I was not here often, though each time I came was memorable to me. I'm Tere, Tere Chizzit. Thank you...?"

"Oh, begging your pardon, master," the heavy woman said. "I'm Tolly. You just let me know if you need anything else. We takes good care of our regular customers, we do."

"Thank you, Tolly. We will not hesitate to ask if we need anything."

Aeden looked at the older man quizzically. For someone who lived in a forest, the man seemed to know a lot about cities and different locations. Not for the first time, he wondered about him. He was about to ask the archer of his past, but Tere yawned exaggeratedly.

"Well," Tere said, "I'm a little tired. I believe I'll turn in. Tomorrow we can begin getting supplies. I want to be ready the second the boat boards three days from now. Goodnight, everyone. I'll see you in the morning."

Tere got up, bowed his hooded head to Tolly from across the room, and lightly ascended the stairs. Aeden could only shake his head; Tere was a sly one.

The next morning, after everyone had eaten their breakfast, the party split up. Tere and Urun went to get supplies and see about repairing some of their weapons and gear. Fahtin and Aila went along to visit some of the shops in the market district.

Aeden wanted to train and try to increase his understanding of the clan magic that seemed so new to him even though he had learned the motions and the words of power so many years ago. Khrazhti and Raki went with him, the first because being outside the city would allow her to be away from prying eyes, and the second to translate for Aeden.

The three left the city from the southwestern exit and walked to the edge of the forest. The trees were thick up to the city walls, and within a half a mile vegetation swallowed the trio. They found a suitable clearing and Aeden began some light exercise to warm up.

There were a few large rocks scattered about the clearing, but the space between them was roughly thirty paces long and twenty wide, more than enough room for him to practice. Aeden had brought his swords—he was rarely without them—and once he had warmed up, he spun them and danced about the open space performing strikes and defensive techniques. His muscles fully loosened, he moved on to practice some weapons forms.

While Aeden moved, Khrazhti let down her hood and appeared to be enjoying the breeze on her face. She chatted with Raki, though Aeden couldn't hear what they were talking about. Even if he had, he probably wouldn't have understood most of it.

The Croagh finished his forms and sheathed his blades smoothly. To get his mind into the proper condition, he performed the spells in the order he had learned them. There were sixteen main spells that, he had found, corresponded to the sixteen quatrains of the Bhavisyaganant, the Song of Prophecy. Additionally, there were four other auxiliary spells. He moved through the motions for one spell at a time, whispering the words of power so as not to cast magic about unnecessarily. He was so focused, he didn't see Khrazhti staring at what he was doing.

Though Aeden had found it was easiest for him to work on the spells in the order they were taught to him, he had recently been focusing on the tenth spell. It was unlike the others and it piqued his interest. After running through the entire list, he started experimenting with that spell, trying to figure out a more efficient choreography for the motions involved, if possible.

It was called Darkness to the Hunters, and it created a shadow or dark cloud that would hide him from his enemies. It seemed to be of limited value, especially since the animaru were more comfortable in the dark than in the light, but the enhanced versions of the Raibrech spells often were much more powerful, and even different, from the ones his clan taught.

He started with the simple movements and words of power the clan had taught him. A series of circular motions with the hands were the main gestures for the spell, as well as the words. He repeated the simple form several times.

"*Airuh, Dheta, Shikuta.*"

A small cloud of pure darkness puffed out from Aeden's body, wrapping him in the umbra. He could still see through it, but from the outside, his form would be obscured. At least, he thought so.

The main purpose of the spell, as taught by his clan, was to obscure evidence of his passing or his existence from one searching for him. Aeden could control the dark cloud and pass it over where he had been to erase tracks or trails that might lead to him. It could also hide him, especially if the area was dark or dimly lit.

Khrazhti did not hide her interest in what Aeden was doing. Her perfect posture became even more rigid as she craned her neck and widened her eyes so as not to miss anything. Aeden noticed it in his peripheral vision, but he did not address her or Raki, who was also transfixed.

The process Aeden went through to enhance his clan magic was more trial and error than anything else. The forms of the Raibrech he had learned were either incomplete to start with or had been diluted over hundreds of years as the clans practiced them. His goal was to go deeper, to get back to the original spell, to the roots of what made the magic work, and to enhance each spell, making it stronger.

He had only successfully worked out one enhanced form he could repeat, but he was confident he could tackle them one by one and increase his power. Once he had discovered that the spells followed the order of the quatrains in the Song of Prophecy, he was able to meditate on the words of the song and pick out their true power, their resonance. This allowed his casting of his clan's spells to be stronger than the original Raibrech, but to truly enhance them, he needed more. The problem was that every quatrain, every spell, sometimes every word, seemed to hold power completely unrelated to any of the other spells.

He had figured out how to use the magic for some of the spells more powerfully than any clan member had—in centuries at least—but he had a feeling he had only scratched the surface of what was possible. With every spell he learned to choreograph movements to, with every word he discovered the nuances for, there were hundreds, if not thousands, of other hidden pieces of power he had no clue about.

It mattered little, though. He would keep learning, keep discovering, and continue to gain understanding and power. Eventually he would gain a mastery that would be unbelievable at his current level.

If only he had a teacher. He longed to get to the Academy. The masters at Sitor-Kanda would be able to help speed his progress along.

But he wasn't there yet, so he had to do what he could until that time. He pulled his thoughts back from his musings and focused on the spell.

Aeden closed his eyes as he performed the gestures and mouthed the words. He went deep within himself and registered every little change, every fluctuation of power with his movements and with the formation of the words.

It seemed to him that he should be able to call the power forth without actually having to say the words of power. True, sound manifested the magic more forcefully, but his masters had taught him to hold the word in his mind, caress each sound before he released it through his mouth and let out into the world. He thought it should be possible to call forth the magic in the words instantly, faster than speech.

But that was something to work on later. That felt too advanced for him at the current time; he had to learn other things first. Step by step, he would build to a fuller understanding.

The gestures were simple, though by their nature very precise. The Raibrech dealt mostly with the hands and arms, with fewer motions of the legs or the rest of the body. Aeden had found that with the other spell he had enhanced, additional motions increased the power. Once he figured out what the other motions were.

Picturing the sounds of the words of power in his mind, he turned them around, inspected them. They were fantastical shapes, all edges and curves and lines. As he pondered the first word, he had an urge to move his right foot ahead of him, placing it lightly with the toes pointing directly forward. The left desired to move behind, exactly behind and in line with the right.

The shape in his mind flashed brighter. It seemed to like the positioning of his feet.

Aeden repeated the words while moving his hands and arms in the same circular fashion as previously.

"*Shikar.*"

The darkness that was emitted from him was...darker. It didn't seem possible, because it had already seemed to be the darkest black possible, but now it seemed to be a total absence of light. It also responded more quickly and completely to his manipulation of it. Interesting.

Khrazhti couldn't contain herself any longer. She stood and stalked to Aeden, stopping right at the edge of the cloud the Croagh had summoned. Her eyes narrowed as she looked at the shadow. Then she started speaking.

Raki ran up to the other two, cocking his head at Khrazhti.

"She says she didn't know you spoke Alaqotim."

Aeden dropped his concentration and the cloud disappeared. "I can't. Well, not much. Just what she's been teaching me."

"She says you were speaking words, but in a way that is special. You were pronouncing the magical core of the words, not just the labels that are used when people speak. She doesn't know the words, but she could feel them."

"Really?" Aeden said. "Jehira told us the words were in Dantogyptain. I've heard both languages and they don't sound anything alike to me."

Khrazhti rattled off words so quickly, even Raki couldn't keep up. The boy said something Aeden couldn't understand and put both hands out, motioning them toward the ground as if he pushing something down. The animaru gave a frustrated huff and started again, more slowly.

"She says she can help you," Raki said. "The magic you are using is the magic of darkness. The magic she uses."

Aeden eyed the blue woman who tapped one foot while Raki translated. He hadn't seen her look impatient before. It was strange to see the tall warrior out of sorts. She had always looked to be in complete control since he met her. Still, he was a little concerned.

"How does she want to help me?" he asked Raki.

"She says she will help you with the position of your body. Your hands and feet, mainly. The way you are standing and moving is blocking the flow of magic."

"And how does she know that?"

"She is a master of dark magic," Raki translated. "She can

see the flow of magic and how you are restricting it. She can help you to use it more efficiently."

Aeden admitted that it made sense. What was he afraid of? He had beaten her before. Besides, he did believe her vow. She seemed to have honor, even if it was a strange kind of animaru honor.

"Tell her I am grateful for her help." Aeden bowed slightly to Khrazhti as he said it. Surprisingly, the woman's blue lips curled up into a smile. Aeden forgot for a moment that she wasn't human. Her coloring was different, but looking at that mouth, he felt his own rise in an answering smile. How odd.

Khrazhti stepped over, looking Aeden in the eyes.

"This," she said, placing her feet precisely in almost the same way Aeden had been trying.

Aeden's eyebrows raised. She had said it in his language. He stared at her for a moment, then shook his head. Of course she had picked up a few words of Ruthrin after spending several days with him and the others. He mimicked her stance, the two facing each other.

"No," she said. "This." She turned his right foot slightly and pushed on his knee to have him move it into place. She tapped on his back leg and he tightened up the muscles. She nodded and then put her hands in front of her. After demonstrating how to create the circles with her arms and hands, she jerked her head toward Aeden. He understood. It was his turn.

This went on for several minutes, Khrazhti coaching Aeden and adjusting his movements. He was surprised when she did the same with his pronunciation of the words of power. They weren't even in her language.

Finally, it seemed as if she was satisfied with his understanding. She stepped back and moved her hand in a circle, instructing him to try the spell again.

Using her suggestions, he went through the gestures and

pronounced each word as he had been coached. On the last syllable, a sphere of darkness sprung around him, large enough to almost envelop the other two standing near him. It was black, but it also seemed to blend in with everything around it.

Aeden was shocked. He *felt* the difference. It wasn't just that the visible effects of the spell were more powerful. He sensed a connection with the dark sphere he had produced. It felt like part of him. He was so excited, he lost his focus and the cloud of shadow disappeared.

"That was amazing!" he said, rushing toward Khrazhti. "Thank you, Khrazhti. That made me understand much more about the magic. I can't tell you how much that will help me." Impulsively, he reached out to the animaru and wrapped his arms around her in a friendly hug.

Khrazhti's eyes went wide and she tensed as if she was going to defend herself, but then she relaxed, maybe recognizing the human ritual Fahtin had performed before. She didn't hug Aeden back, but she didn't strike him, either.

"Oh," Aeden said, releasing her. "I'm sorry. I didn't...I mean, Fahtin hugs me when we have something to celebrate. I guess it rubbed off. I am sorry if I offended you. Animaru probably don't hug, huh?"

Raki translated in between his chuckles. Aeden felt his face grow hot.

"She says she took no offense," Raki said, his voice light with laughter. "Once she realized you were not attacking her, it was fine."

"Tell her I am very thankful for her help. It means a lot to me. It will allow me to progress even further in my magic."

Raki translated and listened to Khrazhti's response. "She says you are welcome and that you should not hesitate to ask if there is anything else she can do to help."

Aeden smiled and bowed to the animaru. "Also tell her

that if she notices anything else that can help, she should feel free to mention it. I am in her debt, too, so if there is anything I can do for her, she only has to ask."

Raki sighed. Aeden knew he was probably getting tired of translating everything. He would do his best to learn Khrazhti's language and then the boy wouldn't have to translate constantly.

"She said she would like to train together sometime. Physical combat. She has seen that you are very skilled and would like to train and spar with you."

"Absolutely. I would love to do it," Aeden answered.

The two went back to sit down so Aeden could practice what he had learned a little longer. By the time he was done, he had choreographed the spell, repeating the entire tenth quatrain as he did it. When he spoke the final word, a sphere almost ten feet in diameter exploded into being. He was able to move it around at will, covering up tracks that the three had made in the grass and hiding any one, or even all three, of them. When he placed it on Raki and Khrazhti, the sphere faded away, turning itself and Aeden's two friends invisible. When he moved it, the ball became black again.

Aeden had a feeling this would be a useful spell. He dispelled it, smiled at his two friends, and walked over to join them. As he did so, he stumbled, his legs suddenly weak. The magic seemed to have taken something from him, like he'd been pushing a wagon uphill. Maybe he'd overdone it. It seemed reasonable that creating more power would take more effort. He'd have to remember that.

The trio made their way back to the inn, Khrazhti and Aeden comparing notes on magic and combat, mainly with Raki as a translator. They were able to communicate better than before, using both the animaru Alaqotim language and also the common Ruthrin tongue. Though it probably wouldn't have been intelligible to anyone else listening, Aeden found that they understood each other more and more.

It helped to keep eye contact and to note the different facial expressions of the animaru, though any gestures she made were slight and he had to pay close attention. He realized halfway back to their inn that he could pick up the intent of what she was saying by her gestures and expressions. Was it like that with all animaru? He didn't remember there being any human-like qualities in them. Was it because they were foes and he simply didn't give them a chance, or was Khrazhti different? He hadn't seen any other of the dark creatures with color—let alone light color.

But it was a mystery for later. He was enjoying the conversation about fighting and weapons. He could almost see the things she talked about.

Khrazhti complimented his weapons, said they were well-made. Aeden replied that he had only seen a few of the animaru who used weapons. She clarified that many of the animaru in Dizhelim were simple soldiers, shock troops called seren. There were a few commanders and the assassins Aeden had already met. Her face darkened slightly when she mentioned the assassins. Was that a blush?

Still, she continued, the more sophisticated and more skilled warriors in the animaru ranks used weapons. At least, the ones who had arms and were humanoid did. The other types, with other shapes, had their own ways of damaging foes.

Khrazhti preferred curved swords. She could wield two at a time, but often only used one so she could cast her magic with the other hand. She claimed to be an expert in physical combat as well as with magic. Aeden believed her. He had fought her, and if it weren't for his friends and their magic, he may not have survived it. Khrazhti moved closer and examined him carefully, and Aeden realized he was flushing, thinking about how she could have beat him. He changed the subject quickly to the animaru world of Aruzhelim.

As they got closer to the city, Khrazhti pulled the hood of her cloak down to cover her face. Aeden let out a little sigh. He could no longer see her facial expressions, and their communication suffered immediately for it.

He didn't learn much more because they didn't want to speak an unknown language when too many people were around. They arrived at their inn less than an hour before the evening meal, so they went to their rooms to clean up before meeting with the others in the common room.

Tere arranged a private dining room, one in which they kept the door barred so Khrazhti could leave her face uncovered.

The companions shared a delicious meal of roast boar and vegetables, freshly baked bread, and the famous Stouth ale. Conversation was light, each person telling about what they did during the day.

They had found within the first couple of days that Khrazhti didn't eat or drink. At least, she didn't need to. Using the reasoning that she was half human, Aeden had asked what would happen if she did eat. She had tried a small piece of roasted rabbit. The way her eyes widened and she turned her head to him in surprise made him laugh out loud. She said, through Tere, that she had never experienced anything like it.

It wasn't just the pleasant sensation of taste, though. She realized an hour later that she had more energy. Something in her human half must have been able to harness the nutrients in the food and add to her normal power.

Since then, she had eaten a little now and then when the others took meal breaks. Aeden thought part of it was simply a social thing—it probably made her feel more a part of the group—but there was no discounting anything that could give her more energy to fight or do magic.

For this meal, however, she didn't partake. She looked thoughtful, as if pondering something. She still listened to the conversations, leaning forward and narrowing her eyes when she was interested in the topic or understood the words they used, but she still seemed distracted. Aeden could tell; he spent most of the meal glancing at her to see how she was acting.

5

When Aeden mentioned that Khrazhti helped him to learn more about his magic, everyone stopped their own conversations to look at the animaru.

"She did?" Fahtin asked. "That's great, Aeden."

"It is," he agreed. "She recognized the dark magic in my spell and helped me figure out the choreography for it. Without her help, I'd still be trying to come up with the correct motions. I wish I spoke more of her language. I'm sure with her thousands of years of experience, she could really clear up some things I don't understand."

Raki was translating as Aeden spoke and when he got to the end, Khrazhti dropped her eyes to the table. Aeden felt a spear of regret drill through him. He hadn't meant to embarrass her. She probably wasn't used to being complimented or even being thanked for her help. From what he had seen, the animaru were all toughness and emotionless.

Khrazhti said something, and while Raki was getting ready to translate, Tere laughed and slapped his knee.

"What is it?" Aeden asked.

Raki was smiling, too. "She said it's fine, that you promised her you would train with her and spar with weapons, so you would be paying back any aid she gave you."

"Did you really?" Aila Ven asked. "You promised you'd spar with her? It took all of us together to beat her—no offense intended," she nodded her head to the blue woman. "You're very brave for wanting to cross weapons with her, Aeden."

"Not really," he said. "She is very skilled, so she won't hurt me by accident. If anything, I will increase my skill. Besides, I trust her. It'll be fine."

As he said it, it hit him. He did trust her. She had been the commander of all the animaru on Dizhelim—and the high priestess for the god of the animaru—responsible for sending them out to slaughter people and, more specifically, to find and destroy *him*. All this, and he did really trust her. He wondered why for only a moment before realizing it was the rapport he had built with her as an honorable warrior. She had turned against her god when she found that what she was doing was dishonorable. She had joined them, knowing there would be prejudice and mistrust.

He sat back in his chair, dazed at the conclusion.

"I can see that it has finally hit you what you agreed to," Urun said. Aeden barely caught it in his stupor. "It's fine. I'll be around to heal you. If there's anything left to heal." The nature priest cackled a laugh and took another drink of his ale.

Aeden flashed a fake smile at the man. He had learned something about himself and no one's opinion was going to taint it for him. He glanced at Khrazhti, who was staring at him. His smile became more genuine as he nodded to the woman. The obvious surprise in those eyes made Aeden want to chuckle.

When everyone was finished teasing him, they decided to

go down to the common room where a minstrel was supposed to be entertaining. They filed out until only Aeden, Raki, Fahtin, and Khrazhti were left.

"Will you go with us?" he asked, tilting his head toward Raki to indicate he wanted his words translated. "Do they tell stories in Aruzhelim and sing songs?"

After considering her words, Raki said, "Stories, yes. She doesn't know what songs are, though."

"Then you may be in luck," Aeden said. "You can hear the minstrel sing one or a few. Come, please. Unfortunately, you'll have to put your hood on, but we can find a table in the back so you can see everything without people seeing your face."

Without thinking, he held out his hand to the animaru to escort her politely to the common room. She looked at him quizzically before he cleared his throat and dropped his arm. Instead, he waved it toward the door. She understood that gesture and stepped out of the room, covering her head with her hood.

Aeden put his hand out again and this time Fahtin took it with a smile. She understood the polite gesture. They left the private dining room and headed downstairs with the others.

Tere had apparently already thought of Khrazhti because the group was just sitting down at a table in a shadowed corner of the room. Aeden and Fahtin took their places. The minstrel, a middle-aged man with a belly that strained his velvet tunic, sat on a tiny stage off to one side of the common room and sang a lilting melody, providing the music with a lute. It told the story of a maiden and her love for a knight from an enemy country.

Aeden missed the music he had grown up with in the caravan. He missed the fiddle Fahtin's father had given him and which he had learned to play. Truth be told, he missed singing with his family as well. As the minstrel's tune washed over him, his heart swelled and then dropped along with the music. He sighed.

Khrazhti sat very still. Aeden couldn't see her face under the cloak, but her body seemed rigid, almost like she would flee. Or attack. He wondered what she thought of the song.

He scooted closer to her. Raki was on her other side, but he wasn't translating at the moment.

"What do you think of the song?" he asked her quietly. He tried to say it in Alaqotim, but he only managed "What think song?"

The animaru started as if she had been in a trance and had been struck. She swung her head toward Aeden.

"It is...different," she said in Ruthrin. In her own language, she followed up with something Aeden couldn't quite understand. She patted her chest as she said it.

"She says it's surprising," Raki whispered. "It makes her feel...something. Right here." Raki patted his own chest.

The minstrel finished the song and began another. This one had a faster beat and told the story of a man who was trying to get his mule to carry his belongings. People in the audience laughed and more than a few kept beat with either clapping hands or stomping feet.

This time, Khrazhti's body was not as tense. She seemed to vibrate with the music, but not in a rigid manner. It seemed as if her body wanted to move to the tune, but didn't know how.

Aeden smiled. It was too difficult to try to talk to her with all the sounds of the minstrel and the people around him. He'd ask her about it later. For now, he enjoyed seeing how the animaru reacted to the new experience.

After a few more songs, the minstrel put up his lute.

"Would any of you fine people care for a story, a tale of heroics and derring-do?" he said in his deep, rich voice. He had no problem cutting through the chatter so that he was heard in every corner of the room.

"Yes," several people shouted.

"Ah, very well. But which story?"

"Lis," one patron shouted.

"Vesta," another said.

"Forden the Risen," another yelled.

"Those are all very fine stories, indeed," the minstrel said. "But on a moonless night as tonight, when creatures of darkness roam, I've a mind for something else. I would tell of the Godan Chul, the evil spirits, and how the gods waged war with them."

When the minstrel uttered the words "creatures of darkness," Aeden wasn't the only one to look toward Khrazhti. He tensed for a moment, more than half expecting that the story would be about the animaru. He released a sigh when the entertainer finished his sentence.

He had heard of the Godan Chul but didn't know of any war with them. Feeling as if the tension had passed, he settled back on his bench and leaned his back against the wall.

ॐ

KHRAZHTI SAT RIGIDLY AT THE TABLE WITH THE FESSANI who were now her only companions. It was strange that she would feel more comfortable with them, more a part of their little group, than she ever did with the animaru. It was probably the prejudice she had always faced growing up.

Once she revealed her talent and obtained S'ru's favor, it had shifted to sidelong looks and gestures the others thought she did not see. She had been in a position of authority, but she had never felt as if she were where she belonged.

With these new comrades, she did.

There had been so many new experiences, so many new

feelings, since she had forsaken her god. It amazed her that she was able to even think it without feeling as if she had failed or betrayed S'ru. The simple fact was that the God of Darkness had set down rules that must be followed, but then did not follow them himself. She had been convinced of the veracity of those laws long ago and given the choice, she would follow them. She had always thought S'ru embodied the laws he handed down, but he did not.

It had been a surprise when the one who was Gneis-prumay—he called himself Aeden—began to use the magic of darkness in that opening in the trees. If she had not been so occupied with seeing the sedentary living things all around them, Khrazhti would probably have sensed the power in him.

Or maybe not. This world was strange and with each experience, it grew stranger.

Take, for example, the song the fessanum was singing in the very room in which she now sat. She had never heard such sounds. And to have meaning on top of it? That was remarkable. And now he would speak of the Godan Chul? How was it that light-dwelling creatures knew of such things? She could hardly wait to hear the tale.

Animaru rarely told tales for entertainment. They told them to brag of conquests, to frighten others, or to recount important history. While it seemed that occurred on the light-world as well, the tale she was about to hear was solely for the amusement and entertainment of the others in the room. How odd a ritual that was.

But he was speaking now. She would listen, try to under-stand what she could, and rely on the small one and the old, blind one to translate the rest. The flutter in her chest might be what the others referred to as excitement. It felt some-thing like what occurred to her before battle.

"Long, long ago, during the Age of Creation," the minstrel said and the boy Raki translated, "there were the Voordim.

"They were supreme, the caretakers and creators of life on Dizhelim, granted their might from the Power itself. They used their abilities to shape the world, to populate it, to initiate the future."

The voice of the minstrel was deep and sonorous. It carried well across the crowded room. Khrazhti thought he might have been a good commander. Much of skill in leading others was a forceful voice. Though she had to wait for the translation for most of it, she could hear the cadence, the way he modulated his voice. Sadly, her translator did not. She could see why the others would listen to a tale from such a creature. She focused on his voice, trying to pick up the meaning as he spoke it. Between what she could understand and what the one called Raki translated, she could follow the story.

The translation did not do the original words justice. She picked out how they blended together, pairing with other words in a pleasing way. They had no such thing in the translation to her own language.

"During this time, the God of Magic, Migae, from whom the term 'magic' comes, pondered the highest level of magical thought. At night, when he laid down to sleep, his mind continued to work through problems even the other gods could not fathom. In his mutterings during those dreams, a fantastic thing happened.

"The nighttime mutterings of the god came to life. They fluttered and swirled from Migae as if their very existence depending upon them escaping. Perhaps it did. Over the course of decades, then centuries, the diminutive god inadvertently created thousands upon thousands of the Godan Chul. For that is what the name means in the most ancient form of Alaqotim.

"Spirit's whisper.

"The Godan Chul were clever, though they did not possess the ability for thought you and I share. They did hide, however, and they did so effectively. It was not until their number was almost endless that Migae found them out and took measures not to mutter any longer in his sleep.

"Yet, he did nothing to the Godan Chul already existing, once he had studied a few of them and found them to be no threat to himself, the other gods, or the few other forms of life that existed at that time.

"But Migae was wrong. Over time, the Godan Chul began to feed upon the population of Dizhelim. The fledgling human race, the astridae, even some of the higher forms of animal life, were food for them. They floated as mist, nearly invisible, until they desired to strike. When they did, they engulfed their prey and drained the magic from them.

"The magic and the life force as well. If enough gathered together, even the gods were susceptible to their insidious power.

"Mellaine, Goddess of Nature and Life, first realized what was happening, and she roused the other gods and the great heroes such as there were in the kingdoms of mankind. Humans stood beside the gods and waged war on the Godan Chul. In the end, almost all of them were destroyed, with very few fleeing to the dark, hidden places of the world.

"And still they are there today. Occasionally, one of the magical spirits will emerge, searching for prey, but they lack their former strength since the gods have left and taken magic with them.

"Still, be wary, one and all, for the Godan Chul live still, and perhaps they are simply biding their time to gather their strength so they can attack when the prophesied time comes."

The minstrel bowed and stepped off the stage toward the

long table at the edge of the tavern. It had ended so suddenly, it took Khrazhti by surprise.

Too, the story had shocked her. Where did these fessani come up with such ideas? She snorted a scoffing sound, resisting the urge to laugh out loud.

Everyone in the room looked toward her, including her companions. She pulled the hood down further. Aeden's eyes stared into the darkness of her hood, confusion written on his face.

Not knowing what else to do, Khrazhti stood up abruptly and headed up the stairs. She was vaguely aware of feet stomping up after her. When she reached the private dining room where they had eaten, she entered, took a few steps in, and wheeled to face her pursuers.

It was Aeden, Raki, and Fahtin.

"Are you all right?" Aeden said and Raki translated.

"I am fine," she responded in Ruthrin. She had learned that much of the language. When no one said anything else, she continued, in her own language. "I am sorry if I acted inappropriately. The story he told was ridiculous. There were very few fibers of truth in it, and even those were stretched thin."

"Are you telling me," Tere Chizzit said in her language as he walked in the door. All of the others followed him in. "That the Godan Chul didn't exist?" He repeated it for the ones who could not speak the proper tongue.

"I am saying no such thing," she said. "I am saying that nearly everything he said about them is incorrect. Fanciful lies."

"I see," the hunter said. He rubbed his chin and seemed to chew on the thought. "Would you be so kind as to tell us the correct version, then? If you know it, that is."

Khrazhti stood up taller and lowered her hood, revealing her glowing eyes. "Of course I know it. I will tell you, though it may destroy some of what you believe about this world and its history."

"Very well," the old man said.

The others sat down again at the table while Tere Chizzit closed the door and bolted it. That one was shrewd, always thinking of the little details. She appreciated it. He would have made a good general, Khrazhti thought.

The animaru was no storyteller. She was competent at relaying information to others, even giving narratives of battles in debriefings, but she did not have the flair the minstrel did. It was just as well. The translation would change her words anyway. She wanted only to communicate the information she knew to be true. The facts that were contrary to the fanciful tale they heard downstairs.

She began, relying on Tere Chizzit and Raki to translate for the others. To that end, she spoke slowly, enunciating precisely.

"A little of what the minstrel said was true. The Godan Chul indeed were formed of the night whispers of the God of Magic, Migae. The name itself means 'spirit's whisper,' as the minstrel said. It is also true that a great period of time passed before anyone knew of the existence of the Godan Chul.

"The rest of what the minstrel said is untrue. The Godan Chul had always been furtive and shy, hiding in the dark places of the world and doing their best to be unseen. Some years after Migae discovered them and took action to correct his inadvertent seepage of power, the Godan Chul began to change.

"It is unclear how long it took, but the Godan Chul took form, inhabiting the dark stuff they found in the world. Each one would somehow mold the material and infuse themselves into it, gaining solid form for the first time. A form that could not only be touched, but one that could touch back.

"These dark forms were the animaru."

Khrazhti paused, anticipating the reaction once her words were translated. She could follow along, though she didn't need to. Both Tere Chizzit and Raki finished their translation with the word "animaru."

Several of her companions gasped. All of them looked at her. Their faces ranged from questioning looks to ones of horror. She continued unaffected.

"Soon, the numbers of the newly formed animaru were in the thousands, even tens of thousands. Within a few short years, they had all been formed, almost as if the Godan Chul had been planning it and implemented it in the most expedient manner possible.

"It was done far away from communities or places the gods were known to frequent. If there was one Godan Chul coordinating it, or a small group, it has been lost to history. What has not been lost was what they did next.

"The Godan-Chul-turned-animaru attacked.

"There were some, a handful, of Godan Chul that did not become animaru, for some reason. The vast majority did, however, creating an entire race at once. Their leaders were clever and all of them were powerful. With their numbers, they could not be ignored. The gods feared they might be overwhelmed.

"The animaru could not be killed. They were much more powerful then, but still unalive. They could be injured, brought low, but not destroyed.

"In the end, after many years of battle, a great magic was employed, channeled by Surus himself, and every last animaru was forced through a tear in the fabric of the magical matrix and deposited on a new world. It was in fact a physical world, as Dizhelim is, but far away, one of the lights in the sky you fessani are so fond of gazing at.

"The animaru were banished there, along with the dark

god S'ru, though whether he had been a god who took the animaru's side or was a very powerful animaru who had attained the power of godhood is not known. There the animaru have stayed ever since, almost twelve thousand years. That is what happened to the Godan Chul."

Khrazhti thought she was finished, but another thought occurred to her. Scanning the faces around the room, all looking at her in rapt attention, she gave them one more thing to think about.

"Only once has there been contact with those on Dizhe-lim. Once, three thousand years ago, a small group of explorers with magical power came from your world to ours. They were...incompatible with Aruzhelim. One lived long enough to bear a child by an animaru who forced himself upon her, something that no one could have predicted would happen.

"That child is me. Whether that means I somehow have a new Godan Chul in me or somehow the one inhabiting my father split into two, I am half fessanum. That is, human. I am the only new animaru to exist in the last twelve thousand years.

"And now you know the truth. Now you know the origin of your enemies who have invaded your world."

The others looked at her, apparently speechless. Khrazhti gazed back. Eye contact and silence did not bother her. In fact, she often used them as tools to manipulate others.

"Thank you for telling us," Aeden finally said in broken Alaqotim.

The others mumbled to themselves or to others, but none spoke directly to her. Fahtin smiled at her.

Within minutes, everyone went off to their own rooms to sleep. The revelation that the evil spirits they had all thought were out there waiting in the dark to get them were actually the dark creatures that had come from another world to get them, seemed to sap everyone's desire for conversation. As she headed up to the room she shared with Fahtin and Aila, Khrazhti hoped she had not been wrong in telling them.

🌿 6 🌿

In the morning, Fahtin went down to the common room to have breakfast, as she had done the day before. Aila and Khrazhti went with her. Before the serving girl had even brought them their food, Aeden and Raki came down.

"Good morning," Aeden said. "What are you planning on doing today?"

"Aila and I are going to explore the city a little more," Fahtin said. "Raki, can you ask Khrazhti if she wants to go with us?"

The youngest member of their party did so, but Khrazhti begged off.

"She says she wants to go with Aeden to train," he said. "She doesn't like being in the middle of so many people. In the forest, she can let her hood down."

"I can understand that," Fahtin said, smiling at the animaru. "I just thought I'd ask. We'll probably join you tomorrow morning to train."

Tere and Urun came down a few minutes later, and everyone chatted idly while finishing their breakfast.

"I want to go get more supplies and pick up the weapons I dropped off to be repaired yesterday," Tere told them.

"And I'm going with him," Urun said. "There's an herb shop I wanted to check out. We should be back well before dinner time."

"Let's meet at sixth bell," Tere said. "There is an inn I want everyone to try. It has some of the best food in the city."

The group all agreed, some apathetically and others with excitement, and then they split up. Fahtin and Aila headed out toward the market district.

They hadn't been looking through the shops for long when Fahtin caught a flash of color from the edge of her sight. She moved around a couple of women haggling for a scarf at a stall and spied a young girl walking quickly through the crowd.

"Aila," she said to the other woman. "I have to go that way. I can meet you back at the inn Tere told us about, if you want."

"Why," Aila asked. "What's going on? Did you see something you want to buy?"

"No, nothing like that. I have to go. I'll see you later."

Aila frowned. "Can I go with you?"

Fahtin was still trying to track the girl she had seen. She quickly turned her head toward Aila. "Uh, sure. It may be boring for you, though."

"That's fine. I don't want to buy any of this stuff anyway. Boring or not, it's more interesting than shopping."

"Okay, fine," Fahtin said. "Come on then."

The Gypta woman moved at a pace just short of a run, swiveling her head and craning her neck as she tried to find her target again.

There. The girl was going around a barrow full of meat pies. Her clothing was wispy and colorful, voluminous skirt billowing out as she hurried along, and the shiny bits sewn to her tight cropped vest glittered in the morning sunlight.

As expected, Fahtin also saw the furtive figures following the girl. Three of them, all fairly large men, and they didn't look like they were looking to do good deeds. Fahtin quickened her step as first the girl, and then the men, headed down an alley toward a less populated area.

The girl made her way through the warren of alleys and side streets. Fewer and fewer people were around until it was only the girl, her three pursuers—it was undeniable now that they were indeed following her—and Fahtin, who stayed far enough back so the men wouldn't see her if they looked behind them.

The girl turned to the right up ahead and made a squawking sound. Fahtin couldn't see what happened, but one of the men grinned at his companions. She hurried to catch up, all thoughts of stealth forgotten.

Aila seemed to know exactly what was going on and padded silently beside Fahtin. If the Gypta woman was honest, she'd admit that the shorter woman was much better at moving silently and stealthily. Truth be told, she was glad Aila was with her.

Heart beating madly, Fahtin came around the corner. A fourth man had gotten around the young girl and trapped her between him and the other three. In the narrow alley, there was nowhere for the girl to run. The walls on either side, as far as Fahtin could see, were blank and windowless.

"Come on now," one of the men said as he leered at the girl. "We're just wanting a bit of fun. Cooperate and we won't have to hurt you. Much. Scream or fight and we may just have to cut up that pretty face of yours." He brandished a knife and the girl folded in on herself, tears streaming down her face.

It didn't look as if the men had touched the girl yet.

Fahtin planned on making sure that didn't change.

"I'm first." The largest of the men swiped a lock of greasy hair out of his face. "It's my turn this time."

The other men grunted, but none of them protested.

The man licked his lips and stalked closer to the girl, who huddled up against the wall weeping.

A knife sprang up from the man's back, under his right shoulder. He screamed and turned toward where the knife had come from.

Fahtin cursed and threw another knife. This one struck the man's collar bone, but deflected so it lodged in his throat. He gurgled his last sounds and dropped to the ground, clutching at the knife as his life ended.

"Who are you?" one of the other men spat, but his words were cut off as one of Aila's blades, on the end of a chain—she had told Fahtin they were called vinci—sliced through his throat so cleanly he didn't even seem to realize it until he put his hand up to his neck. He held his hand out, saw the blood there, looked up toward the two women, and fell to his knees. As the blood cascaded down his chest, he fell over onto his side.

The two remaining men took off running, apparently not interested in fighting someone who could fight back.

One of them received a knife in his lower back. His legs collapsed under him, and he fell hard onto his face and skidded several feet in the alley. The other found his legs wrapped in a fine chain that caused him to trip and fall as well.

Aila sped to the man she had wrapped in her vincus and gave him a savage gash with her blade. He was dead even before she untangled his limbs from her weapon.

Aila turned to Fahtin. "Are you going to finish that one?" She pointed to the man lying in a heap a dozen feet from her.

"No. I damaged his spine with that last throw. I doubt

he'll ever walk again. He definitely won't be attacking any young girls again."

Aila nodded as she cleaned her weapon on the clothes of the man she had just killed.

Fahtin carefully approached the girl, who was still curled up, though she was watching the other two women. She could have been Fahtin's sister, with long, dark hair, a slender figure, and clothes that left no doubt she was Gypta.

"*Mei sain avar, avar sai ik,*" Fahtin said.

The girl's eyes widened even more than they had before, and her mouth parted as she stared at Fahtin.

"Does your family not greet its other members in this way?" Fahtin asked, her eyebrows rising in confusion.

Without a sound, the girl leapt to her feet, crossed the distance to Fahtin, and threw herself at the woman, holding on as if the ground were falling away below her and Fahtin was the only solid thing to cling to.

Fahtin patted the girl's back and cooed to her. She looked to Aila and shrugged.

After a bout of sobbing, the girl's breathing slowed toward normal and she gulped air, causing her to hiccup.

"Don't gulp," Fahtin said softly. "Try to control your breath. Breathe slowly and evenly. I'm Fahtin Achaya. What is your name?"

"S-Sarya," the girl said. "Sarya Chinda."

"It is an honor to meet you, Sarya. I have met your family twice before. Are they here, outside the city?"

"Yes." Sarya buried her face in Fahtin's shoulder and sniffled, still trying to control her crying.

"Can you show me where? We will go back with you to make sure no one else bothers you. This is my friend Aila."

Sarya looked toward the smaller woman. Aila waved and smiled. The girl waved back.

"I can take you."

7

The three headed toward the west part of the city. Fahtin knew the caravan would not be in the city itself. Even the larger cities were hesitant to allow an entire family of the People into their city all at once. Besides the obvious problem with finding enough space for all the wagons, there was still a distinct prejudice against the travelers. She had experienced it often enough.

"Sarya," Fahtin said as they walked. "Why were you in the city alone? Don't you know it's not safe for a pretty young girl all by herself?" Sarya had released Fahtin, but she walked very close to her, as if her proximity alone would keep her safe.

The girl's face grew pale and her eyes became liquid. "Yes. I wanted to see the city. I wanted to get my mother something from the market. They told me I couldn't go, that times are not safe. Not for us. Not for anyone, really. I snuck away."

Fahtin frowned at the girl, whose lower lip trembled. The older Gypta patted the younger's shoulder. "I understand. Please, though, don't ever do that again. As you saw, what your parents told you is correct. It is a dangerous world, especially for the Gypta. But you're safe now and I think you have learned that lesson. Let's get you back to your family."

It took almost an hour to get through the edge of the city and down the west road to where the wagons were all parked in a large opening in the trees. As soon as Fahtin caught sight of the first wagon, her heart lurched as if she had been struck in the chest.

The wagons looked so much like those of her own family. Only the colors were different. They were tall and narrow, rounded at the top, painted in the most delicious combination of hues. The people bustling between the rolling houses wore clothes much like the ones she had worn when she was with the caravan. Filmy, soft material in many different colors. She currently wore a muted facsimile, tougher and thicker, with the colors more subdued.

Would she ever see her own family, her own familiar wagon, again?

"Sarya!" a man shouted as he saw the girl. He ran from among the wagons at a full sprint, reaching them in no time. As he swept the girl up into a hug, Fahtin looked him over. He had the same dark brown hair as the girl, and the same cocoa eyes. Their noses were nearly identical, oddly crooked and leaning toward their right side. While the girl was stick-thin, the man was merely slender.

"Where have you been, child?" he asked her. "Did you go into the city? I have told you it is dangerous there. Did you have trouble? What do you mean by leaving without telling anyone where you went? Why are you not answering me?"

"Papa!" the exasperated girl finally said. "You are smothering me. I can't get a breath in to speak. And you are being rude to my friends."

The man released Sarya and looked toward Fahtin and Aila. He jumped a little, as if they had snuck up on him. "Oh.

My apologies. I was concerned over my little Sarya's welfare. Please excuse my bad manners."

Fahtin smiled at the man. "We completely understand." She bowed to him formally and repeated the ritual greeting. "*Mei sain avar, avar sai ik.*"

The man started again and then his already wide eyes went wider, finally noticing how Fahtin was dressed. "*Jai avar sai ik, ais bhi mei sain ik,*" he said, returning the bow. "I was not aware any other family was in the area. Where are your wagons parked?"

"I am afraid I am not traveling with my family. At least, not with all of them. Two only are with me."

The man eyed her doubtfully. "Who has ever heard of one of the People traveling alone? It is not safe."

Fahtin smiled even more widely at him. "I know. I told as much to Sarya just moments ago."

"Yes, yes." The man shifted nervously from foot to foot and glanced down at the girl. He took a deep breath, then took another. "I am afraid I'm out of sorts. I am Tejin Chinda, Sarya's father. Welcome to our camp. May I offer you some water, wine, or an early lunch? We can talk, and perhaps you would tell me why so few of the People are in one of the great cities without their family around them."

"It would be an honor and special privilege to partake in a little water," Fahtin said. "We ate breakfast only two hours ago and do not need food, however. I am Fahtin Achaya and this is my traveling companion and friend Aila Ven." She noticed Tejin's eyebrows raise slightly when she stated her name. "Do you know of my family?"

"I do. Your father is Darun, the Preshim of the Achaya caravan?"

"He is," she confirmed. "Do you know him?"

"I have met him a few times. He is a fine man, a fine Preshim. I hope he is well?"

"Perhaps we should sit," Fahtin said. "I will tell you all about it."

Tejin led Fahtin and Aila to a few stools set out around a cold fire pit and motioned for them to sit. He himself sat down next to his daughter on a larger seat, almost a bench, and waited patiently for Fahtin to start.

She told Tejin about her family. To provide the necessary background information, she explained how they had found Aeden nearly dead and nursed him back to health. As she delved into finding the village in which he was born destroyed by the dark creatures, it almost brought tears to her eyes. Everything Aeden had of his childhood was dashed to pieces and presented in such a way as to almost taunt him.

Fahtin had a hard time describing when Aeden found his father and came to realize the weakness of the animaru, their susceptibility to life magic.

From the corner of her eye, Fahtin saw not only Aila leaning forward, hanging on every word, but others of the family slowly gathering. She figured that Aila hadn't heard most of the tale and wondered if it would matter, if it would change the way the mysterious woman interacted with the rest of them.

Fahtin explained how the family was attacked and Aeden decided to leave to protect the others, and how Fahtin demanded to go with him. She downplayed how difficult a decision it was and minimized the sacrifice she had made for Aeden. She also left out how Raki ended up with them, only saying that there was a third member of the family as well.

She didn't go into detail about the adventures they had since they left the family, only saying that Jehira had told them Aeden was the Malatirsay—which elicited gasps from some in the audience—and that they were heading toward Sitor-Kanda to get help and to tell them about the dark creatures.

"And so," she said finally, "I honestly don't know how my father or my family are. When we left, they were all well. I hoped, when I first saw Sarya here, that your family would have news of mine."

"I am afraid I don't know anything of them," Tejin said, so caught up in the tale that he hadn't noticed an older man stepping up to them. He was very small, barely larger than Raki, and had lost much of his hair. Fahtin put his age at more than seventy. Probably much more. His eyes, a subtle hazel color, showed the wisdom of those years, but also a light that told her he was not a frail and feeble-minded man. Those eyes held power, though what kind she couldn't begin to guess.

"It is true," he said. "We have heard nothing of the Achaya family, though it is wonderful to see you, Fahtin. Do you remember me?"

She inspected him more closely. A little more hair, a few less wrinkles, and maybe she would recognize him. A memory struck her of a man smaller than others, though still bigger than her, who snuck her sweet cakes whenever their families met.

"Uncle Repun?" she asked, not sure she remembered correctly.

The man's face split into a smile and then she was certain. She would know that look anywhere. She stood and went to him, wrapping her arms around him.

"Yes, yes," he said. "You do remember, though it has been years since I have seen you. You have grown into a tall, beautiful young woman, while I have...well, the years hang heavy on me. But I am still young enough to remember your father, my friend, and your beautiful mother. And you, of course. I am glad the treats I secretly gave you did not cause you to grow too fat to move around." His eyes twinkled as he said it.

"Fahtin has helped my Sarya, Preshim Repun. She told me

what brought her to this city without her family, though I still do not understand how she is here if she is going to Sitor-Kanda."

"We had some other troubles along the way," Fahtin said. "We have booked passage on a boat going north. It leaves tomorrow. With luck, we will be at the Hero Academy in a week or so.

"I do have to warn you, Uncle. These dark creatures, these animaru, they will tear apart any they come upon. They destroyed several villages of the Croagh warriors in the highlands. They would have killed everyone in my family if it wasn't for Aeden."

"He is that powerful, this Crow who has been adopted into your family?" Repun asked.

"Yes. He is still learning to use his magic, but we have battled the dark creatures time and again and he has saved me many times over."

"We have heard of strange monsters stalking the north and east. We were heading in that direction." The leader of the family sat on an empty stool and looked into Fahtin's eyes. "Maybe it would be wise to go another way?"

"Yes," she said, almost too loudly. "Please, Uncle, go west. If we don't stop them, the animaru will eventually reach other parts of Dizhelim, but for now, they are in the east. There may be many hundreds, thousands even, following us here. It would be best if you left soon, before they get here. I have seen them attack towns. They will attack a city to get to us."

Fahtin discussed the issue with Repun and the other older men of the family, and by the time she took her leave of them, she had extracted a promise that they would leave that evening. It made her feel much better that they would be out of the city and going the opposite way from where the animaru seemed to be gathered.

On the way back to the city, Aila was silent. When they

reached the first buildings at the edge of the city, she turned to Fahtin.

"All of that was true, that stuff you told the old man?"

"Yes," Fahtin said. "That and more. Many things have happened to us since we left the caravan."

Aila made a humming noise, but didn't say anything else. At times, her mouth moved as she silently mused about something. Fahtin let her be. She had her own thoughts to wrestle with. She had been so busy trying to stay alive, she hadn't thought about how much she missed her mother and father. How much she missed her wagon and the whole family. She hoped she would see them again and that they were safe.

8

Khrazhti followed Aeden and Raki to the same clearing they had gone to the day before. Aeden had promised her they would spar with the wooden weapons he had obtained. It would be good to be able to move, to feel the exhilaration of combat, even if it was just sparring. It had been too long.

She had left her weapons behind when they departed from Broken Reach. She was essentially their prisoner and so needed to remain unarmed. The last look at her blades—weapons that had served her well for hundreds of years—would forever remain in her memory. Perhaps they could be replaced someday.

As soon as they arrived, Aeden set down the bundle he was carrying, and he and Raki began going through some strange motions. They almost looked like martial forms, but not quite.

"What doing are you?" she asked, rather proud that she could make the entire sentence in Ruthrin, the common tongue of this world. It made her feel even better when

Aeden seemed to miss a step as he looked over, wide-eyed, then smiled hugely at her.

"Warming up the muscles," he said to her slowly. Putting fire into the body tissue? Why would they do that?

"If we get our bodies warm, then we move more freely and don't have to worry about getting injured from stretching too far," Raki clarified in the strange form of Alaqotim he and Tere Chizzit spoke.

Shrugging that they should need such a thing, she joined them, watching Aeden as he led Raki in the exercises. After a few moments Khrazhti realized she liked how it felt to move slowly and carefully. A heat did grow in her arms and legs, as Raki had said. Maybe they had the right idea.

Raki seemed to be favoring one foot as he performed the exercises. Khrazhti was going to ask if he was well, but Aeden stopped.

"Raki, are you limping?"

The boy's face changed color. "I have some bad blisters on my foot from some gravel that got into my shoe. It's fine."

"I'm sure it is," Aeden said, "but maybe you can help me with something. I've been practicing one of the spells of the Raibrech called Life to Un-Life. It's a healing spell, but a really weak one. Can I try it on you, maybe see if I can heal your blisters?"

"Uh, sure. I guess. What will it do if it doesn't work?"

"Nothing, I think. The warriors in my clan used it, though like I said, it was almost too weak to even bother with. I'm hoping I can practice enough to make it stronger."

Raki nodded and Aeden had him sit on the ground where he was. He pulled off the boy's boot and looked at the bubbled skin. Then he made a few motions and softly said a few words.

It was hard to tell, but Khrazhti thought the bubbles deflated a bit. Aeden frowned, then repeated the process.

This time, she was sure of the effects. The skin went back to normal, losing the reddish color it had before. Raki let out a soft breath.

"That feels great, Aeden. You did it! Thank you."

"I'm glad I could help, even if it did take me two tries to heal a simple blister."

"Maybe if you keep practicing it, it'll get stronger, like you said," Raki told him.

With his foot healed, Raki put his boot back on and the three began going through the exercises again.

Aeden stopped after a few minutes, bouncing around on his toes and swinging his arms. Again, Khrazhti emulated him and, again, she enjoyed the sensation.

"I brought something for you," Aeden said to her. Raki translated, but she hardly needed it. He brought something? For her? Was it another one of their strange customs? He handed her two wooden swords. They were shaped like her swords she had left in the fortress, though a bit thicker and heavier since they were made of wood. "For practicing fighting," Aeden continued, and Khrazhti understood what the wooden weapons were for. He obviously didn't want her to hurt him.

Khrazhti took them and smiled at the warrior. "Thank you." She said it in Ruthrin. She needed to practice so she could speak with all her companions in this world.

Aeden took out another pair of wooden swords, replicas of his own real weapons, though they were thicker and heavier, too. He crossed them, bowed toward her, and then took up a ready stance, left sword in front pointing up and right sword in the back, pointing toward Khrazhti.

She had seen such things before, most recently when Aeden had been practicing his skills. The other animaru remembered salutes from before they were banished to Aruzhelim, but they had no need for them. It had been explained to her that they were an outward show of honor, another thing that was foreign to most animaru. Only those who were acquainted intimately with S'ru's commandments knew of such things.

To her, they seemed necessary, as water and food were to the fessani. What use was carrying out S'ru's commands if they were not done with a right mind? She had long understood this, and it made S'ru's failure to obey his own rules that much worse. But it was no time to be thinking on such matters.

She emulated his salute and charged.

Khrazhti threw several feints at Aeden, whirling her swords around at a speed faster than any fessani could possibly follow.

He parried each strike and countered with two of his own. She stepped back and gauged him again. How old did he say he was? Not yet a score of years? How did he gain such mastery and speed in so short a time?

With a feral smile, she went at him again. Soon, the clack of the wooden weapons on each other made an almost regular rhythm in the still forest air. It was nearly soothing, if it hadn't been for the fact that she was being pressed as she had not been pressed for many years. He truly was a skilled warrior.

For more than five minutes, the two danced around each other, striking, parrying, occasionally blocking, and of course, always counterattacking. Finally, she was able to sneak a strike through, scoring a hit on his left leg with the sword in her right hand. She stopped as soon as she felt the strike.

And found his sword resting at the side of her neck.

She blinked at him. Had he just...did he lure her in and allow her to strike him so he could land a more serious blow? Her eyes met his and she was sure of it. Not because there was victory there, or any kind of gloating. She was sure because his eyes held nothing but pure concentration and confidence. He had bested her, something that had not happened in centuries. If one did not count when all of them together had bested her a week past.

Then, just like that, his eyes went back to their normal intelligent blue and he smiled at her.

"Whew," he said. "That was fantastic!"

After Raki translated—he wasn't able to figure out how to say that first word, but Khrazhti assumed it was an exclamation of some sort—she crossed her swords and bowed to him again, as before. He laughed and returned the salute.

"How do you like the practice weapons?" he asked her.

"They feel good in my hands," Raki translated for her.

"I'm glad," Aeden said, limping toward their things lying on the ground. "I brought you something else, something I found in town when I was looking for the practice weapons." He held out another bundle to her. It was covered with some kind of animal skin.

Khrazhti's eyes lit up. She would have to ask about the customs on this world later. She did not want to seem impolite. Presenting gifts to companions seemed to be commonplace.

She accepted the bundle from him and unwrapped it. It was a pair of swords, real swords, encased in lacquered scabbards. Her mouth dropped open slightly as she looked over the weapons to Aeden and a smiling Raki.

"Take them out," he said, but she didn't really catch his meaning until Raki translated. Her mind seemed fuzzy for some reason.

She drew one of the blades. The steel glistened in the sunlight, so bright it hurt her eyes. The sword was remarkable, nearly identical to the ones she had before. The blade was curved, more fully than Aeden's swords. The handguard was full but not so large that it affected her movement.

Touching the curve of the blade, she felt a sting and watched as she bled a few dark red-brown drops onto the ground.

"Why?" was all she could think to say.

Raki translated for Aeden. "You left your swords at the fortress and I thought you might like to have another pair. It's a dangerous world, even more dangerous now that all the animaru want to tear you to shreds. I figured you might have a use for them."

"But...I am animaru. You would arm your enemy?"

"No," Aeden said in Alaqotim. "I would arm my friend."

9

Tere Chizzit had left Urun back in the city, telling the priest he had some scouting to do and that the younger man couldn't keep up with him. Urun knew Tere well enough to recognize it as the truth and simply told his friend to be careful.

"Always am," Tere said with a grin. He "saw" the exasperated look on Urun's face, though it looked different than it would have had he still had his normal sight. As he headed out of the city to the north, he pondered his abilities. Again. For the ten thousandth time.

He had never heard of anyone having his talents. It was a good thing he had them, or he would be just another blind, old man in the world. He had once thought that would be enough, but no longer. He had a purpose again, a place. The little party of companions was almost like his family, and as the elder person, he would do his best to protect them. Thus his third trip in as many days to scout the area.

He would not allow enemies to surprise him.

Before two hours had passed, he reached his destination: a hill with an unobscured view of the north. It was one of the higher mounds in the area, and the only one he'd found that wasn't cluttered with trees. He could see for miles from his vantage point. Much farther than any sighted person, if the target was right.

In this case, his target could not have been more suited to his magical vision. The animaru had a magic all their own, but it was still magic, and so he could see it from much farther away than if he had to spot their actual bodies. He believed he could even see their particular glow before he'd see the huge dust cloud they must create as they came charging toward the betrayer, Khrazhti. Daylight or night, he would be able to give his friends the earliest warning.

Each time Tere had come up to the hill since they reached Satta Sarak, he hoped against hope that he would not see anything, that the animaru were either too far away or somehow following the wrong trail. He had the same feeling as he scanned the horizon, looking for that which he did not want to find.

Halfway through his sweep of the land in front of him, he stopped. There was something, a glimmer from far away. He continued swiveling his head to his right, seeing nothing else. Then he swung back to where he had thought he saw something. There it was again, in the same place. Not so much a glimmer as a flash this time. Mentally blinking, he focused all his vision on the one speck of light ahead of him. There was no doubt. It was a concentration of movement through the magical field of the world, and he recognized the form of it. He had battled the dark creatures enough in the past couple of months to know. They were coming for Khrazhti, and by extension the rest of the party.

By the time Tere Chizzit reached the bottom of the hill and threaded his way through the vegetation between it and the city, he had already calculated the animaru army's rate of speed. They would arrive before the boat left, somewhere around two or three hours before dawn.

He and his friends had to decide what they would do to escape. Hopefully without bringing thousands of dark monsters down on the city of Satta Sarak.

Tere rushed back to the city just in time to meet the others at the restaurant he had told them about earlier. He went through different scenarios as he traveled, dodging people in the city without thinking, guarding his purse and cuffing two small pickpockets as he passed.

He decided to allow his friends their meal before he broke the news to them. Why did he feel so guilty about that? An hour or two would not make a world of difference, and they had to discuss the matter thoroughly before taking action. It wasn't so easy as simply running. There were too many other considerations.

Luckily, he had arranged for a private dining room, so they were free to talk about anything they liked. Tere tried to act normally, but both Aeden and Urun glanced at him much too often, even staring at times. Surprisingly, Khrazhti favored him with a quizzical look as well. He let everyone get well into their meal before he cut through the soft chatter with his announcement. He had decided to take the middle road, letting them enjoy at least half their meal before springing the news on them.

"I have seen the animaru. They'll be here a few hours before dawn at the rate they are traveling."

The room exploded into sound, everyone asking him specifics. At least one or two questioned why he waited. There was nothing to do but to continue onward. He raised his hands, beseeching them to silence. When the questions had stopped, he spoke again.

"I see...farther than most people. I did see the mass of our enemies, but they are still hours away yet. They're moving fast, but we can leave the city with plenty of time to avoid them. At least, I think so. Khrazhti,"—he turned toward the animaru—"do you still possess the glow?" Raki translated for the animaru, so she was able to answer immediately.

"I am not sure," she said. "I cannot see it in myself. I would assume it is still in effect, though I do not know how powerfully."

Tere rubbed his chin. "We'll just have to assume you're correct and that they can follow us. That's good news in a way. If we leave, they won't attack the city. I suggest we go south, into the Mellanor Forest. At the very least, the heavy vegetation will break up their ranks so they can't attack all as one mass."

"We're just going to leave the city?" Fahtin asked. "We're not going to try to catch the boat?"

"If we do, we'll bring the entire force down upon the city. They'll attack and cut through the city to get to us. A lot of people will die, and in the end, we won't be able to leave with the boat anyway. We can't hold out for three or four hours against all those animaru while hoping the boat will leave on time. I'd not like to be backed into a corner by all those creatures. Do you disagree, Khrazhti?"

The blue woman shook as if surprised to be dragged into the conversation. She recovered quickly, though, and Raki translated her response. "I agree with your assessment. If they know we are in the city, the walls and all the people will not stop them. Flight is the only option." She stared blankly at the wall for a moment, before speaking again. "If I were to leave the city and let them have me, you would be safe. They could not track you, or even know of your existence."

"They already know me as the Gneisprumay," Aeden said. "You told me that much. They will continue to try to find me and kill me, even if they don't look in the city right now. And we will *not* be letting you sacrifice yourself for us. I don't want to hear of it again, and by your oath, you will *not* sneak away and give yourself to them."

The animaru's lips tensed into a flat line. Tere had the urge to chuckle. That expression was the same he had seen on women disagreeing with men his whole life.

"We stick together," Tere said. "We need to go back to the inn and gather our gear, then head south. If anyone has a better idea"—he held a finger up—"one that doesn't involve sacrificing yourself, say it now. We've time to finish eating, but not for arguments." The archer looked each person in the eyes, but no one had anything more to say. "Good, let's finish up and then get going."

They only stayed for a few minutes more. The others picked at their food, but didn't eat. Tere was glad he'd waited until they were nearly finished, that he didn't completely ruin the meal. As everyone got up to leave, Khrazhti reached toward the wall to pick up something. When Tere got a good look, he realized she was buckling on a sword belt with two scabbarded swords attached to it. He raised an eyebrow.

"I got them for her. A gift," Aeden said.

"Trust her that much already, do you?"

"I do. I've spoken with her quite a bit since she joined us. I think she is sincere in her belief that life is not to be taken if it can be helped. She has a kind of honor that leaves no room for betrayal. If she was going to harm us, she would have tried to do so already. With her combat skills and her magic, she's the match of any two or three of us."

"That sounds a lot like admiration, Aeden," Tere said, winking at him.

"She's really remarkable." Aeden shook his head. "Anyway, is there a problem with giving her weapons? She is only slightly more dangerous with them."

Tere patted Aeden's shoulder. "No, no problem. It was a surprise, that's all. Truth to tell, if it comes down to a fight with the creatures chasing us, I'd much rather she have something to fight with. You know, other than her magic and her unarmed combat skills."

"My thoughts exactly," Aeden said, looking around the room and finding that everyone else had left while he was talking with Tere. He followed the older man out onto the street toward their inn.

It took twenty minutes to return to the inn and another ten to get their belongings. They met out front, leaving in ones and twos so as not to make themselves even more memorable. Minutes after they had all gathered, they moved through the darkened streets toward one of the south gates.

The party was passing through a darkened area two streets down from their inn when the attack came.

❧ 10 ❧

Something from the corner of Tere Chizzit's perception screamed for his attention. Not sure at first what it could be, he directed his virtual eyes toward it. Something was coming at them, something traveling very fast. Almost without thinking, he took an arrow from the quiver on his back, nocked it, drew, and released it.

It struck the other object mid-flight, shattering it. It was an arrow, and aimed at one of them. But which one?

Another came, and then another and then another. One person was firing them. If there were more, they wouldn't be coming from exactly the same trajectory. It was all he could do to continue shooting his own arrows to intercept the ones coming at them. There was no chance of him firing an extra arrow at the actual archer.

"Get behind some cover," he yelled to the others. He didn't have the time to look at them, to see how they were reacting. He imagined they were probably confused. He doubted any of them could see the arrows he was targeting.

A red flash from another direction, in front and to the left of him, almost made him pause too long in releasing his next arrow. The flash intensified as it hit something. The flare briefly illuminated what had to be an invisible magical shield around Aeden and the two people closest to him: Khrazhti and Raki. Tere didn't know whose magic it was, but it was good they weren't relying completely on him.

Seven arrows into it and Tere decided he had to take a chance. Moving faster than he had ever moved before, he shot another arrow out of the sky, prepared and released another one, and then barely got another one off to intercept a projectile that had almost reached him.

He zoomed his focus in on the intended target of the middle arrow. A person was on a nearby roof. A woman, if his eyes did not deceive him. Her arms were bare. In fact, all she had on her torso was an item of clothing consisting of two small scraps of cloth—or leather, or armor of some kind—covering her breasts. Her lower body wasn't visible, so he couldn't see if her wardrobe was consistent, but he could see the important part: his arrow embedded in the top part of her right shoulder. Even better, she was right-handed, holding her own bow in her left hand. She wore her quiver just as he did, angled so that the fletching poked up over her right shoulder.

He couldn't hear her, but the way she moved her mouth and shook her mane of red hair, she wasn't happy with the development. Good. She wouldn't be shooting arrows at him anytime soon. It was really too bad she was mostly behind the wall of a building or he could have put the arrow in her eye. She seemed to move faster than even his sight could track.

The shining red objects were still striking the shield in front of Aeden, Khrazhti, and Raki. By the look on the animaru's face, it wasn't her magic that created the shield. Surprise mixed with anger showed in her scrunched brow and her glowing eyes, which were fixed on a figure thirty feet away, throwing what appeared to be knives on fire. No, the knives were actually *made* of fire.

The fire-wielder showed no emotion as she threw fire-knife after fire-knife. Her crimson dress, tight in the torso and waist but flowing below that, swirled as if in a strong wind as she walked almost casually toward the group, launching the fiery projectiles.

From the other side of the intersection of alleys, a large shape emerged into the pale light of the lanterns. He was large and all solid muscle. It was easy to tell because he wore only pants and boots, his entire torso bare. Tattoos swirled around his body, leaving only narrow spaces of un-inked flesh. He came too quickly for anyone to react, on the other side of the shield protecting Aeden, spoiling any shot Tere might make.

No, that was not correct. The man did move as fast as lightning, but he wasn't too speedy for Khrazhti. She drew her swords in an elegant movement and was battering at the man even as he got in range. Tere would have to leave the animaru to it. The shield keeping the fire weapons from Aeden flickered. Once it fell, there was nothing to stop the magical projectiles from finding their target.

Tere fired three arrows at the woman. His sight told him how she would move, if at all, and all three should find vital areas, removing her from the fight.

But it didn't happen that way.

Never in his life had his ability failed him. He was able to read how his opponents would move. He could still be over-whelmed, but when he fired an arrow, he never missed. Never.

But he did.

Perhaps it was not accurate to say that he missed. The woman didn't dodge the arrows or deflect them in any way. She merely called upon her power and blasted the shafts from the air with what looked like fiery swords.

Somehow, the woman's magic seemed to be all but invisible to Tere's sight. That was not something he thought possible, and not something he wanted to deal with at the moment.

At least four projectiles glinted in the lantern light and the red of the woman's fiery weapons. Raki and Fahtin had entered the fray.

Tere glanced toward the archer and found that she had disappeared. The party should be able to take the two remaining.

"Go," the fire-wielder said. Tere thought at first she was talking to him or one of the party.

The huge, battle-axe-wielding man huffed a curse, swiped at Khrazhti, who had kept him at bay with her swords, and then turned and sprinted away back from where he had come from. A half dozen fiery daggers flew out from the woman's outstretched hand as she also turned to run.

Khrazhti slapped one of the knives out of the air with her sword—which was glowing with magic—and dodged another one. Raki, Fahtin, and Aila dove to the ground to dodge three more of them. The rest struck Aeden's shield, causing it to flicker again and then pop out of existence.

"Is everyone okay?" Aeden asked. The others looked around at each of their companions, some voicing confirmations and some just nodding. "Good. What in the name of the nine hells was that?"

"That," Tere said, "was an attack."

"Thank you," Aeden deadpanned. "Are we going after them? Can you track them, Tere?"

"I can, but we won't be going after them. There's no reason, but there is adequate reasoning not to."

"What do you mean?" Fahtin said, still a little breathless.

The archer swiveled his head toward her. "I think it was an opportunistic attack. It seems to me that this was a rush job. As an ambush, it was poorly done. With their obvious skill, I would expect a trap to be much more effective than this. I think they were watching us but didn't expect us to be leaving the city so soon. We forced their hand."

"But who are they?" Aila asked. "I kind of expect animaru to be chasing us down—no offense to you Khrazhti—but humans? What did we do to them?"

"They're probably after you," Urun said, glaring at the girl. He seemed to be irritated with the woman lately for some reason. "What is in your past that might cause a group of people to want you dead? *Another* group of people, I mean."

Aila shifted her gaze to Tere, opening her mouth to speak. She was smart enough to figure out what Urun was talking about. The older man had told the rest of the party how he had met Aila that night outside Drugancairn, how the group of men wanted to kill her.

"No," Tere said before the two of them could start bickering. "The first arrows and fiery knives were aimed at Khrazhti. The targets only shifted once the rest of us got involved. As difficult as it is to believe, it almost seems like these three are on the same side as the animaru. Is there something we should know, Khrazhti?"

Raki translated out of habit. Tere usually took up the job when someone else was speaking, but when Tere used Ruthrin, the Gypta boy did translation duty.

Khrazhti answered and Raki translated for the others. "There are humans involved with the animaru. Who do you think opened the portals to Aruzhelim?"

Questions exploded from everyone. Raki put his hands over his ears both to block out the sound around him and to indicate his frustration with trying to translate.

"Enough," Aeden shouted. "This is getting us nowhere. The animaru will be here soon. We need to get out of the city before that happens. And before those three come back with a better plan or with backup, or both. We can talk on the way, or once we're in the forest."

The questions died down to soft murmuring as Tere nodded and headed toward the south, the others following. He wasn't looking forward to hearing what Khrazhti had to say.

One thing he was sure of was that he was happy Aeden had given the animaru those blades. She may have been able to hold off that axe-wielding mountain of muscle without them, but they made the job easier and she did use them on the party's behalf. He hoped she would continue to do so.

As he unwound the long cloths from his arms and then re-wrapped them to be snug but loose enough to allow him free movement, Featherblade listened to the heavily muscled man in front of him. The axe-wielder explained how he, and the other two assassins tasked with watching their targets, had tipped off their prey and then themselves had to flee. This was the reason Featherblade preferred to work missions alone. When other people were involved, issues inevitably cropped up.

Some caused more issues than others.

"What were we supposed to do?" Keenseeker asked. He gestured with arms that had more muscle—and wider girth— than most people's legs. "They had all their gear. They were obviously leaving."

"You could have followed them," Featherblade said calmly. "At a distance." He looked the man up and down. "Or one of the other two with you could have. I understand that your talents do not lie in stealth."

Keenseeker stopped his gestures, and his blue eyes met

Featherblade's even paler cool-blue orbs. "Yeah, I'm a bit too big to be sneaking around like some kind of skinny shadow. So what of it? We're on this team because we all have talents. Can you cut two men in half with one swing of your weapon? I can't dance through the darkness, but I can kill just as well, better, than the rest of you."

Featherblade sighed. For better or worse, he was tasked with leading this brace of assassins. There was nothing to be gained by scolding the axe-wielding killer. The man would never see that he did anything wrong.

They were in the warehouse they occupied as they planned to ambush their target. It was a large, empty place, wooden walls cracked and splintered. There were beds set up in the corner of the massive central room, but not much else in the way of amenities. Featherblade had been in worse.

Along with Featherblade were eleven others of the Falxen. Hardly anyone called the assassins by that name, though. In general conversation—granted that it was morbid conversation—they were referred to simply as Blades. The elite assassins had no equal in all of Dizhelim.

"I can track them," the beautiful red-headed archer—Phoenixarrow—said.

Featherblade glanced at her. "No. You have failed me once tonight already, and you need to see to that shoulder or you'll be worthless for this mission. Fleshrender, go and track them. Do not engage them. Simply determine where they are going. We will meet you at the south entrance of the city."

The tall woman with long sand-colored hair nodded and headed toward the door. Featherblade really didn't know how she did the things she did in that dress. It seemed very tight to him, but he had seen her in combat many times and she moved like the wind, her vicious serrated blades at the ends of chains whirring with expert precision and cutting into her enemies' flesh. She enjoyed that, the cutting. So much that she earned the name Fleshrender.

Despite her morbid preoccupation with cutting people, though, she did have the useful talent of sensing where her prey had gone. She would be able to track the target through the city. The blue woman could not evade the sadistic assassin for long.

Featherblade had been surprised when his tablet indicated that new information had been obtained and not only was he —and the rest of the brace—to return to Satta Sarak, but they were now to target the blue woman. Apparently something had changed and their employer no longer cared about the group of people he had described before.

He had not argued, of course. Orders were not changed often after plans were set in motion, but it did happen occasionally. His task was to make sure death was dealt swiftly and surely, regardless of whether the target was a handful of people or one that was distinctive. They would do their job.

Phoenixarrow pouted prettily, but it had no impact on Featherblade. He appreciated her beauty, shaped in such a way that men fell over themselves to get near her. It didn't help that she also wore attire that accentuated and displayed her figure. What little attire there was. But to him, she was just another assassin under his command. One who had failed in the simple task of keeping an eye on their target.

"Everyone gather your gear," Featherblade said. "I'll contact our employer through the communication tablet and tell him we found the target but that we are still bringing her to ground. As soon as I'm finished, we leave."

The leader of the braces at down, took out a small tablet, and began to write on it with the special stylus he removed from a sheath along the side of the slate. When Featherblade was finished, he put the tablet away and stood up. Everyone else was ready to go. It was late, and their employer may not read the message until the morning. It was no matter. The assassins had their target to find. Featherblade could check the response later. He would receive the response when Izhrod Benzal awoke.

For now, it was time to hunt.

"WILL THEY BE FOLLOWING US?" AILA ASKED ONCE THE party made it to the trees of the Mellanor Forest.

"Yes." Tere led them further into the foliage to the south of the city. "We surprised them. It won't happen again."

"How can you be so sure?" Fahtin asked.

"They're Blades."

"They're what?" the Gypta said.

Tere turned to the young woman. "Blades. Falxen. Elite assassins. Haven't you ever heard of the Falxen?"

"No. Who are they, and why do you think the ones who attacked us are assassins?"

"Did you see the mark on the right ankle of the one who threw those fire knives at us?" Tere asked.

"Uh," Fahtin said. "No. I was too busy being afraid I was going to die."

"Well, trust me on this. It was the Falxen sigil. Someone has hired killers to track us down. Or maybe I should be more clear. They were obviously after Khrazhti. I think we just got in the way."

"But who are they?" Fahtin asked. "We're pretty tough. Why do we have to worry about three assassins?"

"Not just assassins. Falxen. The name, when it is spoken at all, is spoken with respect, even reverence. The Falxen are the most elite assassins in Dizhelim, an organization that transcends boundaries and ethnic distinctions. They are simply the most dangerous group of assassins in existence.

"It would be an understatement to call them a clan or guild. They are much like a kingdom of their own. They maintain a training facility—a location only they know—that trains people in the deadly arts. It's the finest training facility in Dizhelim, aside from the Hero Academy itself.

"Most don't refer to the assassins as the Falxen, however. They're more commonly known by their nickname: Blades.

"And there will be more. Those three were left to keep an eye on us. They'll be gathering the other members of the brace—that's what a group of them is called—and they will be coming after us. It'll be better for us if they don't catch up. I'll tell you about them when we have to stop. For now, though, keep your mind on what you're doing. We need to try to get lost in the forest. Maybe they don't have a tracker with them, though I can't see them making that kind of oversight."

They traveled for another hour, the others following Tere, who unerringly found the easiest path through the dense vegetation. When they finally stopped to get their bearings and decide what they would do next, everyone was darting glances at the archer, anxious for his promised explanation.

Tere knew that some—even all—of them didn't believe him. A normal person wouldn't readily accept that elite assassins were coming after them as a group. He had no doubt, though, even without the mark on the woman's ankle. There was no other explanation for it. If the others they brought with them were as skilled as the three they met, there would be trouble indeed.

"Okay," the archer said. "I will give you a quick explanation of what the Falxen are and then we need to get moving. If we can lose them in the forest and stay ahead of them the entire way to Sitor-Kanda, maybe we'll survive."

The others settled in, quietly drank some of the water they brought, and looked to Tere.

"Hundreds of years ago, three of the finest assassins of the age combined their talents and started a school of sorts. In it, they trained promising children in the art of killing and espionage. They named their new organization Falxen, from the Alaqotim word for blade. Thus, they are most often called Blades, for not only is that their name, but that is what they are: living weapons trained for one purpose—to kill whichever target they are hired to eliminate.

"As the organization grew, they were recognized throughout all of Dizhelim as the best killers-for-hire in the world, and their price reflected that. They have no loyalties, are not political in any way, and are not burdened by conscience. If someone has the money to hire a Blade, the target does not have long to live. The assassin will complete the mission or die trying.

"As I said, the Blades are trained from young childhood in various methods for ending life, as well as infiltration, moving silently, and other useful techniques, such as tracking, cryptology, disguise, and assorted types of magic. It has been said that a Blade is the single most dangerous living creature in Dizhelim. I do not believe that is far from the truth.

"It appears that we have at least three, and probably more, Blades who have been hired to eliminate our new ally." Tere motioned toward Khrazhti. "A brace is typically three Blades but can be up to six, when the Falxen are not working alone, which they most often do. I think there are more than the three, possibly even more than six. It could be two or three braces following us. It would be better if we never found out for sure.

"Don't doubt me when I say we need to flee from them. They most likely have a way of tracking us down, either with good old-fashioned skills or with magic. Either way, we will have to move quickly. They have been trained to hunt prey, and we are that prey; or at least, Khrazhti is. If my explanation is enough, I suggest we start moving and don't stop until we get to Sitor-Kanda. If it's not, well tough. We need to get moving."

As Tere was speaking, Raki translated for Khrazhti. When the Gypta boy translated the last part, Khrazhti emitted an exclamation. To Tere, it sounded a lot like a curse, though he couldn't place the words. She spoke quickly after that, almost as if she was talking to herself. Berating herself.

"Uh oh," Raki said, and Tere agreed.

"We have more trouble," Tere said to the rest of the party. "Khrazhti says she has been so caught up in everything that she lost track of time. The human who created the portal used to bring the animaru over had planned on opening another portal. To do so, he had to plan well in advance, many months. He will open it in less than three weeks.

"*Andorin recoat du acci rudis flagranti,*" Aeden spat. Khrazhti stumbled a step, looking at the Croagh in horror. "Ah, sorry," he said, not quite meeting her surprised gaze. Tere barely kept his mouth from twisting into a smile. The boy should know not to use Alaqotim curses around the animaru.

"Who is this human?" Aila asked.

Tere answered, translating for Khrazhti. "His name is Izhrod Benzal."

"Wait," Urun said. "Are you saying that this Benzal guy will be bringing even more animaru to Dizhelim?"

"That's what she's saying," Tere said. "Yes."

"How many of these creatures are there? How many are here already?"

Tere looked at Raki, and the Gypta waved toward Khrazhti. The archer took the hint and translated for the animaru woman and listened to her response. He translated for the others, "There are approximately two thousand animaru left in Dizhelim, though as far as she knows only two generals remain. As for how many there are in Aruzhelim, there is a total of three hundred fifty-two thousand, one hundred twenty-four, not including her. Minus those we have managed to destroy."

Urun's mouth dropped open and he stared at Khrazhti. He wasn't alone.

"I...had no idea," Aeden said. "How can we fight against that?"

Tere translated without really thinking. It was hard to conceive of numbers that large. Especially when one was talking about enemies. Khrazhti had to repeat what she said twice before Tere realized she had spoken.

"She says our best course of action is to go and stop Izhrod Benzal from opening the portal."

"Sure," Urun said. "That would be great. How, exactly, can we do that? We don't even know where he is."

"Khrazhti does," Tere said. "At least, she says she can find the place. She's been there before, and she can sense his power."

Fahtin edged her way between Tere and Urun. "But that means we can't go to the Hero Academy. Not unless the portal is on the way there."

The archer cocked his head and listened to Khrazhti. "No, it's not on the way. It's to the northeast, essentially the opposite direction we need to go to get to Sitor-Kanda." He faced Aeden. "There's nothing for it. We're going to have to split up, half of us going to stop Benzal and the others going to warn the Academy."

"We weren't just going to the Academy to warn them, though," Aila said. "Aeden was going to get help in figuring out what he's supposed to be doing and how he can use his magic. That means he's going to have to be with the group going to the Academy."

"No, it doesn't," Tere said. "He's also the only one who can do real damage to large groups of animaru. I'm afraid Aeden is going to have to go after Benzal. There will be many animaru there, even if he can make it in time to stop the portal from opening. Khrazhti has to go because she knows where Benzal is, and as long as she has the glow, the animaru chasing us will follow her. So, Khrazhti and Aeden have to go northeast."

"I'm going with him, of course," Fahtin said as if it was already agreed.

"And me," Raki added. "Not only because of Aeden, but so I can translate for Khrazhti.

"I'm going with Aeden, too," Aila said, sidling up to him.

"No, Aila," Aeden disagreed. "You have to go with Tere and Urun. They'll need your help. There are animaru out there, but there are also the assassins and other dangers."

Everyone present seemed to stop whatever they were doing to look toward Aila. Even the forest seemed to quiet down in anticipation of the tantrum that must surely be coming.

"I..." the diminutive woman started. She paused, closed her eyes, and took in a deep breath. "I guess that's logical. I'll help however I can." She turned to Aeden. "But we will gather everyone together again. We will."

Aila moved off a few feet, making a show of scanning the dark forest.

The others studied each other, though no one directed their gaze at Tere. He knew how discomfiting it was for people to look into his blank eyes. That gave him a good vantage point to observe the others, all of whom had confusion painted all across their features. Fahtin even shrugged.

"Well..." Tere said. "Okay. I will take Urun and Aila and head north. If we can catch a boat farther up the river, we will do so; otherwise, we'll go cross country. Khrazhti, where will you be heading?" That last part he said in Alaqotim and again in Ruthrin.

The former high priestess explained where they would go and Tere translated.

"To the north and east. She has only been there once, but she can home in on the power signature from Benzal's magic. She's not sure exactly where it will be, but when she's within a few dozen miles, she can find his precise location."

No one responded. They continued to look at each other as if they didn't recognize the people around them...or like they might never see them again.

Aeden shook his head, dispelling the sorrowful expression on his face. "We better get moving. There's no telling how close the assassins are, and if they're half as dangerous as Tere says, we would be better not to meet them."

"True," Tere said. "Be careful, you four. Danger is in front *and* behind you now. Move quickly and be safe. Meet us at the town of Dartford, near the north bridge to Munsahtiz, the island the Academy is on. Better there than at Sitor-Kanda itself. We should arrive before you, so we can warn the masters and wait for you in town."

Fahtin flew at the tracker and wrapped her arms around him. "You be safe too, Tere Chizzit. And keep our friends safe." She nodded her head toward Urun and Aila in turn. "We need to meet again safe and tell each other stories about the adventures we've had."

She went to Urun and hugged him as well. He was lost in his own musings, and when she embraced him, his eyebrows shot up and he nearly jumped out of her arms. Once he realized what was happening, he returned her hug and patted her back. When Fahtin approached Aila, Tere wasn't sure if the smaller woman would rebuff the Gypta, but she put her arms out and the two squeezed each other tightly.

"You make sure to take care of yourself," Aila said. "And the others. I'll not lose my friends after I have just found them." Unshed tears glistened in her eyes.

A round of handshakes, back pats, and well-wishes commenced. Khrazhti stood off to the side, looking like she wanted to be somewhere else. Fahtin made a cooing sound when she saw the animaru's discomfort and went slowly toward her and showed her what a hug was. The blue woman was hesitant, but once Fahtin had her wrapped in a hug, she seemed to relax, if not exactly enjoy it.

Aeden clasped wrists with Tere, looking directly into the man's white eyes. "Tere, I can never repay you for—"

"No, there will be none of that," Tere said. "This is not goodbye, so don't make out like it is. We are separating to perform our missions and then we'll regroup. It's what warriors do." He patted Aeden's shoulder to soften the sternness of his voice.

"Yes," Aeden said. "It is. Thank you, my friend. We'll see you in a few weeks and we can compare stories like Fahtin says."

The archer winked at the younger man, and Aeden nearly winced. Maybe winking wasn't the best way to communicate camaraderie, Tere thought, not with his eyes. "By the way, you'll probably want to head north before you get to the eastern edge of the Mellanor Forest. I hear there is a hag there, one that can cause problems. I believe she is actually an ilyu. At least, she was there a couple of decades or so ago. So the rumor has it."

"An ilyu?" Fahtin asked.

"We don't really have time," Tere said. "Just be careful and leave the forest to go north before you reach the eastern boundaries. Well before."

He wished Khrazhti well in her own language and thanked her for her help thus far. He showed her how to clasp wrists, but then impulsively pulled her close to give her a soft hug. "You are one of us now. Family. Be safe and successful in your mission."

The blue face, so alien at times, softened. The glow in her large blue eyes seemed to dance, generating their own light.

"It will be as you say. My destruction before that of my companions."

Raki's mouth dropped open. When Tere translated for everyone else, theirs did too.

❧ 12 ☙

Aeden felt the loss of his three friends immediately, as if a piece of his middle had been torn out and tossed away. He had become accustomed to having Aila, Urun, and especially Tere around. For the first time in quite a while, he was unsure about the immediate future. He didn't know what was wrong with him. He knew how to travel through the wilderness, how to fend for himself. He realized he had been taking Tere's skills in tracking and woodcraft for granted.

He took the lead, catching the hesitant motions of his companions as he headed east, following the edge of the Mellanor Forest as it curved up toward the north. They would travel in the relatively thinner vegetation while still using the forest as cover until they got near the eastern boundary of the trees. Then they would go north across open country and then follow Khrazhti's directions.

If they floundered and delayed, the assassins would catch up to them. If they followed in the first place. Aeden hoped the pursuers lost the trail completely, but if not, he would prefer they go after Tere's group, not because he was being selfish, but because the old tracker was more skilled at disappearing or obscuring his trail. It would be best if none of them had to battle with those trying to kill them.

Khrazhti entered the side of his vision, her blue eyes glowing faintly. Her body didn't seem to be glowing as much as earlier. In fact, it didn't seem to glow at all.

"Khrazhti, can you tell if the mark is disappearing from you? You don't seem to be glowing as much as earlier, or at all."

Raki translated his words and then her response. "She can't tell. She can't feel the mark. It should disappear as time goes on, hopefully within the next day or two."

Aeden nodded, but didn't say anything. He hoped they had a day or two. Between the assassins and the animaru chasing them, he could do with a little good news.

"It needs to stay in effect for a little while," Fahtin said. When Aeden, and even Raki as he translated, gave her confused looks, she continued. "If they sense her leaving the city, the animaru won't attack Satta Sarak. Once they have changed direction, then the mark can fade, but the city will already have been spared the trouble of an army of monsters attacking it."

"Good thinking," Aeden said. "You're right. Hopefully we can lead them away. Better they chase us than to attack thousands of innocent people."

Khrazhti nodded also.

The former high priestess had to be concerned. She was a beacon, putting the entire party at risk. She was in a strange world all alone, with people she barely knew, fleeing from danger into danger. It wasn't an ideal situation.

"Thank you for guiding us," Aeden said in broken Alaqotim.

The blue face turned to consider him for a moment. "It is to you that thanks should be given. You allow me the honor of sharing your quest and treat me as a friend." That last word was in Ruthrin. Did animaru Alaqotim have a word for friend? Even if it did, she probably never had one before. He got the feeling that she had been as alone with the animaru as she was with them. The thought made him sad.

Featherblade had been in Satta Sarak four days ago. He and his brace had finished an assignment and were to have a few days without a mission. That was until Izhrod Benzal contacted him through the communication tablet, one of two he carried at all times.

The tablets were made by the artificers in the Academy at Sitor-Kanda, apparently. His current employer gave Featherblade instructions through the devices. The other brace that would join his had their own tablet, and they had received similar instructions.

It was almost unheard of to have even one of the Falxen on retainer, but Izhrod Benzal had several. Even Featherblade didn't know how many, and he was usually utilized to lead any brace to which Benzal gave a job.

The message was simple enough: go toward the ruins of the fortress at Broken Reach to eliminate several people. He gathered the brace he commanded and headed to the old fortress.

Halfway there, he received another message. The target had been changed to a woman with blue skin. Blue skin? Maybe she was an actress who had dyed her skin or perhaps had a rare disease. Either way, she had been spotted in Satta Sarak. Curiously, she was in the company of others that met the descriptions he had been given previously. Featherblade was to rendezvous with the spy who had seen her and find the target's location.

After that, he was to kill her and those traveling with her.

Featherblade had interacted with the spy before. His name was Tilsin Mont, a skeletal, gangly man who seemed so uncoordinated that he shouldn't be able to walk. In fact, though, he was very good at skulking around and not being seen. Perhaps it was because of peoples' preconceptions of the man. Whatever the reason, he had seen the one Featherblade was to kill. They met him at the cobbler shop he owned.

"I saw it in the company of real people," Tilsin told him of the blue woman. "They were at the dock. Booking passage on a boat, no doubt. I sniffed 'em out quick-like. They seemed like they were different than the rest of the folk around, standing too proud and moving too confidently. When a wind took the hood from its head, I saw. Blue skin, just like the message said. Some kind of monster, it was."

"Very good, Master Tilsin," Featherblade said in his soft, soothing voice. "And you know where they are staying?"

"Of course, of course." Tilsin ducked his head. "I followed the lot of them to the Spotted Frog. Been here two days, they have. I reckon they'll be taking the boat soon, though."

"You don't have to worry about that. Please take these three—" He motioned to Fireshard, Keenseeker, and Phoenixarrow. "—to the inn. The rest of us will be in the safehouse on Chandler Street. After you have shown them the inn, please come and see me. I would like to know any other information you might have."

"Yessir." Tilsin bobbed his head again. "I'll do just as you ask. I'll be at the safehouse within half an hour, to be sure."

The spy ducked his head to the others and stalked off, looking like a water bird wading through the muck.

A few minutes later, the assassins glided into the safehouse, skulking in the shadows until they determined it to be empty. It was a small warehouse kept for planning Blades' activities in and around the city. There were few furnishings. A simple table, four chairs, and two pallets. Missions rarely required more than one or two of the Falxen. There was plenty of room for everyone, though, even if they couldn't all use the furniture at the same time.

Featherblade turned his attention to the eight Blades still with him. A slight motion of his hand brought his second-in-command for this mission, Darkcaller, to his side.

As always, the woman was dressed all in black. For that matter, most of them were. They were assassins, after all. With many Falxen it seemed to be obligatory, though there was nothing requiring it. The difference was that Darkcaller wore very revealing clothing, tighter than seemed necessary... and less of it than seemed wise. Her black hair swirled around her as if was a part of the cloak that covered the vast amounts of skin the clothing underneath left bare.

She moved like she knew how attractive and alluring she was. In the past, some men had taken her mannerisms as an invitation. Some were allowed to live, but not many. Alongside her beauty and her pleasing form, she was a killer, through and through.

She was a graduate of the so-called Hero Academy, and the staff she carried was more than a physical weapon. True, she could wield it skillfully, but its value was greater as a focus for her magic.

"That Keenseeker is a pig," she said to Featherblade as she stomped over to him. "I saw his eyes caressing me. If he tries anything with me, I will kill him."

"Please don't." Featherblade sighed. "Punish him, show him his error, but I'd not like it if we start killing each other."

Her light hazel—almost amber—eyes scanned his own. After a moment, she nodded, hesitantly. "Fine. I will hurt him, though. I know the type. Big muscles and nothing but rotting wood inside his skull. He thinks he's better than everyone else, especially women."

It was an old topic. "He thinks he's better than *everyone* else, including men, women, encalo, pouran, astridae, even some of the gods, most likely. It is what we have to tolerate. As long as he only blusters, it will not be an issue. If he jeopardizes the mission, *I* will take care of him. Do not take it upon yourself. Please. It is my responsibility."

Darkcaller blew out a lungful of air. "Understood. It is your brace, after all."

"Thank you. Now, how have your Blades been performing? I'd like to know what to expect in case we run into something more than a blue-skinned woman running away from Izhrod Benzal."

"I only had Edge and Phoenixarrow with me before. The others were simply told to meetup with us at Satta Sarak. Of course, that was before the messages in the tablets. Have you received other orders that all of us should be included? I was under the impression that there was some large mission in the works and that's why we were being called together."

Featherblade considered his second. He had received communication that she had not. "I don't know why we were being called together, but for now, our mission is to track down and kill this blue-skinned woman. She has apparently compromised the client's plans. But what of the two you had with you?"

Darkcaller nodded almost imperceivably. She had been a Blade long enough to know information would be given only as necessary. Featherblade, as the leader, would have information she didn't.

"Edge is, as always, the perfect team member." She nodded toward the man she spoke of. He wasn't large, not even as tall as she, but he was compact and solid. His black hair was pulled into a knot on the top of his head. The soft tunic and pants marked him just as readily as a warrior from faraway Teroshi.

"He rigidly adheres to his honor regardless of the situation. He would gladly die rather than to act contrary to his precious honor, not to mention fail. His skills are as I've always heard, even more impressive, truly, but he follows every order given by anyone put above him. Me in this case. I am glad to have his swords at my disposal.

"As for Phoenixarrow, we have always cooperated well. Are we not both powerful and skilled women? Her strange preoccupation and adulation for the hero Erent Caahs notwithstanding, she is also a good ally. Her skills are useful and her attitude is agreeable. I have had no problems with either of them."

"That is good to know," Featherblade said. "And of the others? Do you know nothing of them?"

"I know of the *joker twins*, Loneblade and Twoblades, of course," she said. "Always playing games and jesting with each other. If it weren't for their obvious skills, they would be worthless. I have worked with them only once, but their abilities more than made up for the frustration I had to deal with. Once I made it clear I would tear their intestines out and feed them to the other if they acted toward me the way they act with others. With women."

Featherblade had worked with them once before as well, and shared her opinion and experience. Without the threats, of course. He rarely resorted to such base actions. He had many more effective weapons in his arsenal.

Featherblade cast his gaze over the others as they prepared to leave. The tall, lanky, blonde-haired White-shadow gracefully repacked the things in her pack. She moved smoothly despite the sword hilts sticking out from every part of her body. Really, it was only the four main hilts of her primary weapons, but it seemed like more. She used two mid-sized swords, almost the length of long swords, and two short swords. She was never without them.

Her garb was...interesting. She wore voluminous pants, reminiscent of those used by ancient sword masters of Teroshi. Her tunic was wide in the shoulders and tied down tight with a sash at the waist, giving her torso a triangular look. Also, wrapped around her pale skin and yellow hair was another sash, covering not only the bottom of her face but also the top of her head, leaving only her cool blue eyes visible. Featherblade had never worked with her, but he knew something of her. Her skills would be assets to the mission.

Then there was Shadeglide. The woman's dark eyes darted around the room from within her darker shoulder-length hair. She had the odd habit of dyeing her hair a very deep blue color, claiming her natural black color was darker than the shadows and could compromise her stealth.

Featherblade didn't believe it. He had heard her ability to disappear, though based on her training and natural skill, was akin to magic.

Strapped to every conceivable part of the woman's body were blades and other edged weapons. Knives, spikes, stars, discs, and other sharp metal implements were her specialty. Some claimed she could cut the wings off a fly from twenty feet without killing the insect. She smiled at him when his eyes stopped on her. He would see if the rumors held true.

Including himself, Featherblade had a full dozen of the most skilled assassins in the world. It should be enough to remove any king in the land, regardless of the guards or army protecting him. But would it be enough to kill one highly accomplished target? He wished he had more information about what they were trying to accomplish and who this blue-colored woman was. All he'd been told was that she was skilled and dangerous.

It had only been a handful of minutes since Fireshard,

Keenseeker, and Phoenixarrow had returned, bringing with them the account of engaging—and then subsequently letting escape—the blue woman and her companions. They now waited patiently to allow Fleshrender to track their target before the Falxen went to meet her. That is, Featherblade waited patiently. Some were not so tranquil.

"What?" Keenseeker said, standing several feet in front of his seated leader. "We're just going to wait here, doing nothing? Why aren't we going after them?"

Featherblade considered the man towering over him. The barbarian from one of the Sittingham Desert tribes was a good four inches or more taller than the leader when he was standing. Sitting like Featherblade was, the bulky warrior was nearly double his height. "Yes, we are."

"Why?" Keenseeker growled.

"Because most of us could not hope to keep up with Fleshrender, and even if we could, we would give ourselves away. It would be better for our presence to be unknown at this time."

"*It would be better for our presence to be unknown,*" the barbarian mocked. "So, we just sit here. I've never heard of such a large group of Blades working on a single mission other than during war, and here we sit, doing nothing."

"It is evident that you do not understand strategy and the details of assassination work," Featherblade said calmly, his eyes never leaving the larger man's. "To avoid undue stress and concern, it would be better if you would turn your mind to something it can understand, such as sharpening your weapons for when we enter combat."

"Are you trying to say I'm stupid, little man?" Keenseeker stepped toward the leader, gripping his axe so tightly the haft creaked.

Featherblade merely looked at the larger man. Blankly and calmly.

"Go sit down." Darkcaller raised a hand and called an unnatural darkness to surround it. "Or I will sit you down."

Keenseeker shifted his attention to the second-in-command and visibly swallowed. He was not a coward, not by a long shot, but the simplest of men knew better than to press matters when dealing with a magic user of her caliber. The warrior must have known she had been itching to use her power on him. Their superiors would not blame her—or the others, should they join her—if they harmed or killed Keenseeker.

Featherblade knew Keenseeker believed he was the match of anyone in the party, even the dark witch, but the barbarian knew better than to press the issue when two or three might band together against him. Better to retreat. He did so.

Featherblade sighed inwardly. He disliked confrontation between the Blades within a brace, but it was inevitable with a group this large. He would simply have to try to make the best out of the situation.

"Fleshrender has had enough time," he said to all of them, rising from his chair. "Let us go meet her at the south entrance and see where our target has gone."

They made it to the designated spot in little more than ten minutes. As they walked up, Fleshrender peeled herself out of the shadow of a building and nodded to Featherblade.

"They've left the city and are heading south toward the forest, as predicted. I can follow their trail. They're moving fast, though. Almost as if they knew we were after them." She flashed her too-white teeth and jerked her head toward the open gate. "Shall we?"

❄ 13 ❄

Khrazhti was amazed at the Mellanor Forest. The sheer amount of life within this world astounded her, but the forest? It seemed to *be* life. She felt it so strongly she could almost touch it.

She wondered if all animaru were able to sense the life in things as she did or if it was because of her human half. Whichever was the case, she took the time during their flight from the city of Satta Sarak to investigate the strange phenomenon. She went down deep into herself and tried to learn everything about the magic around her, taking it mentally and turning it around for closer inspection. It was fascinating.

The introspection was also the reason she felt it so strongly when the glow suddenly faded. Not the glow from the life around her, but the glow of S'ru's disapproval. It was like an uncomfortable itch suddenly disappeared. No, that was not correct. The itch was scratched to satisfaction. She suddenly felt the absence of something she had not realized had been chafing her.

Khrazhti stopped mid-stride and gaped at those she was traveling with.

Aeden was the first to notice, just a few steps later. He stopped and met Khrazhti's eyes.

"Are you...well?" he asked, obviously searching for the words in Alaqotim.

She smiled at the effort and answered in broken Ruthrin. "The glow is gone. It winked." His eyebrows climbing his forehead showed that he did not understand fully. She repeated herself in Alaqotim.

"Oh," he said. "Winked *out*. That's great."

Raki and Fahtin had stopped, too. The boy asked her if she meant the other animaru could no longer track her and she clarified that she thought so. All they had to do now, she said, was to get out of the area. Their pursuers would continue to where they had last sensed her, so it would be advantageous for them to be gone from there.

"Once we get far enough away," Aeden pointed out, "all we'll have to worry about is the assassins hunting for us. Unless they follow Tere."

Khrazhti, still reeling from the loss of the mark that would allow the others to find her, stepped toward where they had been heading. The weak tugging in the corner of her mind guiding her toward Izhrod Benzal was still there. Jerking her head in the direction they needed to go, she took the lead.

As they traveled, the four companions remained relatively silent. Their pace was not so fast that it required them to be so, but Khrazhti thought the others were also enjoying quiet introspection. So many things had happened since she came to this world. It was dizzying to think of it all.

She thought of Aeden and the magic he used. He was powerful, there was no doubt, but she got the sense that he was not as fully trained as he had first appeared. In physical combat, he had the grace of years of training, but with magic, he was still halting, rough, unrefined. She wondered how he could wield such powerful magic yet not seem to understand how he did so.

Her wondering would not let go of her. The need to know became more insistent in the silence as they passed through a more lightly wooded area, one in which they could move quickly but effortlessly. She scanned the surroundings for danger, of course, but her restless mind held on tight to the subject of Aeden's magic. Finally, she could stand the silence no more.

"Aeden," she said. "How did you learn to use your magic?" Raki translated as she spoke.

His blue eyes widened slightly, but then went back to normal. He let out a breath as the corners of his mouth dropped a small distance.

"I learned forms—gestures—when I was young, but was unable to call the magic forth. It wasn't until later that I heard about the Song."

"Song?" she interrupted as Raki reached the word. "Like the minstrel was singing? What does a song have to do with it?" She still pronounced the word strangely, not quite used to it.

"The Bhavisyaganant, the Song of Prophecy," he said.

"Prophecy? You fessani—humans—have prophecy?" She tried to use the term Aeden and the others used for themselves so as not to insult them in any way.

"Of course. During the Age of Magic, there were several important prophets. The most famous, of course, was Tsosin Ruus. He created the Hero Academy."

Khrazhti shook her head. It was too much, what Aeden was telling her. "Please, slow down in your speech. Hero Academy? Prophecy? Song? I do not understand."

"I'm sorry," Aeden said as he walked around a group of

small boulders in his path. "Let me think for a moment." They continued on for a few minutes, Khrazhti waiting for the information, Aeden chewing his lower lip, and the other two watching both of them.

"Start with the war," Fahtin offered, and Raki translated it immediately. Khrazhti was learning more and more of the Ruthrin language. She hardly needed the translations any longer, but she didn't want to ask Raki to stop yet. She apparently had an affinity for the language, or maybe languages in general. It could have been the similarity between Ruthrin and the pure Alaqotim she spoke, she didn't know. Ruthrin was obviously a derivative of the older language. Fahtin's suggestion sounded good, though. War was something she understood. It would give her a basis for the rest of the information.

"That's a good idea," Aeden agreed. "Thank you." He turned his eyes to Khrazhti and continued. "Three thousand years ago, there was a great war. It is simply called the War of Magic. The entire world was involved, all the great nations and empires of Dizhelim, battling over the use of magical energies. It almost destroyed everything.

"During the war, the greatest prophet in all of history, Tsosin Ruus, announced his most important prophecy. He penned it in the form of a song. It is called the Bhavisya-ganant—or Bhagant for short—the Song of Prophecy. It tells of a time when darkness will invade our world and the future of all things living will be in danger.

"He did not say exactly when this time would be. In the Song, he mentioned the Malatirsay, the one who would be our world's only hope against the dark invaders. To try to provide this hero with the best training possible, the great prophet began to build Sitor-Kanda, the Hero Academy. It had one purpose: to train the Malatirsay so he could defend Dizhelim.

"In the prophecy, Tsosin Ruus gives information to identify the Malatirsay, but even more important, the Song itself is powerful. It was originally written and sung in the language Dantogyptain, and the words have magic. I have learned the Song, and the words and its tempo and cadence seem to be the origin of my clan's magic. That's why I practice, trying to learn how to apply the Song's words to the gestures. When I find the right combination, my clan's magic is much more powerful."

Khrazhti listened intently to Raki's translation. With nearly three thousand years of experience with magic, she recognized immediately that Aeden was correct. Any time a caster could compound different techniques for calling forth magic, the effects were greater.

However, she was aware of very few magics that utilized more than one or two components. Typically, there were gestures of some kind as well as a spoken component. Complex movements were rare, and even rarer still were the mental spells wherein the caster brought her mind into the appropriate state and withdrew power directly from the surroundings. She had never heard of a spell that gained power from song, but since the animaru had no songs, that was to be expected.

"Please sing this song for me," she said to Aeden in Ruthrin, hoping he understood.

Judging by the way his mouth dropped open, he either did understand or she had just insulted him in some way. It was strange how these fessani—humans; she had to remember to call them that—had a bright part in their eyes, with different colors within them. At the moment, Aeden's looked to be popping out of his head, the bright white background shining brightly, almost glowing, while the cool blue seemed to crackle.

"I...uh...it's in Dantogyptain," he said. "Do you understand that language?"

"No. Please, sing." Even if she didn't understand it, she wanted to hear. She had never heard a magic song. She had only recently heard her first song of any type. How would this one compare?

"We'll have to stop for a moment," he said. "I don't think I can sing while traveling."

Khrazhti needed to hear all of Raki's translation before she understood completely. Why could he not sing while moving? He was a warrior, fit and capable of breathing easily while pacing across the terrain.

"Please do so," she said, trying her best to communicate without using the young translator. She looked to Aeden as his eyes locked onto hers. The intensity there shocked her and calmed her at the same time. She had grown up with combat, with warriors. His focus made her feel...at home.

"Okay," he said. "Quickly."

Aeden cleared his throat and began to sing.

From the first word, Khrazhti realized this was not a song like the minstrel's. It quivered with power, each pure and perfect note resonating in the air, vibrating everything around it. She wasn't sure if it was because of her skill and familiarity with magic or if it affected everyone so, but she knew without a doubt she had never felt such raw potential. It would have been frightening if it weren't so exciting.

Aeden went on, singing through the entirety of the Song of Prophecy, as he called it. She noticed his limbs twitched as if wanting to move through the gestures he had learned or was still developing. She was glad he restrained himself. The power may have been too much for her.

When the Song ended on one flawless note, Aeden slumped as if he had just finished the hardest battle of his life. Every part of Khrazhti's body tingled with the wash of power. She blew out a breath and relaxed muscles she had not even known she had tensed.

"I have never witnessed power like that, not even when S'ru deigned to use his own in my presence." She stumbled a step and Aeden was there, catching her arm, holding her up. She looked into those crystal eyes surrounded by white and shivered for a moment. If this man had utilized the power he was capable of wielding when they fought, she would have been utterly destroyed. She had no doubt of that.

"Anyway," he said in her own language. "That is the Bhavisyaganant. We need to keep moving now so the animaru and the assassins don't catch up to us."

Khrazhti grabbed Aeden's arm as he turned to continue their journey. "Wait. This Malatirsay, I know of him."

Aeden's eyes grew suspicious, or at least contemplative. "You do? Did the animaru have the Song also?"

"No. Animaru do not have songs. We have prophecy, but not yours. I have met this Malatirsay. We are going toward him now."

Both Fahtin and Raki swung their heads toward Khrazhti, but Raki spoke first, probably because he understood her attempts at speaking their language better than the other.

"We're going *toward* him? Khrazhti, Aeden is the Malatirsay."

That was something she had not expected. She looked at the small human for a moment, working her mouth but making no sound. Finally, she got out, "Aeden?"

"Yes," Fahtin said. "The Song identifies him, and the way he can use its magic proves it."

"But," Khrazhti said. "Izhrod Benzal told me he was this chosen one."

Aeden hadn't responded yet and Khrazhti wished he would do so, that he would tell her she was mistaken and that he was this special warrior. He didn't say a word, though. He continued to look at her as if pondering what she said. Why was he not correcting her?

"That's impossible," Fahtin said. "The sole purpose of the Malatirsay is to destroy the animaru invaders."

Khrazhti had to rely on Raki's translation. The former high priestess could not understand the humans' language when they were agitated and speaking quickly. Once Raki translated—reluctantly—Khrazhti's eyes dropped to the ground.

Fahtin noticed. And her hand flew to cover her mouth. "Oh, I'm sorry, Khrazhti. I meant that he is supposed to protect our world from those trying to destroy it. The prophecy says that's his primary responsibility. Izhrod Benzal is helping the animaru to come to this world to kill all life. He can't be the Malatirsay."

Khrazhti knew the human woman was not trying to insult her, but she felt a stab of guilt when she thought of how she had come to this world to do her god's will. Come to end the lives of all who lived here, though she didn't understand the extent of it until Aeden and the others had explained it to her. She regretted she ever had a part in it.

"I only know he told me he was. I do not know of this Song of Prophecy, so I do not know how to disprove him. Our own prophecies do not mention this one. At least not by that name. The Prophecy of S'ru mentions only one enemy, the Gneisprumay, though it may be more than one."

"What do you mean?" Aeden finally said. "Why do you say there may be more than one enemy?"

"The word, it means first or most important enemy, but the form means more than one. The form could signify great honor or exaltedness, but there is the sense of being more than a single entity. Perhaps it is a group of people, a class of great warriors of your world?"

Aeden listened to the translation and he stood excitedly as if he was impatient to speak. "Wait. Is it the *-ay* part of the word that indicates this exaltedness or plurality?"

"Yes. That is the way of it in Alaqotim."

"It's the same thing as in *Malatirsay*," he said. "At least, that is what I have been told. I was told that it meant someone who was worthy of great honor."

"It is so," Raki translated for Khrazhti. "You understand."

"Would you tell me this prophecy of yours?"

"It is not my prophecy, but that of S'ru. He gave it to the animaru more than five thousand years ago."

"Five thousand?" Fahtin said. "That means it's older even than the Song. From two thousand years before the War of Magic, even."

Aeden frowned. "Will you tell me the prophecy you refer to, the one given to the animaru?"

"I will, but translation may not be accurate. Alaqotim has many nuances and what Raki translates may not be exactly correct."

"I understand. I would still like to hear it, though, if you are willing to tell us."

"Very well," Khrazhti said. "But remember, animaru do not sing, nor do we write or speak in poetry. Here is S'ru's prophecy of the time of the end of our banishment.

Ages pass, isolation in the darkness, century after century
In the end time, the door will open
A world of light, but of plenty, open for conquest
The fessani will unlock the portal, to their dismay
Animaru shall flood forth, preparing the way
Darkness, unlife, all will be changed
For the glory of S'ru
The enemy will stand forth, Gneisprumay
Wielding light, animaru will fall
Destroy the Gneisprumay they must, or face eternal isolation
S'ru will empower them, to his own glory
As at the first, so it will be again

Balance for time unending

An earned reward."

The ancient words burned in her throat. They were part of the holy knowledge of S'ru, and she had been his high priestess.

But no longer.

"Thus were the words given to us by our god," she said.

Aeden was silently looking at the ground, his eyes half-closed in concentration. Was he memorizing what Raki translated? The former high priestess wondered if he had done it accurately. She could not hear him as he told the other two what she said.

"Thank you," Aeden said in Alaqotim. "It has given me much to think about. For now, though, we must go."

Khrazhti dipped her head to him in understanding. There would be more questions, from Aeden and from her, but he was correct. They had stayed in one place for too long. Enemies stalked them, and they had their own prey to catch. After, though. After they had stopped Izhrod Benzal, the self-proclaimed *Malatirsay*. Then, at the latest, the questions must be answered.

She hitched her pack upon her back and moved toward where she sensed Izhrod Benzal. They had a long way to go yet.

❧ 14 ❧

Darkcaller swept through the forest along with the other eleven assassins. Fleshrender was in the lead, her sand-colored dress barely visible even though she was only two people ahead of the dark witch. It was funny. She had never been called a witch at the Academy, even though she learned to use her magic there. It was only since she had left that anyone called her that name.

She didn't like it.

The word, as many others, seemed to diminish her abilities just because she was a woman. Did anyone ever call a man a mage or a warlock and mean something derogatory? She thought not. The entire world and its man-centric views could burn, as far as she was concerned.

Keenseeker tried to push past her, but she angled her body to block his forward progress. The man was a pig. Maybe he would get upset and try to attack her. Then she could tear the soul from his body and claim it was self-defense. He huffed, but did nothing further.

Too bad. Maybe next time.

Fleshrender and Featherblade stopped in a small clearing.

They were discussing something quietly when Darkcaller approached them. The leader nodded to her as she took her place next to him and waited for the others to gather around them.

"Our lovely Fleshrender has tracked them to this point." He nodded toward the beautiful young woman whose blue eyes seemed to glow with fervor in the darkness of the forest. Darkcaller was sure it was just a reflection from the moon, not some magical radiance.

Featherblade continued. "She tells me that their group split up here, not more than two hours ago. The group with the blue woman went north and east, somewhat back toward the city, while the other went north and west, toward the mountains."

The slender man met the eyes of each member of the brace briefly, as if he was reading their intent.

"Which will we follow?" Edge asked, his topknot swaying as he moved his head from Featherblade to Darkcaller. The Teroshi warrior knew who was in charge.

Featherblade opened his mouth to answer but was interrupted by Keenseeker. "We go after the blue woman, of course. Why are we wasting time talking about it?"

The leader of the brace considered the barbarian. If Darkcaller hadn't known better, she would have said there was a tightness around Featherblade's eyes. It must have been a trick of the dim light, though. She had never seen the man show any kind of emotion. He was the ultimate calm, cool professional.

"You are not in a position of authority, Keenseeker," Featherblade said in his smooth voice. "Unless Darkcaller or I ask for your opinion, please refrain from voicing it."

"What?" the ax-wielder said. "Are you telling me to shut my mouth?"

Featherblade cocked his head slightly, looking at the huge man as if he were some new and fascinating bug. "Yes, I am."

"That's it. I've had it with you and your giving orders. We'll see who's strong enough to lead this group."

The warrior's ax had hardly been lifted before a blur passed across Darkcaller's vision. Featherblade was suddenly standing near Keenseeker. Very near. He had somehow traveled more than ten feet, drawn his blade, and placed it so precisely at Keenseeker's throat that as the big man took in a deep breath, the skin on his neck broke and blood trickled down onto his chest.

"I have treated you with patience and more respect than you deserve," Featherblade said. His voice, while still low and soft, now had an edge that made Darkcaller chill. "I will overlook your impertinence this one more time, Keenseeker. The next time you challenge me or anyone else I put above you, I will remove your head before you can even think about lifting your weapon. Do you understand this?"

Keenseeker swallowed, causing the blade to bite into the skin of his throat again as his Adam's apple passed. "Yes."

"Very good." Featherblade flicked his sword, sheathing it so fast it was simply at Keenseeker's throat and then it was in its scabbard. The slender sword master wiped the blood from his forefinger and thumb—having cleaned the blade as he sheathed it—on Keenseeker's pant leg. He turned to the others, apparently unconcerned about Keenseeker being at his back. "Now, we also will split into two parties."

"We're going after both of them?" Darkcaller asked before she thought better of it.

"Yes. Our mission is to kill the blue woman, but it is within my discretion to track the others as well. I believe the intent of the original orders was to eliminate all involved. Are there disagreements? If so, please voice them now. I am not averse to people disagreeing with me, as long as it is kept civil."

"I just want to cut them," Fleshrender said. "Doesn't matter who or where."

"Yes, my dear," Featherblade said. "To that end, you will go with me."

The woman smiled and Darkcaller recognized that Fleshrender was probably the most beautiful woman she had seen in her lifetime. That didn't stop the dark magic wielder from feeling a little fear at the assassin's sanity, or lack thereof.

"No other questions? Then here is what we will do. I will take with me Whiteshadow, Twoblades, Loneblade, Bolt-shadow, and Fleshrender. The rest of you will go with Dark-caller. This mix of skills will give us the best chance of success. I believe we may be tested by those we are to kill."

"Tested?" Whiteshadow asked. "You mean, like, they'll ask us questions as they do at the Academy?"

"No, Whiteshadow," Featherblade said without even a hint of the exasperation Darkcaller felt. "I simply have a sense that some of us may not survive this mission. I thought out carefully who should go with which party." He turned to Phoenixarrow. "You will be glad to know, my fantastic archer, that you will be tracking the bow wielder you encountered earlier. Feel free to look at it as a competition, so long as he ends up dead and you alive."

The statuesque redhead smiled widely, showing perfect, white teeth.

"So then, let us not waste any more time. Darkcaller: Fire-shard, Keenseeker, Edge, Phoenixarrow, and Shadeglide are your team. I expect you to command it with the skill and professionalism I have witnessed of you previously."

"We will be successful." Darkcaller nodded, as close to a bow as any man would ever get from her.

"I'm sure you will. I have linked our communication tablets so you can report your progress to me each day. I will retain the tablet to our employer in case he requires updates."

There were no goodbyes. Each Blade was accustomed to working in groups and alone, whatever was necessary. One group simply followed Fleshrender to the northwest and the other followed Phoenixarrow to the northeast.

As she headed out with her group, Darkcaller wondered about what Featherblade had said. Some might not survive. Just how powerful were those they were tracking? Nothing she had ever met could stand up to half a dozen Blades. She wasn't sure she wanted to meet anything that could.

৩৯১৩

"YOU HAVE ACTUALLY WORKED OUT HOW TO DO IT?" Ulfaris Triban asked, nearly bouncing on his toes with excitement.

"Of course, Ul. Did you ever doubt that I could?"

"No, not really, but it's amazing. I never did understand the Conjuration/Invocation or the Magical Transmission schools. Plain elemental magic is easier to understand. I was never good with calculations."

Izhrod Benzal took a drink of wine from his goblet. "I remember. Do not bother yourself over it. We all have our own talents."

"True, true. Still, I can hardly believe you were actually able to open a portal to the dark world. And bring creatures over into Dizhelim! If only the masters could see."

Another swallow of wine went down. "I'd just as soon not share this bit of information with the masters. They don't understand it is the only way. I have heard what they believe the prophecy means, but they have it all wrong. I will lead what is left of humanity into a glorious new age. All others will cease to exist. It is a necessary thing."

"There's no need to convince me," Ulfaris said. "I am here with you, am I not? I'm part of the movement."

"Yes, I suppose you are at that."

"Tell me about the portals. Not all the calculations and theory. Just the basics. How did you ever figure it out?"

Izhrod smirked as he raised his chin in acknowledgment of his mastery. "It was fairly simple once I had thought it all out. You know the basics of teleportation: the magical constructs are built in two places and then their affinities for each other are used to open a gateway in between them."

"Yes. I've read about it, and seen a small-scale demonstration a few years ago."

"I have found that the teleportation gates and a portal share some characteristics. Instead of a process that consumes or destroys the constructs, however, I used equal parts light magic—for the Dizhelim side—and dark magic—from the Aruzhelim side—to create an opening that spans the vast distance between the worlds without building constructs at all."

Ulfaris scratched his head. "But, if that works, then we should be able to make a teleportation gate without the need for the magical constructs."

"Ah, yes. Perhaps you are correct, but I haven't been able to teleport without building the constructs. In order to create my portals, I discovered how to tap into the lines of power, or more precisely, the nexuses of the lines, to charge the portals with the actual lines of energy inherent in the world, a task usually handled by the constructs. True, it limits the locations for such portals to those nexuses that are strong in both light and dark magic, but once I found the locations, a series of experiments allowed me to refine my technique and my spells to successfully bring over some of the animaru."

"That is wonderful, Izhrod. You're brilliant. With your spells, we should be able to bring all of them over quickly and take over the whole world in no time."

"Things are never that easy, Ulfaris," Benzal said. "Magic is complex, and the interaction of different types of magical energy is even more so. With the pulsing of the different types of magic, the timing is critical. I can predict the ideal times for creating portals up to a few months in advance, but even done at the perfect time, there is a limit to how much energy can be used and matter can be transported.

"Though the animaru are not really alive, there appears to be some value associated with each of them. A more powerful creature may be three or four times as costly to transport as a weaker creature. The first group I brought over consisted of three thousand animaru. Of those, less than a dozen were the more powerful types. I decided to opt for more numbers rather than the more potent creatures. This time, I intend to bring over more of the latter. I am unsure how many total I will be able to transport, but those I do bring over will be leaders, more powerful than the average animaru."

"I understand," Ulfaris said. The excitement in his eyes dimmed a bit as he asked, "When will you open the portal?"

"In less than three weeks, on the twentieth day of Sangen. And you, my friend, are going to help me."

❧ 15 ❧

"**W**e're close now," Fleshrender said.

The woman had waited for the others to catch up to her. For two days they'd trailed the small group with their primary target, the blue woman, in it. During that time, Featherblade had communicated with Darkcaller via the tablets twice. Neither of the assassin groups had made contact with their prey.

"Are you sure, there, sweetie?" Whiteshadow asked.

"I'm sure." Fleshrender's blue orbs reflected the light of the full moon. It gave her a manic look. Just like when it was daylight. "I can feel it, and the feeling is stronger than it was."

"Are you sure it isn't an upset stomach from Twoblades's stew?"

The beautiful sadist tilted her head.

"Pay her no mind, Fleshrender," Featherblade said, glancing briefly at the tall, pale woman with four swords visible on her person. "She's just trying to bait you."

Whiteshadow shrugged and sat on a small rock.

"I'd like to bait her," Twoblades said under his breath to

Loneblade. He apparently didn't realize that Featherblade's sense of hearing was excellent.

"Mmmm," Loneblade agreed, just as quietly. "I can think of lots of things I'd like to do." Out loud, he said, "Whiteshadow, why are you teasing our beautiful tracker like that?"

"It's Witshadow," she responded without even looking at him.

"What?" Loneblade looked at the others. "I...I thought it was Whiteshadow."

"Why would I call myself Whiteshadow? What kind of name is that? Now Witshadow, that's a witty name. For a shadow."

Twoblades chuckled and Loneblade stared at him for a moment before laughing, too. "Oh, I get it." He added more softly to his friend, "It is Whiteshadow, though, right?"

"Yes, it is," Twoblades answered. "She's messing with you."

"So," Featherblade heard Whiteshadow say, "your name is Loneblade. Shouldn't it be Longblade? Or does that mean...?"

Featherblade shook his head and scanned the trees around them. They were not in a forest any longer, but the distinction was probably academic. The land through which they passed was still fairly thickly wooded, providing cover so they were not seen during the daytime but also presenting more difficulties in moving quickly.

He disliked that they hadn't caught up to the small group they tracked yet. He didn't know if they had sensed the assassins, but they were making surprisingly good time, even through the rough terrain. Would they prove to be difficult targets? They had easily evaded three of their number when ambushed in the city, but from the accounts of the short battle, it seemed that the archer had much to do with their escape. The archer that was being followed by Darkcaller's brace.

A few things had been obvious about the tracks they had

found. The party they were pursuing had split, and—judging by the lack of good prints from the group that went to the northwest—the archer was with them. His skills seemed to mirror those of Phoenixarrow's: archery, long knives, and an ability to follow subtle trails. Trackers also worked hard at foiling anyone trying to track them. Yes, the archer had gone with the others.

Featherblade wished he knew more about those he was chasing. What were their strengths, their weaknesses? There were apparently four of them, based on the tracks he himself had picked out as they went. He wasn't an expert tracker, but he had some skill. Nothing to rival Fleshrender's ability to sense those she was after, but adequate for most jobs he had been assigned.

Four. The blue woman, who remained a mystery, a smaller person, perhaps a boy or young woman, the one described as a warrior, and a taller woman. This last one had been described as wearing Gypta garb, of all things. For that matter, the three who had seen him said that the warrior also dressed like a Gypta. Interesting, that. The curiosity tingled in his middle, threatening to make him anxious to reach them and answer his questions.

He would be patient, however, not only because the patient man made fewer mistakes, but because it would allow him to savor the hunt and the anticipation. Without these things, the task would be hollow.

But they had rested long enough. It was time to continue.

"Fleshrender, if you would?" he said to the lovely sadist.

The woman flicked her nut-brown hair as she turned and stalked off into the surrounding trees. She was on the scent, and Featherblade knew it was only a matter of time until they caught those they were after. Then he would have some answers.

The pursuit stretched on for another two and a half days,

much to Featherblade's surprise. Even Fleshrender shot him confused looks each time she thought they were close, but then continued to find the terrain ahead empty.

On the fifth day after their departure, the assassins finally caught a glimpse of movement ahead of them. The terrain had changed slowly from heavy trees to more widely spaced vegetation, not only easing travel, but occasionally affording them the opportunity to see farther ahead.

They had crested a small hill and a flash of color pulled Featherblade's eyes to an area perhaps two or three miles ahead. He turned to see Fleshrender looking at him. When his eyes met hers, she broke into a smile so exquisite he could almost forget how truly insane the woman was.

"It seems we are finally catching up," he told her.

"Yes." It came out like a hiss, and the leader of the brace of assassins almost felt pity for their prey.

Despite catching sight of the targets, they saw nothing but their tracks for another three days, never quite catching up. On the third day, all trace of them simply disappeared.

Fleshrender was nearly manic. She stalked back and forth, her head shaking even as it searched for any sign of those they pursued.

"If any of you so much as steps into this area," she said as she threw her arms wide, gesturing to a very large area of the forest, "I will kill you and eat you. Not necessarily in that order."

Twoblades looked toward Featherblade, the whites of his eyes shining in the sunlight and his mouth parted. Featherblade put a hand up discreetly so the angry woman couldn't see it and shook his head. Sometimes it was better to let people have their way. Especially if they were more than a little imbalanced.

The leader put his hand out to his side, palm up, then rotated his wrist so the palm was down and sat down to wait. His team understood and seated themselves also, waiting.

It took Fleshrender forty minutes to stop her stomping and muttering.

"It was right here," she said, pointing to a spot she had seemed to always come back to. "Their tracks were moving along as they have since we started after them. Then, poof, they disappeared. No trace, not a sign of any kind of scuffle or abduction. They just stopped. It's almost like something picked them up and flew away with them. Except that I checked the trees and there is no sign of their passing that way either.

"What's worse, I can't sense them. Not at all. That has never happened. Even if they were killed, I should be able to find their bodies. But I can't. Nothing. It has to be magic, though I can't sense any of that either. If they used magic or it was used on them, I should be able to sense something. Anything."

"What do you propose we do about it, Fleshrender?" As always, Featherblade kept his tone cool and neutral. Speaking emotionally was a good way to alienate people and to undermine authority.

"I...I don't know." The beautiful psycho plopped down on a log next to her leader. "I can't tell where we should go. I almost want..."

Featherblade waited for a time, but the woman did not finish her sentence. "What is it? What do you want?"

"I want to wait here. If they disappeared, maybe they will reappear at the same place."

Featherblade first thought to deny Fleshrender's request. If she lost track of their prey, so be it, but they would not compound the error by wasting precious time waiting for something that would never happen.

Then he really looked at the young woman. She was biting

her lip, eyes darting from Featherblade to the others, and then to the ground. She was frantic. Whether it was because she thought she would be blamed for the mission failing or if it was some personal thing, she was manic.

What harm would it cause to allow her that comfort? Eventually, she would figure out their prey were not coming back, and then they could get on with business. He would like to be done with this mission, but there didn't seem to be a time limit on it as far as Izhrod Benzal was concerned.

"I will give you two days," he said, watching her eyes flash. She very nearly smiled, until he finished. "You will be responsible for food for those two days. I suggest you start hunting and get a fire ready."

The beautiful, deadly assassin sighed and shrugged her shoulders.

❧ 16 ❧

Aeden looked back to the direction they had come from one more time. He felt uneasy, like there was an itch right in the center of his back and he couldn't scratch it to save his life.

As if it weren't bad enough that they traveled toward a powerful mage and probably a bunch more animaru, they had assassins tailing them. He was sure of it now.

He had hoped that the group would follow Tere and the others—though he felt guilty for even thinking it—and that he and his group would be left alone. After all, Tere would be able to keep his party out of trouble. The man could disappear in the forest, and he had a nature priest with him.

But it was not to be. Khrazhti said she could feel them closing in. She said one of them was using a kind of magic to track them. At first, Aeden thought the animaru was being paranoid, but then, just a few days ago, she exclaimed suddenly that they were within sight. Aeden himself had caught a glimpse of several people in dark clothing miles away, on the top of a hill, looking right at them.

He didn't doubt her anymore.

Another significant thing that happened in their frantic flight was that Khrazhti started speaking Ruthrin. She said she'd always had an affinity for languages, and when she put her three thousand years of experience to use, she could learn things much faster than others.

She mostly spoke without Raki to interpret now, though occasionally she'd run into something she didn't know how to say. Aeden asked her to still work with him on his Alaqotim. It was always useful to have an extra language, especially one that was so ancient and suffused with magic. He wasn't learning it as quickly as his blue friend learned Ruthrin, but he was getting better all the time.

As he learned, Aeden never let his eyes stay in one place. It was especially important in the current situation because with a group of assassins after him, he couldn't be too careful. He was sure they had many varied and exceptional skills. What if one had a skill that allowed them to overtake Aeden's group with a burst of speed? He was sure they had seen him as he caught sight of them.

Raki was just ahead of the Croagh, to the left. Khrazhti was slightly ahead of him and to Aeden's right. Fahtin was alongside Aeden. When Raki suddenly disappeared, Aeden started. A chuckle from his side irritated him for a moment, but then he smiled at Fahtin.

"He's getting very good at that," she said. "Not that he wasn't good before. He's going to be a genuine thief soon if he keeps that up."

"Yes. Or an assassin. Still, they are good skills to have. I'm glad he had Tere show him enough so he could practice when they're separated like this."

"Tere trained Raki?" Khrazhti said. Aeden realized she had stopped and allowed them to catch her.

"Sort of." Aeden pulled his fingers through his hair. "Raki has a natural ability for stealth. It's like magic."

"It *is* magic," Fahtin said. "Magic runs in the families of the Gypta."

"Gypta?" Khrazhti asked. "Despised one?"

"What?" Fahtin asked as she wheeled on the animaru. "Why are you calling him a despised one?"

Khrazhti pulled back as if stung. "I meant no disrespect. In Alaqotim, *gyptumin* means a lowly or despised one. I thought that was what you referred to. I am sorry if I offended you."

Aeden watched the conversation play out, fully intending to jump between the two women if their argument heated up. There seemed no need, though. Fahtin deflated, her rigid shoulders drooping.

"Oh," the Gypta woman said. "That's all right. I'm just a little tense right now, with assassins chasing us and all. Plus, I have heard it my whole life, how my people are not really people but wandering thieves, how they are worthless to other people."

"It is so?" Khrazhti asked. "Why is it others say that of you? Have you offended them, declared war on their families? Have they beaten you in fair combat?"

"No, none of those things. It's a long story."

"We have a great distance to travel," Khrazhti said. "Stories will make the time pass more easily."

Fahtin cocked her head at the blue woman. "Do your people believe that, too, or do you just learn much too fast to be believable? Didn't you tell us animaru don't tell stories?"

Khrazhti showed her teeth in what Aeden figured was meant to be a smile, but it was disconcerting, almost like the smile a highland cat might wear before eating its prey.

No longer having any excuse, Fahtin told Khrazhti the story her father had told Aeden, that the Gypta were conscripted to travel and declare the glories of the king of Agypten. Because of their origin nation, people began to call them the Gypta. It was unfortunate that the Alaqotim word for despised or lowly shared a root with the nation's name.

"Throughout the centuries, my people have been looked down upon and refused the right to settle in one place," Fahtin finished. "But for most of us, that was a blessing rather than a curse. We are travelers, constantly finding the wonder of the world."

Khrazhti was silent for a moment, and Aeden thought that maybe she needed Raki to translate. Then the animaru spoke. "I am sorry such occurs on your world as well.

"In Aruzhelim, some classes of animaru are lesser and they are treated poorly. I myself am familiar with this prejudice because of my heritage. I am the only animaru that is half human, the only one not created along with all others. I have faced such treatment by others because of my...uniqueness. Is that correct, uniqueness?"

"Yes," Fahtin said. "It is the perfect word. You are one of a kind and you should be proud of that."

"I am proud," the former high priestess said, straightening her posture and pulling her shoulders back. "I am proud of my skills and of my accomplishments, but not of my heritage. I was born of hatred and cruel curiosity. I wish I had known the one who bore me, but she failed in the environment of my home."

"You can be part of our family, then," Fahtin countered. "Aeden was not born Gypta, but we brought him into our family, and he is as much a part of it as any other." She smiled at Aeden, who returned the gesture.

"You were not always with the *family*?" Khrazhti seemed to have trouble pronouncing the word.

"No," Aeden said as he stepped around a log. "I—"

The world spun in a wash of color just before everything went black.

Aeden recognized something. It was bright, even through

his eyelids. What was it called? Oh, right. Light. He opened his eyes, regretted it immediately, and blinked to focus and adjust to his new surroundings.

He was definitely not in the wooded area through which he and his three friends were traveling.

"What...?" His mouth felt like it was full of sand. He swallowed, working moisture into it, and tried again. "What happened?" He wasn't asking anyone in particular. He wasn't even sure why he said it aloud.

"You were called here," a smooth, sophisticated voice said. "To me. By me."

Aeden snapped his head toward the sound, scanning in his peripheral vision while doing it. The first thing that registered was that his friends were scattered around him, in different stages of regaining consciousness.

The second thing he saw was the monster in front of him.

"Did...did you just speak?" Aeden asked.

"Of course. Do you not think me capable of such an action?"

Aeden blinked several more times, then rubbed his eyes. When he opened them, the monster was still there. It had to be over fifteen feet tall, covered in...something. It looked like furry scales. Its hands and feet both ended in wicked claws, something Aeden didn't feel completely comfortable with.

The thing's head was covered with the same fur scales as the rest of its body, and its face was very nearly human, except for the overlarge eyes and the mouth full of more sharp teeth than Aeden had ever seen in one mouth. Intelligence glowed in its yellow eyes, though. No, this was no mere monster. It was smart.

"I...am still disoriented. I meant no offense." He looked around as he said it, trying to get his bearings. It appeared he was in a massive audience hall, marble pillars in rows holding up a ceiling that was too high for him to see. The air had a misty, sparkly quality, as if he was seeing it through a window covered in frost. The ground was spongy, but appeared to be stone tiles of exquisite workmanship.

"Ah," it said. If Aeden had closed his eyes, he would have thought he was talking to someone of noble birth. The way it spoke reminded him of nothing so much as nobility. "No offense taken. It is understandable that you are out of sorts. The transfer from your world to my domain can be taxing for many creatures."

"I'm sorry," Aeden said, "but did you say that you brought us here?" Off to the side, he saw his friends regaining their feet, though they were still wobbly.

"Of course I did. Who else could or would bring you to my domain? It is ridiculous."

"Why have you brought us here?" Fahtin said, picking up the conversation.

"Why, to eat you, of course," the monster said without a hint of malice or conscience.

"Eat us?" Raki rubbed his eyes as Aeden had done, looking at the monster.

"Yes. I am afraid so. I only eat every few decades, but now is the time, and you were the ones chosen by me."

"What is your name?" Khrazhti asked, staring at the creature as if she recognized it somehow.

"My name? I am the Epradotirum," the monster said with pride in its voice.

Khrazhti gasped, her coloring going to a lighter blue.

"She asked your name, not what you are," Fahtin said. Aeden wondered why she was antagonizing the creature.

"It is my name and it is also what I am. There is but one Epradotirum, and that is me. You may call me the Epra for short, if it pleases you. I do try to be accommodating before I devour my prey."

None of this made any sense to Aeden, nor did it matter what the thing was called. Khrazhti seemed to be terrified, and anything that scared her was not something to be taken lightly.

"Khrazhti, what's wrong?" Aeden asked.

"Have you no legends of the Hunter?"

"We have many legends of hunters, but none named Epra."

"No, not *a* hunter, *the* hunter. Epradotirum in Alaqotim means one who hunts, or hunter. But this one," she jerked her head toward him, "he is *the* Hunter. The ancient word came to be used only for him and others were added to the pure language so none would confuse him with a common hunter. *Epradotire* ceased to be used in a common fashion to prevent the speaker from calling his attention to them.

"He has been alive as long as the gods and he is as powerful. The gods are the only ones who have nothing to fear from his hunger."

"I see you have heard of me," the Epradotirum said, bowing its menacing head toward her. "It has been long since anyone recognized my name. I sense in you...yes, you are animaru, but yet not. Curious."

Aeden's mind raced. He had to figure out how to get back to his own world. Besides the ending of his life, and that of his friends who were with him, all of Dizhelim depended on him facing the animaru threat.

"It takes people from different worlds?" he whispered to Khrazhti.

"There is no need to whisper," the Epra said. "I can hear anything uttered in my domain. And, in case it is not apparent, I am a *he*, not an *it*. To answer your question, yes, I take my prey from whichever world I happen to fancy when my hunger strikes. This time it was Dizhelim. Sometimes it is other worlds. Including Aruzhelim." He nodded toward Khrazhti as he said it.

"Is there no way to stay your hand?" the blue woman asked. "A way to keep you from eating us? Such things have happened before. It is how we know of you to begin with."

"True. If the only ones who knew my name through meeting me died, there would be no stories, no legends. However, those few cases are rare and, as I have said, I am hungry. I do enjoy a good tale, though. Perhaps you can enlighten your comrades. They appear to be confused."

Aeden wasn't in the mood for stories, but anything that would delay their being eaten was fine with him. He shared a look with Khrazhti and, frowning, she nodded.

"It happened over five thousand years ago, long before I was born to the human woman who had come to explore Aruzhelim and become trapped there. One of S'ru's chief minions, a general of one of his armies, disappeared suddenly. S'ru apparently knew or guessed what had become of him.

"The god communicated with the Epradotirum in whatever way he does, and they discussed the capture and eventual consumption of the animaru general. S'ru proposed that the

Epra instead take three others, all skilled in magic, if he would return S'ru's minion.

"The Epra, seeing it as a good deal for him, agreed, and he released the one he had taken. He accepted the three S'ru gave him and sealed himself away with them in his domain, as is his custom. He apparently enjoys conversation before he dines, if the one released is to be believed. Based on our own experience right now, I would say it is the truth.

"The one released, a powerful animaru named Suuksis, told the tale many times, and what he had experienced became the basis for much of the legend of the Hunter. Two thousand years later, Suuksis would again be involved in significant happenings. It was then that he impregnated the human woman. My mother."

The Epradotirum rubbed his furry, scaled chin with a clawed hand. "I did not know that part. Your father was strong in magic. I can see where you got your talent. The strength of your magic is one of the primary reasons I detected and chose you to begin with."

"But," Fahtin said, "isn't there any way we can convince you not to eat us? I don't like the thought of someone else taking our place, but we're on an important mission."

"I am afraid it is not that simple, my dear. Unless you have a god who is willing to intercede and to make an offer that is advantageous to me, I am afraid you will be my next meal. It is nothing personal, I assure you. The four of you together have the requisite amount of magic to constitute a good meal. I should not have to eat again for at least three or four decades."

"You can't just take people and eat them," the Gypta woman said. "It's not right."

"As you would no doubt have found if you were allowed to live, 'right' is a relative term. It is perfectly right for me to select and take those who will feed me most effectively. Do you not do the same thing with the animals in your world? Have you eaten meat lately?"

"But Aeden is the Malatirsay!" Raki shouted. "The whole world depends on him. You can't just eat him. If you have to, eat the rest of us, but let him go. If he's not there to fulfill his purpose, everyone in our world will die."

The Epra's eyebrow rose. "The Malatirsay, you say? You refer to the Bhavisyaganant? That *is* something else, now, isn't it?" He turned to Aeden. "Is this true? Are you the one named in the prophecy?"

Aeden dropped his eyes to the stone floor. "I...I don't know. Others have told me, and I believe them, I guess, but I don't know for sure. I can use magic in relation to the words of the Song, though."

"Can you, now? Show me."

Aeden glanced at his friends, one at a time, meeting each of their eyes. He didn't know if it would do him any good to prove himself to this creature, but maybe he could gain some leverage and get the monster to free one or more of them. But which ones?

He needed to impress the Epra with the power he could wield, but also decided it would be best to cast something he was sure would not fail. He had only one spell he could use reliably in its enhanced form, so he proceeded to use the seventh spell of the Raibrech: Saving Force.

Aeden dropped into a deep, square stance and brought his arms up together in front of his body. As they raised to eye level, he rotated them and pushed out to the sides. He repeated the motions three times, pronouncing the words of power at the specific point in the casting to call forth the magic.

"*Chadu. Nidar. Kavach.*"

The spell manifested as a shimmering shield surrounding him. The sight of it shocked Aeden at first; when he'd cast it before, it was almost completely invisible. Something about the Epra's domain made it more apparent. As he completed the spell, the Epra did something completely unexpected.

He frowned.

"You use the magic of the Bhavisyaganant, something that should not be possible if you were not the one referred to within it. Even though your skill with the magic is woefully lacking, this presents us with a conundrum. To tamper with the fulfillment of prophecy is a thing of great magnitude, something I am loath to do. Yet, I still hunger.

"What is this mission you embark upon?"

"We go to stop a human from opening another portal to Aruzhelim, letting more animaru into the world of Dizhelim," Khrazhti said. "Added to the number of animaru already here, it could be devastating to this world if more are allowed to come. I am leading them to the portal, for I can sense it."

"I can see the importance of such a task in the fulfillment of the prophecy. But are all of you required for this task? The one referred to by the prophecy is necessary, of course, as is the animaru, since she can sense the portal location. It is unclear whether the other two are necessary, however. Please explain their purpose."

"Their purpose is that they're my friends," Aeden said. "They help me in my tasks."

"I see," the Epradotirum said. "They have no necessary role in the mission."

"They do. They are required." Aeden stood up straighter and crossed his arms across his chest.

"Come now. It is clear they have no intrinsic value for this mission. I could still eat them and eject you and the animaru to continue on your way. Hmm…"

The Epra pondered for a long moment before speaking again. "However, though they have a touch of magic, they are not sufficient to satisfy my hunger by themselves. Therefore, in the interests of fulfilling prophecy, I will allow all four of you to continue on your mission. I will have to look for other prey to eat."

"Wait," Fahtin said. "That's it?"

"That is all," the Epra agreed.

"You'll let us go?"

"I will. It is most likely that I will eat you when your mission is complete. When the prophecy is fulfilled."

"I, uh, okay." Fahtin shook her head, confusion blossoming in her eyes.

"Leave it alone, Fahtin," Aeden admonished. Turning to the Epradotirum, he continued. "Thank you, Hunter. We appreciate your mercy."

"Oh, it is not mercy guiding my hand. I have lived a long time and know that it is never good policy to work counter to prophecy. The words of the Prophet are merely a communication tool. The core of prophecy is as binding as the physical laws in each world. There is at once room for multiple possible conclusions and for consequences to those who would inadvertently, or especially purposely, tinker with the workings of a major prophecy. It is much safer for me to stay clear of trying to affect it too strongly.

"Do not toy with me, however," the Epra said. "I will require your oath that you will perform the duties of the Malatirsay with all your power. I will not have you escape your fate only to shirk your responsibilities."

"I will do so. I swear it," Aeden said. What had he done? Aeden realized he was fully committed now. Compared to death right at the moment, it seemed a good decision, but a queasy feeling in Aeden's gut told him that no matter what else happened, he would need to see this thing through to the end. Even if the Academy refused to help him, he would have to continue on.

"Perhaps the situation will change as time goes on, but my

senses tell me that your part in the prophecy will only grow stronger as time passes. I care not to test myself against such strong magic."

"I thank you anyway," Aeden said. "Your actions will help our world, maybe even save it."

"We shall see. The future is not set so firmly that anything is guaranteed. Perhaps we will meet again, and perhaps at that time I will eat you. Use the time you are being given well."

With a flick of a great clawed hand, the world spun and Aeden lost track of the colors and shapes around him. When he opened his eyes, he found himself lying on his back looking up at a familiar canopy of trees, sunlight filtering through and striking his face.

Off to the side, closer than he would like, were six other figures. He didn't recognize them, but he was familiar with the aura of skill and death around them.

The assassins had found their prey.

❧ 18 ❧

Tere Chizzit looked back toward the forest where they had left their friends. A chill washed over him at the thought of what was ahead of them. He had lived a fair amount of time, seen his share of adventure—more than his share, to be honest—but his current situation seemed different. More real. More permanent.

"Will they be all right?" Urun asked from beside the hunter.

"Will *we* be all right?" Aila asked from his other side. "Do you think those people, those assassins, will follow us or them?"

"I think it is never a good idea to underestimate Aeden," Tere said. "His combat skills are fantastic and he's learning more about his magic every day. Fahtin and Raki have their skills, too. And Khrazhti, that woman is a powerhouse. She's lived a long time, trained for combat during most of it, and she has strong magic herself. Hopefully it's enough to get them through. They are going to where possibly thousands of animaru will be entering our world.

"As for us, we'll get by. We have a mission, and I don't

intend to fail. Aeden needs us to notify the Academy, and that's what we'll do.

"They seemed to be after Khrazhti for some reason, so I would expect the assassins to follow Aeden's group. I wish we didn't have to split up. I could have hidden our trail, or maybe doubled back to pick one or two of them off before they could reach us. But we all have our own parts."

"So we'll have a smooth road to the Academy, for a change?" Aila pressed.

Tere clucked his tongue. "I don't think there are any smooth roads in this. Animaru are still out there, and other dangers. We'll have to travel fast, keep our senses peeled, and try to make the best time we can."

"What's the plan, then?" Urun asked.

"We'll head north, past the Teats and up through part of Sutania, and then Tarshuk, and eventually enter the island at the north bridge. We might be able to catch a ship from Kanton point, but it would have to go all the way around the island to get us to the Academy, so that's probably not a good option."

Urun scoffed. "Oh, it'll be that simple? We'll just go north until we get to the bridge, cross over onto Munsahtiz, and walk up to the Academy? What are we waiting for? Sounds easy enough."

Tere turned to the nature priest, swiveling his white eyes at the younger man. "I am simplifying, of course. What is the problem, Urun?"

The priest of Osulin ran his fingers through his dark hair and he sighed. "Oh, I don't know. I don't like it that we had to split up, and I don't like that I'm separated from Aeden. Osulin instructed me to help him, specifically him, to fulfill the prophecy. I don't like it that I'm relegated to being a message boy."

"I know, my friend. I don't like it, either, but it's the right choice. Malatirsay or not, Aeden will need the help of the Academy and any troops they can bring in from the nations. We're facing possibly the end of our world. Our part is important."

"Yeah, I guess."

Tere directed his attention to the north. From the hill on which the small party stood, they could see the Gwenore River winding off into the distance, a turquoise snake that shimmered in the light from the setting sun. He wished things had worked out so they had caught their boat. They'd have boarded later that day, and then all of them would have been relatively safe and together on a boat on the river below.

There was no use in dwelling on it, though. Their situation was what it was. He had learned long ago not to dabble in *what if* and *what could have been*. As the saying went, "If wishes were coppers, they wouldn't be worth gold." Or something like that.

"Let's keep moving," he told the other two. "We have daylight left yet to travel by. No sense in wasting it."

Aila groaned.

They headed down the side of the hill opposite from where they had scaled it, sinking into the thicker trees there. Soon, they were swallowed up completely.

For the rest of the afternoon and into the evening, the three trudged through the heavy forest. Actually, Aila Ven trudged. Tere Chizzit was accustomed to traveling in heavily wooded areas and unerringly found the easiest path. Urun Chinowa used his magic and the vegetation seemed to peel away from him, allowing him to use a gait much like he was strolling on a level path.

Two hours after dark, they finally stopped to camp. Tere could have continued all night, his sight not relying on light to make his way, but the other two had been casting looks in his direction for some time and he decided it was time to stop.

"I'll take first watch," he said. "Urun, if you don't mind taking the middle watch, Aila can take the last."

Urun grumbled at his assignment but nodded, and Aila simply grunted, "Uh huh."

"But first," he said, "we should eat something. "We're not sure if any of the assassins are following us, so no fire tonight. It's cold rations for dinner."

Tere settled into his watch when his two traveling companions went to sleep. The forest near Satta Sarak didn't feel nearly as wild as the one where he had lived. Then again, he didn't think there *were* other forests like the Grundenwald in the world anymore. He'd been through most of the great forests left in Dizhelim, and nothing compared to the place where he had set up his home.

Their sheltered campsite was probably safe enough that he could leave his friends for a little while to scout. What he had seen of the assassins in the city had him worried. Had they followed Aeden and his group, or were they still trailing him? He didn't like not knowing.

He immediately thrust the thought from his mind. If he went out looking for the assassins, he'd leave his friends defenseless. Better to wait until Urun's watch so he wouldn't expose them unnecessarily.

Tere's musings were cut short as a growing sense of danger invaded his mind. The weight of something's gaze settled upon him and every instinct he had flared to life.

He swung his head back and forth. His magical sight didn't need to be pointed as precisely as normal sight—he had a wider range of vision looking straight ahead—but to look all around him, he needed to swivel his head at least a little.

A flash of color behind and to his right caught his attention. It was a magical signature, sure enough, but one that seemed...off. He couldn't see whatever had been there and moved, but it had been something.

He didn't like the feeling that something got so close before he detected it. He couldn't remember anything that had been so elusive to his sight. And that concerned him. Greatly.

Tere spent the rest of his watch looking for any similar movements but found nothing. He almost believed he had imagined it. But no, he couldn't have created it in his own mind.

Could it have been one of the assassins? Were they staying just out of range of his sight, waiting to pounce?

He very nearly went off to look for them, but recalled himself when he remembered his two friends. Time enough to search for them later. He hoped.

Tere was still considering the phantom trail when Urun woke up for his watch.

"Anything interesting or dangerous?" The nature priest wiped the sleep from his eyes.

"Actually, yes."

Urun blinked at the grizzled hunter. "Really? That was meant to be wry."

"Even so, there was...something. I felt as if I was being watched and caught a trace of a trail in the magical matrix over there." He pointed toward the area where the trail had been. It had dispersed quickly, too quickly for Tere's liking.

Urun stepped over and inspected the place Tere had pointed out. "There does seem to be something wrong with this area."

"Something wrong? What do you mean by that?"

"I don't know. This section of the foliage feels like it should be diseased, but it looks fine. At least as much as I can tell in the dark."

"At least it means I'm not imagining things," Tere said.

"I'm not sure how whatever it was got so close without me detecting it. I don't like it. If it can sneak up on me..."

"Don't worry. I can set up a ward around us to notify us if something crosses. Anything larger than a rat will trigger it. I should have thought of that earlier."

"Do you have to be awake for it to work? When Aila takes her turn, will she be vulnerable?"

"No. Once I cast the spell, it will remain in place until I make it dissipate."

"How will it notify us?"

"Oh, don't worry about that. You'll know if something triggers it."

Tere gazed at the spot where the anomaly was. "Good. I don't know if it could be one of the assassins or not, but I'd rather not take chances. I was thinking of going hunting."

"Hunting? Now, in the middle of the night?"

Tere leveled a flat glare at the priest.

"Oh, right. Scouting for them. Got it. Maybe it would be better to do it when we're both awake, in case something gets by you."

"Yeah, maybe you're right. I could use some sleep anyway."

Urun nodded and then seemed to fold in on himself. He tended to do that, especially since they had split from Aeden and the others. Tere didn't like the trend.

"Urun," the archer said.

The nature priest raised his head.

"Be careful. Things seem a little off to me for some reason. Not only the magical shadow I saw. The world feels strange right now."

Urun cocked his head as if he was considering discussing it, but then he blinked and the look was gone. "I will. Good night."

Tere rolled himself up in his cloak and was asleep in seconds.

When he woke, the sky hadn't lightened with the dawn yet, but it would soon. Aila was sitting on the same rock he and Urun had used for their watch.

The girl hadn't noticed he was awake yet, so he took the opportunity to study her. What was her story? Not the nonsense she had given them so far. Her real story. She was an accomplished fighter, a fair hand at stealth, and seemed to be well-educated, though without the breadth she really needed. More importantly, why was she with them? What did she want, besides Aeden? Or was that all she wanted?

"Good morning, Tere," she said before swinging her head toward him.

How had she known? He didn't think he had moved his head. Maybe his breathing? "Good morning, Aila. Any trouble during your watch? No, you would have woken us. Anything interesting, then?"

"Nothing but normal animal sounds out in the forest. Urun told me about the wards he set. They weren't set off, though I'm not even sure what would have happened if they were."

Tere got to his feet and wrapped his cloak about him to combat the morning chill. "Our priest does like his little secrets." *And he's not the only one*, Tere thought. *You and I have our own, don't we, my mysterious friend.*

Aila stood and stretched, then walked to her pack and took out a piece of dried meat and began chewing it. "Not the breakfast I dream of, but at least it's something."

Tere's brief smile didn't reach his white eyes. "We got spoiled eating meals at an inn the last few days. I'm afraid this'll be normal for us for a while."

The small woman sighed and kept chewing.

Urun grunted from his makeshift bed a few feet away. "Ugh. Is it morning already? I hate the middle watch."

"I'll take middle tonight," Tere said. "You can take the first watch and get it over with."

"Uhng," the priest moaned, sitting up.

"Did your wards detect anything last night?" Tere asked Urun.

The young man grumbled as he disentangled himself from his blanket and stood. "No, nor did anything try to probe them. Either your wraith moved on, or it sensed the magic and stayed away. I can't be sure which."

"Hmm," Tere said. "I've never imagined seeing a magical signature before, no matter how tired I got. I suppose it's better that we be careful anyway. With the skills some of those assassins showed, it wouldn't surprise me if some of them could use magic."

"If we meet them again, I'm sure we'll find out," Urun said, rolling up his blanket and stuffing it in his pack.

The three ate in silence for several minutes until Tere spoke.

"We have about twenty miles of the Mellanor Forest to traverse—and no, we can't leave the forest; it'll expose us unnecessarily—and then maybe another two hundred miles to the Academy.

"There is the southern route through Praesturi and the main route, the northern one, on the western side of the Molars. I'm thinking the northern route would be faster, simply because the roads are more established going that way. Probably safer, too. The last time I went to the south of the island, there were no trails through the Verlisaru Forest separating it from the Academy. It's dangerous there."

Aila waved the hand holding dried meat. "But if we can't leave this forest because it leaves us too exposed, then we probably won't be taking the roads to the north anyway, right?"

"Yes, I suppose," Tere said with a sigh. "We can figure out which path to take over the next few days. We have a hundred miles or so to think about it before we need to make the choice."

They ate quickly and started on their way again. Tere nonchalantly looked back occasionally, but saw nothing, magical or otherwise, following them.

Midway through the morning, the terrain within the forest changed to rolling hills. The trees and underbrush were still as thick as ever, but they found themselves hiking upward and then down again, repeatedly.

"Of course," Aila grumped. "This thick vegetation isn't enough. We have to go uphill, too."

"Be glad that we don't have to travel steeper terrain," Tere said over his shoulder. "These are the mildest inclines in the area. If we had to go a little farther west, we'd be in the mountains, Ianthra's Breasts."

"Thank Vanda for that."

Tere shook his head. "Actually, while we're feeling fortunate, we can probably be thankful that we haven't run into anything nasty yet. The Mellanor Forest, though not nearly as dangerous as the Grundenwald, is wild. With so much area of thick, old-growth trees, some very dangerous things live here."

"I'd almost rather fight than to slog up and down hill after hill," Aila said, kicking at a small fern that seemed to have offended her.

"You may get your wish," Urun said as he walked past her, pumping his legs to get up the hill more quickly, "especially if you keep making obvious trails like that the assassins can follow."

When they reached the crest of the rise, they found a

spot where two large trees had fallen, clearing a small opening in the surrounding trees with their demise and crash to the ground. Through the space, they could see to the northeast, over the boughs at the northern limit of the Mellanor Forest.

The edge of the vegetation seemed to come suddenly, as if a line was drawn in magic to keep the trees back from the open land of the nation of Sutania.

Tere stepped up next to Urun, who had stopped to look. Aila huffed behind him as she joined them.

As Tere scanned the horizon, he noticed something that made him blink. He didn't know why he still had that habit after so many years without his real sight. Blinking did nothing for his perception of the world around him, and he certainly didn't need to lubricate dead eyes.

The strange emanations were still there.

The archer was used to seeing the magical matrix. After all, disturbances in it helped him to "see." But looking out over the terrain ahead of them, he almost didn't recognize the way the magic appeared. It had intensified and somehow also grown fuzzier. Just a little, but looking out over such a vast distance, it was more recognizable.

"Urun," he said. "Have you noticed anything lately about your magic?"

The nature priest eyed the older man for a moment, a glint of suspicion in his gaze. "What do you mean? Noticed what?"

"I don't know. Has it changed somehow? Does it feel different? The matrix—the way magic diffuses our surroundings—it looks different to me, though I can't explain exactly how."

Urun's suspicious look was replaced by a concerned one. "Yes. The last few days, things have felt...off. I can't explain it, either. It doesn't seem to have affected my use of the magic, but there is definitely some kind of change. I didn't want to mention it earlier because I wasn't sure if it had anything to do with what you saw. I wanted to be sure."

"I'm glad it's not just me," Tere said. "Hopefully it's something peculiar to the area, though I never felt it when I traveled through here before. Please tell me if it changes again or if you notice something new. I'll do the same."

Urun gave Tere the smile that made him look like a mischievous boy, complemented by his shaggy hair and too-young face. "That's fair. I'm sure it's just something local."

"I hope so."

❦ 19 ❦

They traveled for several more hours, until the forest around them grew even darker and the brief glimpses of the sky above through the canopy showed only the deep purple of night.

"We need to find a defensible place to camp," Tere told them. "We'll stop at the next likely place we find, a small clearing or some such."

The other two nodded. Conversation had grown sparse in the last few hours. The travel seemed to be wearing on all of them.

They found a place and set up camp. There would be no fire again. Aila grumbled about it, but not too forcefully. She knew the reason.

The young woman ate and then rolled up in her cloak and fell asleep quickly. Urun set himself on part of a fallen tree in preparation for his turn at watch. Tere lifted a few of the arrows in his quiver to make sure they would come out easily and picked his bow up from the tree he had leaned it against.

"Going somewhere?" Urun asked.

"Yes. I saw flashes of something twice today. Small

magical swirls like the one I saw last night. I'm still not sure what it is, but I'm going to go and see if I can find out. If it's the assassins, I want to know about it before they can plan some kind of ambush."

"And if you don't return?"

Tere huffed a breath. "Then it's likely we couldn't have withstood their attack in any case. I don't say that to be arrogant, but this," he swept his arm out toward the trees around them, "is my domain. Heavy forest in the dark of night. If they can kill me outright without me warning the two of you, I doubt the two of you would last long, even with your skills and abilities."

Urun ran his fingers through his messy hair. "Agreed."

"Will I set off your wards if you put them in place?" Tere asked.

"I can make them recognize you so they won't alarm when you cross them."

"Good, then do so. I won't go far, just enough to be confident they're not close by. If everything goes wrong, I'll at least try to shout to warn you. If you hear it, you run out of here as fast as you can."

"And leave you?"

"If I shout, I'm already dead."

Urun nodded, his lips a thin line. "Be careful, my friend."

Tere grinned at the nature priest. "I always am."

Tere Chizzit ghosted through the forest like a wraith. It felt good to be able to pass between the foliage at his own pace, not having to worry about others. He had spent so many years alone, sometimes it still grated on him to consider other's feelings and abilities—or lack thereof—when deciding what to do.

He supposed it was worth it. He had missed human interaction. If nothing else, it made him appreciate these times where he could use his skills to the fullest and not have to worry about someone else not keeping pace.

But then, he wasn't out in the darkness for fun. He had a job to do, so he'd better get to it.

The archer moved quickly, slipping through the underbrush and dodging trees as if it was the brightest daylight. He would leave no trail; he had been moving without leaving a recognizable path for decades.

And in all those decades, he had never had anything slip away from his magical sight. Not once, let alone several times like had happened in the last two days. If he admitted it to himself, it was infuriating, and more than a little worrying. He still wasn't completely sure what he had been seeing was real. People with normal sight occasionally thought they saw things; why couldn't he?

None of these questions helped, so he changed his thought process. If what he had seen was one of the assassins, where would that skulking person be right now?

Tere made a wide circuit a mile or more back toward where they had come from, searching for any clue that someone had passed. He shook his head when he saw the devastation Aila had wrought as she made her way through the underbrush. Urun had not left a trail, with the way his magic gently shifted the vegetation out of his way as he passed, and Tere didn't leave a trail, but that young woman, she might as well have been setting out a line of paint in her passing. Bright, glowing paint.

But there was nothing he could do about it short of actually carrying her. Until he could get the group to somewhere that didn't take tracks as well—maybe solid rock or a busy roadway?—he would deal with what he had.

His search took two hours, but in the end, he went back to their little campsite disappointed. Not disappointed that he hadn't seen the assassins, but that he still had no idea what he had seen the day before.

What could cause a trail through the magical matrix, but then disappear? Nothing that he knew of. Maybe his age was catching up to him.

Tere stepped out of the darkened trees right next to Urun. The priest started at the archer's appearance and began waving his hands and chanting to cast a spell before he realized who it was.

"Gah!" the priest exclaimed. "Don't do that. You scared five years off my life."

"Sorry," Tere said. "I'll try to remember to make a noise before I step into camp from now on."

"Yes, that would be appreciated." Urun cocked his head and his eyes drilled into Tere's. "You didn't find anything."

"No. While it's good news that the assassins are either not following us or are farther back than I went, I'm beginning to doubt my sanity."

"Hmm. If it makes you feel any better, maybe they have magic that kept you from seeing them."

"That's not helping, Urun."

"Oh, right." The priest ran his fingers through his hair. "Don't worry too much about it. We both noticed that magic is acting strangely. It could just be that."

Tere sighed. "Yes. Maybe. Keep your eyes—and your wards—peeled. I'm going to get an hour's sleep and then I'll take my watch."

Urun nodded and scanned the forest. Tere found a relatively level spot, wrapped himself in his cloak, and went to sleep.

The end of Tere's nap came in the blink of an eye. He woke, worked his mouth to get rid of the gritty taste that had somehow taken root in such a short time, and levered himself to his feet. Why did he feel stiff? He had just lain down an hour ago. He rolled his shoulders, grabbed his bow from the tree it was leaning against, and then shuffled over to Urun.

The nature priest watched the archer with curious eyes. When Tere made it to the log where Urun sat, the younger man spoke, "Is something wrong?"

"Huh?" Tere said. "Oh. No, just a little stiff from lying on the cold ground. I think I was sleeping with a rock wedged in my back."

"Ah. Here you go." The nature priest made a motion with his hand and said something under his breath.

The aches disappeared and Tere felt like he had slept for a full eight hours on a soft bed.

The archer blinked at Urun. "Thanks for that. Sometimes I forget about your healing magic. It did the trick. You're handy to have around sometimes, you know?"

Urun gave him a tired smile. "You're welcome. I'm going to get some sleep. I can't cast that spell on myself, so I have to take care of fatigue the mundane way. The wards are set, so we'll get a warning if something tries to cross them."

"Good enough," Tere said. "I'd not sleep over there." He pointed to where he had been sleeping. "If you want to avoid an aching back, anyway."

✿ 20 ✿

"So," Aila Ven said as they made their way through even more of the Mellanor Forest, "what's your story?"

Tere didn't realize at first that she was talking to him. He was scanning the thick vegetation in front of him, as always, and Aila had come up to join him, crashing through the brush with enough noise to notify anyone within three miles of their presence.

"I don't have a story," he answered.

"Everyone has a story, though granted, most people have a boring story. I'm sure yours is not."

"You're wrong again, young lady."

He watched her at the edge of his vision. She worried at her bottom lip.

"That thing you do, seeing even though you don't have eyes, it's amazing. I think you actually see things better than we do."

He shook his head. He didn't like her questions. "I do."

"And the way you can shoot that bow, it's amazing. I've never seen anyone do what you can do."

"Perhaps you need to get out more often," he said.

"So, what's the story? Who are you and where did you come from?"

"I'm Tere Chizzit and I came from the Grundenwald. I sprang spontaneously from the seed of an ash and an eagle's feather. What's your story, Aila Ven?"

Tere continued scanning for threats, but he caught the young woman opening her mouth to speak and then closing it again. Twice. She dipped her head and slowed to her normal pace, following him and Urun as they chose the path forward.

A dull, throbbing pang of regret stabbed through Tere. He didn't mean to be so defensive, but neither did he want to talk about his past. He did wonder about Aila's past, but he had been polite enough to let her have her secrets. He swung his head toward her to see her expression, but she had pulled her hood up and looked downward, not meeting his eyes.

The archer sighed and turned his attention back to the path ahead.

The day seemed to stretch on, the trio quieter than normal. A mood seemed to have slipped onto them, and they marched through the forest with single-minded intensity.

They entered a small clearing. Right away, Tere felt its wrongness, as if they had entered something that shouldn't have been there.

"Tere," Urun said. "I don't like the feeling of this area. It's unnatural. I think we should—"

A shape appeared before them out of thin air. Even to Tere's sight, there was nothing and then the thing came to be in a way he had never seen, almost like the magical matrix was torn and the creature before them had stepped through.

On all six of its legs.

The visitor looked like a gigantic ant. It had a three-sectioned body and limbs like an ant, but its face was more intelligent-looking. More human.

Tere recognized the magical tracks it left in front of him.

They were the same he had seen before, the ones that had disappeared.

They did so now again, along with any other evidence the creature had ever existed.

"I hate bugs," Aila said. She already had her vinci out. She had told the archer only the name of the weapons, not how their chains seemed to lengthen and shorten, as if by magic. Another secret.

The insect appeared again, directly in front of Urun. It struck out at the priest with one of its forelegs.

Urun glowed in Tere's sight, magical protection springing up around him, and the blow was deflected, though the force of it threw Urun back and knocked him off his feet.

Tere had already drawn an arrow and released it. The shaft passed through the creature's head.

But it didn't.

Just as the missile would have struck, the insect phased out, all trace of it disappearing. The arrow passed through where it had been and stuck in a tree twenty feet away.

The creature, and three more just like it, popped into existence in front of the three humans.

Tere was surprised to see a heavy weight attached to a long chain sweep through the creatures, or rather, where the creatures had been. All four of them had flickered just as the weapon passed through them. The archer reminded himself that though Aila complained and often acted petulantly, she was a warrior. He had seen her fight with the strange chain weapons she wielded.

"Damn!" the young woman said when her attack caused no injury to the insects.

"They phase out of existence when we try to attack," Tere said. "We'll have to try something else. Urun? Can you do anything?"

"I'll try." The nature priest threw his hand up to rebuff one of the monsters that was trying to get at him.

Two of the attackers went after Urun, both rearing up on their back two sets of legs and trying to strike with their forelegs and the pincers above their huge eyes. Below those eyes, mouths and noses that looked far too human wore expressions of concentration and—could it be?—anger.

While Urun tried to keep his magical shields in place, the other two creatures disappeared and then winked back into view, one each in front of Tere and Aila.

"Urun?" Tere yelled, rolling out of the way of the attack aimed at him. He let loose with two arrows, one after another in the blink of an eye. His target was the insect attacking Aila.

The first missile passed harmlessly through where the creature had been, though there seemed to be nothing there any longer. As the second followed, the flicker of something flashed in Tere's sight. It looked as if...

Aila darted out of the way of the pincers as the insect attacking her became solid again. She struck out with the blade end of her weapons, but did no damage to the enemy that had become incorporeal once more.

Tere swung his bow at the creature attacking him, knowing it could not be struck but hoping that it had to become solid to land its own strike. He thought of ducking through where the monster had been, but then rejected the idea. He had no desire for the creature to become solid again with Tere inside it.

He went to swing at it again and rolled to the side instead. This time, he shot three arrows, faster than the eye could see. Again, his target was the insect harrying Aila.

The first arrow passed through empty air.

The second arrow did the same, though there was a flicker or something there as it did so.

The third arrow almost made it through the unoccupied space, but then the creature solidified just as the shaft was exiting the area. The monster screamed as a chunk of the other side of its head was torn off.

A fourth arrow went through one of the monster's eyes, knocking it away from Aila. It didn't get back up.

"They're limited to how long or how many times they can go insubstantial," Tere said.

Then he grunted as the monster that had been trying to strike him finally did. A line of fire traced down his shoulder from the thing's pincer. It felt like poison.

Tere drew one of his long daggers as he spun away from the insect and slashed out. He was fast enough to catch a piece of one of the pincers before the monster phased out. It made a slight *tchk* sound but didn't do any apparent damage. His attacker came back in at him for another attack, this time with its forelimbs, one from either side.

The archer backstepped, throwing out his dagger and his bow to block the strikes. He timed it so that as the limbs became solid, they met the human's weapons and were deflected.

As Tere was busy fending off his foe, he caught sight of Aila running toward him to help. Ten feet away from her, the nature priest was down on his knees, his hands glowing with power, a dim shield surrounding him.

"No," he yelled at her. "Go help Urun. His shield is weakening."

The young woman changed direction in an instant. That was good. Tere was afraid she would argue, but she was reliable when it really counted. That was an important thing to know.

As for his own foe, Tere had a better idea of what he needed to do. Leaving Aila and Urun to their own devices, he backstepped from the insect creature in front of him and slashed at its striking forelimbs. As expected, only the tips, the part it was trying to strike him with, were substantial. The rest of the monster's body remained phased out.

The trick was to either catch the parts of its body the thing made solid or to fatigue its ability to be ethereal.

Now that he had determined the monster's weakness, Tere began to maneuver it into place. Using his bow stave as a cudgel in one hand and his knife in the other, he timed his parries so that any of the blows he didn't avoid, he was able to bat away from him. The mouth on that insect face had gritted teeth and displayed what, on a human face, would be frustration.

Good.

Occasionally during his game with the creature, Tere would take a fraction of a second to fire off an arrow or two at one of the two insects assailing Urun. They seemed to put a high value on downing the priest, all but ignoring Aila. The woman had landed a few blows to the creatures as they became more solid when they clashed with the nature priest's shield.

Just a little longer.

Tere saw his chance. The insect he was fighting threw a flurry of frantic strikes at him. Left forelimb, right forelimb, pincers, then back to its forelimbs. He dodged two, batted aside another blow, and met the last two attempts with his knife. As he did so, he dropped his bow, drew his other knife, and slashed out at the creature's head.

It had grown so frustrated, it stopped taking advantage of its ability to appear in another location. Instead, it focused entirely on striking the human in front of it.

Tere slashed through the insect six times before it began to flicker and solidify. Still, it did not blink out of existence and into another location. The faint magical signature was still in front of Tere, though he wasn't sure if anyone else would have been able to see it with their regular eyes.

When the insect finally became solid, the look on its face said it all. It realized it had gotten carried away with trying to kill the human and it had gone too far. Its huge eyes seemed to get wider and its mouth shaped itself into an O as it became fully solid in time for Tere's knives to come from either side of its head and cut into it.

The top quarter of the thing's skull, along with its antennae and part of one eye, spun off as they separated from its body. Sickly blue brain matter sprayed out as it began to fall.

By the time the insect's body had reached the ground, Tere had sheathed his knives and picked up his bow.

Now it was time for the other two to die.

Tere launched three arrows in rapid succession at one of the insects. As the first one passed, Aila's eyes went wide as if she thought she was being attacked, but by the time the third went by, she had obviously realized what was happening. She struck just as the last arrow hit a nearby tree.

Her strike, though demonstrating impressively fast reflexes, only accomplished a glancing blow off the creature's forelimb. By the time her other weapon swung around, the creature had regained its ability to phase out again.

Tere shrugged his shoulders, focusing on the feeling of it. He only had twelve arrows left. He was unaccustomed to wasting the shafts as he needed to with these foes.

He thought of a better way.

Urun chanted under his breath, moving his hands sluggishly, trying to keep the shield up around him. It seemed all he could do to maintain his protection, with no power left for attack. Aila continued to dance around the two remaining insects, both still focusing on the nature priest, though the one that Aila had struck quivered its antennae at her as if trying to decide if it should target her.

What was it about the priest that the creatures found so important?

The archer started toward the four combatants, firing three more arrows at the same one he had targeted before. Again, after the third arrow, Aila struck out at it, this time with three coordinated attacks one after another.

The third time paid for it all. The weighted end of Aila's weapon smashed into the side of the monster's head, breaking one of its antennae and disjointing its mandible.

Another arrow punctured the creature's skull, spilling the bluish fluid over Urun's shield and the front of Aila's tunic. The monster fell away, leaving only its companion, still trying to get through Urun's protection.

Tere reached the three remaining fighters and dropped his bow in favor of his knives. He slashed at the creature, knowing his strikes would pass through it. Aila, to his right, swung her weapons at the insect, though she couldn't have seen it but in brief flashes when it actually struck Urun's shield.

The monster finally took its attention from the priest, turning toward Tere and solidifying its forelimbs to strike. Tere slapped one away with his knife and leaned back out of range of the other. Then, like an ocean wave, he leaned back in and sliced at the creature again.

Tere's internal clock told him that very soon, the insect's ability to phase in and out would be fatigued. That was when they needed to strike.

"Get ready," Tere told Aila. He saw her nod in his peripheral vision.

Something came over the creature then, a look on its face that, on a human face, would indicate a realization. The monster shifted its head, taking in its foes with its black eyes, then completely disappeared from Tere's sight.

For all of a second.

It appeared again, its entire form solid, mouth frozen in a wide O. It twitched, but that was all.

Tere cut into the monster with both his knives, the left at its skinny neck and the right at its left eye. At the same time, Aila slashed at both sides of its head with her own weapons.

The result was devastating. The head literally exploded from the force of all the strikes as it was cut free from the monster's body. The sickly blue liquid splashed over both of the combatants and the headless body of the insect dropped to the ground.

Aila spat and retched. "Blech! Sour. That is as foul a thing as I have ever tasted. Why did it just stop like that at the end?"

"That would be me," Urun said. "Once it stopped attacking, I could use some power for an attack instead of just maintaining my protective shield. It looked like it was going to try to disappear and flee, so I froze it."

"Froze it?" Tere asked. "As in, turned it to ice?"

Urun sighed. "No. It was a figure of speech. I manipulated its body to make it stand still and reappear."

Aila looked back and forth from the monster's carcass to the nature priest. "You can do that?"

"With this creature. It was close enough to an insect that my power worked on it."

Aila shivered visibly. "Ugh. I hate bugs."

Tere stepped over to pick up his bow. "I understand the sentiment. I've never seen one quite like this before."

"*Formivestu*," Urun said.

"What?" Aila asked.

"Formivestu. That's the name of those creatures."

"That sounds like Alaqotim," Tere said. "How do you know what they're called?"

Urun prodded the carcass in front of him with his foot. "Osulin told me about them. The goddess occasionally tells me of ancient things to bring home a lesson she is trying to teach. The creatures have a peculiar type of magic, one that erases any trace of them when they wish it. They haven't been seen in Dizhelim for over three thousand years, around the end of the War of Magic or the exodus of the gods. Old magic."

"Old magic." Tere rubbed his beard. "That answers why I wasn't able to see them, or at least not more than a trace or two. Not until they attacked, in any case. When they did that, I could track them, though they were faint."

"You could see them?" Aila said. "I only saw flashes of them when they became solid to hit something. Maybe they can only use one of their magics at a time, so when they phase out, they can't erase traces of themselves."

"That sounds reasonable," Tere said. "The question, though, is why they were here to begin with. Did our enemies somehow create them again or bring them back from wherever they went?"

The three were silent for a moment, but then Urun answered. "No. I think it has something to do with the strange way magic is acting here. Maybe there's a pocket of power in this general area. I think they chanced upon us and tracked us, probably planning to eat us. If anyone sent them against us, the master would be here to finish us off."

"That is a valid point," Tere agreed. "This thing with magic, though, it bothers me. If it's just here in this local area, then it's all well and good, but if creatures of old magic are coming again, will they stay only in this area? I don't like the implications. What else is changing? Maybe more importantly, what has caused the changes to begin with?"

❧ 21 ❧

Phoenixarrow knelt on the forest floor.

"It's almost as if there is only one person traveling. The archer leaves no trace and the other one, the young man, it's like he doesn't exist at all." Their contact with Featherblade's group through the tablets had allowed them to deduce which of their enemies were in each group.

"Are you saying you can't track them?" Fireshard said.

"No, that is not what I'm saying. I figured out which of those we saw in the city were in front of us, didn't I? I have kept track of them up until now, haven't I?"

"Enough." Darkcaller adjusted her hood to scan the seemingly unending forest ahead of them. "The other one, the one who leaves tracks, you can lead us to him?"

Phoenixarrow scoffed. "In my sleep. That one—she's female, by the way—leaves enough trail for double their number. I'm sure she makes enough noise to scare all the animals away, too, judging by her tracks."

"Why are we even wasting our time following these?" Keenseeker complained. "Our target is supposed to be that blue creature. She went the other way."

Fireshard scowled at the big man, but that was nothing out of the ordinary. Her default look was a scowl. As typical, she said nothing. She turned her glare on the trees around them, as if they were responsible for all the ills in the world.

"We've been over this," Darkcaller said. "We are following them because it is our job. You will be paid the same regardless of your task in this mission. When we have completed it, we'll receive our normal rate and you will move on to your next assignment. It almost seems as if you're afraid to catch the ones we're chasing. Is that it, Keenseeker? Do they make you nervous, cause you fear?"

He hefted his great battle axe on his massive shoulder and opened his mouth to speak, but Shadeglide interrupted him.

"We can look at it this way: two of them move through the forest as if it's not even there, leaving no trail that even our expert tracker Phoenixarrow can detect." The dark-haired woman nodded to the red-haired archer. "It's a challenge. They obviously have magic or skills. What else can they do? It's very exciting."

Keenseeker's mouth dropped open and he stood looking at Shadeglide.

Darkcaller smiled. She liked the smaller woman; everyone did. She was overly optimistic for her profession, but she kept their infighting from turning bloody. The leader of the party chastised herself. She shouldn't let that pig of a man goad her into responding in kind.

"Let's go," Darkcaller said. "Our prey won't be stopping and neither should we. The sooner we catch them and kill them, the sooner we can be done with this mission. We may even be able to circle back and meet up with the others in time to help kill our primary target."

Keenseeker glanced her way. He gave an almost imperceptible nod. She knew he'd like that last part.

Phoenixarrow headed off into the trees, following the one visible trail.

Darkcaller waited as the others passed her, following Phoenixarrrow. Edge went first, back ramrod straight, his formal Teroshi garb moving silently as he made his way through the foliage.

Fireshard went next, her intense eyes looking for enemies in every frond and leaf. Darkcaller knew the other woman liked to work alone, but the same could be said of many of the Falxen. The fiery woman was perhaps a little bit more insistent in her preference, though. The leader of the group hoped the fire-wielding assassin would not cause problems.

Speaking of problems, Keenseeker passed next, walking straight ahead, not looking to the left or right, simply strutting through the forest as if it was a street in a city and he was the king. How did the ridiculous man ever accomplish his missions? The same way he did everything else, Darkcaller realized, bulling his way through it with brute force. It could be useful. Maybe she would sacrifice him in some battle soon.

Shadeglide glanced at Darkcaller, as if to politely offer to allow the leader to go first. The mage waved her hand toward the others. Shadeglide smiled at her and gave her a little wave back. How did she assassinate people with that attitude? She would have to talk with the shorter woman, find out her history. Being too polite and consistently happy like that could be a liability to the entire group. Darkcaller's brief research into the different members of the brace had been interesting. Shadeglide had killed more targets than any of the others in the group. The leader was confused by that. She did not like being confused.

Darkcaller watched the smaller woman for a while. While she had enjoyed men physically, their superior attitudes toward women sickened her. She was at times attracted to females as well, even going so far as to experiment with them in the past.

Shadeglide was definitely one she found attractive. Her form, lithe and compact, was enjoyable to observe. If Darkcaller didn't miss her guess, the other woman had a mixture of blood of one of the northern races and another more southern. Even her blue hair, dyed to blend to the darkness better, was interesting and distinctive.

But that was about all the leader knew about the pretty assassin. Other than Shadeglide always appeared happy and optimistic, and that she seemed to like interacting with people. These things were unusual in a Falxen. Darkcaller herself would rather not deal with people at all. Except for killing them, of course.

"Shadeglide," Darkcaller said. "Drop back, please."

The younger woman flashed one of her many smiles at the leader and did as asked.

"What is your story?" Darkcaller asked.

"My story?"

"Yes. How did you become a Falxen?"

Most Falxen wanted their life history kept secret. They treated it as if it was no one else's business. Darkcaller understood that, but it wasn't forbidden to ask someone, just treading on the border of propriety.

Shadeglide nodded and continued smiling. "Oh. Well, it's not all that exciting."

"Perhaps it's not exciting to you because you lived it. Others may find it so."

"I guess that could be," Shadeglide said. "If you want to hear it, I'll tell you. Walking through this forest without speaking seems like it will make the trip longer anyway."

If anyone else had said those exact words, Darkcaller probably would have been annoyed, but she couldn't seem to muster annoyance with this woman. She was like a child in a way, seeming so innocent that her words only seemed to indicate her genuine joy in finding another point of view on the matter.

"I was born on the border of Arania and Shinyan," Shadeglide started. "My mother was from the first and my father from the second. They both died when I was young, so my grandfather raised me.

"He was retired from his position as an assassin for the Aranian king. Because the Borderlands were so dangerous, he trained me in all the skills he had developed over his lifetime.

"It was like a game to me, learning to fight and move unseen, and all the rest of it. It brought us close. He became the parents I didn't have, the most precious person in my life.

"Then he died as well. He was old and his body simply wore down until it was too weak to go on. For such a great man, it seemed an insult.

"There was nothing for me in the borderlands anymore. Everything about my house and the surrounding area reminded me of him, and of my parents. I left, never to go back.

"Making my way outside in the wider world was more difficult than I thought it would be. Most of my skills were not suitable for making a living. Eventually, I began doing jobs for money, stealing things, even killing people.

"I would only accept jobs to kill evil people, of course. I'm not one of those who enjoy taking a life. I am good at it, but I do not take it lightly.

"One day, a woman approached me. I knew the way she held her body, the furtive looks as she scanned the surroundings. I figured she had a job for me to do. It was much more than that.

"She was a recruiter for the Falxen. She said there was a place for me in the Blades, that my skills made me desirable. I would do what I had been, but it would be steadier work, not hit and miss as things had been. More importantly, there would be others, a family to call my own. That last appealed to me more than all else, so I agreed."

Shadeglide paused. Was she finished? Darkcaller waited for several more seconds before speaking herself.

"And the jobs you do for the Falxen, do you not have issues with them?"

Shadeglide's mouth turned into a slight frown—the first one Darkcaller had ever seen on the beautiful face—before it disappeared with a more neutral expression. "I try to take only jobs where bad people need to be killed."

"Bad people?" Darkcaller asked. Didn't this girl know that most of her new *family* were bad people?

"Yes. For example, the last man I killed beat his wife regularly. The one before that tormented his children with horrific stories that made them afraid to sleep at night."

"Those things don't deserve a death sentence."

Shadeglide bit her lower lip but then seemed to realize what she was doing and stopped. "No, but it makes them bad, less deserving of life than others."

Darkcaller decided to change the subject. "How are you so successful? You have made more kills than any other of the Falxen I know. Your personality is so happy and carefree. How do you play a role and gain trust of the people you need to manipulate? I know that you do more than kill. I remember hearing of a mission where you infiltrated a thieves guild in order to find the hidden leader and kill him."

"Oh, that one," Shadeglide said as if it were nothing. Darkcaller marveled that the woman had been able to pull it off. Three other Falxen had tried and had been found out, losing their lives. "It's really nothing. My grandfather taught me to take on the persona of anyone I chose."

"I don't believe it," Darkcaller said. "I have observed you. You simply cannot keep a smile from your face. Please don't take offense if I tell you that you are much too tender-hearted to ever really convince someone of a, shall we say, darker nature, that you are a like personality."

Shadeglide smiled even wider at that. "I do okay. Do you consider yourself having such a 'darker nature'?"

"Yes."

"Fine."

The woman seemed to change before the mage's eyes, as if a dark shadow passed over her. Darkcaller would have sworn that the other woman's bright blue eyes darkened and the smile that had been there a moment before turned to something of a sneer that chilled the taller woman's heart.

"What do you think now?" the woman said in a voice that was different than her normal, perky tone. It somehow sounded more serious, more ominous. Was there something else underneath the simple words she had uttered?

"I, uh..." Darkcaller stuttered, at a loss for words.

In a blink, the expression on Shadeglide's face changed again. This time, her hard eyes grew soft and her lips puckered into a shape that looked like she was preparing to kiss someone. She gazed longingly at Darkcaller, scanning her body in a way that suddenly made the mage feel like she needed to cover up...or to remove her clothing completely. She tingled with excitement.

Another few seconds passed and Shadeglide's bright eyes and happy smile had returned. She fingered a few stray hairs from her face and looked questioningly at Darkcaller.

"That is simply amazing," the dark mage said. "That first look made me think you were the most dangerous of people and the second...I was convinced you wanted to ravish me right here in front of everyone."

"I know," Shadeglide said, chuckling. "It's scary, huh?" She reached over and rubbed Darkcaller's shoulder, the warmth helping the goose bumps that were still there subside.

"Point taken. You are very good. I know masters at the Academy who could learn from you."

"Academy? Are you talking about the Hero Academy? Sitor-Kanda?"

"Of course. I was trained there. Come on now, I'm sure you know that. With what you just showed me, I won't believe for a moment that you haven't investigated the histories of every one of the members of this brace."

Shadeglide shook her blue hair to fall back over her shoulder and gave Darkcaller a wry smile. "Maybe."

"Tell me what you know."

"Well, I know that Fireshard has magic that lets her create tangible items made of fire, and that she was taken from her parents when she was just a few years old and trained at the Falxen training facility.

"I know that Phoenixarrow wants to be Erent Caahs, and she has spent her entire life trying to be just like him. Except the whole becoming an assassin thing instead of a hero, anyway.

"Edge was an elite bodyguard and assassin for the emperor of Teroshi, but when the emperor was killed while he was away on a mission, he became masterless and joined the Blades instead of taking his own life.

"And I know Keenseeker is an arrogant asshole whose one tactic is to run in and chop everything in sight to pieces with his axe."

Darkcaller laughed. "That is all accurate, but hardly a bucket of secrets. What do you know about me?"

Shadeglide's smile turned crooked, making her look like a mischievous child. "Enough not to tell you what I know about you. Let's just say that I can agree that being a woman does not make one lesser, though I don't think it makes one greater, either. I have no desire to argue about this point. I try to treat everyone as they deserve, male or female."

Darkcaller sniffed, but didn't press the issue. "Very well. I'm glad you're with my team. I look forward to talking with you again. It's so hard to find stimulating conversation."

Shadeglide gave her a thumbs up and then bounced ahead to follow the others. Bounced! Darkcaller found herself wearing a small smile. She liked the woman. But was she manipulated into it? She really didn't know.

Despite Phoenixarrow's statement that the one leaving tracks made it too easy for the assassins to follow, the little group Darkcaller was following was making good time. She was not fond of forests with all the messy foliage and the bugs. Mudertis knew that with how much skin her clothing showed, she was getting her share of bites, though why she thought the god of thievery and assassination would care was ridiculous. It really was a pity she hadn't studied more nature magic at the Academy. She might be able to keep the foul creatures from her.

When they stopped for the evening, Darkcaller approached Phoenixarrow.

"When will we catch them?"

The statuesque archer shook her mane of red hair from her face. "At the current rate? When they get out of the forest and into the plains. We're falling behind a little more each day. Unfortunately, the rest of you can't move fast enough through the underbrush. If I could go on ahead and—"

"No," Darkcaller said. "We can't take the chance. What if they killed you? You are the only one who can lead us through this...this mess."

"It's not that bad. Anyone could follow the tracks the sloppy one is leaving, even Keenseeker."

"Perhaps, but what happens when they do leave the forest? How could we track them then?"

"I think you are underestimating my skills," Phoenixarrow

said. "I won't be seen. I'll find them and then come back. We need more information about those we're chasing."

"You can't promise you'll not be seen. As you say, we don't know anything about them. Do they have magic, special talents, some other advantage? It's too risky. We'll have to continue on. Maybe we can travel through the night?"

The archer sighed. "No. That wouldn't be a good idea. We could miss their trail or something else important. Plus, most of the brace can hardly keep from tripping in the daylight. It would be a disaster to try to travel in the dark."

"Then we continue on as before. As long as we don't lose the trail, we will catch them eventually. There is nothing north of the forest for a hundred miles. We'll have time. We simply have to be patient."

"I'm a hunter," the red-haired woman said. "I'm always patient."

❦ 22 ❧

eden blinked and tried to focus on the forest clearing he and his friends had appeared in. He recognized it as the same one they had entered just before they were transported to wherever the Epradotirum had taken them.

The dappled sunlight gave the small meadow a peaceful air. It should have been soothing, but for the figure that rushed toward them.

He blinked again, but the person was still there.

She was stunningly beautiful with long blonde hair flowing behind her as she ran. She was wearing, of all things, a dress that was tight enough for him to see every curve on her exquisitely toned body, at least down to her waist. Below that, it widened out into a long, flowing mass of cloth that seemed impractical for combat. As impractical as the amount of skin the rest of the tight clothing showed.

Aeden opened his mouth to speak to her until he looked into her eyes. In those bright blue orbs he saw pure insanity, a fervor that made him draw his swords and go on guard.

It was only because of that that he was able to deflect the first knife she threw at him.

Luckily, he was closest to her or she may have targeted one of the others. The blade she launched wasn't so much thrown as it was swung. He noticed as it clanged off his sword that it was attached to a chain stretching back toward the woman. An unorthodox weapon, but one she seemed to know how to use effectively. It reminded him of Aila.

As Aeden parried the other knife—she had one for each hand—other movement flickered in the underbrush at the edge of the clearing. Five more people rushed into the open.

"*Vermi cuta tuu caernant,*" he spat.

Khrazhti already had her swords out, and Fahtin and Raki were preparing for combat in their own way. The Gypta girl went into a defensive stance with her long knives, and Raki disappeared from view.

"Fleshrender."

One of them had spoken and the woman with the chain blades ducked her head as if she had been struck. She looked back toward the others, sighed, and with a flick of her wrists called her blades back to her. She casually snatched them from the air, lifted her chin, and slunk back toward her five companions. Her walk accentuated her firm body provocatively.

The one who had spoken took a step forward. He was of average height and slim build, but seemed to radiate power, or at least command. His jet-black hair swayed loosely at shoulder length and his blue eyes, contrasting with the dark hair and the dim light of the clearing, burned a path to Aeden and his friends. He had curious bits of cloth wrapped around his arms, almost like bandages.

"We want only the blue woman. The rest of you may leave. We haven't been paid for your deaths, only hers. This is the only time I will offer. Leave and we will allow you to go.

Stay, and we will, unfortunately, have to kill you as well. The choice is yours."

The entire situation was strange to Aeden. Why would someone stop to talk in the middle of a battle? His mind raced to think of a solution. He wasn't interested in fighting these assassins. There were much bigger things to concern himself with.

"Why do you want to kill her?" he asked.

"Want?" the man said. "It has nothing to do with desire. It is simply my job. We were paid to see that one"—he pointed toward Khrazhti—"dead. The reason we received those orders is irrelevant."

"Not to us, it isn't. Who are you?"

"Ah, forgive me." The man's voice was soft, almost calming, but he could easily be heard across the clearing. "How rude of me. I am Featherblade. My companions are Whiteshadow, Loneblade, Boltshadow, Twoblades, and of course, our dear Fleshrender." As he spoke, he pointed to a tall woman with such light blonde hair it was almost white carrying at least four swords, a taller man with a blade that had to be more than five feet in length, a muscular man who was nearly crackling with power, a man dressed in dark, flowing clothing and carrying two curved swords with strangely shaped blades, and the beautiful woman who had just attacked him. She was currently licking one of her knives.

"We are Falxen," the man said finally.

Falxen. Tere had been right.

"Can't we come to some arrangement?" Aeden asked. "We have money. How much would it take for you to leave?"

The leader gave Aeden a wry grin. "I'm sorry. Once we take a contract, no amount of money in the world will cause us to give up the chase. The only thing that can do that is if the contractor cancels the arrangement. And before you ask, no, I will not tell you who the contractor is. It is irrelevant.

"You have one choice to make. Give over the blue woman and we will let the rest of you go free, or do not and we will kill all of you. Decide."

Aeden looked to Khrazhti and she met his eyes. A sadness crossed hers and her small frown was disappointed. She said in her dialect of Alaqotim, "I will surrender to them."

Aeden's eyes widened and he shook his head. He answered her in her own language. "No." Then, remembering himself, he said it again in Ruthrin. "No."

Featherblade took a deep breath and let it out slowly. "Very well. It is a shame, but so be it. Falxen, complete your mission."

All six of the assassins moved at once.

"Fortassi deisant testin tuu," Aeden cursed and he caught a small smile on Khrazhti's face. It was in Alaqotim, so she no doubt knew what he'd said.

The tall blonde assassin drew her two longer swords and charged Fahtin. The woman had some kind of mask wrapped around her head, showing only her eyes, with her light-colored locks protruding from the back in a long tail.

The leader joined the man with the very long sword, heading straight for Khrazhti. The dark-cloaked man with the two strangely shaped swords came at Aeden, while the crazy woman—Fleshrender, was it?—continued to pelt him with her chain daggers.

Peculiarly, the muscular man the leader had called Bolt-shadow stayed where he was. He was dressed like a Teroshi Shaku assassin, with a jacket belted over an undershirt with a sash, and with loose pants tucked into boots laced up his calves. A hood with a face cover hid everything but his eyes, which seemed to glow with power.

Aeden attacked the man coming at him aggressively, throwing fast combinations with his two swords, taking his foe by surprise. Between the blur of the four swords dancing and one of the chain daggers coming as if from out of nowhere, Aeden scored a shallow gash to the double-sword opponent's leg.

It was enough for him to be able to turn and run toward Fahtin. There was no way the Gypta would be able to defend herself with her knives against a seasoned fighter, especially one with two swords. He had to protect her. With a glance to Khrazhti—the animaru was capable of taking care of herself —he went to help the woman who was as close as a sister.

Before Aeden had taken two steps, and before the two assassins running toward Khrazhti could reach her, a flash of blinding white light zipped across the clearing, causing Aeden's hair to lift from his scalp.

From the corner of his eye, he could see a bolt of pure energy arc from Boltshadow to Khrazhti, striking her full in the chest.

"Nooo!" Aeden screamed, but continued toward Fahtin. If one of his friends was lost, that did not mean he had to abandon another.

But Khrazhti was not lost. The energy struck her and widened, as if it was battering against a stone wall. Or some kind of shield. Then, the bright light dissipated, appearing to be sucked into the blue woman's body.

She began to glow.

Aeden didn't know what it meant, but the animaru was still standing. He would find out what happened later. After he and his companions defeated their foes.

Whiteshadow began swinging her swords at Fahtin as she neared the Gypta. Aeden yelled and pushed more energy into his legs. He reached the blonde woman as her sword was about to strike Fahtin.

Aeden's adopted sister had brought her knives up to block the blow, but she hadn't seen the other sword, coming around in a wide arc to cut her down from her right side.

As the blades were about to strike flesh, Aeden caught up to the assassin and slammed his sword into the woman's left blade while swinging at her neck with his other.

With her strike going wide now that Aeden had deflected it, she twisted the blade in her right hand to block Aeden's strike to her neck. The awkward angles of all the strikes and blocks caused her and the Croagh to tumble to the ground in a mass of arms and legs.

Aeden was up in an instant, scanning the area around him and finding Fahtin who was, thankfully, still standing and not bleeding. She gave him a look of desperation and he could see the fear in her hazel eyes.

By instinct, he brought his sword up and it clanged loudly as the chain dagger aimed for his head bounced away harmlessly. He took three large steps to Fahtin's side and spun to face the three assassins.

The dark-clad man with the double swords—the leader had called him Twoblades—had regained his balance and was slowly circling Aeden and Fahtin with a limp for his damaged leg while Whiteshadow moved around in an opposite direction. Another glimmer and Aeden parried the other chain dagger from its trajectory heading toward Fahtin.

A quick glance toward Khrazhti showed that not much had changed. She was still glowing and the two swordsmen were doing their best to slice her to ribbons. It may have been a trick of the light or that Aeden was trying to focus on everything at once, but the leader, Featherblade, seemed to move faster than the eye could track. None of them would last long if they didn't do something drastic. But what?

Whiteshadow cursed and twitched as if she had been struck. Aeden smiled as she pulled out a small dart from her side. Raki was doing well to keep hidden, but he had not abandoned them.

The pale assassin glared, her eyes angry and wide. She

scanned the area, but then moved in toward Aeden and Fahtin along with her dark-cloaked companion.

Boltshadow swayed on his feet as if all the power had been sucked from him. Khrazhti was trading blows with the two assassins attacking her, mostly in a defensive manner. She had not taken more than a few small cuts, but she couldn't keep that up for long. One mistake would cause more than the gashes that dribbled blood a darker red than ran through human veins.

But he had his own problems. As he parried and blocked strikes from Whiteshadow and Twoblades, his mind raced to figure out what could help him, and more importantly, his friends, survive this encounter.

A chain dagger got past his guard as he stretched to keep one of Twoblades's swords from cutting Fahtin. The small weapon slashed his left shoulder, but not deeply enough to limit his mobility.

"*Aucioch aet mam!*" he hissed.

Fahtin did her best to stay out of Aeden's way. She threw her knives but only one struck her intended target. Whiteshadow growled as one of the small blades punctured her right forearm. She glared hatefully at the Gypta girl and tried more frantically to get to her.

"Run, Fahtin," Aeden grunted as he blocked one of Twoblades's swords and dodged the other one, kicking out at Whiteshadow to upset her balance so she couldn't complete a swing at Fahtin. He twisted to barely avoid one of the chain daggers as it whizzed by him, but the other flicked downward and deposited a slice to his right calf.

Fahtin looked as if she would argue, but then backed away from the three fighting and ducked behind a tree. Another chain dagger sliced the bark near her head.

Aeden glimpsed Khrazhti several feet away. She took a blade to her thigh and dropped into a kneeling position just as Featherblade's sword cut the air where her head had been.

They were simply outmatched. If they didn't have to cover for Fahtin, he and Khrazhti may have prevailed, but unless he could use his magic, they would not survive. Pressed so closely, though, he couldn't hope to complete the motions for any of his spells before he was cut down.

He hoped Raki and Fahtin got away. It was obvious he and Khrazhti wouldn't.

"*Jacete!*" Khrazhti yelled in her own language. It took a fraction of a second for Aeden to realize what she had said and then he threw himself to the ground. He wasn't sure what she was warning him against, but he trusted her.

A wave of power exploded outward from the animaru. Even lying flat on the ground, it threatened to pick Aeden up and fling him away like straw in a windstorm.

Aeden leapt to his feet immediately after it passed. All of the assassins had been thrown a dozen or more feet away from him. Khrazhti stood unsteadily where she had been, no longer glowing. Luckily, Fahtin had been with her back against a thick tree, so she was standing, though it appeared the wind had been knocked out of her. Raki picked himself up off the forest floor on the other side of the tree, having missed the brunt of the explosion because he was leeward of the trunk, and because he understood Khrazhti's language even better than Aeden did.

The assassins were beginning to move as well, though more slowly, as if dazed. Now Aeden had the time he had needed.

There was really no choice in what he needed to do. Combat against the assassins' superior numbers wouldn't work. He needed to use his magic, and not the relatively weak spells he had been taught during his training. What he needed now was one of the enhanced spells he had been working on.

He took a wide-legged stance, stable and strong. He breathed in deeply and then began. His arms swung outward and upward gracefully, describing a circle in the air. He sang the first quatrain of the Song of Prophecy, so softly that even he could barely hear. At the apex of the motion, he sang the first word of power more loudly.

"*Fantim.*"

His hands grew warm as he brought them close to each other in front of his chest and gestured as if pushing a ball downward, continuing with the Song. When his hands reached his center, just below his navel, he rotated his hands and pulled them upward while drawing breath deep into his lungs.

"*Lishant.*"

When Aeden's hands reached the level of his heart, he rotated his hands again, this time outward as if he was going to push someone away from him. He pronounced the final word with a forceful exhalation of breath, pushing his hands out rapidly.

"*Katha!*"

The entire clearing exploded with light so bright, all of the assassins were blinded, even those who were not looking at him or had their eyes closed. They were also picked up and thrown a second time, tumbling head over heels, some striking trees and stopping with pained grunts.

When the light faded, the assassins were dazed and blinking rapidly, obviously trying to focus their eyes.

"Move now," Aeden said to his friends. "I'm not sure how long it'll last."

The spell had not affected his three companions. Fahtin stood still, shocked at what had happened.

"What...?" she said. "Why didn't it affect us?"

"Talk later, Fahtin. Move."

That snapped her out of her stupor, and she ran where Aeden was pointing. Raki followed her, then Khrazhti. With one last look at the assassins, Featherblade waving his hand in front of him to compensate for his blindness and Fleshrender trying to stand but falling back to the forest floor, Aeden ran after his friends.

❧ 23 ❧

Khrazhti rushed after the humans who had become her friends. The word still seemed strange to her. There was nothing like it in her native tongue. Raki had told her the term in the Alaqotim he knew, but the pure version of the language had no need for such terms. At least, that is what she had thought.

Fahtin and Raki seemed relatively uninjured, a testament to both Raki's skill in avoiding notice and Aeden's dogged determination to protect his friends. The thought of it sent an unknown energy through her body. Why? What was it about the interactions of these light creatures that prompted such sensations? She hoped she had not been afflicted with one of the many illnesses that seemed abundant in this world.

The battle had been a short one, but furious. She could only thank S'ru that the large one, the one the leader had called Boltshadow, had used magic she could harness. He was powerful, for a human, but his attack was ill-conceived. But how could he know she could take the energy as her own and use it to power her own magic?

Dark Explosion was not a spell she used often. She had not

been challenged for centuries the way she had since she came to Dizhelim. The problem with the spell, though powerful, was that it drained her considerably. If she cast it without using Power Drain first, she risked using so much of her own energy that she would be too weak to continue fighting. If Dark Explosion didn't finish her enemies, it could mean her own defeat.

But the spell hadn't been enough. It had injured the assassins, but not greatly. She would have been defeated once they gathered themselves again and attacked. Her choice to use the spell less powerfully than she could have, to protect her friends, left them vulnerable. It was why caring about others was a weakness. So had she thought before. She was unsure now.

The former high priestess turned to look at Aeden behind her. She showed her teeth to him, something she noticed many of the humans did to bond in some way. At first, he looked surprised, blinking at her in confusion. Then, the edges of his own mouth curved upwards and he flashed his teeth at her.

Khrazhti didn't know exactly what the ritual signified, but she liked that expression on his face. She would work to utilize the tactic more often. It increased the warmth building within her, and she found that it was not unpleasant.

But her mind wandered. The best way to improve her abilities was to analyze each encounter, especially each defeat, and learn from it. She turned her thoughts to that end.

What was that thing Aeden had done? Much of what he had said was too low for her to hear, but she had picked out a few words he had spoken more loudly. They were not in her own pure language, but hearing them gave a sense of what they meant. They must have been in that other language Aeden spoke of, the language of magic.

Still, it amazed her. She had seen Aeden practicing,

working through his magic and trying to determine the gestures and timing to make the spells more effective. The words themselves were not potent on their own. If she pronounced them—and she had tried to do so in the same order he used them—they did not create the effects he managed.

The magic he had cast was as powerful as any she had experienced. What's more, not only was it strong, but somehow it differentiated between foes and allies. The wave of power threw the assassins like aliten feathers in a gale but did nothing to her or their other two companions. How was that possible?

When they had a moment, she would ask Aeden. He probably did not know, of course. He seemed as surprised by the effects of the magic as anyone else.

She wondered again, for the hundredth time, how the animaru prophecy fit into everything that was happening. Was it as valid as the human prophecies, or was it more so—or less so? With a last passing thought at the strange situation she had found herself in, she continued to run.

The next three days, the little party did not sleep much. They rushed—as much as the vegetation and terrain allowed them to—as if death itself was chasing them. They had no doubt it was true.

Khrazhti had questioned Aeden during one of their stops. She was aware that the humans needed more rest than her, so she did not press for a long conversation.

"Aeden, that thing you did when we were fighting the assassins, what was it?"

The reddish-haired man looked at her, then blinked. His eyes had dark circles under them, something that happened when the humans did not rest acceptably. A tingle that transformed into a painful prick assaulted the middle of her torso.

She had felt much worse pain, so she did not react, but worried that something in this world was affecting her.

"That was called Dawn's Warning," he said. "It's a spell I was taught by my clan, but it's also one of the few for which I have worked out the movements that coincide with the part of the Song of Prophecy."

"But what does it do?"

"In the simple version I was taught, it causes a light that can be used to blind an enemy or to signal someone. The enhanced version is more powerful, it seems. It blasted them backward, like your spell did."

Khrazhti considered this. "No, not like my spell. Yours harmed them but did not affect the four of us. My magic does not have such...discrimination. How did you do it?"

Aeden blinked again. "I don't know. Of course, I didn't want it to affect my friends, but I can't remember doing anything specifically to keep that from happening. Maybe the spell interpreted my will, or I did something without knowing it. There is too much I don't know about the magic and the Song."

That sounded strange to Khrazhti, but then she was trained to use magic and had centuries to explore her power. It was all new to Aeden.

"How long will it have kept them down?" she asked.

"I don't know that either, and that worries me. We need to come up with a plan for escape. They'll follow us like they did before, and they'll be wary of me using that magic again. When we meet them again, we have to be ready to fight to the death. We probably should have killed them while they were stunned, but I don't know how long the effects last and we could have been surrounded and defeated before we finished them off."

"It was a sensible thing to do. The animaru, we rarely

think of such things as self-preservation when the battle feeling comes upon us. I am glad you are wiser than that."

He smiled at her. "Thank you. We better get moving again. There's no telling how close they are to us."

They continued their frantic pace for two more days until, suddenly, they broke out into the open. Khrazhti thought it was another clearing at first, but then she noticed the wide-open land with a few scattered clumps of trees that had sprung up in the midst of the grasses of the plains. To her right, gently rolling hills stretched on as far as she could see.

"Oh, thank Codaghan," Aeden said.

It was strange to Khrazhti when any of the humans mentioned their gods. She had been the high priestess of S'ru, her service to him her life. She had not seen any such devotion to the deities the others mentioned, except maybe from the man Urun Chinowa. Perhaps service to their gods was handled differently than what she was accustomed to.

Fahtin sat down on the grass as if she had finished a contest, a race to a destination, and now she was done and would rest. Was that what she really thought?

Raki stood nearby, his gaze switching between the girl sitting on the ground, the land ahead, and back to the forest from which they had just emerged.

"Come on, Fahtin," Aeden said. "We can't rest just yet. We have to get out of plain sight, behind some kind of cover. If the assassins see us, they will never let us go."

Fahtin sighed. "Do you think they're still following us? That thing you did seemed to do a lot of damage. Maybe they'll give up."

"They won't. The Falxen don't give up. Ever. Once they have a contract, they'll keep coming until they or the one they're after are dead. The most we can hope is to get far enough ahead so we can prepare for them the next time we fight. Either that, or put off the confrontation long enough to give me a chance to work out more of my magic."

The girl's face fell in resignation. "Okay." She grunted as she gained her feet and stepped over to where Raki still scanned the area.

Aeden turned to Khrazhti. "Where do we go? Can you still feel where Benzal is?"

Khrazhti only pointed, disappointed enough in her knowledge that she didn't want to speak. Aeden's face hardened as he sighted down her arm toward their destination.

"Really?" he said. "Still north? Are we going back to Broken Reach?"

"Yes," Khrazhti answered. "I believe that is where the portal will be."

"*Cuir aet biodh*! We could have saved a lot of time if we had just stayed there." He seemed to deflate, the anger going out of his eyes. "Oh well. I guess we were in no condition to fight all the remaining armies of the animaru. Not that we are now, either, but there is no changing the past. Let's move out. We still need to find some cover. At least we'll travel faster than we did in the forest."

They made their way to a small hill half an hour later. Once they were over the top and traveling down the other side, Aeden seemed to relax a little, his stiff shoulders and neck regaining some of their normal pliability. Khrazhti did not believe a simple hill would prevent the assassins from finding them, but she could understand not wanting to be seen.

In no time, they had crossed several other rolling features in the landscape and came to a small group of trees that provided some shelter from roving eyes. Aeden stopped them, suggesting they rest for a few minutes and eat.

While they nibbled on hard baked wafers and dried meat, Fahtin kept glancing at Khrazhti as if she was doing something strange. Khrazhti tried out the smile she had been prac-ticing and the Gypta girl smiled widely back. It made Khrazhti's mouth widen of its own accord. Strange.

"You eat," Fahtin said.

"I am eating," Khrazhti responded. Why was the girl giving her orders?

Fahtin's face changed color, as Khrazhti had seen human faces do. She still was not sure why this happened.

"No, no," the girl said. "I'm sorry. I wasn't telling you to eat. I was just pointing out that you do it. You eat things."

Khrazhti cocked her head at the girl.

"I'm not making any sense, am I? What I mean is that you eat food when we do. When I was taken captive by the animaru, I noticed that they didn't eat or sleep. They did hide out in the middle of the day, but they didn't actually sleep. I never saw them eat anything."

"Yes, that is correct," Khrazhti said. "We do not do these things."

Fahtin bit her lower lip and her eyebrows raised. "Umm, but you *are* doing it. I've seen you do both."

"That is also correct. At first, I did so to make you comfortable. I did not want to impress upon you how different we are. Then I found that when I did these things, the power in me increased.

"Did I say that correctly? My power was increased?"

Fahtin smiled at her again. Khrazhti found that she liked it when the girl smiled at her as well. "Yes. You found that eating and sleeping gives you more energy, allows you to do more?"

"Yes, that is it. I do not need these things, I think, but if they are helpful, then I will do them. An effective warrior will use every weapon at her disposal."

Fahtin laughed. "Now you sound like Aeden."

"Not just me," Aeden said. "Any warrior will tell you the

same thing." He turned to Khrazhti. "That's good that you found a way to be more powerful."

"Yes, that is my opinion also. I do not want to become dependent upon these things, but it is good that I can choose to do them if they are helpful."

"I agree," he said. "It can also help us when we need to keep watch while most of the party sleeps. You can take longer watches, if that's all right with you."

"Of course. It would be my preference to allow all of you to sleep and keep watch myself the entire night, if you trust me to do so."

"We trust you," he said without pause, "but I don't want to make you keep watch all night. You should sleep at least an hour or two to keep your energy level high. We'll need it when the assassins catch up to us.

"Speaking of which, we better get moving. It's not time to settle in for the night yet. There are still several hours of daylight left."

The party got up and started off again. As they did, Khrazhti thought of what Aeden had said. They had been enemies, her sole purpose on Dizhelim to kill him, and now they trusted her to guard them at their most vulnerable condition. The idea of it suffused her with warmth. She wondered if her own face was changing color. Was this what it felt like?

Her mouth had turned up into a small smile, but she hadn't put the expression there. There was so much to learn about these humans, about her own human half. She hoped she survived to do so.

For two days more, the four fled from the assassins. They ate as they moved, or took short breaks to do so, and their nights consisted of just a few hours of sleep before moving on again.

The relative lack of tall trees allowed them to navigate by

moonlight, Khrazhti in the front because of her keen animaru eyes. Surprisingly, Raki often ranged up front with her during the darkness, his eyes picking out details even she had not noticed. It seemed strange that a human could see better in the darkness than her, but it seemed to be so.

During their journey, all of them scanned the terrain around them, especially that behind them. There was no doubt the assassins would catch them again. It was merely a matter of time. The Falxen did not need to rush and force themselves to go without sleep. They were professionals and would maintain their readiness for battle. That is, they would do so if they were anything like the assassins Khrazhti had used in the past. Those had been animaru, of course, but she believed the principles were the same.

Khrazhti took full advantage of the other three in improving her Ruthrin. She practiced it even when she was not speaking with them, quietly pronouncing the words until they sounded correct.

While she worked on her language, Aeden was trying hard to improve his magic. He was often withdrawn, mouthing words and moving his hands or other parts of his body as he traveled. Khrazhti recognized some of the words that passed his lips, even if she couldn't hear them.

He was figuring out the gestures for that song he spoke of so often, the one that granted him power like she had never seen.

Then suddenly, as they passed over a grassy hill with a few scattered bushes, the party dropped to the ground as one.

Ahead, in a shallow depression that was not quite a valley, but may as well have been, an army sprawled out in all directions.

※ 24 ※

The dark figures of the animaru thundered through the foliage, heading north. The twisted black bodies were as Tere remembered, though he hadn't had an opportunity to observe them this carefully before. Previously, he had always been too concerned about killing them before they reached him to look at them closely.

He scanned the area for stragglers, suddenly glad that Urun and Aeden had worked out a way for the nature priest to use his own magic to imbue weapons with life magic and had been doing so each day for Tere and Aila. When it was certain all the creatures had passed, Tere let out a breath.

"Damn ugly monsters," he said.

The other two didn't speak at first. Tere swiveled his head from the bushy terrain ahead to his companions.

"That's the third group we've seen in as many days," Urun pointed out.

"Are they looking for us, you think?" Aila asked.

"Honestly," Tere said, "I have no idea. I doubt it, though. They wouldn't know we were here. Even if they did, what good would it do them? As far as the creatures are concerned, we're nobodies. It's Aeden they want, not us."

"And it's a good thing we're not Aeden," Urun said. "They can sense him, track him. If he was with us, we wouldn't be able to hide from them like this."

The archer swung his white eyes back to the surroundings. "Maybe, maybe not. We should have asked Khrazhti how they tracked him. Maybe it was luck or educated guesses. Who knows? We can only hope she's helping him stay out of trouble now."

"Stay out of trouble?" Aila scoffed. "He's being chased by assassins and heading toward where the animaru are gathered. He's running *into* trouble."

Tere chuckled at that. "Yeah, I guess he is. Highlanders!" The smile left his face quickly as the old hunter swept his gaze over the terrain again. "We have a choice to make, and I don't think we can put it off any longer."

He knew the others already understood what he was talking about. When they topped a small hill earlier that morning, they had seen the Kanton Sea and, more importantly, the thin strip of land within it. It was the edges of the island of Munsahtiz. The home of the Hero Academy.

But they weren't there yet.

"I have always favored going across the bridge to the north to get to the island—not that I've done it often, mind you—because the southern route passes through Praesturi. Not only that, it also requires passing through the Verlisaru Forest to get to Sitor-Kanda.

"The problem is that the animaru seem to be heading to the north. How they're doing that without the Academy knowing about them or what they're doing up there, I have no idea, but I don't favor the idea of trying to pass through the lot of them."

"I think there are animaru everywhere," Urun said. "It's

like the strange feeling in the magic around us. Something significant is happening. Now is a time of prophecy. Everything is chaos."

Aila stared at the two men as they discussed the issue. "They're still hunting Aeden."

"What?" Tere asked, surprised not only that the young woman joined the conversation but that she didn't seem to be using the opportunity for some snide remark.

"The animaru," she said. "They're still looking for Aeden. They would have returned to that fortress of theirs, finding a lot of their friends killed and their leader gone somehow. There had to have been commanders with them. Once they sorted out who took control of the forces, that animaru would continue with the mission given to them by their god.

"After we left Satta Sarak, if that glowing thing that affected Khrazhti had gone out, the monsters would have spread out, going in different directions to try to find Aeden, their primary purpose in Dizhelim.

"Those commanders, at least one or two of them, would probably know the significance of the Academy and that the Malatirsay would want to go there. In fact, Aeden was trying to go there before Fahtin was taken. Knowing where he wanted to go, it would be logical for them to try to put up groups to block him from getting there. They're probably scouts with a larger army somewhere else that can respond to any reports the scouts find.

"So, yeah, that's why they're here. They're still looking for Aeden."

Tere found that his mouth was open and he closed it slowly, noting that Urun also wore a startled expression. "That's...well, that is a very good analysis, Aila. You sound like a military commander. How did you get such a good grasp of strategy?"

The woman flushed, something Tere didn't know she

could do. "It's not strategy, just common sense. Let's get going. We still may have people following us."

Aila started down the hill. Tere and Urun shared a look and rushed to catch up to her. Tere would press her for more information later, after he'd thought about it. The woman was full of surprises. He hoped none of it would prove harmful to him or the rest of Aeden's allies.

As they headed northward, the terrain transformed from one of scattered stands of trees and vegetation to a more arid environment. The plants became tougher, with thorns and saw edges, and streams disappeared. The trees seemed to squat close to the ground as if waiting for an attack.

It was the Tarshuk region, a patch of desert-like territory just to the southwest of the Heaven's Teeth Mountains rising up in the distance. It was strange to struggle through the dry, heated land and at the same time see snow on the mountains that seemed so close. They weren't, of course. The mammoth size of the Heaven's Teeth Mountains just made them seem so.

Aila was back to muttering her dislike of their means of travel. Tere caught a few words of it: horse, wagon, someone to carry her.

"It's only another twenty miles or so," he said to the air. "Tarshuk isn't all that wide going from south to north. We can consider ourselves lucky that we don't have to traverse it from east to west."

Urun had gone into one of his episodes in which he didn't respond to the others. He followed along, but as he did so, he sang little songs and sometimes had lengthy conversations with himself.

Tere shook his head. This is what he had for support: a whiny girl who could at the snap of his fingers transform into an intelligent, competent party member and a half-crazed nature priest with antisocial tendencies. They were all he had, though. Maybe it was slightly better than traveling alone.

No, he reconsidered. It was better being alone. He sighed.

A flash of power off to Tere's right caught his attention. He snapped his head toward it, but it disappeared quickly.

"Did you—" he said to the others.

"Yes," Urun said. "I saw it. A flash, like a great mirror off in the distance. What was it?"

"I don't know, but it was magic. A powerful burst of it, almost as if something magical exploded. I don't know how far away it was, but that kind of power...it had to be immense."

All three of the travelers scanned the horizon in the direction of the flash, but nothing else happened.

"What is going on, Urun?" Tere finally asked. "Do you sense anything? Has Osulin given you any guidance?"

The young priest shook his head. "I'm sorry, Tere. Things feel the same as what we discussed before. My senses are jumbled and the entire natural world seems to be out of balance somehow, but I can't pinpoint what it is. Osulin doesn't often speak directly to me. I imagine she has work to do with the lack of equilibrium. If she has a task for me or needs to tell me something, she will do so. I have been trying to commune with her, but if she hears me, she is not yet ready to speak to me."

"Are you saying that your goddess doesn't answer the prayers of even her own priest?" Aila snapped.

Urun turned his head slowly toward the woman and his eyes became hard. "And your grand god Vanda has spoken to you? He has spoken to anyone? Ever? Don't compare the Goddess with a fabrication of storytellers. Osulin has many other things to do than to coddle her priest. She has given me a task, and until it is finished or something more important comes up, I am to continue with it."

Aila opened her mouth to speak, holding up a finger for emphasis, but then she dropped her hand and closed her mouth. She angled her body toward where the flash had occurred one more time and then gazed longingly toward where they had been headed.

Tere stepped in between them to reduce the tension. "Whatever it was, it already happened. Let's get moving. It'll have to be a mystery for another time. We have plenty of other things to think about right now. For example, Urun, don't you find it strange the way magic has changed over time?"

"What do you mean?"

"In all the stories set in the Age of Magic, there are grand spells and fantastic displays of power. Mages battled and caused destruction that's hard to believe. Relatively few had magical abilities, but they were powerful."

Urun shrugged. "Yeah, well there was more magic back then, before it was all used up and the gods left Dizhelim. What's your point?"

"I don't mean that. There was more magic, but things were different. I mean, back then it was a few people with abilities. I think now, there are more people with little magics. The total amount of magic in the world may be less, but I think it's also spread out across a larger number of people. I think the form magic takes now is little abilities, things like my magical sight, rather than the devastatingly powerful spells in the history books."

"I never really thought about it," Urun said, "but you may be right. You can ask the masters at the Academy when we get there."

"I suppose. It's just a random thought." It was true. Tere had been wondering about it, but the main purpose he had brought it up was to keep the peace between his two companions. It seemed he had accomplished his goal.

The three traveled in silence for the better part of an hour, Tere slightly ahead of the other two scanning the area for signs of danger.

Aila finally broke the silence. "Tere, you're old—"

"Thank you for that," he said.

"No, let me finish. I probably should have worded that differently. What I mean is that you are experienced. You've seen a lot in your lifetime."

"I have."

"Would you care to tell us about it?"

"Would you care to tell us about your own life?" he said.

Tere glanced at the woman in time to see her face screw up into a look of disgust. She recovered quickly and changed her request. "Umm, well how about something you learned... or heard, or read? It may make the miles go more quickly."

"Hmm," Tere said. "I might have a tale or two buried somewhere in my old brain. As do the two of you as well, I'm sure. We can play this game, but we all have to play it. I'm sure each of us has something to say that the other two haven't heard."

"Oh," Aila said. "Like a game? We'll each tell a story?"

"Sure. Like a game."

"That sounds good. Will you go first?"

Tere stopped and faced Aila. "Aren't you forgetting something? There are *three* of us. If we do this, we all will take turns."

Urun didn't seem to be paying attention to the other two. He was slipping into one of his quiet phases. Tere thought it might be just the thing to help the young priest feel more a part of the trio.

"I'm fine with it," Urun said, surprising Tere. "I have a few stories Osulin has told me of the Age of Magic."

"Ooh," Aila exclaimed. "I've always loved stories from the Age of Magic. You can go after Tere tells his."

"We'll see," Urun said.

Tere shook his head and chuckled at the girl's enthusiasm as he started walking again. He remembered how much he had loved the old tales and mythology when he was younger. Was he ever as young as this woman? He had trouble remembering such a time. He didn't *remember* being as innocent as she seemed. But yes, telling stories might help make the endless trek seem less boring.

"Fine, fine," Tere said. "I'll go first. Let me think for a few minutes and I'll see if I can come up with something suitable."

Aila clapped.

The fool girl probably thought he'd tell one of the many stories about Erent Caahs. Between her and Raki, he had been pestered almost to distraction about the man who had also made his way through life using his bow and his uncanny ability to hit anything he aimed at.

Well, she would be disappointed. He was good and tired of all the puffed-up stories of the so-called hero. They seemed to get grander every time someone told them. He was only a man, for Surus's sake. He disappeared, so why not just leave him alone?

No, he wouldn't be telling a tale of the hunter of men.

An idea came into his head. Younger people always wanted to hear about heroes. So be it. He had just the story, one of his favorites when he was a child. His old trainer had told him the story—many times, on request—but it wasn't something that was widely known. Every time he had mentioned it or told the story, his listeners had never heard of it before.

Yes. He would set the tone for their new game of telling tales.

❧ 25 ❧

"I've thought about it and I have decided on a story," Tere said as the three walked on.

"This story," he started, still examining the terrain ahead for enemies, "is from the time of the Great War. The entire world of Dizhelim seemed to be involved, all the great nations and empires vying for land when their territories were already vast. Even though it started as a contest between those exploiting the world and those claiming they wanted to save it, it changed into what all wars are eventually about: getting land and riches.

"At that time, there did not exist the many smaller nations and kingdoms of today. Three great juggernauts ruled by the sword and axe—and magic, of course—and a handful of smaller nations only hoped to be left alone. I won't speak of the specifics of the war or of who may have started it or ended it. Instead, I will focus on one seemingly insignificant piece of the larger world. A parcel of land that would forever change rulers' opinions and understanding of what was possible for a small group of dedicated people with unconventional resources.

"At the time, Dizhelim was essentially separated into three different governments, as I said before.

"Salamus was far to the west, its territory stretching from the mountains called the Wall of Salamus—today called the Shadowed Pinnacles—to the Aesculun Ocean. The Souveni Empire held much of the eastern half of the main continent of Promistala. Gentason sat between them in the crescent surrounding the Kanton Sea. Though their land masses were wildly different, each of these three powers had nearly the same number of people, which many believe prolonged the war as long as it did.

"Fifty-eight years into the War, Gentason was in trouble, as one would expect for the kingdom crushed between the other two. Each day, reports of more cities falling either to Souvenia or Salamus reached the ears of those not too focused on surviving to hear the news. As land was gobbled up a piece at a time, it was clear that soon, Gentason would be no more.

"When the capitol city of Gentason was finally crushed and the Souveni armies marched northwest to meet the Salaman armies coming southeast, nothing would stand in their way.

"Clear, that is, for all but a relatively small group of harried citizens of Gentason holed up in a place called Sintrovis.

"They totaled fewer than three hundred fifty people, comprised of scattered groups of soldiers fleeing the armies that had decimated their forces as well as the population of a few tiny villages in the area.

"In the midst of all the people, there was one man with any kind of military rank. His name was Thomasinus, the son of Daven, and he was a sergeant. As he and the group with him ran north, trying to find a place to elude the Souveni armies following him, he ran into the soldiers coming south, fleeing the Salaman armies that had devastated the areas they were escaping from.

"'Who is in charge of your forces?' he asked the ragtag group that looked to have been dragged down a hill of sharp shale.

"'No one,' one of the men said. 'All the officers were killed, as were all the sergeants or anyone with any authority. We're all that's left.'

"Thomasinus shook his head as he took an accounting of the group. There were less than a hundred of them, perhaps a third of them women. At that time, women shared in military service with the men, and the women soldiers of Gentason were every bit as dangerous in a battle as the men. Of course, when faced with overwhelming numbers of Salaman or Souveni troops, none of that mattered.

"Because of his rank, the others looked to Thomasinus as their leader.

"'Is there any way we can survive?' one of the men from his own group asked. 'There are armies in front of us and armies behind. Soon, they'll meet in battle and we'll be crushed between them.'

"Thomasinus was at a loss. He had hoped to be able to get far enough ahead of the armies to circle around, taking to the mountains and then making their way south. There wasn't time for that now. The mountains were home to the wild Ghodlek barbarians, as well as many wild beasts and monsters. The only trails he knew were fifty miles north.

"The armies of Salamus were twenty miles away.

"'There is one place,' another man said. Thomasinus recognized him from his own group. He was not a large man. In fact, he was shorter than average and could even be called scrawny.

"'What place?' Thomasinus asked.

"'It's toward the Sea of Kanton, maybe twenty-five or thirty miles east of here. It's called Sintrovis.'

"'Sintrovis,' one of the women from the other group of soldiers said. 'Isn't that the place with all the ghost stories?'

"The man continued. 'Yes, there are tales of that place. It's a place of power, of mystery. But it is our only hope of evading the armies.'

"Thomasinus scratched his chin, rough with three days' growth. 'And you know how to get there?'

"'I do. I grew up not fifteen miles from here.'

"'What is your name?' Thomasinus asked.

"'I am Kebahn Fatir,' the man said. 'I am...was...a scribe and scholar for Captain Adahn.'

"Thomasinus inspected the faces of those around him. Looking deeper than the panicked eyes and nervous looks, he saw hope, if only a little. He made his decision.

"He addressed the crowd in front of him. 'I am Thomasinus, son of Daven. Kebahn here says he knows the way to a place where we may be able to elude the armies closing in on us. I will go with him, for I fear there is no other chance to survive. If you would like to come as well, you are welcome, but we must move swiftly. I don't know if it's possible to slip away, but to stay here would be certain death as the armies of Salamus and Souvenia clash. Will you join me?'

"The people before him had been through hardship already, first in battle then in fleeing the armies that overwhelmed their fellow soldiers. They all agreed and filed into line behind Thomasinus and Kebahn.

"On the way to Sintrovis, they passed through two villages and a town. At each, they warned the people there of the coming armies and the numbers of those seeking safety grew. At the end of the second day of travel, they traveled through a mountain pass an old tracker from one of the villages knew, just as the sun was touching the horizon. Thomasinus and those with him stood looking down into the strangest location they had ever seen.

"Sintrovis could have been described as a massive crater. It was a bit over twenty miles across and surrounded by high natural walls. The granite cliffs were unforgiving.

"Within the bowl of the crater was a vast forest, but also areas devoid of trees. Through the vegetation, Thomasinus spotted glitters of blue, several streams or rivers.

"'There is water there,' the leader said. 'And with all that forest, there must be game to hunt. We should have food to eat and water to drink, then.'

"'Yes,' Kebahn said. 'Maybe the armies won't bother to find a pass and to explore this area. Maybe they'll leave us alone.'

"'We can only hope.'

"The exhausted travelers found a suitable place to camp and scouted almost a week before they found a way into the valley. It took them four more days to find a location that they could use for the long term, a sheltered clearing within the forest, near a river and with several avenues of escape. Escape to other parts of the bowl, of course. There seemed to be only one entry or exit into the bowl from the outside.

"Over the next several weeks, the refugees built their community and explored the area surrounding their encampment. Though there were cases of experienced scouts losing their direction and other minor strange occurrences, nothing happened to indicate that the area was the mysterious location of the superstitious tales.

"All the while, Thomasinus commanded the soldiers, making sure they trained and, more importantly, setting in place a guard rotation to monitor the only entrance to the place they had found. Some of the villagers, and even a few of the soldiers, grumbled that no one would ever find them so there was no need to set a guard. Thomasinus insisted.

"Eventually, he was proven to be right. A runner from the guard reported that they had detected small groups of soldiers wearing insignia of the Souveni Empire scouting near the entrance to Sintrovis.

"The first group to actually find the narrow pass were killed to a person by Thomasinus's troops, shooting them with arrows from the boughs of trees. The next group to come was larger, but they, too, were rebuffed. Soon, a full company, nearly two hundred soldiers, made their way toward the entry of the refugees' new home.

"The pass was a winding, narrow thing, so with a good supply of arrows and fighters hidden along the way, it seemed as if Thomasinus and his group could hold off an army. And they would have to.

"Wave after wave of soldiers came at them, but they were always repelled. At times, the forces of Salamus also took a turn at trying to get in.

"'How is it possible that the forces from both of our enemies are taking turns trying to kill us?' Thomasinus asked Kebahn. He had started relying on the scholar in his decisions, calling him Kebahn the Wise. It was a half-joke at first, but more and more, it became the man's title.

"'It has to be that they are still fighting nearby,' Kebahn said. 'As the front lines move north or south, the land in which the pass lies comes under control of the other army.'

"'That is not good news. It means whichever army wins, they already know of us.'

"'Yes.'

"And so the refugees fought to keep the invaders from entering their sheltered valley home. They were remarkably successful for their tiny number. For weeks more, the fighting alternated between the armies of Salamus and those of the Souvenia. Thomasinus knew that as long as the two opposing armies fought each other, they would not commit many troops to trying to force their way into Sintrovis.

"Then there was a lull in the attacks. It lasted for several days, longer than the pass had been quiet since it had first been discovered. Thomasinus did not welcome the news, though many of the people with him rejoiced.

"'Many of the villagers, and some of the soldiers are celebrating, Thom,' Kebahn said. 'They think the armies gave up because they haven't been able to get through the pass.'

"'Let them have their celebrations,' Thomasinus responded. 'We will not relax the guard or the preparations for battle. The worst is yet to come.'

"'I agree. Both armies are too proud to give up after being rebuffed for so long. They most likely think we are hiding something of great value in here. There is only one reason they would have stopped attacking.'

"'Yes,' Thomasinus said, putting his hands to the side of his head and squeezing as if he was trying to force out his pain, 'but which army was victorious?'

"'Does it really matter?' Kebahn asked.

"'No. I suppose it doesn't.'

"As expected, the next week brought reports from the scouts that a great number of soldiers was massing near the opening to the pass. They wore the colors of Salamus, burnt orange and grey.

"Thus began the siege of Sintrovis. Every day, soldiers tried to batter their way into the valley, and every day, the refugees repelled them.

"But it became harder to do so. The Salamans were throwing everything they had to break through, and Thomasinus's soldiers began to take casualties. Worse, scouts saw parties of the opposing soldiers circling Sintrovis, obviously looking for other ways into the great bowl.

"In one particularly vicious battle, it seemed that the Salamans would break through. The refugees fell back to the very mouth where the pass entered the valley and still the attackers pushed.

"The defenders had resorted to melee combat, all the archer stations overrun. Thomasinus was in the thick of it, his sword and shield appearing to be the only thing holding the invaders back. He expected to die, but hoped it would be enough to stop the attacks one more time.

"Then Kebahn stood atop a rock overlooking the battle, a book in his right hand. He began to read in a language Thomasinus didn't understand while waving his arms in complex gestures. The words built in volume and came faster and faster. When they finally reached a crescendo, Kebahn clenched his left hand and thrust it toward the battle.

"It was as if a huge fist of the gods themselves landed on the soldiers of Salamus. Bodies flew dozens of feet backward and troops were knocked down ten ranks behind the front line.

"Thomasinus felt the power infuse him, giving him strength and erasing all vestiges of fatigue. He looked up to his friend, wondering what Kebahn had done...and how he had done it. But the time for explanation was later. He took the opportunity to wade into the enemy's disarrayed ranks, dealing death wherever he went. Behind him, his own troops followed.

"The day ended in a rout, the Salaman troops fleeing before a power they were not prepared for. The refugees took back the pass, repopulating the archer stations and guard posts. As the sun went down, Thomasinus finally caught up with Kebahn.

"'What in Surus's name did you do?' he asked the scholar.

"'I'm afraid I didn't tell you everything about my role in Captain Adahn's company. I was a scholar and scribe, yes, but

I was also apprenticed to Rahul Thakur, the mage. I would eventually have learned to use magic in battle.'

"'From what I witnessed today, I would say you have accomplished that,' Thomasinus said.

"'Yes, but that's what is troubling. I had just started my training with Rahul. I couldn't work the simplest of spells yet. When he was killed, I took his tome of spells, but though I've read from it each day, and even tried to practice the magic, I had never been able to make a spell work. Until today.'

"Thomasinus looked askance at his friend. 'That was your first spell? What could you accomplish once you've practiced and learned more?'

"'I don't know. My master told me that if I tried a powerful spell, one beyond my abilities, it could burn my body to ash, the magical power building within me with no proper outlet. I fully expected to go up in a pillar of flame today. I had to try, though. If they had entered the wider area of the bowl, there was no way we could have defeated them. Somehow, I was able to make the magic work, though it was different than I intended.

"'Different or not, you saved us all, my friend. I hope you have more tricks hidden in that book. The next group to attack will definitely include mages.'

"Kebahn swallowed and nodded.

"As expected, the Salaman army did attack again, and two mages accompanied them. Kebahn was able to mitigate their magics and counterattack with his own. Day after day for more than a week, the troops of Salamus crashed against the walls of flesh and magic the refugees had set up in the pass, and each day, they had to retreat in defeat. The refugees began to grow confident that they would be able to hold the pass indefinitely.

"In the end, the Salamans besieged Sintrovis, permanently

stationing troops on the inhospitable mountain slopes. They would rarely attack, only maintain their presence, waiting for any perceived weakness from their enemies within the pass.

"The refugees, of course, were largely unaffected by the siege. There was plenty of water and game in the bowl, and they had created farms to provide further food. The people settled into their new home, many of them forgetting how close they were to an enemy that would see them all dead.

"Thomasinus did not forget, however, nor did Kebahn. They increased the fighting strength of their soldiers as the years went by, and Kebahn worked out magical ways to help with the defense. The years turned into decades, then centuries, and the armies of Salamus, and the grand kingdom itself, eventually faded away into history.

"Never was Sintrovis, renamed the Great Enclave, invaded or defeated. Time passed and it became a kingdom in its own right, starting with the first king, Thomasinus Davenson. For the rest of his life, his friend and advisor, Kebahn the Wise— now officially the royal mage—stood by to help his friend with the governance of what would eventually become one of the world's greatest military forces.

"And so, though everyone knows of Thomasinus Daven-son, now you know the story of one equally important in the creation of the Great Enclave, Kebahn Fatir."

Tere cleared his throat and took a sip of water from his skin. He eyed his friends to gauge their reactions to the story. Urun had a thoughtful look on his face, but Aila had an expression that could only be disappointment.

"What's wrong, Aila?" he asked. "Did the story not suit you?"

"What?" Her eyes flicked up to him, and then away. "Oh, no. It's fine. It's just that I already know that story. I was hoping for something new."

"Sorry," he said. "I'll try to do better next time." As he

said it, Tere wondered about the young woman again. How had she heard that story? He had traveled widely in his life, studied things most people had never seen. Not once since learning the story all those years ago had anyone admitted they knew it when he retold it. This young woman was full of surprises.

Tere shrugged. He'd eventually solve the mystery of his companion. No rush. He had his secrets, too. He felt the slight twinge of guilt at resolving to pry into her past that way, but it would be safer for all his allies—safer for him as well—if he knew what she was about and where she came from. He couldn't care less about what personal secrets she was hiding as long as they didn't affect himself and the others.

"Maybe you can show me how it's done," he said to her. "You can tell the next tale. I'm looking forward to—"

Mid-stride, the world went the darkest black and Tere felt himself falling to the grass.

❧ 26 ❧

"*Andorin recoat du acci rudis flagranti!*" Aeden hissed under his breath, making Khrazhti snap her head toward him.

"What is an army doing here?" he continued, in Ruthrin this time. "And what's it for? There aren't any kingdoms around here. We just passed into Lusnauqua. It's deserted, or at least it's supposed to be. How many are there...?"

Raki watched Khrazhti as she listened to Aeden. She focused on the groups camped in front of them. From what the Gypta boy could see, they were all human. The camp butted up against a set of cliffs to the west and spilled out nearly to the cliffs to the east.

"There are four hundred of them," Khrazhti said.

"What? Aeden said. "How do you know?"

"It is what I do. I led one of the largest armies in Aruzhelim. War is a big part of my calling as high priestess to S'ru. Assessing troops became second nature to me hundreds of years ago.

"For example, I can tell you that they came from the west and are heading northeast. Also, their sentries are as lazy as an urtumbrus. There are many holes in their guard patrols. It would be easy for a lone soldier or small group to enter the deeper parts of their camp and sabotage their efforts or kill some of their officers. Do you want me to do so?"

Raki shook his head and blinked. Just enter an army camp and kill officers? Was she serious? Of course she was. She still hadn't quite gotten the hang of humor.

"Uh, no," Aeden said. "It would be nice to get more information about why they're here, though. It's getting dark fast. We won't be able to see them from here for too much longer."

"I can do it," Raki said. He was right next to Aeden, and the Croagh's eyes widened when Raki spoke. His friends did that a lot. "I can get into the camp and see if I can find any information that would be helpful."

"No, Raki," Fahtin said. "You are *not* going to sneak into a camp of four hundred soldiers. It's too dangerous."

"But how else are we going to know if they're friends or enemies? If we had an army to help us, we would be able to beat the animaru for sure. They would probably even scare the assassins away, at least for a little while."

"Do you think you could do it without being seen or detected?" Aeden asked, earning a glare from Fahtin.

Raki nodded furiously. "I definitely could. Even those assassins couldn't find me when I wanted to stay hidden. If they couldn't see me, how could just a normal soldier spot me?"

"He does have a point there, Fahtin," Aeden said. Her glare had become a concerned look, her eyes pleading and her bottom lip between her teeth.

"It'll be fine, Fahtin," Raki said. "Please let me help out. I'm the best one for the job, and we do really need to know what's going on."

Fahtin continued to chew her bottom lip. "I know you

have skills, Raki. I've seen you disappear right in front of me before. Still, you're talking about strolling through a camp surrounded by soldiers, any one of whom could probably cut you in half, let alone bring the rest down on you, if he even catches a glimpse of you."

"They won't see me. I'll be careful. Just a quick trip to see what it's about and then I'll be right back."

"I don't know..."

Aeden looked like he was going to say something. He was probably going to try to talk Fahtin into it. Raki appreciated it but he didn't always want someone to stick up for him.

"Fahtin," Raki said. "Our lives are full of danger now. We have to think about everything and weigh our actions against what they could achieve and what could go wrong. The entire world is depending on us. Sometimes we have to take a risk. This one is pretty small compared to the life of everyone in the world, don't you think? It's time for all of us to act like heroes. Please let me do my part. You can't keep me from danger forever."

Fahtin blinked and flinched as if she had been struck. Her hazel eyes went liquid and Raki thought he had hurt her feelings. He raised a hand to say he was sorry and that she was right, but she spoke first.

"Oh, Raki. When did you get so wise? When did you grow up? You're right, of course. We are in danger all the time now. It's just so hard to see the little boy from the caravan becoming a man. It's hard to think of you putting yourself into danger. But you're right. You are the right person for this task. Just be careful. Don't let anyone see you. Go only as far as you need to and then come back, okay?"

Raki smiled but felt pressure building around his eyes. He would not cry. He would not. "I promise. I'll find out what's going on and then come right back so we can decide what to do."

Fahtin nodded and sniffled. She reached out and brought the younger Gypta into a hug and squeezed him as if she wouldn't ever let go. Raki hugged her back, a comfortable, warm feeling spreading over him.

When Fahtin released him, Raki turned to Aeden, who also surprised him with a hug.

"Be careful," the Croagh said. "I have faith in your abilities, but I want to remind you to focus. Don't let your concentration slip for any reason. Go in, find any information you can, and then come back out quickly. We'll be waiting here."

"Yessir," Raki said. He looked to Khrazhti, who was observing all the hugging and negotiation with an interested look on her alien face. She smiled at him—she had a little work to do before it looked natural, but it made him feel good that she was trying—and he smiled back and waved at her as he turned toward the army.

With a flexing of his will, he melted into the rapidly lengthening shadows and headed toward the encampment, wondering if he had made a mistake.

The young Gypta looked back toward his friends, but they were barely visible in the failing light. Raki swallowed and continued on. He had a mission to accomplish and other thoughts would only make him vulnerable.

He had seen the patrols Khrazhti mentioned, but he hadn't thought of their timing or their routes until the animaru said something about it. Now he could spot the holes in their defenses. He waited for a moment, crouched in the grass, as a group of three men walked by.

They didn't look like any soldiers Raki had ever heard of. Their clothing didn't really look like uniforms so much as the raiment of brigands or street toughs. Only one had armor, and that was simple soft leather pieces, not even boiled. The other two had dark trousers and tunics.

The men's weapons looked serviceable, though not of the best quality. One of the men drew his sword and showed it to the others, explaining something about how he had obtained it. It had a prominent notch halfway down the blade, along with scratches in other places along its length. It would still kill, but it didn't seem to be the weapon of a professional soldier. From what Raki had heard, they took much better care of their weapons.

The patrol passed and Raki started moving again, angling toward the main body of the camp. Now that he was looking more carefully, he noticed that there were different clumps of soldiers scattered about the main, larger grouping of people and fires. If there was a place to get information, it would be with the bigger group.

He avoided two other wandering clusters of guards. They had a rough pattern for their patrol, but it was obvious even to Raki that they disdained their duty and didn't expect to find anyone sneaking about. Raki could see why they had that attitude. Who would try to sneak into an army camp?

Just me, he thought, and a sly smile found its way onto his face.

Raki still wasn't exactly sure how he blended into the surroundings the way he did. Tere had taught him to move more quietly and to leave fewer tracks, but judging by the expressions on his friends' faces, he actually disappeared in front of them when he willed it. How had he learned that? Had he always been able to do it, or did he somehow gain the power recently?

He had so many questions. Maybe when they finally made it to the Hero Academy, he could ask the masters about it. They knew everything there was to know about magic.

Raki stopped again and crouched, surveying the area. Magic? Was that what he did to become invisible? The thought thrilled him and, to be honest, scared him a little. He was just a poor Gypta boy. What business did he have dabbling in magic? His Nani always said his people had magic in their blood. Could it be true?

He shook his head. There was no use in letting his mind wander. He needed to focus.

Raki had made it to the edge of camp, a few dozen feet from one of the smaller groups sitting around a fire. He skirted the pool of light and angled toward the fringes of the bigger group. Those around the fire never noticed him. How could they when their dark vision was ruined by the fire and they were busy laughing, telling crude jokes, and drinking.

These weren't the soldiers of the stories Raki had heard. Proper military soldiers would be respectful and sober and... well, clean. These men definitely were not that.

It occurred to the young man as he made his way closer to the main group that he hadn't seen any women yet. In most of the kingdoms of the world, there were few women soldiers compared to the number of men, but he hadn't seen *any*. Maybe there would be some in the main group.

Raki kept his eyes open for any sign he could take back to the others of who was in charge. Some kind of crest or standard or something would be nice. But he didn't see anything that looked like a symbol. The men were all dressed differently, and none of them seemed to have any insignia. There were no banners, either. At least, not in the areas he had gone through.

He didn't know much about armies—except what he had heard in stories—but shouldn't they have a way to identify themselves? If it weren't for the number of people, Raki might have thought that this was a group of bandits.

He stayed in the shadows and moved carefully toward a large group of men sitting around a fire farther into the center of the camp. They still didn't have uniforms on, but their gear looked to be better quality and the tents near them looked in good repair in the splash of firelight. Maybe these were the officers.

"We just got here and now we need to march east again?" one of them said.

"That's our orders," said a large man with two swords strapped across his back. "Benzal wants us to head toward where they'll be staging the troops."

"That's what he told us about this forsaken wasteland," a third said. "We had a hard march to get here in time and now he changes his mind?"

"Quit your complaining," the big man said. "He pays us regular. What is it to you if we march all around the world? Better than having to deal with those dark monsters. Those things give me the creeps."

"We're really going to side with them?" another man said. "I hear they tear people up just for fun."

The first man laughed. "I've heard the same about some of us here. Listen, Benzal put us in charge, so don't let the men hear you squawking about this. We get paid and we don't have to fight those creatures. I hear they can't be killed. Better to be on the winning side, right?"

What?

Raki caught himself as his knees buckled, his legs suddenly going weak. Did he hear what he thought he'd heard? Were these men actually working *with* the animaru? Didn't they understand the creatures meant to destroy their entire world?

He couldn't believe it. That anyone could turn against their own people—

"Hey, boy," a voice boomed from behind Raki. "What are you doing there?"

❦ 27 ❦

Raki spun. A man who apparently had been walking toward the fire from one of the other, smaller, camps, had seen him. The Gypta mentally slapped himself. He must have lost his focus at exactly the wrong time and compromised his meld with the shadows.

The men at the fire turned to look toward the voice. Raki knew they probably couldn't see him with their light-ruined eyes, but the man who had spoken could. He needed to get out of there fast.

He rolled backward, deeper into the darkness, and willed himself to become part of it. He dodged to his left and sped off on silent feet, back toward where he had come from. The man who had spoken to him stood there, looking around him, confusion painted across his face. He scratched his head and then shrugged, heading toward the others at the fire.

As Raki slowed and carefully made his way past the smaller camps, the men began laughing and teasing the man for imagining he saw something that wasn't there.

His heart didn't slow down until he was already well beyond the edge of the camp and he was picking his way back through the sentries. That had been too close. He needed to practice maintaining his focus even when surprised.

And he had been surprised. He pushed the thought to the back of his mind for the time being, but soon he'd be back with the others and then he could think—and speak—about it some more. A sick feeling welled up in his belly. He and his friends and probably the whole of humanity were in trouble. Big trouble.

Raki appeared suddenly in the midst of his friends, dropping his focus and allowing himself to separate from the shadows surrounding them. Fahtin gasped, Aeden calmly blinked, but Khrazhti had been looking right at him when he appeared. Could she see him when he was trying to go unseen?

Fahtin was the first to speak. "Oh, thank Danta. I was beginning to worry. You were gone for hours."

"Are you well, Raki?" Aeden asked.

"Yeah." They didn't need to know about his close call. There were more important things to discuss. "I overheard some men that I think were the officers."

"You *think* they were officers?" Aeden asked.

"Yes. They didn't have any rank insignia or anything to identify them. No one did. They're not even wearing uniforms. They're dressed in normal clothes, only some of them in armor. They look like bandits. I looked for any kind of crest or banner or anything to identify who they were, but there was nothing.

"That's not the worst part, though. They're on the animaru's side. I heard them talking about how Benzal wants them to work with the dark monsters and how they're supposed to be meeting up with other armies, both human and animaru."

"What?" Fahtin said. "They're joining the other side and fighting against all the other people in the world? Why would they do that? The animaru are trying to destroy the world and kill everyone in it."

"They think they will be left alive," Khrazhti said. "Whoever is leading the animaru now no doubt gave Benzal and others promises that they would be left alone."

"But...but how can they do it? They're turning their backs —no, actually taking up arms against—their fellow humans. How will they live with themselves afterward, when they know they helped to destroy their families and everyone they know?"

"They will not," Khrazhti said. "When the world is transformed and S'ru arrives, all the remaining humans will be killed. They will not be left to possibly rebel in the future. The existence of creatures of light will be an annoyance."

Raki felt even sicker than he had earlier. "You mean, they're going to fight against the humans and then they'll be slaughtered if the animaru win?"

"Yes."

"I don't know if I can even feel bad for them," Fahtin said. "The whole thing is terrible."

Khrazhti shook her head. "It is war. There will be no secret alliances, no special favors given. The animaru have been fighting amongst ourselves for thousands of years. Either we will be defeated, or the humans will be completely destroyed. There are no other possible resolutions to this conflict."

Fahtin threw a look of disgust at Khrazhti and then immediately adopted one of sorrow. "I'm sorry, Khrazhti. I shouldn't blame you for what your species is doing. We'll beat them and then you'll be here with us, the finest example of what an animaru could be if given the chance."

The blue woman flashed a strained smile at Fahtin.

Raki sighed. What a mess.

Aeden had been silent during the exchange, a pensive look on his face.

"Okay, so they're enemies. Unfortunately, there are too many for us to attack, though I'd like to. The only thing I can think to do is to go around them and continue with our mission. We have to get to Benzal before he opens the portal to Aruzhelim.

"Raki, can we go wide around the army? It looked like they were pretty close to those cliffs when I saw the camp earlier."

"There's no room to go around them, at least not on the western side. I didn't see the eastern side, but I did see flashes of firelight reflecting on the cliffs over there, too. I think they've spread out to fill the entire passage."

"*Daeann daedos ist.* The terrain looks rough on either side. It'll take us at least an extra day to skirt the cliffs and rocks to get back to where we need to be going." He looked to Khrazhti, who nodded.

"It is true," she said. "Our path leads directly through the army. Benzal is that way." She pointed directly at the center of the camp.

"Is he there, with the army?" Fahtin asked excitedly.

Khrazhti shook her head. She had been picking up mannerisms from her traveling companions. Raki didn't think the other animaru usually used those expressions. "No. He is still days away, but the direction we need to go is through there."

"I might be able to get everyone through," Raki said. "I could scout and lead you, maybe."

"We may have to do that," Aeden said. "We may not have time for anything else. I've been working on another of my spells, trying to get the movements right to use the enhanced version. It's not quite reliable yet, even after Khrazhti helped me to figure out the enhanced version when we were in Satta

Sarak. The original spell allows me to camouflage myself so I can't be detected. The enhanced version would allow me to hide more than one person. Using it, though, I am useless for anything else. It takes all my concentration."

"Is that what you were working on while Raki was gone?" Fahtin asked. "Why did you pick that particular spell to practice?"

Aeden chuckled. "It's one of the few I've been able to cast in its enhanced form, but I haven't nailed it down so I can use it reliably yet. It tires me out pretty quickly."

"This magic would be helpful," Khrazhti said. "I can hide myself with my magic, briefly and imperfectly, but I cannot use it on others."

"So it's just Fahtin and me," Aeden said. "Give me a couple of hours to work on it and maybe I can get it to work reliably enough to give it a try. If I can't figure it out, we may have to try to sneak around them the old-fashioned way. If we can get to the other side before they detect us, we could probably escape and evade them. They won't chase us for more than a few miles, I think."

Somehow, that didn't make Raki feel any better.

The two Gypta and the animaru settled in while Aeden experimented with his footing, tried and discarded several sets of gestures, sang bits of the Bhagant, and cursed in several languages.

Raki guessed that the Croagh warrior was testing how each new thing felt. Did he feel some kind of magical resonance when he chanced upon the correct movements? How did one even narrow it down? There were literally an endless number of combinations of movements that could be made.

As Aeden was working, eyes closed in concentration, Raki checked his other two companions. Fahtin alternated between watching Aeden, looking at Raki and Khrazhti, and looking around the darkened landscape.

The moon was sitting half full in the sky and with very little vegetation around them, yet Raki could see almost as if it were daylight. He wondered at that. He didn't recall having excellent night vision before, but it had improved over the last few months. It could have been his training with Tere, learning to strain his eyes for details, but he didn't think so.

Khrazhti sat unmoving near the other two, but her wide blue eyes never left Aeden. Her attention was locked on him so intently, Raki thought enemies might be able to attack them and she would never know.

As if to put a lie to the thought, she turned her head toward Raki and gave one of her smiles. Okay, so maybe she *was* paying attention to the surroundings.

The animaru turned back to Aeden and resumed her statue-like immobility.

After more than two hours, Aeden seemed to have narrowed in on the movements. At least, he kept them nearly the same each time he went through the cycle, making only very minor changes in the way his hands were tilted or his feet were spaced or the posture of the rest of his body.

He chanted low, under his breath, as he did it. No, not chanted. He was singing softly. Raki stepped closer to hear better. Khrazhti leaned forward, probably for the same reason.

> **Airuh** *dah arjisteta sai, Animaru*
> *Prein Malatirsay dah **dheta** dara sai*
> *Mortiyu ko sabment per sarak*
> *Intaa nata deh dah **Shikuta** aun dregutota dara sai*

Raki picked out what Aeden had been calling the words of power. He gave them a bit more emphasis than the other words, and the movements seemed to revolve around them.

Aeden, eyes closed, had his right foot in front of his left. Even though the stance would not be stable—Raki had been training with the Croagh for long enough to know what solid footing looked like—Aeden seemed to be in perfect balance. His arms slowly moved out to the sides, the left going clockwise and the right counter-clockwise, sweeping out and describing circles as large as his arms were long. They came together in the middle, hands not quite touching, and then pushed downward as if Aeden was trying to push himself up on a shelf in front of him.

The air shimmered and Aeden seemed to phase out of existence for a moment, allowing Raki to see the rocks behind him in the dim moonlight.

Fahtin gasped.

Aeden relaxed and breathed out, his body sagging into a casual stance. He opened his eyes and the whites got slightly larger when they locked on his three companions, but then his pupils grew as he focused on them in the dim light of the moon.

"Did it work?" he asked.

Raki opened his mouth, but Fahtin spoke first.

"It was amazing. You disappeared completely for nearly a minute. I thought something was wrong and some power had taken you away."

"I think I have mostly figured out the movements and the way the spell works. Let me try something else. Fahtin, could you please come near me?"

Fahtin did as he asked, watching him through the side of her eyes.

"Now," he said, "stay here. Raki, Khrazhti, please tell me what you see."

Aeden repeated the motions he had made earlier, singing the song under his breath as before. When he pronounced the last word, he faded from view.

Fahtin disappeared also.

"You both vanished," Raki said.

"Fahtin," Aeden's voice said from where he had been. "Can you see me?"

"Yes," her voice said from thin air.

"Good. Move with me."

Raki sensed movement, but couldn't quite place it.

"Can you see us?" Aeden's voice sounded from behind Raki.

"No," Khrazhti answered. "You are still not visible to us."

Aeden and Fahtin suddenly appeared ten feet on the other side of Raki from where they had started.

"I think that will work," Aden said and sat down on the ground. "It takes a lot of energy. Hopefully it will be less taxing after I get more used to it. For tonight, though, I think it will be all I can do just to maintain the bubble around us."

"You do not have to keep singing or moving around in the way you did in order to invoke the magic?" Khrazhti asked.

"No. Once I have activated the spell, it only takes my will to keep it active. I can do other simple things, like walking, but I need to focus on the spell, so complex movements and combat are out. Let me rest for a few minutes and we can try to get through the pass. If we wait too much longer, we'll be risking daybreak."

"While you rest, I'll go out and scout," Raki said. "I want to make sure those patrols haven't wandered closer to us."

"Good idea," Aeden said as he closed his eyes and began to breathe deeply.

❧ 28 ❧

Aeden was more fatigued than a full day of training could make him. He wasn't sure the magic was worth it if it tired him out so completely. What would happen if someone did detect him? He wouldn't be able to fight effectively. He desperately hoped it would be as he told the others, that as his skill grew, the magic wouldn't be as taxing.

Raki was gone for less than half an hour. When Aeden heard the young Gypta talking to Fahtin and Khrazhti, he knew it was time to get moving. He took one more deep breath, let it out, and opened his eyes.

"Let's go," he said, checking that his swords moved freely in their scabbards.

Fahtin's eyes showed concern. Aeden appreciated it, but he simply couldn't rest anymore. They were running out of time.

"Stay close to me," he told her. "Raki, Khrazhti, are you ready to use your own skills?"

Both of them nodded.

"How will we keep track of each other?" Aeden asked.

"Fahtin will be able to see me, and me her, but you won't see us and we won't see you.

"It would be best if I included the two of you in the bubble of magic that would make us all invisible, but I don't have the strength to do it." He slammed his fist into his other hand. "I am so sick and tired of not knowing enough and not *being* enough to do what needs to be done."

Khrazhti moved her hand toward him, as if she was going to put it on his shoulder, but dropped it halfway across the distance separating them. Her face was inscrutable, with a complete lack of expression.

"You must realize that these things take time. It took me more than a hundred years to fully come into my power, and I had those who could teach me. You will not take so long, but it will not happen immediately. I will help you with whatever knowledge and power I possess." She paused and sighed. "But I cannot help you with this. My only suggestion is that we decide upon a meeting point on the other side of the forces before us and then get as close as is safe before hiding ourselves."

Aeden studied the animaru. She was so unlike anyone he had ever known. He had barely any of the revulsion he had first felt for her animaru heritage. It was plain that she was not like the others. In fact, as they traveled together, she seemed more human each day.

He smiled weakly at her. "Thank you, Khrazhti. I will gladly accept your help, once we get through this current predicament. I think your idea is a good one. Anyone else have anything? I can't think of a better plan."

Fahtin shook her head and Raki quietly said, "No."

"Good enough. Let's do like the lady said and try to get through as many of the patrols as possible before we need to all disappear."

Khrazhti's head snapped up and a light flared in her eyes.

Her lips turned upward briefly and then regained their expressionless quality.

"Raki, can you move ahead and lead us through the outer sentries? Bring us to what you think the best place might be to go around the army."

"You bet," the young Gypta said as he headed toward the camp again. "Give me a couple of minutes and I'll show you where to go."

Raki returned a few minutes later, ghosting out of the darkness. "I found where we can go. Follow me."

Aeden allowed Fahtin and Khrazhti to go ahead of him, taking up the rear in case someone circled around them. The risk was low, but he felt better being able to see his friends.

A patrol passed off to their right. The little party stopped and stayed close to the ground as the soldiers continued on their way, oblivious to the intruders' presence.

As they slinked along the border of the army, the stone walls loomed to their left, foreboding and immovable as anything Aeden had ever seen. If they were detected, those walls would effectively trap them, and the army could bring the full might of all the soldiers against them.

Up ahead, a fire lit up the side of the stone obstacle. Some soldiers had set their camp within ten feet of the cliff, in a little hollow area that seemed to have been cleared out from the scree and rockfall. Aeden pondered their stupidity. Didn't they know that rocks often fell as stone cooled in the evening chill? They were putting themselves at risk.

He realized his anger was at himself, though, and the fact that no rocks had fallen to crush the men. Instead, he and his friends would have to try to sneak by them. He cursed under his breath as Raki stopped them out of hearing range of the soldiers.

"I don't know what's on the other side of that fire," Raki whispered. "I can't see any other fires close to the cliffs, but there could be tents or sentries. Anyway, the tough part is going to be getting around the ones within the firelight."

"It's what we planned," Aeden said. "You and Khrazhti disappear in your own way and I'll handle hiding myself and Fahtin."

Raki gulped. Aeden hadn't realized it before, but the young Gypta was nervous. He had shown such professionalism in recent days, Aeden had forgotten that this was all new to the young man. It was new to them all, really.

The Croagh gripped Raki's shoulder. "It'll be fine. Each of us will make sure we aren't seen. We'll head around or through the small camp around the fire, then follow the cliff around the other side. A quarter mile after we pass the last soldier, we'll meet up at the base of the wall."

Raki nodded, as did Khrazhti. Fahtin stared at Aeden with eyes as wide as he'd ever seen them, the whites glowing in the dim moonlight.

"Fahtin, stay close to me. Try not to make a sound. My magic should make it so they can't see us, but they can still hear. With their conversation, it shouldn't be a problem, but be as silent as you can to make sure. Are you okay?"

She finally nodded, wrapping her arms around herself.

He felt bad to put her through the experience. It must be even scarier for her because she had to rely on him completely, with barely anything she could control.

Aeden looked into her eyes. "Grip the hilts of two of your knives—not too hard. I think it will make you feel a little better. You won't need them, but they can be a source of comfort. Trust in me, and in your weapons. We'll get through this, no problem."

She did as he asked. He smiled at her and she returned it weakly, but Aeden felt her panic. He hoped she didn't freeze up.

"It's too bad rocks haven't fallen on them because of their

bad choice of a campsite," Raki said. He noticed Aeden's look of surprise and continued. "You explained it that time when we made camp by the cliffs after we'd fallen in the river, remember? When the warm rocks that have been heated by the sun cool at night, sometimes stones will break off and fall. It would make things easier if they were bounced around a little by falling rocks."

"Yes," Aeden said, proud of the young man and how well he learned. "But we might as well wish for them to simply all fall asleep, which doesn't seem likely since it's nearing daybreak. Is everyone ready? I'm going to start my spell. Once it's in effect, we should move as fast as we can safely. I don't know how long I will be able to hold the spell active."

Fahtin threw a worried look at Aeden, but he ignored it as he started the motions and the incantation for the magic. In less than a minute, he was struggling with the taxing spell. Raki and Khrazhti seemed to have lost track of them, their eyes not focusing on either himself or Fahtin.

"Good?" he asked quietly.

"I can't see either one of you," the young man said. "I guess this is it. I'll meet you on the other side."

He melted into the shadows and Aeden wondered again how he did it. He thought he could sense a small tingle of magic, but it was so faint, it could have been in Aeden's mind. He shook his head. Raki couldn't use magic. He was just very skilled at stealth. Even Tere had said the boy was a natural.

Khrazhti scanned the area where Aeden was one more time. Her eyes stopped when they met his. At least, that's how it seemed. He'd probably imagined it. She whispered something in her native tongue, something Aeden couldn't quite understand, but whether because he didn't know the words or because it was too faint, he didn't know. The animaru faded from existence in front of him. That time, he definitely felt a buzz of magic.

"Are you ready for this, Fahtin?"

She swallowed once and nodded, gripping the hilts of two of the daggers at her waist.

"Okay," he said. "No more talking until we get beyond the soldiers. Stay close to me and try to make as little sound as possible. I'll pick a path and you can follow in my footsteps. We'll be fine. In just a little while, we'll be on the other side and heading away from the army."

She nodded again and turned her head toward the fire by the cliff.

Aeden moved slowly forward, soundlessly picking a way across a long rock that didn't have as much gravel as the surrounding ground.

He wished he could see the others. He also wished he could handle the spell's magic without it taxing him so. With every step, he became more fatigued. At the current rate, he would barely make it beyond the fire before he was too exhausted to walk, let alone maintain the spell.

They passed more closely to the fire than he would have liked, but there were other fires with groups of men sitting around them on his other side and he would choose being closer to the one than skirting the edges of several others. Did these men ever sleep? It was nearing dawn and they were still up and talking, drinking, and telling stories.

At least they were loud. With how much noise Fahtin was making as she moved, he cringed each time she took a step.

Just a little farther...

"Oi," a voice said off to Aeden's right, near where Fahtin was. "Find your own spot. This one's taken."

Fahtin froze, her eyes wide. Aeden could tell from where he was that she was holding her breath.

A man was standing next to a clump of bushes, one of his hands in front of him. A soft splashing sound came from the ground. He wasn't facing toward Fahtin, so he hadn't seen her. He must have heard her.

Aeden waved for her to move toward him, but Fahtin shook her head, her wide eyes frantic. Aeden waved again, more insistently, but the young woman closed her eyes tight. She was beyond reason. He'd have to take care of the man before the soldier realized he couldn't see anyone where the sound had originated.

Aeden was going to have to kill him.

The thought of the unnecessary death pricked at Aeden, but he pushed the feeling aside. If the other man sounded an alarm, Aeden and his friends would die. He moved toward the man slowly, making no sound.

As Aeden reached Fahtin, about halfway to the man, he felt a pulse of magic ahead and to his left. A brief flash caught his eye, quickly followed by a rumble.

Aeden reached out and grabbed hold of Fahtin, her eyes going wide open and her mouth opening. The Croagh put his hand over her mouth and held her to him, waiting.

As expected, the soldiers at the fire next to the cliff wall scattered, running toward the main body of the camp. Closely following them, rocks of different sizes bounced and skidded down the wall, crashing through trees and bushes clinging to the terrain. Even the man who had spoken had taken off, hurriedly closing up his trousers as he went.

Aeden, holding Fahtin, focused on the spell that felt like it was wrestling him for control. When someone got close, he would twist or step to the side, pulling Fahtin with him so no one would run into them. In seconds, the scree had settled and the pair were standing alone near where the fire had been. A cloud of dust filled the air where the dirt and rocks had put the blaze out.

"Are you okay?" he whispered into Fahtin's ear.

She nodded.

"Don't speak or make any noise."

She nodded again.

He slowly removed his hand from her mouth, grabbed her hand with it, and pulled her toward where they had been heading. As he did, voices rose from the direction of the closest fire.

"We told you not to camp so close to the cliff, you morons! 'It's no problem,' you says. 'I ain't never seen a rock-slide fall on anyone,' you says. Ha! Maybe next time you'll listen."

There was some low muttering, but it was drowned out by the laughter at the soldiers' misfortune. Aeden didn't stick around to listen. He pulled Fahtin along and was soon out of the dust cloud and into the darkness on the other side of where the fire had been.

Aeden shuffled away from the soldiers' previous camp, barely able to lift his feet to walk. He maintained his spell, though it felt like it was draining the very life from him. Fahtin was at his side, but nothing else around registered in his mind.

He kept tight hold of one thought: he must get past the soldiers to where he was to meet the others. Agonizing foot-step after footstep, he continued onward.

When they had gone at least a quarter mile from the camp—though it felt like it was fifteen miles to Aeden—he stopped. He looked around, searching for any sign that there might be more soldiers. They should have had sentries on this side of the army, too, right?

He tottered as he scanned the area around him. Fahtin had stopped next to him, looking at him worriedly. He didn't detect any enemies, so he allowed himself to sit on the ground. The motion was more like a controlled fall than anything else.

He was so tired.

Motion from his left jolted his senses and he drew one of his swords in the blink of an eye. He was barely able to hold it steady in front of him, but he would be damned if he would let anything happen to Fahtin after all they'd been through.

The shadows coalesced into Raki. Aeden's sword dropped to the ground, too heavy for him to maintain his hold. Somewhere in his mind, he realized he must have ended the spell or Raki wouldn't have seen him.

"Are you two all right?" Raki asked, stepping up to Aeden.

"He's exhausted," Fahtin answered. "He can't even stand up right now."

Raki got out his water skin. "We'll let him rest. Here, Aeden, have some water."

Aeden blinked at his friend. "Khrazhti?"

Another shift in the shadows and the blue woman appeared in front of him. "Here."

"We made it," Aeden said, taking the proffered skin and gulping down a mouthful of water.

"Yes," Raki said. He turned to Khrazhti. "Was that you, the thing that made the rocks fall? I thought I saw something just before everything went crazy."

"It was me," the animaru said. "Aeden and Fahtin had been detected by that man. I needed to create a distraction."

"That was good thinking," Fahtin said. "Thank you."

"You are welcome."

"I'm going to look around and see if there are any sentries around here," Raki said. "Aeden, rest up. We should probably move out a little farther soon, but I think we're okay here for right now."

Raki disappeared and the two women sat down near Aeden. He leaned back and let himself fall to the dirt. It wasn't comfortable, but he felt like he could sleep on the hard soil for ten hours.

"I just need a few minutes," he said, already thinking more clearly. "The magic took a lot out of me."

"You're fine," Fahtin said. "We'll keep watch. Take a nap and we'll let you know when we need to move."

"Nap," Aeden said. "Yes. That sounds good. Thank you."

Aeden closed his eyes to stop the world from spinning. As he drifted off into slumber, he heard Fahtin.

"We have how long? Are we going to make it in time to stop him from opening the portal?"

Aeden clawed toward lucidity, desperately trying to open his eyes to join the conversation, but the weight pulling his eyelids was too great and he lost all sense of where he was.

🎕 29 🎕

Tere Chizzit was confused.

His face was resting against something that felt like grass. How was that possible? He had just been telling a story, hadn't he? What was going on?

Urun's voice broke through the fog over Tere's mind. "Tere. Tere, are you okay?"

The archer felt the tingle of magic touching him as he tried to sit up. His stomach roiled and he turned his head just in time to keep from vomiting all over the young nature priest.

"Blech," he spat. "Don't use magic on me right now. It'll make me throw up again." The sensation stopped abruptly.

Tere wiped his mouth and moved his head slowly to see where he was. It looked like the same place he had been walking as he finished his story.

"What happened?" he asked as he fumbled to get his water skin to wash out the sour acid taste in his mouth.

"You were in mid-sentence and just fell down," a feminine voice said. Aila. Right, Aila Ven. He was thinking a little more clearly now.

"What hit me?" he asked.

"Nothing that we saw," she responded. "It's like you lost your ability to control yourself."

Tere put his head in his hands and squeezed his temples. His skull felt like it was full of rocks. And molten lava.

"Did you..." Urun said, putting his face in front of Tere's, looking into his eyes with a worried expression on his face. "Did you feel anything before you blacked out? Can you remember anything?"

Tere closed his eyes to shut out the world and thought. "No. I was walking and talking, and then I was here on the ground."

"I thought I felt something right as you fell," Urun said. "Some kind of magical pulse. I am not as sensitive to the overall magical field as you are. I think something changed dramatically. Like what we talked about before, but stronger and all at once."

Tere opened his eyes again. Both his friends stared at him. "Ugh. Don't gawk at me. It's bad enough the world seems to be crooked. I don't need you looking at me like I'm a pixie in a cage. Give me some room."

The two backed off a couple of steps, still watching him carefully, as he climbed to his feet. The landscape was settling down, hardly moving at all now.

"Do you notice anything about the magic around us right now?" Urun pressed.

"No, there's nothing..." Tere stopped. He looked out over the terrain, but it did seem different than before. He could still see in the peculiar way he always did, but the tracks in the magical field were gone. There was no trace of where Urun or Aila had been even a moment ago.

"What is it?" Aila asked.

"The tracks," Tere said. "There are no tracks in the

magical field. I can still see, to an extent, but I can't pick out where you or anything else has disrupted the field."

"What, exactly, are you saying, Tere?" Urun asked. The two were hovering around him like he was a dangerous animal or something.

"Just what I said," he snapped. "I can't track movements in the magical field."

"So you can't track. And...?" Urun had an edge to his voice Tere had never heard.

"And I can't predict where something will move. One of the reasons I never miss what I'm aiming at is that I can sense which way it will move by the precursor disturbances in the field."

"Precursor disturbances?" Aila repeated as a question.

"Yes, damn you all to the abyss. I'm not just talking about tracking things we're looking for. I'm talking about my ability to hit things in combat, to avoid attacks that would otherwise get me, either ranged or close quarters. Do you not understand? My ability to fight has just been taken away."

Tere's two companions shared a look that he was sure they hadn't meant for him to see. It was worried, but there was also a bit of pity and, even worse, a healthy dose of fear. They finally understood. He would be like a baby if they were attacked by something powerful like those ant creatures again.

"Is it permanent?" Aila asked softly.

"How in the hells should I know," Tere spat. "It's a first for me."

Urun stepped closer, inspecting Tere. "Well, if I can't use magic to read what's wrong with you, we'll have to try to detect the problem another way. Other than that, I think we'll have to wait it out. Judging from your reaction to my magic when I was trying to scan you, trying to heal you with magic wouldn't be a good idea."

"No," Tere said. "It wouldn't."

The hunter took a deep breath and blew it out forcefully. "Listen, I'm sorry to snap at you. This has me worked up a little. I know it's not your fault. Just chalk it all up to me being a crotchety old man."

"That's usually what I do," Aila said, smiling widely at him. When he didn't smile back, hers faded. "Too soon?"

Tere chuckled a little. "Definitely too soon. Let's get moving. We still need to get to the Academy. If this thing doesn't get better by then, maybe they can help me."

They started out again, traveling north. They didn't need great tracking skills to do so. They could see the Molars in the distance, beckoning them onward.

"At least we don't have to fight," Aila said. "It would be really bad if—"

Tere's head snapped up as she cut her sentence off in the middle. Why had she done that? He followed her gaze ahead and to the right, understanding immediately. A dark blur was moving ahead of them, coming closer.

"What is that?" Aila asked.

"I think you know," Tere answered, unlimbering his bow. "'Ask for trouble and it will beat a path to your door,' so the saying goes."

"*Fortassi deisant testin tuu*," Urun spat.

"I didn't know you spoke Alaqotim." Tere selected an arrow from his quiver and nocked it.

"I don't. Despite my best efforts, I've learned some of Aeden's curses. I have no idea what they mean, but it does feel good to say it."

"You probably don't want to know. Let's move to that patch of trees there. It will restrict their movement and make it tougher to surround us."

"They who?" Aila readied her own weapons.

"The animaru," Tere said. "It's the only thing that shape

can be. Nothing else I know is so dark and moves like that. Let's hope it's a small group, or we've got some big trouble."

It was not far to the shelter they sought, but Tere knew it wouldn't throw off the creatures after them. He was sure they had seen the three humans out in the open. No, it would come to a fight.

"Should we climb up into a tree?" Aila eyed a large maple.

Tere thought about it for a brief moment. "It won't do any good. Those things can jump and climb better than we can. I might be able to get off an arrow or two more, but then they'd knock me down. With your weapons, it's better to stay on the ground."

Aila nodded and wiped her hands on her pants before drawing her vinci.

Urun didn't say anything. He was a few feet from the others, moving his arms and chanting something that had the sound of a prayer. Tere was disappointed that he didn't see a glow or any other manifestation of power around the nature priest. He always had before. What was he going to do when the monsters came?

The archer gauged the distance between him and the fast-approaching animaru. The creatures' bellows and screeches preceded them.

They sounded excited, almost hungry. If he didn't know better, he would think they were ready to eat all three of the humans.

The monsters moved like wolves, on all fours, though they were humanoid in shape like most of the others they'd seen. They were the same ugly grunt animaru they were used to. Khrazhti had called them seren. Some had hair while others didn't, but one thing they had in common was their sharp claws and their uncanny speed.

A hundred yards out, Tere fired his first arrow at the lead animaru. It easily slipped to the side without missing a step.

The ten other creatures following it howled in anticipation of the fight.

Beads of perspiration formed on Tere's forehead as he launched another arrow at the group charging them. Again, two of the monsters slithered around the missile without breaking stride.

The glowing bubble Tere had seen before blossomed around Urun. That must be visible to normal sight.

"I'm sorry," the nature priest said, "but I can't expand my shield to you two. That's not the way the spell works. I'll do what I can, though."

Tere nodded his understanding and Aila set her feet in a side-facing stance, preparing for the onslaught of the creatures.

With the animaru twenty yards out, Tere closed his eyes and breathed deeply to calm his racing heart. Panic would do him no good here. He needed to think clearly. So his ability to predict where his targets would be was gone. That didn't make him helpless, right?

Huffing out a breath, he watched one of the animaru in particular, one a bit larger than most of the others and not quite as fluid in its motion. Tere tracked the creature as it barreled toward him, judged the distance and its available space for movement, and fired another arrow, not at where the creature was but where Tere guessed it would be.

The shaft, glowing faintly from the spell Urun had cast on all their weapons, struck true, glancing off the bridge of the creature's flat nose and rebounding into its eye socket.

The animaru went down in a heap, tripping up the two right behind it. Another two reacted quickly enough to leap the corpse of their companion as it tumbled to a stop.

Tere smiled as he pulled another arrow free from his quiver and nocked it. Maybe he wasn't so worthless after all.

His thought was interrupted by Urun throwing out his

hand toward the fast-approaching monsters. A pale, yellowish green blob shot forth, shaped vaguely like a triangle with its point in front. It slammed into the lead animaru and blasted it apart, pieces of the creature spattering the other creatures. Urun's shoulders slumped a bit, but then he straightened his posture and began moving his hands again.

Tere was able to punch another arrow through the head of an animaru before the creatures reached Urun and Aila.

There were eight left.

❦ 30 ❦

Aila flowed around the two charging her, slashing at one with each hand, delivering long gashes to their abdomens. The spell that had been cast on their weapons allowed the animaru to be injured, even killed, and Tere was glad of that. He thought of the outcome if their weapons had not been anointed with life magic and shuddered.

But it was no time for thought. Tere shot another arrow, then another, then another, at nearly the same time. The first struck one of the other animaru going toward Aila, striking its open mouth, punching through its palate, and angling up into the brain.

The second arrow missed his target altogether. The third grazed another of the creatures as it came toward him and twisted out of the way.

Three of the animaru focused on trying to get through Urun's shield to tear the nature priest apart. The two Aila had injured had circled around to attack the young woman. The remaining two were already too close for Tere to use his bow.

At least, they were too close for him to use it in the

conventional way. He swung it like a staff at the animaru he had injured. With a loud crack, it struck the monster's head, causing it to lose its balance and fall into a roll to Tere's side. By the time it had righted itself and moved in to attack the archer again, Tere had dropped his bow and drawn his two long knives to meet the other animaru swiping at him with its claws.

Tere met the creature with an assurance born from decades of combat, both ranged and up close. His confidence was misplaced.

The creature slithered away from Tere's knives and slashed at the archer, tearing a gash in his forearm. It wasn't deep enough to force him to release the grip on his blade, but it hurt like he had lost his arm.

Tere backstepped, slicing at the creature's claws, barely parrying them aside. Without his ability to predict where the next blow would come from, he was at a severe disadvantage. He had to become more fluid. His lack of precognitive sight had made him uncoordinated and rigid.

He tried to go on the offensive, sliding to the side as the monster tried to reach him and pivoting to cut at it. He scored a very shallow cut along its shoulder, but it barely broke the creature's momentum. He was going to be in real trouble if—

A rake of pain lashed across his back and Tere rolled forward by reflex to minimize the damage, so awkwardly that half his arrows flew from his quiver and scattered on the ground. He made it just under the attacking animaru's razor claws, coming to his feet and turning in time to see that the other dark creature had attacked him from behind as he was engaged with its fellow.

Stupid, stupid! He chided himself. The creature never would have been able to sneak up on him if he had his full sight.

Tere threw the thought out. Now was not the time to deride himself. He had two monsters before him, both faster and less injured than he. He was going to have to figure something out or he would die here.

The longer of the animaru, the one Tere had injured slightly, cocked its head in a gesture that was entirely too human. The other slowly moved to circle around Tere as its black eyes drilled into Tere's face. He wondered off-handedly if that gaze would be worse if the archer saw the world through regular sight.

Without any indication they were communicating, both creatures lunged at Tere. He rolled backward, fire shooting up his back where he had been cut as it contacted the ground. As soon as he regained his feet, he jumped up and over one of the animaru that had reached down low to slash him. As Tere passed over its head, he thrust his knives out and slashed the creature before ending his flight in another roll that pained his back again.

There was no time to think about how bad his injury was, though. Both of the monsters pivoted and charged him again, the one he had just injured screeching its anger, or maybe its pain.

Tere backed up, one painful step at a time, batting away claws and slashing out. He couldn't think of a technique or a trick to use to take down the animaru, and he was tiring quickly. He must be losing a lot of blood from his wounds. In mere moments, he would be unable to fight them off, let alone attack.

Desperately trying to think of a tactic to use, it hit him like a punch in the face: he was panicking. How long had it been since he had been truly fearful for his life, such that he tried to formulate complex plans in his mind during combat? He knew better. Overthinking would only to send him to his grave. He needed to stop thinking and feel.

He rolled again, this time to the right, barely avoiding the slashing claws of the monsters. As he did, he cleared his mind. He had no time for thought. Live or die, he would simply move with the flow of battle, even without his full sight.

The longer animaru overextended to reach Tere, gnashing its teeth in frustration. The archer slipped to the side just enough to dodge the blow and slashed out with his knife to score a cut along its torso. It bellowed and swung at him again, but he was already out of reach, engaging the second monster.

Tere feinted with his right blade, causing the other creature to move its head aside slightly to avoid the blow.

Right into Tere's left knife, which cut deeply into its eye.

The monster backed off and shook its head, bringing a clawed hand to its ravaged eye. Tere went in to take advantage, but aborted his attempt when the other animaru came at him again.

He spun while ducking under the animaru's swipe, cutting at its legs with both knives as he did so. With a yelp, the animaru dropped to the ground, its right leg so damaged it could not support the creature's weight.

Tere launched a series of slashes and lunges at the one-eyed creature, finally getting through its desperate parries and punching one of his knives through its other eye. The blade traveled into the brain and the dark monster dropped to the ground, dead.

It was an easy matter to finish the crippled animaru off now that Tere didn't have to worry about its companion. A few slashes through its throat finished it off.

Tere looked up from the two corpses at his feet to see Aila still fighting with the two animaru attacking her. She had slashes on her arms and shoulders, but none so deep that they kept her from fighting. Still, she seemed to be slowing down and the animaru attacked with renewed vigor.

He picked up his bow, only a few feet from where he stood, nocked an arrow, and took aim. He couldn't predict where any of the combatants would be using his magical sight, but he was not defined by that sight. Not totally.

The ability was not his entire skillset. He had practiced for years to be able to hit the smallest of targets, and to do so quickly. He couldn't be sure exactly where the animaru would move now, but he would hit where he aimed.

He would need to. Putting an arrow into Aila would do none of them any good.

Tere had to hand it to the woman: she could move. Her compact body twisted and spun, dodging most of the attacks from the two monsters assailing her. But she was over-matched in both strength and size, and while she was notice-ably growing slower, the animaru were not. The archer took aim.

Aila slashed one of the creatures while she parried the other's swipe with the weapon in her other hand. The one she had struck spun with the strike, however, spinning and back-handing her, throwing her back before she could close in for the kill. That provided Tere the space he needed to loose his arrow.

The shaft sped toward the animaru Aila had just injured, but the monster moved slightly at the last minute, so the arrow glanced off its torso, tearing a small cut but not killing it. Tere cursed as he pulled another arrow from his quiver and nocked it.

The three clashed again, too close for Tere to risk shoot-ing. He moved his bow to follow the dark creatures, but didn't release for fear of hitting his friend. The three combat-ants were moving too quickly and erratically for him to take the shot.

Then one of the monsters broke through Aila's guard and landed a solid blow to her midsection. Its claws tore through her leather armor. By Aila's scream and the spray of blood, the razor-sharp claws tore through her flesh as well. Her body spun with the force of the blow, thrown away from her attackers.

Tere launched four arrows in the blink of an eye. The first three struck, with different degrees of damage. The first took one of the animaru at the base of its neck as Tere was just launching the fourth. The second drilled into the other animaru, high on its chest, with the third following closely lower on the chest. The fourth nearly missed the target altogether, putting a slash on its cheek.

The monsters screamed and locked their black eyes on Tere. None of the arrows had killed their targets—damn it—but they no longer seemed to put killing Aila as their highest priority. The one with the arrow in its neck was losing thick, mud-colored blood quickly and seemed confused that it couldn't move as fast as it normally did. The other tore at the ground and charged.

Tere nocked, drew, and loosed two more arrows before the creature made it to him. The second arrow was a perfect shot, entering the monster's eye and punching partway out of the back of its head. It dropped to the ground and slid almost to Tere's feet.

He paid it no mind because he was already drawing back an arrow to finish the other animaru. There was no need, though, because despite her injury, Aila was on her feet and tearing out the animaru's throat with both of her weapons. She and the animaru corpse both dropped to the ground.

Tere swung his bow in the direction of Urun and the monsters still trying to get through his shield. There wasn't anything he could do for Aila at the moment. His best choice was to end the confrontation. And that meant killing Urun's attackers.

The shield provided a little space between the nature priest and the creatures attacking him, so Tere was not concerned about hitting Urun by mistake. Besides, that shield of life magic, though not great for physical attacks by something neutral like an arrow, would deflect a shaft enough to prevent him from being injured even if Tere's aim was horribly off target. With his head buzzing and the weakness leaching into him, Tere didn't think that to be unlikely.

He released the arrow and struggled to nock another and loose it. Yes, he was definitely slowing down. It was probably due to blood loss from his gashed back, but it could be animaru poison. Some of them seemed to have that.

The two arrows struck their targets, though not exactly where Tere had wanted them to hit. One pierced the upper arm of an animaru and the other punched through a second creature's skull. That last one was deadly, but the first only succeeded in enraging the monster, which turned and charged Tere.

The archer scooped up a few more arrows scattered at his feet, dumping most of them into his quiver and quickly nocking one. Before he could draw it, a muffled boom threw the two animaru away from Urun as a flash of light erupted from the priest.

The monster closest to Urun was thrown off its feet, sizzling as if on fire. The one heading toward Tere was pushed forcefully toward the archer, screeching in pain.

Tere released his breath along with the arrow. It sped the fifteen feet and rammed through the animaru's eye, blowing out the back of the monster's head with its force. As the archer pulled out and nocked another arrow, Urun flung another of those bright triangle missiles at the remaining animaru, blasting a hole in its chest as it tried to regain its feet. Its body flopped to the ground and stopped moving.

Tere relaxed his bow, scanning the area for any other enemies. All he saw were dead animaru, Aila lying on the ground unmoving, and Urun slumping to his knees. There hadn't seemed to have been any of the ones that disappeared when killed.

"I'm sorry I'm so generally worthless during combat," the young priest said, shaking his head. "It's all I can do to keep my shield up and maybe throw out an attack once in a while. I really need to have a talk with Osulin about it. I wasn't trained for fighting like this."

"You did fine," Tere told him. "We're all learning." He limped toward Aila. His battle rush was subsiding, and his injuries painfully reminded him he was not invincible.

When Tere got to the young woman, he felt for a pulse in her neck. At least she was still alive. He turned her, positioning her on her back so he could inspect her wound.

It didn't look good. She wasn't bleeding as quickly as before, but the slashes in her abdomen were deep.

He turned to find Urun three steps away from him, shuffling toward Aila. "Can you do something for her? It's pretty bad."

Urun sucked in a deep breath and let it out, almost falling over with the effort. "Yes, of course." He dropped to his knees next to Aila and closed his eyes. "Give me a moment to gather what energy I have left."

Tere eyed the young man. His face was drawn and pale, and he had dark circles under his eyes, almost dark enough to look like he had been in a tavern fight. He wondered if priest magic was like mage or sorcerer magic. Could he harm himself, even kill himself, by trying to use too much power when he was exhausted? He wouldn't ask. Urun knew what he was doing. He was young, but he had been Osulin's priest for years.

The young man's grey eyes opened, hard as chips of stone. He put his hands over Aila, inches from her skin, and moved them over her whole body. They ended up hovering over the wound.

"The good news is that she doesn't have any other serious injuries than this one," Urun said. "The bad news is that this one is really serious. I'll need more than just magic."

He brought out a packet of leaves from his pack, put them in his mouth and chewed them to a mushy consistency, and placed them on Aila's abdomen. His hands glowed slightly as he moved them in what had to be practiced and choreographed patterns. He chanted something, low under his breath, continuing in this way for several minutes.

Finally, he dropped his hands to the ground, barely catching himself to prevent falling on top of the young woman in front of him. He pushed himself up, pale face coloring slightly.

"That's as much as I can do right now," he said, his voice barely a whisper. "She's out of danger, enough that I can rest a little before finishing.

"Thank you, Urun," Tere said, taking a towel from the pack he had retrieved from the ground while the priest was healing Aila. He wiped the blood from her side and found that the gashes had closed up. They weren't completely healed, just tender pink skin that looked as if they would tear open again if she sneezed, but she wasn't bleeding. Magic was a useful thing.

The archer dribbled a little water into Aila's mouth from his waterskin and turned to offer it to Urun. As he reached out to hand the skin to the priest, the world did a flip and then went dark.

When he came to, Tere was lying on his side, propped up

with a pack on either side of him so he wouldn't roll over. The animaru corpses were nowhere in sight.

"Welcome back," Urun's tired voice said. It sounded hoarse, like the priest had been screaming, though it was probably just exhaustion.

"What happened?" Tere asked.

"You passed out. That's what happens when your back is shredded and you lose a bunch of your blood."

Tere moved his shoulders a little, but stopped immediately when a hot lance of pain shot up and down his back. "Oh, the back."

"Yeah. I was able to heal it partially, enough so that you won't die soon, but I couldn't do that whole job. I don't have the strength. I'm sorry. I did move us away from the dead creatures. Hopefully far enough that scavengers won't come after us."

"Thank you, Urun. Why don't you get some sleep? I'll watch over things."

Urun laughed, a raspy, horrid thing. "I would normally reject the idea, but as things are, I probably couldn't defend myself even if we were attacked. We're both in bad shape."

"Aila?"

"She's on the other side of you. She is sleeping, but she'll live. At least until I can gather the strength to finish healing her. And you."

"Get some sleep. Did you eat and drink?"

"Yes, mother."

The priest hadn't lost his humor, even if it was acerbic as ever. That was good. Still, Tere worried for him. He worried for all of them. They were in a precarious position. Until Urun could regain his strength and heal them, they were vulnerable. It wouldn't take animaru or assassins to completely destroy them at this point. A couple of hares could probably do the job. Maybe just one.

The thought of rabbits made Tere hungry. He sat up, with difficulty, and dug through his pack—the one that had been in front of him, propping him up. He tore into the dried meat he pulled out and fumbled for his waterskin. His body reacted sluggishly, but he thought he'd be able to stay conscious to watch over the other two as they slept.

"I'll make a loud noise if you're needed to help defend us," the archer said. "Maybe say a prayer to your goddess that nothing comes across us while we regain our strength.

Urun chuckled softly. "Already done that. Many times. Okay, I'll sleep. Try not to tear your back open again. It'll just make my job harder when I am finally able to heal you more."

"I plan on sitting here as still as a tree. Rest up. I'll see you when you wake."

The priest nodded, then rolled himself up in his cloak and was asleep in seconds.

Tere scanned the area. They were surrounded by trees, though they weren't too thick. He couldn't see where they had fought the animaru. Just how far had Urun dragged them? Tere was suddenly glad he had friends, and immediately felt a pang of guilt. No, it wasn't what his friends could do for him that was important. It was the fact that they were there at all, that they existed.

He had missed that, living alone in the Grundenwald. It was nice to have people to care about again, and to have them care for him. He smiled, just a little, but even that hurt. How long had it been since the old days, when he and his friends shared adventures? Too long. Much too long.

The aging archer shifted his thoughts before he delved into the subject too deeply. Physical pain was one thing, but remembering—no, he didn't want to visit that torment. Instead, he turned to look at Aila.

The young woman was lying on her back, breathing deeply and regularly. She was resting easily, it seemed. That was good. He had been concerned about her. Quite a spitfire, that one. He reached over and swept a lock of her hair out of her face.

What *was* her story, anyway? He still had so many questions about her. She was a mystery wrapped in a conundrum and tied up with a confusing knot of misdirection. He liked her, though. She was the bratty little sister all young boys complained about but would never give up in a million years.

"Sleep well, little sister," he whispered, realizing as he did that at her age, she could easily have been his daughter. "We have a way to go yet. A long way, I think."

𝕾 31 𝕾

Phoenixarrow wrestled with her memories of the encounter with that archer, one of the targets they were out to eliminate. How *had* the man done what he did? It was impossible. She had trained her entire life to become the best archer ever. Well, the best archer since Erent Caahs, in any case.

The brace was gathered in a small clearing, barely large enough for the six of them. Something was going on, though she couldn't figure out what. Darkcaller and Fireshard were out of sorts.

"We will remain here for a time," Darkcaller said. Her posture communicated exhaustion. And pain. She slumped, slightly, but enough that Phoenixarrow could see she was aching from her core and wanted to curl up into a ball to try to relieve the agony.

"Why?" Keenseeker asked. "We're getting closer, even if little Miss Red Archer over there can't seem to find them."

Phoenixarrow didn't bother glaring at the oaf. It wouldn't make a difference anyway. It would probably just entice him to continue.

"Because I say we are going to stop momentarily," Darkcaller said. Her voice had an edge Phoenixarrow had rarely heard. The leader did not show anger easily, but she was getting there now. "Something just happened with the magic of the world. I need to think."

Fireshard's normally stoic face opened up in surprise. The slight widening of her eyes was more emotion than Phoenixarrow had ever seen in the woman. So she was feeling the effects of whatever magical occurrence happened as well.

Keenseeker grumbled but didn't push the issue. The unlikely looking assassin set his muscular body onto a rock to wait.

"What do you think is going on?" Shadeglide asked Phoenixarrow. The smaller woman was just a few feet from the archer. The redhead hadn't realized she was there.

"I don't know. I didn't see or feel anything, but I don't use magic, either. Darkcaller knows what she's doing. She'll tell us when it's time to go."

"I guess." The dark-haired woman suddenly smiled. "You weren't trained as an assassin in the Falxen school, right?"

Phoenixarrow scrutinized the woman's smiling face. She had learned to be wary of people trying to get personal information from her. It was one of the first things she had learned growing up on the streets. "Why do you ask?"

"No reason. I didn't train in the school, either. My grandfather trained me himself."

The woman's smile did look genuine, though that didn't mean anything. She had observed Shadeglide, and it seemed she just liked people. Few of the Falxen were truly social. Shadeglide was one of them, it seemed.

It wasn't that important. Many of the assassins she had worked with knew her story. What was one more? Talking with the shorter woman would help time pass.

"I trained myself, for the most part," Phoenixarrow said.

"I made my way, living on the streets, learning things the hard way. I developed skills and the Falxen pay for such things."

"You grew up on the streets? Wow, that must have been tough. How did you get so good with a bow?"

"Practice. Lots of practice."

"She fancies herself the reincarnation of Erent Caahs," Keenseeker said, following his statement with a booming laugh.

"Really?" Shadeglide asked.

Phoenixarrow already regretted the conversation. "No, not really. I know I'm not Erent Caahs reborn, but I have lived my life trying to be like him. He was the best archer who ever lived."

"Ooh," Shadeglide said. "I did love to hear stories of him when I was a child. He went everywhere, did everything. Very exciting."

Phoenixarrow nodded. "He was smart and competent and didn't use his incredible skills to take advantage of others. If he were here, he would have figured out a way to catch our prey and taken them out."

Keenseeker bellowed another laugh. "You do know that Erent Caahs was a *hero*, right? You are an assassin. How does that work, with you trying to pattern your life after his?"

Phoenixarrow nocked an arrow and drew her bowstring to her cheek in one blurring movement. "Shut up, Keenseeker. It's none of your damn business."

Darkcaller hissed. "Put the arrow away, Phoenixarrow. Keenseeker, mind your own business."

Phoenixarrow slammed her arrow back into her quiver. "I'm going to scout around us. The air is beginning to stink around here."

"Can I go with you?" Shadeglide asked. "I won't hold you up. I have too much energy to sit around right now."

"Sure, fine."

The taller, red-haired woman led the shorter, blue-haired woman into the trees. Her anger was still a fire within her. How she would love to put some arrows into that bastard Keenseeker. It wasn't any easier to hear what he said because he was totally right. She had dedicated her life to the memory of Erent Caahs, but if she were to meet him, he would probably kill her. Heroes and assassins rarely saw eye to eye.

"Tell me more about Erent Caahs," Shadeglide said.

Damn. Phoenixarrow had forgotten the woman was with her. She sighed and began to talk.

"I first heard a story about him when I was three years old, when I still had a family..."

❧

"QUIT SCRATCHING AT IT," LONEBLADE SAID. "OR IF YOU won't, at least go somewhere else to take care of the itch. It's making me uncomfortable."

"I can't help it," Twoblades responded, turning his back to the other assassin and scratching furiously at his crotch.

Featherblade observed the interaction with a single raised eyebrow. What was going on with the two now?

"I don't understand it," Twoblades continued. "It just started all of a sudden."

Loneblade considered his friend. "Did you avail yourself of any services when we were in Satta Sarak? Maybe you caught something."

"No, of course not. Even if I had wanted to, we didn't have time for that. It just started after the last time I had to piss an hour ago."

Whiteshadow, who had been sitting quietly off to the side, burst out laughing. That was different. Featherblade had rarely seen her laugh outright, though she jested nearly constantly.

"Didn't your mother ever tell you to wash your hands before you hold it?" Whiteshadow asked. "No telling what might happen if you don't."

"What did you do?" Twoblades demanded.

"Just a little ground itchweed. Nothing serious."

Loneblade guffawed. "Oh, good one, White. Very nice."

Twoblades glared at the tall, pale woman, but then cracked a smile which turned quickly into a laugh. "Damn you. That *was* a good one. Okay, okay, one for you. You better watch your back."

"I do that better than you watch your front, apparently."

"Hmm," Twoblades said. "The thought of watching your backside is stuck in my mind now. Turn around for us, let me see if there's anything you might need my help with."

Whiteshadow gave him a wry smile. "Thanks, but there's nothing I can't handle. Speaking of which, you need to be more careful about what you handle."

Loneblade laughed again and slapped his friend on the back. "My advice is for you to quit while you're *behind*." At that last word, he raised his eyebrows to Whiteshadow.

"Oh, fine. For being such good sports, here you go." She turned slowly and when her back was to them, she bent at the waist as if she was picking something up off the ground.

Featherblade noticed the reaction of the two men. He appreciated Whiteshadow's form, though she was not what was commonly accepted as beautiful. She was a little thin for the tastes of the time, but she was fit and shapely and her clothes conformed to her figure well.

Twoblades and Loneblade whistled exaggeratedly and Whiteshadow turned to face them, bending again, but this time in a bow.

"Now go and wash so we don't have to watch you scratch at yourself all day," she said.

"You wanna help?" he responded.

"I think I've done quite enough. Putting itchweed on your hands is as close as I'll be getting to you. I'm like a wild animal. I kill and eat those I mate with."

Twoblades raised his hands in front of him like they were arms on a scale, raising and lowering them. "It just might be worth it."

"Go," she said. Her face was stern, with not a hint of a smile or joke indicated anywhere on it.

Twoblades huffed and headed for the small creek on the other side of the jumble of rocks they were using as a resting spot.

When he was no longer in sight, Whiteshadow winked at Loneblade, who laughed again.

"Sometimes, I don't know how to read you," he said. "But I'm glad you're on our side."

That got him a slight smile.

Featherblade leaned back against a small boulder. They were waiting for Fleshrender to return from scouting. She was trying to find out what happened to...

The chainblade-wielding woman slipped from the trees and came straight for the Falxen leader.

"They got around the army," she said when they were two steps apart.

"Army? It is truly an army then?" The brace had seen the group of men, of course, but it had been unclear what it was. Bandits? Refugees? Something else?

"Yes. There are about four hundred of them. They don't have uniforms, but they seem more organized than a group of thieves would be, if not by much. They were camped close to the cliffs last night and the targets passed through them at the edge."

"Through them," Featherblade mused. "Really?"

"There was some kind of rockfall. Their tracks go straight toward it and then emerge on the other side."

"Interesting. Where is the army now?"

"They moved out toward the east this morning. They've only been gone for a few hours."

"You're sure, then, that the ones we seek went through the army when it was still there?"

Fleshrender turned her azure eyes to his. Strange, that. She rarely made eye contact unless she was about to kill, or there was a significant reason for it.

"Yes," she said. "The layering of the tracks tells me so."

"Very well. Thank you. An excellent job, as always."

The woman nodded and dropped her eyes to the ground.

Featherblade tapped his chin with a finger. The blue woman was less than half a day ahead of them. That was good. He brought up a mental map of the terrain ahead. The targets were going toward Broken Reach. But why? What was there that they desired? They had been there three or four weeks ago, according to the report he had gotten from Izhrod Benzal. What was it they forgot there? Why go back?

Even more troubling was the Falxens' last encounter with them. They had displayed power Featherblade had not been aware they had. He disliked not knowing dangers he would face. He had no qualms about combat with powerful enemies —in fact, he thrived on it—but the surprise at what these could do was troubling. He wouldn't underestimate them again.

To the contrary, he was beginning to think the four they sought were a match for the brace charged with ending them. There would be casualties when they met again. He would have to plan carefully to ensure they were as light as he could make them. Death was inevitable for all, but that didn't mean he wanted it to visit his brace. He would have to be careful with where and how they attacked the next time.

"It's time to leave," Featherblade said softly. "Let's go. We have targets to catch."

❧ 32 ❧

Tere watched over his sleeping friends for several hours. He lost track of the time, moving around to keep his eyes open, using the pain he still felt from the incomplete healing to give him the edge to stay awake. The afternoon turned to evening and the land was slowly plunged into the darkness of night.

Urun's breathing changed tempo and he snorted, then rolled onto his side.

"How are things?" the priest said in a raspy voice. He cleared his throat. "Anything happen while I was sleeping?"

"Nothing," Tere answered. "Just me wrestling with trying to keep awake and aware. How are you feeling?"

"Like I've been beat up and locked in a small box for a week or so. That's much better than I felt before, though. Did Aila wake up?"

"No. She's as exhausted as you are."

"I appreciate you taking watch, Tere. I needed that rest. How long did I sleep?"

"Maybe four or five hours."

Urun got to his feet and shuffled toward Aila. "It'll have to do."

The priest checked the woman for any signs her wounds had been more serious than he had surmised. He waved his hand over her, and Tere figured he was scanning her with his magic. He would have seen the magic working, before. Now he didn't detect even the faintest traces of power.

"How is she?" Tere asked.

"She's fine. Well, I mean, she's in the same condition I left her. No serious injuries, just the half-healed ones from before."

Urun stood and took a step toward Tere, but the archer waved him away. "I'm fine, just like you left me. If you're going to use your magic, finish healing her. I'm good for now."

"Are you sure? Those wounds you took weren't small."

"Oh, I expect you to heal me, when you have the strength. I would rather you finish with her for now, though."

Urun ran his fingers through his hair. "Okay. I'll finish what I started here, but I should be strong enough to heal you at least a bit more."

"That's fine. Just remember those assassins may still be on our heels. Don't weaken yourself too much. We have a long way to go yet."

Urun grunted and turned his attention back to Aila.

By the time the priest finished, Aila had woken and was sitting up drinking while it was Tere's turn. The chill associated with wounds healing ran across the archer's spine as Urun poured his power into him.

"There." Urun leaned back on his feet, which were tucked under him. "That's about as much as I can do right now. Sorry I couldn't finish. At least whatever weird reaction you had after you blacked out is gone. It would be bad if your body wouldn't accept healing."

Tere rolled his shoulders and swung his arms in circles. There was hardly any tugging on the skin on his back and the little there was didn't hurt.

"I feel great, Urun. Thank you. I'm tired, but that's nothing new or serious. We're all three tired. What say you we rest a bit longer and then start heading north? I'd like to leave before the assassins find us. Or more animaru."

"You're already talking about leaving?" Aila asked. "We almost died today, Tere. Can't we rest a while?"

"True, we almost died today. But it's also true that if the assassins catch us in this condition, we *will* die. I'd rather push my endurance a little and get away. No use in making it easy for them."

Aila grumbled but didn't argue further.

Urun stood up and went toward his pack. "I'll take watch for a while, Tere. You've been up all day while we rested."

"No," Aila said. "Urun, you healed us both, to the point of exhaustion. Tere stayed up while we rested even though if he felt half as worn out as me, he shouldn't have been able to stand. I've slept more than either of you. Let me take watch. You guys get some sleep. I'll wake you an hour before dawn and we can head out."

"Thank you, Aila," Tere said. "I appreciate it. A little sleep will make me feel more human instead of the beaten piece of meat I feel like now."

"Are you sure?" Urun asked Aila.

"Yes, yes. Both of you go to sleep. You're wasting time. I'll see you in a few hours."

After thanking her again, both men curled up in their cloaks and went to sleep. Tere hoped that when he woke, his sight would have returned. Maybe exhaustion was keeping him from using it. He laughed bitterly at himself. Sure, like problems in the world were that easy.

Tere woke to Aila shaking his shoulder. As she had

promised, it was still dark out, but not quite lightless as when he had gone to sleep. Dawn would be coming soon.

"Ugh." He climbed to his feet and shook his cloak free of the dirt and leaves that had stuck to it. "I'm too old for this life."

"You've been too old for it for years," Urun said, rubbing his eyes. "But you're still better suited to it than anyone I know, myself included."

Tere picked up his pack and grumbled. "What I wouldn't give for a few minutes next to a fire."

"Maybe later," Aila said. "For now, let's get going. I don't like the feeling of this place. I heard scavengers moving around. I don't think any of them will eat the animaru, but they didn't find their way here yet. It sounded like some of them might. I'd rather not have to fight again for a while, if you don't mind."

Tere stopped what he was doing and considered Aila. She was obviously not in the best of moods.

"Thank you for keeping watch," he told her. "I really needed that sleep."

She sighed. "It was the least I could do. We're a team. You and Urun saved me."

"That's what it's like to work together with friends," he said. "You save me, I save you. It all becomes a blur. I do appreciate the sleep, though. Thank you."

Tere couldn't see colors well with his *sight*, but the way she looked away, he thought she might be blushing. Interesting.

"Okay," Urun said after a few seconds of silence, "which way are we going?"

"North," Tere said.

"I know we're going north. Which way is that?"

Tere laughed and slapped the priest on the back. "It's this way. Come on."

They traveled for another day and a half through moderately wooded terrain. Tere took down a small deer for them, and they risked a fire in a sheltered area in the midst of a field of boulders. It was the first real meal they'd had in more than a week and a half. The archer was happy to know he could still be useful without his full abilities.

Urun licked the grease from his fingers and leaned back against one of the rocks. "So, has your full sight returned?"

"No." Tere said it too quickly, too sharply. He purposely softened his voice. "No, I still can't see tracks in the magical field or any kind of magic. I have to aim the old-fashioned way, leading the target and guessing which way it'll move. I have probably relied too much on the magic."

"That's silly," Aila said. "If you have abilities, why not rely on them? Every advantage that can be gained should be utilized. Who would have ever thought you'd lose it? It's like training with weapons. Do we refrain from training with our arms because one day someone might cut one off?"

"I concede your point," Tere said. "I just wish I could figure out what went wrong and how to get my sight back. Is it gone permanently, or can it be fixed? I'm afraid I'm a liability like this."

Aila waved toward the rest of the meat they were cooking thoroughly so they could eat it over the next few days. "This doesn't seem like a liability to me. Loss of your magical sight hasn't affected your aim. You can still hit an acorn on a branch fifty feet away."

"She's right," Urun said. "Besides, you're more valuable than just someone who joins us in combat. Your experience, your knowledge, the way you know where north is, it's all invaluable. When we get to Sitor-Kanda, they'll be able to fix it. They're basically the center of magic in current times."

"Yeah," Tere said. "Maybe. No sense in whining about it in the meantime, though. I'll be glad when we can see

Munsahtiz and are almost to the Academy. I want this thing done."

Tere led them north and slightly west for several hours. They came up over a large hill and Aila's sharp intake of air made Tere swing his head toward her, thinking she had spotted more enemies. She stood there, looking out over a patch of grassland that ended abruptly at a flat expanse of blue glittering in the morning sun.

"The Kanton Sea," Aila said. "We're almost there."

Tere couldn't help but to smile. "It's still more than twenty miles to the south tip of the sea, but yes, we're closer. Come on, it's no good us standing out in the open like this. We can be seen from all sides. Let's not push our luck."

Aila's wide eyes regarded Tere for a moment before she nodded and headed down the other side of the hill. "I was just excited, that's all."

"I know. It's my job to worry about our safety, remember? That's my role, to be the paranoid old guy."

The young woman chuckled and continued making her way down the hill.

In two more days they neared the edge of the Mellafond, the swamp bordering the eastern shore of the Kanton Sea. To the north, the land was littered with gnarled trees and watery marshland.

"The Mellafond," Tere said. "We'll not be going through that. Too many dangerous things live there and firm footing is scarce. I've been through parts of it before and would like never to go through again. That swamp can swallow people whole. We need to go around."

"Then we'll take the northern route to the Academy, as we discussed?" Aila asked.

Tere looked to Urun. The priest nodded. "Yes. I think it's the best choice. Once we get around to the other side of the Mellafond, it's a straight shot to the northern bridge and

Sitor-Kanda. The distance is a little longer than if we went south, but much safer. And most likely quicker because of the easier terrain."

"Safer sounds good to me." Aila said. "Quicker sounds even better. I'm sold."

Urun threw another look at the swamp. "Are you sure you don't want me to try to lead us through the Mellafond? I might be able to get it to bend a little for us."

Tere shook his head. "It's not just the treacherous surface and the beasts in there. Something is strange about its magic. With how magic has been recently, it may be even worse."

"It may be better," the priest said.

Tere gave Urun a flat look. "Really? No, Urun, I have to insist. There are too many unknowns. Even if we survive it, the shorter distance through it would probably take more time than going around. Better to stick to the path we know."

"I see your point." The nature priest's voice sounded less than certain, and Tere thought he might continue the argument, but the younger man simply stared out over the terrain of the Mellafond for more than a minute, silently considering something.

The area skirting the swamp was heavily wooded, with the River Road passing through. It was the same road they had tried to take a few short weeks ago when they had made their first attempt to go to Sitor-Kanda. The party had not quite made it, instead leaping into the Alvaspirtu River to escape the animaru chasing them.

Was it only a few weeks? Tere counted it out on his fingers. Two months. It seemed a lifetime.

As they traveled, the trio stayed close to the edge of the road. Twice, they melted into the trees as people passed. The first was another group of three, riding horses and galloping as if all the beasts of the hells were chasing them. The second was a small caravan of what looked to be traders. Three wagons and a half dozen horse-mounted guards.

They weren't monsters or animaru, but Tere was uneasy. Without his magical sight, he thought it better if no one or nothing knew he and his friends were traveling the road. Both times, he and his companions watched the other humans fade before they mounted the road again.

Tere began to feel as if he was being watched. It was an itch in the center of his back, one he couldn't scratch no matter what he did. He'd had the feeling before, but he had always thought it was his magic, some special sense telling him when danger was near. Why was it calling to him now? Did it mean anything?

"Tere?" Urun said as they walked on the edge of the road. "Is everything okay?"

"Huh? Oh, yeah. I just have a feeling. Like someone is watching us, stalking us. I'm probably just paranoid."

They turned a corner in the road and Tere hissed. "Off the road. Now."

The three were well accustomed to this by now. They slipped into the forest on the east side of the road—the opposite side as the Mellafond—and crouched inside the cover of the trees and underbrush.

A group of a dozen or so animaru was standing in the road.

"What are they doing?" Aila asked. "Do they usually just stand around like that?"

Tere felt a bead of sweat drip down his forehead. "I've never seen it. It seemed to me that they're always moving."

"Then why are they doing it now?"

"I don't know. I'm not the expert in these creatures. It almost seems like they're waiting for something."

"Or some*one*," Urun said.

Tere wrestled down his irritation. Urun was right. They

seemed like they were waiting to ambush someone. But why stand in the middle of the road? They were close enough to Sitor-Kanda that one of the traveling students or masters might see them.

"I wouldn't think they'd be so in the open this close to the Academy," Urun said, mirroring Tere's thoughts. "From what I've seen, they are trying to hide their existence until they're ready to attack. I always thought they had a plan. You know, kill Aeden first, gather their forces, take out smaller populations like the highland clans, then attack cities when they had the numbers to match their enemies. I assumed they had someone in charge that had a strategy."

"They did," Tere said. "Khrazhti. There had to be one of them to take her place, maybe more than one. With that in mind, we need to ask ourselves what is so important that they'd risk being seen."

"Does it matter?" Aila asked.

"It does," Tere responded. "Anything they're doing that's out of the ordinary concerns me. Besides, this activity looks to me like they're specifically searching for something."

"Aeden?"

"We can hope. He's hundreds of miles away right now, so if they're searching for him here, it's a great waste of their time."

The archer considered the dark figures in the road ahead when they suddenly looked toward the east as if something had gotten their attention and the entire group crashed through the vegetation to chase down whatever it was.

"Let's start moving through the trees on the west side of the road. I don't think it's safe to be in the open anymore."

"The west side is where the swamp is," Aila reminded him.

"Yes. We'll need to be careful to continue to skirt it, stay in the woods bordering it."

Three more times that day, the party saw animaru. The number of the creatures was never more than fifteen, but they definitely had the look of searching for something.

"That's four groups now, and the day's not even over yet," Urun said. "Has the invasion already begun? Maybe the Academy has already fallen. What will we do then?"

"It can't have done so," Tere said. "That place is the home of the most powerful magic left in Dizhelim. Its sole purpose was to be strong enough to be a resource for the Malatirsay. No, the Academy won't have fallen. We'd know, somehow."

"How is that?" Urun spat. "Would we sense it somehow, maybe detect a change in the magic of the world?" The priest raised an eyebrow.

Tere didn't know how to respond to that. He looked toward where the most current group of animaru had disappeared up the road, heading north.

"Traveling along the edges of the Mellafond like this," Urun continued. "It's allowing me to feel the magic of the place. You're right, Tere, it wouldn't be good to go in there. There's something off about the place. Something wrong. There's some kind of rot. I can't explain it, but we should avoid going in there at all costs."

"I'm glad you agree," Tere said. "Any more close calls like this last one, though, and we may be forced to escape into the swamp."

Aila had been silently watching the two men, shifting her gaze between them and the trees on the other side of the road. "Can we switch over to the other side of the road and travel that way?"

Tere shook his head. "All of the groups seem to either come from that direction or leave toward that way. They must not want to deal with the Mellafond either. I'm afraid that if we use that route, we'll run right into a group of them."

"It's only a matter of time until we run into them on this side. How far until we can circle around the northern edge of the swamp?"

"At least twenty or thirty miles is my best guess."

"Tere," Urun said. "Maybe we should backtrack, go the southern route. The animaru won't come after us if we go into the town."

The archer huffed and looked at his boots. "We'd be adding several days to our trip, at least. Plus, Praesturi isn't a large town. It's just a village with maybe a few dozen people. I'm not sure it would be a protection from the animaru."

"They're known to be tough, with a bit of magic themselves," Urun insisted. "Plus, we didn't see any of the creatures south of here."

"There may be some now. I don't know, Urun. I think we can slip through the noose the monsters are trying to fit us with. The northern route is the fastest and better-known route. Let's continue on and see what we can find. Once we make it north of the swamp, there will be more area to try to avoid the animaru."

Urun considered Tere and muttered something under his breath. He closed his eyes briefly and when he opened them, they had a look of resignation in them. "Fine. You're the guide. We'll do as you ask. I feel as if we're running out of options here."

"Me, too, my friend. Me too."

With a last look toward the edge of the swamp, not more than fifty paces through the trees to the west, Tere led his friends north again.

It wasn't more than fifteen minutes later when they detected another group of animaru, across the road and in the trees bordering it. As with the others, they seemed to be searching for something, swinging their heads to scan the surrounding area.

The three humans were kneeling in the bushes on their own side of the road, waiting the dark creatures out. Tere hardly breathed, not wanting the slightest movement or sound to give them away.

Aila nudged him and he turned his gaze to her. She motioned with her head subtly and when he followed her eyes, he was surprised to see another group of animaru moving slowly south on the roadway itself.

They had seen no travelers for at least a day and a half. He wondered if the monsters were killing any they found on the road and hiding the bodies.

The two groups of animaru met a few hundred yards from where Tere and the other two humans were hiding. They spoke to each other, their voices harsh though now he knew —thanks to Khrazhti—they spoke a dialect of Alaqotim. He couldn't make out what they said to each other, the distance reducing the conversation to a series of disconnected sounds.

The two groups of animaru parted again, the ones from the trees turning south to continue their search within the undergrowth there and the ones on the road heading north again.

When both groups had disappeared from sight, Urun opened his mouth to speak, but Tere put his finger up to his lips and shook his head sharply. The priest closed his mouth and raised his eyebrows.

A moment later, Urun snapped his head toward the northwest as the animaru Tere had heard moved out of the trees to gather in the road. Like the others, they paced the area briefly, searching. In a few minutes, they went north again, using the road this time.

Tere waited for several minutes and then finally spoke. "They are definitely looking for something."

"Do you think it's us?" Aila asked.

"I don't know. It doesn't matter. If they're searching the

area that thoroughly, they'll find us. Even if we're not what they're looking for, they'll attack us. We might be able to take down one of those groups, even with my limited abilities, but the area is crawling with them. If we get into a fight, we'll be swarmed."

"What can we do?" Urun asked. His nervous look toward the west didn't slip Tere's notice.

"Damn it!" Tere said. "I think we only have two choices, unless we decide to risk going north. I'm pretty sure we won't survive that. The road is gradually getting closer to the swamp, with the strip of dry ground we've been using getting thinner. So, it's go through the swamp and hope that the patrols lighten up when there is more terrain to cover north of the Mellafond, or turn around and take the southern route through Praesturi and the Verlisaru forest."

"How bad could the swamp really be?" Aila said.

Tere sighed. "I'd rather take my chances with the animaru."

"That bad?"

"Yes."

"While I don't have any experience or know much about the area," Urun said, "I'd agree. The feeling of the place...I'd not like to go in there if we don't have to."

"Then it looks like we're going south," Aila said. She stood and dusted the dirt off her knees. "Let's get going before we find that there are groups of those filthy creatures coming up from the south, too."

A small smile formed on Tere's lips. Just when he thought he had figured the girl out, she went and threw him for a loop again. The archer turned and guided them back toward where they had come. Urun and Aila traced his steps.

Gods make it that Aila's words were not prophetic. Things were already bad enough without being trapped between search parties of animaru.

33

The cracked and barren terrain stretched out as far as Aeden could see, broken only by the rocks that were similarly shattered. Just at the edge of sight, the fortress at Broken Reach beckoned to the small party.

"We're back," Raki said. He didn't sound happy.

Aeden didn't look away from the fortress they had spent so much time fighting to find and to conquer, only to flee once it was done. "Yes. If we only had known, huh? We could have saved a lot of time and pain if we'd simply waited."

"You could not," Khrazhti said. "The animaru would have swarmed you and you would have been destroyed. I could not have held back so many."

"Yeah." Fahtin stepped up to see what Aeden was looking at. "And if we were waiting there after that mark came on Khrazhti, we never would have been able to outrun all the animaru who wanted to tear her apart."

"Both good points," Aeden said, "but I still feel like we wasted time and effort only to come back to the same place. Time is not something we really have, I think." He turned to

Khrazhti. "You're sure you don't still have the mark? Will it call all the animaru from around us to you?"

"I do not think it is still active. I believe that it has faded."

"You think, you believe? You don't know?"

"I am sorry. I do not. I have been cut off from S'ru, but other than that, there is no specific feeling of the disapproval. I may have simply grown accustomed to my new situation of being unworthy."

Aeden gritted his teeth. "You're not unworthy, Khrazhti. You made a decision based on your conscience, on your honor. If that god of yours doesn't like it, maybe he should consider his own actions in light of what his stated purpose is."

The blue woman didn't answer, only looked toward the fortress and then to the ground. There was an ache in Aeden's chest when he thought of it. She had been S'ru's high priestess for hundreds, if not thousands, of years. It was all she knew. He couldn't imagine the courage it took to cast that away based only on her principles. It was the single most honorable act he had ever witnessed.

And it was tearing her apart.

"He's right, Khrazhti," Fahtin said. "We appreciate your integrity. Everyone is viewed as unworthy to someone. We Gypta know that better than anyone. It doesn't matter how others view us, but how we view our—"

Fahtin snapped her head back toward where they had come from in the middle of speaking.

Aeden whirled, scanning the terrain behind them, but he didn't see anything. "What is it?"

"I...I don't know. A feeling just struck me. A loathing for something back there. It's getting stronger." She looked deep into Aeden's eyes. "I think someone—or some*thing*—is heading our way. And I don't think it's friendly." A frantic look blossomed in her eyes.

Aeden still couldn't see anything, but that didn't mean she wasn't right. His adopted sister hadn't ever shown any kind of intuitive powers before, but with all the crazy things happening in the world, he wasn't going to discount her senses.

"Let's get moving, then. We're within a day of reaching the fortress. Maybe we can outrun it. Or maybe it'll go another way if we keep moving."

Relief washed over Fahtin's face. Not, Aeden thought, because she didn't feel they were in danger, but because he believed her. He smiled at her, shouldered his pack, and headed toward where they would hopefully end Benzal and all his plans of bringing more animaru over to the human world.

By the time they made it to the first of the crumbling watchtowers, Fahtin was frantic.

"The feeling is getting stronger. Something is coming right at us. We need to prepare."

Aeden shared a look with Khrazhti. She shook her head subtly. He didn't want to discount what Fahtin was feeling, but he wasn't sure what to do about it. If Khrazhti didn't sense anything with her magic, and he and Raki couldn't detect anything, what were they to do? He was fairly certain that if whatever was chasing them was animaru, Khrazhti would know.

The assassins, maybe? A little thing like distance and an army wouldn't stop them from continuing to stalk their prey.

Aeden had sent Raki out to scout the tower to make sure it wasn't occupied. Even during their last foray into Broken Reach, the outer towers were empty, but better to be safe. The young man had come back to report there was no sign of anything nearby, so the four went into the tower to rest.

"We can probably get to another tower or two today,"

Aeden said. "It doesn't seem to deter whatever is after us, though." He looked at Fahtin questioningly, hoping she had something else to add.

She didn't, only sat with nervous eyes darting back and forth from her feet to the wall in the direction they had come from.

The others were subdued. Between the pace they'd been keeping and Fahtin's insistence that enemies were about to overtake them, they seemed to share Aeden's dark mood.

He wished he could confirm or disprove what the Gypta was saying. He didn't like making decisions on one piece of information, especially since Fahtin had no history of any kind of special sense. If only he could...

Aeden slapped his forehead. The sound made Fahtin jump and earned a quizzical look from Khrazhti. Raki calmly considered Aeden. When had the boy become so calm and confident?

"Why are you striking yourself?" Khrazhti asked.

"I just remembered something. One of the spells of the Raibrech, Light's Betrayal, may help us to confirm Fahtin's feeling. Honestly, I always felt the spell was kind of a waste of time to learn, but I had to master the movements anyway."

"What does it do?" Fahtin asked hopefully.

"It just indicates the direction of the closest enemies. It's kind of like the spell that makes the lights that point toward the animaru, Pieces of Evil. You remember, right? That's the one that I always thought only made pretty lights and was completely worthless, but we found that it actually points toward the animaru. Between the two, maybe we can figure out what's going on."

Aeden quickly performed the movements for Light's Betrayal, a spell he had only cast once or twice since he had gained the ability to do real magic. A weakly pulsating ball of light appeared in front of him. It was about the size of a man's head and seemed to glow and then dim at regular intervals.

He cast it while purposely facing toward the east, not sure if it would make a difference in its effect. He and the others watched as it slowly moved, circling them and settling toward the southwest. There, it remained motionless, pulsing with a cool, yellow light.

"What does it mean?" Raki asked.

"I'm not sure," Aeden said. "It's supposed to show us the direction of enemies. I honestly thought it would point toward the fortress, if it worked at all."

"It's sitting in the direction where I sense danger," Fahtin said. "Doesn't that confirm my feeling?"

Aeden didn't know what to say. He felt ashamed that he had cast the spell just to discount what Fahtin might be feeling. It wasn't that he didn't trust her. It was just that she had never shown any ability to sense things before. Now his magic seemed to be agreeing with her assessment.

Before he could say so, Khrazhti spoke. "We must prepare. That is now two warnings that enemies approach. These things should not be ignored."

Fahtin smiled faintly at the animaru, obviously appreciative of the support.

"Yes," Aeden said. "Of course, you're right. It seems that Fahtin has somehow gained the ability to sense danger."

"Magic," Fahtin said.

"It probably is magic," Aeden agreed.

"No, I mean that I think I'm sensing magic, not danger."

"My spell identifies enemies," he said.

"Then they must be magical enemies. I can't tell you why, but I feel that it's magic I'm sensing. I don't know how, but I think that's what it is."

Aeden looked past the glowing ball that was, even now, fading from existence. Toward where the magical enemies were coming from. "We'll have to talk about this later. Maybe the Academy can help you, too. Maybe you've had magic all along but didn't know it."

Fahtin looked embarrassed. "Jehira always did tell us that the Gypta had magic in their blood, but what are the chances that I have some power?"

Raki fidgeted and Aeden could guess what he was thinking, but now was not the time for such discussions.

"Well, you may have just saved our lives. Chances are good that it's the assassins. We need to prepare, to find a place that will favor us when we fight them. It has to end here."

"Maybe we could fight them here, in the main hall of this tower," Raki suggested.

"I do not think that is wise," Khrazhti responded. "In a closed space such as this, the woman with the chain blades will more easily be able to corner us to strike. The one with lightning magic, too, will be more effective."

Aeden agreed with her. In fact, he was about to say the same thing before she beat him to it. He found himself pondering how he had misjudged her intelligence because of the language barrier they'd been facing. She was not only smart, but she had thousands of years of combat experience. He couldn't forget that.

"Then how are we going to set up the battlefield to win?" Fahtin asked. "They outnumber us, and they have skills and magic that some of us can't match."

"What we need is a place with obstructions we can hide behind," Aeden said, "but with escape routes so we can't get trapped. Half of them will fight us with their blades, but the others—the woman with the chains and the man who throws lightning—those will take some care to neutralize."

"I'll go out and scout for an area," Raki said. "You can work out our strategy while I'm gone and you can tell me about it when I get back."

Aeden nodded. "Fine. Be careful, Raki. We're not sure how close they are."

"They won't see me." The young Gypta grinned as he slipped out of the front entrance to the tower.

Aeden's thoughts swirled in his head, spinning and colliding with each other, stealing his ability to think momentarily. He was no stranger to battle, to facing death. Long before he had lived with the Gypta and ended up on this crazy quest, he had developed the ability to stare death in the face and keep his head.

But his friends...

Not only were his friends at risk of being killed, but the entire mission he had been saddled with was in jeopardy. If he and his friends died here, in the desolate wasteland of Broken Reach, who would carry on to defeat Benzal and prevent the animaru from taking over the world? Could Tere and the others do it without him?

If he was honest with himself, he still wasn't sure about the whole Malatirsay thing. The prophecy was so old and so vague, it could probably be applied to dozens of people, if not hundreds. What made him so special? He could fight, there was no doubt about that, but the war he found himself in made his individual skills pale in comparison to what faced Dizhelim.

"You should go," Khrazhti said, breaking Aeden's ponderings into a thousand shards. "Leave me here. I will slow the assassins before they kill me. They may be satisfied with only my death."

"Khrazhti..." Fahtin said, reaching her arm out toward the blue woman, though she was ten feet away.

"No," Aeden said firmly.

Khrazhti's glowing blue eyes met his. "Aeden, you know it is the right thing to do. You must stop Izhrod Benzal from continuing to bring more animaru into your world. There is no need for you—or Fahtin or Raki—to die. They have come for me."

"No," he repeated. "We need you, Khrazhti. Even if we didn't, you are our friend. We'll not let them kill you. Friends don't abandon each other."

"They are too strong," she said.

"No! They *are* strong, but we are, too. With a bit of strategy, we can take them. I don't want to hear about it again. We are with you, to the death if necessary." Aeden realized how loudly he had spoken and that his face was scrunched up in anger. He consciously calmed his features and softened his voice. "Please, Khrazhti. No more thoughts of giving yourself up. Use your experience and your intellect to help us plan. We *can* beat them; we just need to be smarter than they are."

The animaru's downcast eyes shouted sadness and her mouth turned down into a frown, but she nodded.

The three waited for what seemed to Aeden like hours. His mind would not quiet. Where was Raki? Had he run into the assassins? The thought did not help Aeden's anxiety over the upcoming fight.

Fahtin sat quietly, her arms wrapped around herself and her knees pulled up to her chest. She had closed her eyes and seemed to be napping, but when she snapped her head toward the tower doorway and opened her eyes, they were frantic.

"They're coming closer."

"Fahtin," Aeden said. "Try to stay calm. Raki will be back and then we'll go to where we can fight them."

"I'm sorry I'm such a burden, Aeden. I've been trying to get better with my knives, but all I am in a battle like this is someone you have to protect. Maybe I should go somewhere else and hide while you three fight the assassins. I'm just a liability."

Aeden went to her and wrapped her up in his arms.

"You're my sister, Fahtin. You are *never* a burden. Your skill with your weapons is getting better all the time. Soon, you'll be able to stand up to just about anyone, and I don't say that lightly. Give it some time and be kind to yourself."

"But I may never have that time. Fighting these assassins, it's like I'm a child with wooden knives. In that last fight, it almost cost you your life because you had to protect me. It's bad enough to feel powerless, but when it can kill you or the others, I can't bear it."

"We'll get through it. If you go off somewhere by yourself, one or more of the assassins may circle around and find you, then you'll be isolated. Stay with us, help if you can, but don't take too many risks. If Raki finds the right kind of place, you should be able to stay out of most of the fighting but still be there with us."

"I don't know." A few tears rolled down her cheeks. "I don't want to be the reason any of you dies." She cast her eyes to the ground.

Aeden took her face in his hands, gently moving her head so he could meet her eyes. "Fahtin, you will do fine. Stay behind cover, throw your knives when you have a clear shot, and keep behind me and Khrazhti. Raki will be ghosting about. We will rely on you to alert us to something we might not see. Can you do that for us?"

"I...yes."

"Great. It will be an advantage, having you watch our backs so we can't be flanked."

"I'll try," she said.

Aeden tilted her head down and kissed her forehead. "I know you will. Battle is scary. It's normal to feel fear beforehand. Don't let it interfere with how you think. Keep your eyes open, let us know if something is happening we can't see, and use your knives when you have the opportunity."

She sniffled. "I will."

She sighed and relaxed her body so suddenly, Aeden thought something might have knocked her out. He saw in her eyes that she had merely released the tension that had been holding her.

Raki stepped into the room a few minutes later. Aeden was still holding Fahtin—she was breathing slowly like she actually had gone to sleep—and the young man stepped up to his three companions.

"I found a place that I think will work. Follow me."

❧ 34 ❧

Raki led them at a fast pace, almost a jog, to a location nearly a mile away from the tower. It wasn't quite in the path on the way to the main fortress, but off slightly to the northeast. As they slowed, Aeden immediately saw the advantages of the spot.

It was a wide, flat area almost completely devoid of vegetation—as most of Broken Reach was—but that wasn't what made it distinctive. Scattered throughout were boulders of all shapes and sizes, some barely larger in diameter than Aeden was tall, but others fifteen feet across.

Strangely, a great number of the rocks were squarish in shape, almost like they had been cut that way. Standing outside of the boulder field looking in, Aeden called to mind Kings and Killers, the popular dice game. The area in front of him looked like the board, the six dice used for each turn already cast and scattered by the hand of the enormous player.

"This is perfect, Raki," Aeden said. "Great work."

The younger man flushed and pulled on the hood he had been wearing more frequently so that his face was shadowed.

"The terrain is flat, so we won't have to worry as much about tripping on something, the rocks give some good cover, and the spacing in between them will make it difficult for the assassins to gang up on just one of us."

"Well thought out," Aeden said, slapping Raki on the back. He was already scanning the area for specific locations where they could position themselves.

"It is a good place for an ambush," Khrazhti said. She pointed to a configuration of stones that progressively narrowed the space between them. "That is a good area to funnel the enemies while providing cover."

Aeden nodded, glad to have such competent friends. "I agree. Why don't we walk through it? Fahtin, how are your senses? Are they any closer?"

She had been staring out toward where they had come from. When Aeden spoke to her, she blinked. "They're moving faster than us. Yes, they're closer. Very close. I'd say we have less than an hour at this rate."

"Then we better get started figuring out exactly what we'll do. Hopefully, it's not some other enemy of which we know nothing, or it will be an unpleasant surprise. For us."

They got to work, preparing their plan to end the pursuit permanently.

Aeden hoped it wouldn't mean the end of any of his friends.

"THEY'RE CLOSE," FLESHRENDER WHISPERED TO Featherblade.

The leader of the Falxen brace had the chain-blade-wielding woman on a short leash. Figuratively, though at times he thought it might be a better alternative to tether her literally. A familiar lust in her eyes signaled the thrill of the hunt coursing through her. She licked her lips as her eyes darted from him toward their prey.

He had stopped the group when his little scout had informed him that they were almost upon their target. Mistakes like the ones they had made in the last confrontation could not be allowed. With this battle, all his people needed to have clear direction and must cooperate.

It was really his fault the last engagement went poorly. As the leader of the brace, he should have known the capabilities of every member of the group they were chasing, but he had no time or opportunity to gather intel. He hated rush jobs. How could one take pride in a job well done if he could not prepare adequately for it?

He disliked leaving things to chance.

But then, not everything in life—or death—could be controlled. It was the rule of human existence, and it was something an assassin should never forget.

"We were lucky last time," he said softly to the others. "They are more powerful than I had given them credit for, and their little surprise could have meant the end of us. If they had simply walked up and slit our throats while we were stunned, we couldn't have prevented it. All I can surmise from their actions was that their power is unreliable, or unfamiliar, and they didn't want to take the chance to move in closer when we could have fought back.

"Now we know a bit more about them and what they can do. If we handle this correctly, it will end here. They have stopped, most likely deciding to make a stand. They will be preparing for us.

"Do not doubt me in this: if we go in and attack individually, we will be defeated. Stick close to the plan, and we will complete our mission and be rewarded with a big payout. Fail to do so and we may never have the opportunity for another mission again.

"Here is what we are going to to…"

Once Featherblade was confident each of the members of his team knew their role, he gave Fleshrender the sign to lead them to their prey. He wasn't nervous or anxious—he'd given up those things long ago—but as he watched the others moving as one toward their confrontation, he wished he had taken more of the larger team with him. Such wishes were not worth an exhalation, though. Better to focus on what he had and what he must do.

Not for the first time, Featherblade mulled over the current mission. This blue woman they were to kill, who was she? True, it didn't matter nearly so much as the fact that he had an order to end her existence, but still, he wondered. She was obviously not human, nor encalo, pouran, trabin, demid, immanita, or even astridae, arba, or any other of Dizhelim's denizens he had ever heard of. Just what was she?

He thought she might be one of those dark creatures of rumor, though she was a lighter color. More and more, he heard whispers of some kind of beasts that attacked small villages, wiping them out completely. He had never seen one, but too many tales from too many places meant something was there. The one who had hired him could probably tell him—a few pieces of information in messages to him caused him to believe the employer had some relation to the creatures—but Falxen were not supposed to question their employers over much. Being ignorant of those paying for his services was a good way to do business. Usually.

It probably didn't matter who the woman was. Shortly, she and her friends would be dead and then he would be moving on to his next mission.

That was, if he got his head on his task and stopped his useless analysis. He was an assassin, he had a job, and he needed to focus and complete it. That was the truth of his existence.

The Falxen glided through the rocky terrain. There were few trees or bushes for them to hide in, but there were rock formations and little hills of stone with ravines and depressions between them. They moved swiftly and silently through, doing their best to keep their prey from knowing where they were.

Fleshrender slowed and threw him a look. It was time. He noted the position of the others—they were where they should be, as he would have expected of professionals—and nodded to the woman. She had a hungry look on her face, eyes wide with anxious energy.

They moved into the boulder field ahead.

The blue woman stepped suddenly out in between two rocks, motioning with her hands. Her mouth was moving, but Featherblade didn't hear what she was saying.

Boltshadow did as he was instructed and released the lightning bolt he had been preparing for the last several seconds. Featherblade, Twoblades, and Loneblade sprinted toward their target, racing the magical lightning.

When Featherblade was halfway to reaching the woman, well ahead of the others, the bolt struck. But instead of the charred corpse of their prey smoking in a heap in front of him, the outlines of some kind of bubble appeared. The leader's eyes, averted in anticipation of the lightning strike, barely caught the motion as it winked out of existence. His eyes went wide at that, then narrowed in frustration.

She had cast some kind of shield, anticipating the brace's ploy. He hadn't been sure that was what had happened in their earlier engagement.

No matter. Featherblade reached her long before the other two and attacked with ferocious cuts from his sword. He slashed left, thrust to the right, spun and swung his blade in an arc, circled back around to cut at her from below left, then from the upper right, and kicked at her midsection at nearly the same instant. With his abilities, the blows would have been nothing but a blur.

Somehow, she parried, evaded, or blocked all his strikes. How was that possible? She hadn't seemed this skilled in their earlier confrontation, but she had also been distracted by others attacking her at the same time.

The Falxen leader stepped back momentarily, assessing his opponent. It was hard to believe she was still standing. Standing *and* uninjured after a lightning bolt and a flurry of his own attacks.

The other two assassins reached the woman and launched into their own attacks, Loneblade with a wide, sweeping slash and Twoblades with short, close attacks like the ones Featherblade himself had used. The woman stepped to the side to allow the long blade to pass within a fraction of an inch of her head while she slapped Twoblades's swords away with her own, converting the motion into thrusts toward Twoblades's chest and abdomen. The double sword-wielding assassin jumped backward in time for the weapons to miss their targets, but barely.

Featherblade joined the other two, hoping they were enough to take their opponent down.

From the corner of his eye, Featherblade noticed the red-haired man lunging at Boltshadow. So they would be using the same techniques the assassins themselves were using: they would flank the other group and try to whittle it down.

Whiteshadow intercepted the warrior, raining blows down upon him with two of her four swords. The man moved like a snake, dodging some blows, parrying others, and counterattacking. Neither of the combatants received wounds from their first exchange.

Boltshadow, obviously deciding he couldn't use his magic effectively with his companions mixed in with the enemies, drew his sword and joined Whiteshadow in attacking the man. Fleshrender stayed back and swung her chain blades at their enemy, expertly weaving them between her brace members.

Featherblade monitored the fighting through images he gathered in a fraction of a second, while he was fighting. He'd had that talent for as long as he remembered, the ability to focus on something but still maintain awareness of everything else around him. It was one of the things that made him such a good leader.

He continued to harry the blue woman, trying to find a gap in her defenses. The other two assassins could be used to distract, to move her where they needed her. All he needed to do was to manipulate their positions—and their opponent's—through his own actions. He struck low, toward the woman's legs, to test the response from her and his companions while glancing back toward the other half of the brace every few seconds. They would win this battle. They would.

A flash of motion resolved itself into the young woman with the knives. She stepped out from behind some rocks and threw one of her blades at the exact time the red-haired man lunged to dodge Whiteshadow and press Fleshrender.

The chain blade wielder didn't seem to notice the woman's attack until the last moment. She twisted to avoid the flying knife, but was only partially successful. She grunted as the projectile gashed her shoulder, nearly causing her to fall prey to the man's blades.

Fleshrender screeched in agitation. Featherblade could feel the heat of her rage from where he was fighting.

As directed, the Falxen, had split up and engaged the two best fighters so they couldn't use the spells they had before. It had taken the man several seconds to cast the spell that had knocked them all down in the last battle, so as long as they continued to press the blue woman and the man, they should be safe from what had happened the last time they met.

The red-haired man moved strangely, drawing Featherblade's eyes. His normally fluid motion changed slightly. His hands formed gestures and his mouth moved. What was he doing?

The sudden forceful movement the man made gave Featherblade the sense of finality. Then, his normal smooth battle movements returned as he struggled with three of the assassins.

Then Featherblade noticed it. Fleshrender now moved more slowly. It would have been imperceptible to most people, but the Falxen leader had been honing his combat skills his entire life and could read volumes in small movements. She was definitely fighting with less speed, but not from fatigue. The man fighting her must have cast a spell on her. It was a small thing, but it was used effectively. Just how effectively became clear a moment later.

The dark-haired woman ducked back out of sight and Fleshrender attacked the red-haired man furiously to get past him to kill the other woman. He rebuffed her attacks, all the while fending off blows from Whiteshadow and Boltshadow. He was good. Very good. Featherblade wished he could test the man out himself, but he had other pressing business: killing their primary target.

Before Featherblade returned his attention completely on his own fight, a ripple of shadow became the boy—Featherblade had wondered where he was—who had moved unnoticed behind Fleshrender.

Featherblade thought to call out, but it would have been too late. The boy rammed his knife into Fleshrender's lower back and brought it back bloody. She screamed, twisting to end his life, but he had already rolled to the side and retreated behind some other rocks.

❧ 35 ❧

Fleshrender was as good as dead. Besides how sluggishly she was moving, without healing immediately, she wouldn't last more than a minute. The possibility of her surviving ended as the red-haired man relieved her body of its head.

The man flowed into his next attack, targeting Boltshadow while evading Whiteshadow's attacks. Most of them, anyway. The majority of his attacks focused on the lightning-thrower, no doubt to keep him from using magic against his friends. Clever, clever.

Featherblade had been attacking and defending almost by reflex as he monitored the others' battle, but he turned his mind to finding a way to defeat the blue woman. Her combat skills were very good, but her magical ability was unknown. They needed to finish her off before she used her spells so they could go around and flank the red-haired man and be finished with the entire mess.

He darted in, within the range of his sword, which was shorter than the ones used by his azure opponent. She was fending off blows from the other two Falxen, keeping her blades close to the center of her body so she could move them quickly to block whatever came her way. Featherblade added his strikes to the flurries of the others.

The woman turned slightly, allowing Loneblade's long sword to cut into the bits of clothing covering her chest. She judged the distance perfectly, not taking a cut herself, but allowing the cloth to flap free, uncovering her left breast. It allowed Featherblade to place a small gash on her side, along her rib cage. A fraction of an inch deeper would have done some serious damage.

She didn't flinch, but continued in her frantic blocking.

Impressive.

The woman spun her swords, slamming away Featherblade's weapon so forcefully he nearly lost his grip on it. So strong! In the middle of her twisting evasions, she shouted a few syllables of some language he didn't understand and a misty, dark projectile shot from her hand and punched through Loneblade's right bicep.

Loneblade screamed and then gritted his teeth, adjusting his stance and his motions to fight with only his left hand. Luckily, it was his dominant hand—something the woman wouldn't have known—but though he was very skilled with his sword, he couldn't maneuver it as well with only one fully functional arm.

The woman spun away, lashing out with her longer swords, giving Twoblades a gash in his shoulder and forcing Featherblade and Loneblade back. She opened up a gap between herself and the men, glancing toward her friends.

No, dear, Featherblade thought. *There will be no help coming from that quarter. You're on your own.*

The three assassins lunged in as one, Loneblade's weapon a bit slower than the other two assassins. That sword she ducked under while inverting one of her blades to sweep Twoblades's weapons away. The other she swung in an arc to block Featherblade's sword and kicked out with such speed she actually knocked it farther away with her foot.

She lunged toward Loneblade, who was slightly off balance from overreaching on his dodged strike. She punched her sword into his left forearm. As the sword dropped from his hand, he looked up into her eyes, his own wide with surprise.

The woman ran the other sword through Loneblade's chest. She pulled it out quickly, pivoting to circle behind him, and slashed into the back of his neck as she backed out of the way again, leaving the assassin to fall toward his companions, a look of confusion on his face.

Featherblade used a burst of speed to get around Loneblade's falling body and cut into the blue woman's leg. Another shallow gash, but those could add up in a battle. Her blood, dirtier-looking than any person's he had ever seen, flowed freely. Soon, she'd be too weak to continue. He needed only to wait her out.

The infernal woman gestured while holding her sword and she spat out a few syllables in an imperious tone. For the briefest moment, the air grew heavy, like the feeling of an approaching thunderstorm.

Then Featherblade's entire world went black.

Though he thought himself unflappable, he had to admit that he panicked a little, his breath spiking in a ragged intake of air and his heart tripling the rate at which it was beating.

It lasted only a moment before he brought himself back under control. The witch had cast a spell on him, taking his eyesight. Part of him wondered if the condition was permanent, but that tiny fraction of his brain was wrestled under control as he fought to maintain his battle instincts.

He was in combat. It was not time to grieve over possibly losing his vision. Instead, he centered himself, closing his useless eyes to regain a bit of the familiar. Featherblade had trained extensively with blindfolds—all competent Falxen did —and he was nearly as deadly in the dark as when he could see.

Not a moment too soon, he let his training take over and he brought his sword up to block an unseen strike. The clang of metal and the feel of a solid contact between his blade and another told him he had done correctly.

The sounds of battle—from the other group not too far away, and his own—swirled around him. The whistle of weapons, the rush of bodies moving, and the scuffs on the ground became all for him as he strained his ears and his mind to filter out unnecessary stimuli. He twisted and threw his sword out, parrying another blow.

Featherblade didn't know where Twoblades was. He hoped he wasn't actually fighting with his fellow assassin as he focused mostly on defending himself and not attacking. He did counterattack a few times, relatively sure that the blades coming at him were not those of his ally.

Was that a lightening of the darkness surrounding him? He opened his eyes, hoping against hope he would be able to see, but he could not. The black was definitely grey, though. If he could hold on for a few more seconds, he was sure he'd regain his sight.

Then he would end this farce once and for all.

Three more breaths, and silhouettes swirled around him. They were only shapes, but with every heartbeat, they became more distinct. Colors began to leak into his vision, the blue of the woman and the flowing black of Twoblades's clothing.

Almost there.

His sword was still defending him on instinct. He was not able to trust his sight yet, but soon he would. The woman launched a particularly furious flurry of slashes at him and his existence became the piece of steel in his hands, trying desperately to keep the other weapons away from him. He took two minor gashes, but they weren't serious enough to affect his ability to fight.

His world seemed to slow down. Rather, *he* had slowed down. The blows raining down on him had a familiar feel. Yes, they were maneuvering him, forcing him to put himself slightly off center, partially off balance. He adjusted automatically, coming back into a neutral position, sword acting independently, batting away the woman's blades.

His vision was almost back. He couldn't focus well yet, but detail was increasing.

Too late, he realized what he had done. In parrying both the woman's blades outward, his own guard was compromised. If she was fast enough...

Featherblade got his sword back in place fast enough to block one of the woman's blades, but not the other one. It slipped in, like an eel striking out, and cut deeply into his chest from neck to navel.

Few of the Falxen wore any kind of armor. It wasn't conducive to their activities. So there was nothing to stop the blade from slicing into Featherblade. Only his reflexes that guided his body away from the strike, spinning him, kept him from being killed right then.

Not knowing if he would die in the next few seconds, Featherblade spun around Twoblades, using his companion as a shield while he assessed his condition.

It didn't look good.

Featherblade used his special ability, zipping a dozen steps to get around a large boulder near where he was fighting. He hated to abandon Twoblades like that, but in his current condition, he wouldn't last long against the woman. His enemies had chosen the battleground for their victory. Well, he was not above using their own assets against them.

He unwound the long cloths he kept around his arms for

just such an occasion and bound his wound while looking to see if anyone had tracked where he had gone. The blue woman was still fighting with Twoblades, swinging her head to and fro looking for Featherblade. The red-haired man was too involved with his own fight to have noticed what was happening with the other combat.

In fact, the battle against Whiteshadow and Boltshadow was coming to its end. The dark-haired woman stepped out from her rock again—she apparently hadn't seen Featherblade escape either—and threw another knife, this time at Whiteshadow. The tall pale woman caught the motion and spun, deflecting the projectile away from her with one of her swords, but it left her open to the man's whirling weapons. He cut her forearm, nearly taking her hand off, and continued to exploit the hole it made in her defenses.

Meanwhile, the boy was suddenly behind Boltshadow, lunging with his knife as he had done with Fleshrender. But the lightning bolt caster was more experienced than Fleshrender and parried the knife with such force it twisted the attacker, allowing the big man to cut him down with a long slash down his back. The boy cried out and spun away, collapsing to the ground.

The red-haired man screamed and battered down Whiteshadow's one-handed guard, and then struck her with two killing blows. His left sword went through her chest while his right swung in from the side and cut halfway through her neck. Her surprised face drooped to the side, eyes wide and already going glassy.

The man spun, tearing the sword from Whiteshadow's chest and lunging at Boltshadow.

But he wasn't fast enough. Boltshadow had already started casting. At the dark-haired woman.

The lightning bolt struck the woman solidly in the chest and blasted her off her feet. The force of it threw her body ten feet into the place where she had been hiding, behind two large boulders.

The bolt-casting Falxen knew he was going to die and had chosen the way that would help the brace. Featherblade appreciated that, though he would have tried to find a way out himself if he were in that position. It was too bad Bolt-shadow couldn't use his powers at close range or he could have attacked the red-haired man. Instead, he had to be satisfied with killing the woman, because now he had the warrior's full attention.

Against such a force, Boltshadow didn't last long. Before he could try to cast some other spell, escape, or even effectively block, the red-haired man's twin swords cut several important pieces from the assassin, including his head.

It was time for Featherblade to leave. Even uninjured, he couldn't defeat the two targets left alive. He gave one last look to Twoblades, who was bleeding profusely from a few serious cuts and many minor ones.

"I'm sorry," he whispered. "I could do nothing but die at this point." Featherblade closed his eyes against the pain and the weakness he felt. "I might anyway."

With that, he headed to the west, back from where he had come, as the last of his assassins was cut down by the blue woman.

❧ 36 ❧

Aeden finished his grisly work with the lightning-bolt caster and looked over toward Khrazhti in time to see her cut one of the hands off the final assassin, ram her other sword through his throat, and then kick him off her blade. He twitched for a few seconds and then lay still.

Where was that tall, thin man? He seemed to be their leader. His corpse wasn't in sight, but as long as he wasn't attacking, Aeden didn't care. Raki's body lay close by, but Fahtin's had been thrown back out of sight. How could he have failed them both?

Raki moaned and tried to get up. Aeden went to his friend, surprised the boy was actually still living. His back was bloody, his dark clothing parted cleanly down the middle. He was bleeding rapidly. Too much longer and he *would* be dead.

"Don't move, Raki," Aeden told him. "You'll only make it worse."

"Worse," he said toward the ground. "I'm already dead. It can't be worse."

"Not yet, you're not."

Aeden quickly ran through the gestures for Life to Un-life, the only healing spell in the Raibrech. It wasn't particularly powerful—what he would give to have Urun here to help —but it was better than nothing.

Aeden's thoughts kept trying to slip away from him. He was fatigued, and the thought of not only Raki but also Fahtin dying was enough to scatter any sense of reason he had. When had he grown so weak?

He clamped down on his errant thoughts and focused on the gestures, making them as perfect as possible. It shouldn't be a problem; he had practiced them enough. Arms sweeping to the sides at chest level, then coming in toward the center, the wrists flexible as if he was moving them through water. He repeated the motions while pronouncing the words of power. "*Jiva. Karana. Jivana.*"

Aeden's energy fled from him and Raki jerked, moaning. Then the younger man sighed. Aeden peeled the blood-drenched tunic apart to look at the wound. It still looked bad, but along the edges, it appeared to have grown together a little, though the wound still oozed blood.

Aeden sensed Khrazhti's presence at his side. She'd watch for any other attacks. It was all Aeden could do to keep his eyes open.

He repeated the spell, and then repeated it again. Each time, it felt as if his very life force was being sucked from him. But each time, the bleeding slowed and the edges of the wound grew a little closer together. After casting the spell a fourth time, Aeden was so weak, he leaned over and toppled onto his side.

"Enough, Aeden," Raki said. "You look like you're about to pass out."

"Huh?" Aeden said. Why was it so hard to think?

"I'll be fine now," Raki continued. "Rest. Where's Fahtin?"

Fahtin! Aeden inspected Raki's wound one more time.

The bleeding had all but stopped and the injury looked much better. But Fahtin?

He lurched to his feet, though he didn't know where he found the strength. How long had he been working on Raki? It seemed like hours. Where had Fahtin's body—he stifled a sob at the thought—been thrown? Maybe he could heal her, too.

The world tilted and he felt himself falling. A pair of strong hands caught him and pulled him into a supporting embrace.

Blue hands.

Aeden blinked and turned his head, finding Khrazhti's glowing eyes staring into his.

"You are weak. You must be careful."

"Fahtin," was all he could manage to say.

"I will help you. Come with me." She put her arm around him and held him up as they stumbled toward where Fahtin had fallen.

When they rounded the rock she had been using as cover during the battle, they both stopped abruptly.

Fahtin was sitting up, a dazed look on her face, but otherwise apparently unharmed. She spotted her two friends coming toward her and smiled. It quickly fell off her face as she took in their condition. Both Aeden and Khrazhti were bleeding, and the way Aeden swayed on his feet, even with Khrazhti's support, was not lost on the young Gypta.

"Oh, Aeden," Fahtin said, squeezing her eyes shut and then blinking them rapidly a few times. "Are you okay?"

"Fahtin," was all he could think to say.

"Here, let me help you. I'm a bit dizzy, but I think I'm in better shape than you at the moment."

Aeden traded a confused look with Khrazhti.

"Fahtin, I saw you struck by lightning. The bolt hit you square in the chest. How are you still alive?"

The worry on Fahtin's face grew even more pronounced. She drew her eyebrows down, narrowing her eyes at him. "I... I just saw a flash. It must have missed me and thrown me off my feet. Stunned me."

"No," Aeden said. "I *saw* it hit you. You were struck by magical lightning, and it knocked you aside like you were a twig. Look at your clothes. They're singed."

Fahtin looked down at her chest and twitched as she touched the singed edges. There was a hole burned clear through her clothing. She pulled her top away from her chest and looked down.

"My skin isn't burned. It doesn't even look bruised or red. Aeden, what's going on? How could I have survived that? Khrazhti, did you put one of your shields on me or something?"

"No, Fahtin. I did nothing. I do not know how you withstood the magic, but I am glad you did. We feared that you had perished."

"Perished?" Fahtin frowned at the word. "Hey, where's Raki? Still blending into the shadows? Did we win?"

"He...he is in bad shape," Aeden said. "They cut him down. Can you walk? We have to go check on him. I tried to heal him, but I don't have the strength to do it right. Not just now. I'm hoping what I did will allow him to survive."

"Cut down? Yes, yes, I can walk. Here, let me help you. You look horrible, Aeden. And Khrazhti, you don't look much better. You are both bleeding."

Aeden turned on his heels and headed back to Raki. He would try to figure out how Fahtin survived, but later. Right now, his friend was still in danger. He had to do whatever he could to help.

The three went back to where Raki lay, the two women helping Aeden, who was too weak to walk on his own. Once there, Fahtin cleaned the blood from the young Gypta so she could inspect the wounds.

"So much blood," she said. "I can't believe you're still alive after losing so much."

Raki smiled weakly. "Me either. If it wasn't for Aeden, I wouldn't be."

Aeden was surprised by Raki's cuts. He hadn't been able to see them clearly before because of all the blood. Now, with Raki's back cleaned off, he could see that the largest cut, all the way down the young man's back, had closed up. It was still pink and tender, but it no longer leaked blood. He only had a few other wounds—he had mostly kept out of the battle—but those were already healed enough that Aeden could barely see where they were.

"How are you feeling?" Fahtin asked.

"I'm tired," Raki said, "and my back still hurts. A lot. I'm alive, though."

"I am sorry to mention this," Khrazhti broke in, "but perhaps we should move away from the bodies. When I was here before, I observed scavengers and predatory animals. I do not want to have to fight again so soon, if it can be helped."

"But Aeden and Raki aren't in any shape to move," Fahtin said.

Aeden sighed. "No, she's right. We can move a little." He looked around them, searching for a good place to go. "Ah, there's another tower right there, just up that little hill. That will be perfect for us to rest and heal up a little before going on. I'll feel much better with walls around me and a single point of entry that can be guarded."

Fahtin bit at her lower lip. She looked like she was going to say something she didn't want to.

Aeden put a hand up. "It's fine, Fahtin. We'll move slowly. It's not far. Then we'll rest."

It took what seemed like the rest of the day to make it to the tower. By the time they stumbled in through the door, Aeden's head was buzzing and the world spun. He collapsed two steps into the entry room and lay there, panting.

While he got his breathing under control and the world stopped its movement around him, he sensed someone sit down hard next to him. He cracked an eye and saw Raki there. He looked horrible, about as bad as Aeden felt.

"A little rest," he said to the younger man, "and then I'll heal you the rest of the way. You'll still be weak for a little while. I don't think my healing returns the blood you lost."

Raki nodded. "Thank you, Aeden. For saving my life. For everything."

Aeden smiled—why did his mouth feel like it weighed a thousand pounds—and drifted off to sleep, barely noticing Khrazhti and Fahtin moving around him and talking about guard duty and checking the tower to make sure they were alone.

When Aeden opened his eyes sometime later, Khrazhti sat near him, watching him. It was still daylight, so he must not have slept long, unless he had remained asleep through the entire night until the next day.

"How long did I sleep?" he asked her.

"Only two hours. You must rest more. How do you feel?"

"I actually feel better, but hungry."

She dug in her pack and handed him some dried meat and bread. "Good. Eat and then sleep some more. You look better than you did earlier. You must be careful not to tax yourself. If you are exhausted and use magic, you could drain too much of your energy. It would destroy you."

Aeden's head snapped to her, his eyelids lifting as he stared at her. "Can that really happen?"

"I have seen animaru use too much magic when too weak to do so properly. They were forced into a catatonic state for an appreciable length of time. If animaru had life, I believe it would kill them. Humans are not as resilient to extreme damage. Yes, I believe you would cease to exist."

"Wonderful. I hadn't even thought of that. Now I need to be careful with using too much of the magic I can't seem to figure out how to use."

He dropped his head into his hands. He was so tired. When would it all be over?

"Wait. What day is it? Has Benzal opened the portal already? Are we too late?"

Khrazhti shook her head. It wasn't something animaru did, she had once told him. He wanted to smile at her adopting human mannerisms, but couldn't build up the energy to do so.

"I do not know exactly when it will be, but it has not happened yet. I am sure I would know if that many animaru joined us in this world. I have felt the portals opening twice before. It has not happened yet."

Aeden released the breath he had been holding. "That's good, at least. Still, we need to get there before it happens. To make sure it doesn't."

"It will do no good to be there," she pointed out, "if we are too weak to stop him. You must rest, Aeden. Please."

The pleading tone in her voice was new. He relaxed his jaw, which he had been clenching without realizing it. "I plan to. I feel much better with the little sleep I've gotten and with this food. Strong enough maybe to try a couple of rounds of the healing spell on Raki." He put his hand up to stop her from arguing with him. "Honest, just a couple more times and then I will get some rest. It'll be fine, Khrazhti. Trust me."

She frowned at him again—she was getting almost as good at that as she was at smiling—but didn't argue. "I do trust you," she finally said. "Just as you must trust me."

"I do," he responded. "Two more and then I'll sleep."

"Very well. If you feel pain—not just fatigue—you must stop immediately."

"I will."

Raki had been lying near Aeden, listening to the exchange without speaking. Fahtin, too, listened from her position by the door, watching for attackers.

"I'll be fine, Aeden," the boy said. "Really."

"Yes, you will. In just a moment."

With that, Aeden stood and performed the gestures for the spell as he intoned the words of power. He would need his friends in the best condition possible in the next day or two. He never wanted to see any of them that close to death again.

37

Tere relaxed his bowstring but left the arrow nocked on it. The small group of animaru that had surprised them made their way back into the trees to the east. From what he could tell, they still weren't going too close to where there might be communities of people.

It had taken the three travelers nearly an entire day to backtrack and make it to where they now were. From a wooded rise, they could see the bridge crossing the narrow span of the Kanton Sea to the southern part of the island of Munsahtiz.

Beyond that, a vague shape of the town of Praesturi sat in the middle of a larger clearing in the trees. Smoke from the town formed a haze that hung over it like a filthy blanket.

"I thought we'd never get here," Aila said. "The animaru are really out in force. I'm glad they're not as heavy here as they were on the way to the northern entrance to the island."

The words were exactly what Tere had in his mind. "Once we get to the bridge, I don't think we'll need to worry about them. Which is good, because we'll have other things to worry about."

"Things like what?"

"Praesturi is...different. Originally, it was an outpost placed there by Salamus to keep an eye on the Academy and to remind Sitor-Kanda that they didn't own the entire island. After that nation fell into obscurity, Praesturi went through some changes. Over the hundreds of years, it has become like a frontier town. They don't have any interactions with the Academy, each pretending the other doesn't exist. Because of the forest separating them and the sea separating the town from everyone else, things have become dangerous. I'm not even sure who runs the town, if anyone. It's been decades since I set foot on Munsahtiz, let alone in Praesturi.

"One thing you have to remember is that most people there have something to hide. For some, it's relatively minor, but for others, there is blood in their past and they are not fond of others bringing it up. We'll get through the town as soon as possible and then through the forest to the Academy."

Aila cocked her head and considered what Tere had just said. "Why don't we just bypass it completely, go around and straight into the forest?"

"Well, we might be able to do that. How's your swimming?"

"My swimming?"

"Yeah. The town spreads from shore to shore on the narrow part of the tip of the island. It's just a small spit of land, but the bridge empties right out in the middle of town and the buildings are crowded together, as if huddling like that they'll keep the people safe from whatever lives in the Verlisaru Forest."

Aila scoffed. "Oh, come on, Tere. You're not going to tell me the stories of that forest are true, that it's full of monsters and beasts not found anywhere else."

"I'm not saying anything about the forest. We were

talking about the town. I'm sure we could sneak around it, though if we're caught it won't be good for us. The town folk have a very special hatred for people sneaking around their homes. But yes, many of the stories of the forest are true, so the less time we spend in it the better."

"Okay, so we can't—or shouldn't try to sneak around the town. Fine. Let's get it over with. How dangerous could it be?"

Tere leveled an emotionless gaze at her. She met his eyes for a moment, but then looked away, but he couldn't tell if it was his stare or the fact that his white eyes didn't focus on anything. He knew they made people uncomfortable.

"All right," she said. "Lead on."

He nodded. "You should probably let me do the talking, since I've been there before, even though it's been years. Try not to aggravate anyone while we're there, okay?"

"Me, aggravate someone? I'm very easy to get along with."

Tere shook his head and looked to Urun, who had been silent throughout the conversation. The priest shrugged and motioned with his hand for Tere to lead them. He had been quieter than normal the last half day of their travels.

The last two miles to the bridge were the easiest they had traveled in some time. They finally left the cover of the surrounding trees and traveled on the road, though Tere's head constantly swung back and forth, checking for hidden attackers.

As they neared the edge of the mainland, the tip of south-eastern Munsahtiz could be seen more clearly. Tere thought it had always looked too perfect for its purpose. Almost as if someone long ago had designed the land mass that way. With what mages were able to do back in the Age of Magic, he only half doubted it.

Soon enough, they stood in front of the bridge and ready to cross to the island.

"This is a first for me," Aila said. "I've never been to the island before. Never really had a reason for it."

"I wish we didn't have a reason now," Tere answered. "I would have liked to have gone over the northern bridge. It would have been far less trouble."

"What trouble? The last couple of miles were nice. No one chasing us, no monsters about."

"Just because we didn't see them doesn't mean others aren't chasing us. The assassins are still out there, remember."

"Oh," she said. "Yeah."

"Anyway, maybe it'll work out that the assassins are confused by us backtracking and lose the trail. If we can get through the town and into the forest, I don't think we'll have to worry about them.

"Let's all be clear about this: I want to get some supplies and leave as quickly as possible. Don't answer any questions. Don't ask any of your own. We don't want to stick in anyone's memory. No traces."

"Sure, sure," Aila said. "Is that the end of the lecture, because I'd like to get something to eat and maybe an ale or three."

"Did you not just listen to me?" Tere snapped. "We need to get what we need, talk to as few people as possible, and leave."

Aila glared at him. Urun seemed to be staring off into space.

Tere started down the road toward the bridge. "Let's get this over with."

The narrow sliver of water from the mainland to the island at the point where Praesturi started was only a quarter mile or so wide, but nevertheless the bridge was massive. It had been three decades since Tere had crossed it, and the sight almost took his breath away as it did when he had first seen it. Aila let out a little gasp as they came down a small hill and turned to get their first good look at the entire structure at once.

The pilings were made of stone and each looked to be one piece. How had they carved those? It almost seemed like they had been poured into an enormous mold specifically created for the purpose of making sure the bridge had a solid foundation.

The beams of the bridge's construction were massive as well, making Tere wonder how they had found trees so big. The wood looked almost like rock, it was so old. The bridge's surface was paved with stone. It looked like a street in one of the great cities, not a construct with water flowing underneath it. As the three crossed, Tere could not sense any movement or any echo of sound indicating that the surface beneath them was not on the ground. Truly, the bridge would last forever. It had already stood for three thousand years. There had to have been magic involved.

There were no guards on the mainland side of the bridge, but there were a few at the mouth of the city. Few people were crossing, making it easy for the three travelers to be picked out. As they approached the four men sitting at the end of the bridge, one of them got up.

"What's your business?" he asked in a bored tone. He was a large man, fit and wearing leather armor with a sword at his waist and a shield leaning against the chair he had been sitting in.

"Just visiting," Tere said. "We're looking to resupply and then we'll be on our way."

"Why didn't you go to Dartford? They're more friendly to travelers."

"This was closer to our path," Tere said. "Are you barring us from entering?"

The man frowned. "No. Just curious, that's all. Don't

cause trouble, and you might not get more than you can handle. Then again, even if you don't go looking for it, trouble might find you. This ain't no soft city like Arcusheim or Satta Sarak. It's for hard men." He looked Aila up and down and got a wicked smile on his face. "...and women."

"Thank you for the warning. We'll be careful."

"Best you are." He sat down again and waved for Tere and the other two to pass.

Tere led his companions to where he remembered there being a provisioner.

"We're going to go straight to where we can buy some rations and then leave," he told them. "I had originally thought we might stay the night, but I think it's a better idea to leave the town and make camp on the edge of the forest. It'll be safer than here, I think."

As he spoke, he scanned the street. It had obviously once been paved and capable of handling several wagons passing each other on its width. It wasn't so anymore. Stalls, mounds of trash, and temporary structures that looked as if they'd fall over in a stiff wind cluttered the area, leaving only a narrow, winding path through it.

People eyed the three, and Tere didn't like what was in those eyes. They all had the hungry, greedy look of someone counting the coins in the strangers' purses and already thinking about how they'd spend them when those strangers were lying dead in the street.

When Tere brought them to their destination, they faced the burned-out husk of a building. The fire had long ago been doused and anything of value carried away. They would be buying nothing from there.

"Damn," Tere said.

"Was that where we were going?" Urun asked him.

"Yes. It was a shop when I was here last."

"How long ago was that?"

"A long, long time. This town was a hairy mole on the face of Dizhelim back then. It seems to have gotten worse." He sighed and swept his gaze across the intersection. "Well, we need to find someone who can sell us some food. I hadn't wanted to do any business in the middle of the street where all the stalls were, but it seems we have no choice."

They backtracked until they were again on the main street. Picking a vendor at random, they walked up and Tere addressed the man standing there. He had his hand on his sword and two other men, both large and glaring at everyone within sight, stood behind him with cudgels banded in iron.

"What do you want, stranger?" the man asked.

"Just to buy some travel food and then be gone."

"Where are you traveling?"

"Does it matter?"

"Maybe it does, maybe it doesn't."

"Will you sell us what we need or not?"

"Sure, if you got the money for it."

The men proceeded to haggle over the food he had available. While they did, the two guards scanned the crowd while glaring at Tere. A grey-haired man, obviously older but still in good physical condition approached, looking as if he wanted to trade as well. The way he examined items at random and darted looks toward Tere made the skin on Tere's neck prickle. He turned, looking Tere in the face, and jerked as his eyes widened. The man turned and hurried off into the crowd. Tere needed to get his goods and leave. The man who ran off seemed like trouble.

Tere and the vendor came to an accommodation, though what he was paying for the paltry collection of foodstuffs was ridiculous. There was nothing for it, though. Each moment they stayed in this backward, twisted town was too much.

"Thank you," Tere said as he traded his money for the

supplies. He didn't wait for the man to respond; he figured the fellow wouldn't anyway. Tere, Aila, and Urun headed for the northern part of Praesturi.

The town wasn't large, but even before they made it halfway to the northern edge, Tere pulled up short.

"Uh oh."

"What is it?" Urun asked.

"Not sure, but I feel like we're being watched. Or stalked. Let's get moving. Once we're outside the town, there will be a smaller chance we'll be pestered, at least from the town folk."

"Could it be the assassins?" Aila asked.

Tere scanned the street ahead. "It's possible. I don't know."

The street they were on curved toward the west. Tere took his friends to the right, onto another street, to keep their northerly direction. The path ahead narrowed, almost like an alley, but appeared to open up into a wider area farther on.

Several men stepped into the road before them, blocking their path. Tere cursed under his breath and looked behind them. Sure enough, others were coming toward them from the sides of the street and behind them. They had walked right into a trap.

The snick of Aila's blades being drawn from their sheaths accompanied the soft sound of Tere withdrawing an arrow from his quiver and then the whisper of it being nocked on his bowstring. He didn't draw it, though.

"Too many," he said. "If we were outside of town, I might say we should try to take them. At least a few of them so we could escape in the confusion. Here, though, in the middle of all these people, I don't think we'd survive attacking them. I don't think it's a mugging, not this blatant. Not unless Praesturi has sunk even further than I thought possible."

Soon, they were surrounded by more than two dozen

men, all of them rough-looking. One stepped out in front of them. The man Tere had seen when he was haggling with the vendor.

"You shouldn't have come back here, Alston," he said, looking right at Tere.

Did this man think he was someone else? Tere looked behind him, hoping someone else was there, someone else the man was speaking to.

"Are you talking to me?" Tere asked. "If so, I'm afraid you have the wrong person."

"Alston Squesik. It's been many years, but you can't hide those white eyes. Did you think the Mayor would not remember?"

White eyes? Tere kicked himself. He should have kept them hidden. He should have known that they were too distinctive not to be noticed. Still, the name was not familiar. The last time he was in Praesturi, his eyes were not as they were now.

"I don't know your mayor and I don't know that name. You have the wrong man."

"We'll just leave that to the Mayor. He is anxious to *speak* with you. Come along. No use in anyone getting hurt."

Tere searched his memories. He didn't know the name the man said, and he didn't know anyone who held the office of mayor. "Who is this mayor of yours?"

"Come now, Alston. Have you betrayed so many people that you don't remember what you did to Dared Moran? He wasn't the Mayor then, but still, you couldn't have forgotten him."

The way the man said Mayor, it didn't seem to be a simple position. It sounded like the man had taken it as if it were his name. When he had been to Praesturi last, there was no mayor, only a town council. Something must have happened to shift the power structure.

There was apparently no way out of going to see this Mayor. "Let these two go. They have nothing to do with me or whatever issue you believe I have with the Mayor."

"Can't do that," the man said. "The Mayor wants all three of you. Come along now. These boys are anxious for some action. Let's not give it to them. They tend to get carried away. You won't like what happens to your pretty friend there when they do."

Aila tightened the grip on her weapons and Urun's eyes grew hard. Tere thought through attacking again, but not all three of them would survive. Hells, he probably wouldn't survive himself.

"There are six men with crossbows aimed at you, by the way," the man said nonchalantly.

Tere picked out at least three of them. The odds were too overwhelming. Though he hated to do it, they'd have to surrender. Maybe he could convince this Mayor he wasn't who they thought he was.

Tere put the arrow back in his quiver and raised his hands. "Fine, take me to your Mayor. Maybe he'll see reason."

The man chuckled as he waved his companions forward to tightly circle the three. "Yeah, sure. He's as reasonable as you can get." Several of the other men around him joined in the laughter. That didn't make Tere feel any better about his situation.

At a wave from the man, a few of his companions stepped up and took the weapons from Tere, Urun, and Aila. It was only a small consolation that Urun didn't need a weapon to use his abilities.

At least they didn't bind them with ropes or manacles. Instead, the three were surrounded closely and pushed to start them walking behind the man who had been speaking.

Up ahead and to the right stood what was undoubtedly the Mayor's residence. It was the largest building they'd seen in the town, made from cut stone and shaped like a fortress. It wasn't there the last time Tere was in Praesturi.

But that's not where they were taken. Tere had assumed and started walking that way, but a burly man to his right pushed him hard to the left, almost causing Tere to bowl Aila over as he stumbled to regain his balance.

Their destination was another stone building, this one dirty and dark. They were brought in through a large wooden door and escorted through a large room and a hallway, down a flight of stone steps, and into another hallway, this one dimly lit with torches that left pockets of shadow between their circles of light.

At the end of the hallway stood a door. It looked thicker and heavier than the one they entered through, but it was also narrower and shorter. It had a window with bars on it and a smaller opening on the bottom, covered with a hinged metal plate.

"I thought you said the Mayor wanted to speak to me," Tere said, already inspecting the prison door for a means of escape.

"Oh, he does," the man said. "He just doesn't have time for you right now. You understand, he's a busy man. He'll get to you as soon as he can."

He motioned toward the cell and one of the other men with him opened the door. Others pushed Tere and his friends toward the doorway. There was no use resisting now. They were fully in the control of these men.

The three travelers entered the cell. The man clanged the door shut and, looking through the door's barred window, said, "I hope you have a nice stay. Good luck." With that, he took a torch from the sconce in the hallway and chivvied the other men down the hallway, two of them taking the other torches from their holders.

The cell was plunged into darkness. All they could hear was the men laughing, and then even that was silenced when the door at the end of the hall slammed shut.

38

Aeden swayed on his feet. Raki was almost completely healed, but it seemed the last little bit of magic was too much for Aeden to generate.

"That's good enough, Aeden," Raki told him. "I'm already in better shape than you are. If you have any strength left, use it to heal yourself."

"Can't," Aeden said, sitting down and closing his eyes against the light-headed feeling. "The spell I know can only heal others, not myself."

"Oh. That seems kind of unfair."

Aeden rubbed his temples. He was developing a headache. "I know, but I don't make the rules. I can only do what I can, at least until I figure out how to do more magic or refine the spell of the Raibrech I already have."

"Still, it's good enough. I feel great. I'm barely sore. Save your strength. We're going to need it."

"Okay. I'll heal Khrazhti and—"

"No," the blue woman said. "I need no healing. I have a few cuts, but so do you. They do not affect my ability to fight. They will heal on their own."

"And I don't need healing," Fahtin added from the doorway where she was keeping watch.

Raki looked from Fahtin to Aeden. "Yeah, why is that, anyway? I mean, didn't that guy hit her with a lightning bolt?"

"I'd like to know that myself," Aeden said. "She should be dead. Not that I'm complaining, so don't even act like you're taking offense, Fahtin. It's important for us to figure out how you did it, I think. Are you immune to magic or just lightning? Did you do anything conscious or did it just happen?"

"I've told you, I don't know," the Gypta girl exclaimed. "Maybe I just got lucky and it didn't actually strike me but hit the ground in front of me or something."

"Maybe," Aeden said, "but it looked like it hit you square in the chest, and your clothes are burned right where I saw it hit you. I can see skin through your shirt." Fahtin crossed her arms in front of her chest, looking away from him.

From the corner of his eye, Aeden saw Khrazhti stiffen. It triggered his battle sense and he had his sword half out of the scabbard before she spoke.

The animaru shook her head. "The magic is building. Benzal will open the portal soon. We must stop him."

"Looks like it's time to go," Aeden said, slipping his sword home into its scabbard. "We don't want to have put in all this effort and then not make it in time."

His friends gave him skeptical looks. All three of them.

"Granted, it's not ideal," he said. "I'd like to rest for a few days, maybe have a warm bath and eat a full, hot meal. Those things aren't going to happen, though. Not until we finish this. We've run out of time." Looking into Fahtin's eyes, he continued. "I promised you I would see this through. We could end it here. Stop Benzal and then take care of the animaru who are still left. Done. So, are you going to stand around giving me sad looks or are you going to go with me? I want to finish this."

He walked out the door, past Fahtin, and didn't look back at his other two friends. They would follow. He hoped they would.

They did.

Aeden navigated his way down the path from the tower. He could see the fortress, still a half a day's hike away. The fortress where their last big battle had been. The fortress where they had found Khrazhti and, surprisingly, she had joined them. He smiled at that, but it was a crude defense against the memories of the hardship he had found in this same area.

It would be difficult to make it to the fortress, let alone to infiltrate it and kill Benzal. Why was it up to him to carry out this task? He still wasn't sure if he was the one prophesied to fight the dark creatures. Sure, he was capable of hurting them, but so were others. If he was a bit better at killing than most, that didn't make him into a hero from the Song of Prophecy.

Conversely, if he was the Malatirsay, shouldn't things be easier for him? He didn't have the training from the Academy —the organization set up specifically to train the prophesied hero—but one would think that a chosen person the world had been expecting for thousands of years would have an easier time of it. To him, that indicated he might not be who everyone was looking for.

It didn't matter. He would do as he promised and see it through.

He looked back over his shoulder. The other three were closing the distance to walk beside him. He met Fahtin's smile with one of his own. It was forced, but hopefully the others found it believable. For better or worse, they would have their final confrontation, and soon. Codaghan, let it be soon enough to stop the madness.

Two hours passed and Aeden got into a numb rhythm,

placing one foot after another. He searched his mind for anything that would help him, give him an edge in the upcoming battle. And he knew it would be a battle. There was simply no other way to stop Benzal from bringing more animaru to the world.

He couldn't, for the life of him, focus on trying to figure out more of the enhancements for the spells of the Raibrech. Would the Academy help him with that? Did they know enough to instruct him on how to better use the magic of his clan? It seemed unlikely, but the man he had met from the Academy, Dannel, knew a surprising amount about not only the Croagh but also about the Gypta. Being able to learn more about his magic without blindly stumbling upon discoveries would be a welcome change.

"Khrazhti," he said. "Why are there no animaru patrolling? When you were in charge, there were sentries we had to dodge or eliminate."

"Izhrod Benzal is not a commander," she said. "From my discussions with him, I believe he does not know how to run an efficient camp...or fortress. Also, I do not know if he has any animaru with him."

"Then where are they?" Raki asked. "There are still a lot of them left."

"I do not know, Raki. Perhaps they are here, perhaps not. Most may still be looking for me to the south where the mark faded from me."

Aeden found that strange. "You can't sense them?"

"No."

That didn't fill Aeden with confidence. They might get to the fortress and find only Benzal preparing to open the portal, or they might be greeted by thousands of animaru, ready to tear them apart.

"Raki, Fahtin," he said. "Maybe it would be better if you—"

"No you don't, Aeden," Fahtin said, as firm as he had ever heard her. "You are not going to make us hide while you and Khrazhti take on who knows how many enemies."

"But you—"

She cut him off again. "You are facing death just as certainly as we are. You can fight better, but that won't make a difference if you're surrounded by more than you can handle. We might not be able to do much, but it may be enough to tip the balance."

"She's right, Aeden," Raki said in his soft voice. "It may kill us, but it may kill you, too. It's our world as well as yours. We're going with you."

Aeden shook his head and sighed. He figured it would go like that, but he felt bad about dragging them into this mess.

Fahtin softened her voice. "Aeden, we may find no one but Benzal or we may find something that will kill us whether Raki and I are with you or not. The point is that we go in together. We're not great warriors, but maybe we can help. Let us do so. We're your friends—family, really. Our place is next to you."

"I had to try," he said. "Let's go. We don't have much time."

They settled back into a slog. All the while, anticipation pressed in on Aeden's mind. They should hurry, but he knew well what it meant to pace oneself. Part of his training with the clans had been for endurance. Too many would-be warriors sprinted into battle and wore themselves out, allowing them to be bested by inferior opponents in the latter part of the skirmish.

He was already so tired, though he did his best to keep his posture erect and move as if he didn't feel like he was going to collapse at any moment.

Just ahead of him, Khrazhti missed a step and stumbled. That wasn't like her at all. She was always so graceful, moving with the elegance and efficiency of a warrior who had trained her body for years. Hundreds of years, actually. Thousands.

When she stopped and turned to him, all the heat left his body. Her face was pained, an expression he had only seen hints of when she was battling with the idea that her god had betrayed his own rules when Aeden had first met her.

"It is open," she whispered. "The portal is open and animaru are entering your world. We are too late."

"*Percipius pental tuu caenare.*" Aeden spat. "*Andorin recoat du acci rudis flagranti!*"

Khrazhti's blinked at him, head leaning back as if a strong wind was blowing in her face. "Is that truly possible?"

Oh, right. He *really* probably shouldn't use the Alaqotim curses around Khrazhti.

Aeden grunted and his legs took that opportunity to collapse on him, dumping him to the ground. Raki grabbed at him but wasn't fast enough. "What do we do now? If the portal is already open, there's no stopping the animaru coming through."

Khrazhti still eyed him with curiosity. "Yes, this is true. Perhaps it is too late for this window of time during which he can open a portal, but if we destroy him now, he will not be able to open another portal when the time comes for the magical energies to be aligned again."

Aeden moved into a sitting position. Raki sat next to him. "But wait. If the portal is open, that means hundreds or thousands of animaru are coming through right now. That means we'll have to get through them to get to Benzal."

"It is possible you are correct," Khrazhti said.

"Still," Aeden said, "we're here. So close. I don't know if we'll ever get a better chance to attack Benzal. As he lets more and more animaru into Dizhelim, he'll only have greater numbers of them around him."

"You can't really be suggesting we go and face an army of

animaru to try to get to Benzal," Fahtin said. "You can hardly stand. No, let me rephrase that, you can't even stand. You're too weak to fight through an army to get to him."

Aeden ran his fingers through his hair. "You have a point there. Still, if we could get to him..."

Fahtin looked at her other two companions. "You're not going to actually let him try this, are you?"

"There is some small wisdom in what he says," Khrazhti said.

"I'm with Fahtin, Aeden," Raki said. "The odds are too great. Let's rest and heal up. We can try again. He may stay at the fortress. Even if he doesn't, we can try to get to him as he's traveling."

"We're almost out of food, Raki. We can't stay around here waiting for him. There's nothing to hunt, no edible plants to gather. We try now or we may miss out on our opportunity."

Fahtin and Raki both started arguing, both cutting the other off and making the entire conversation a jumble in Aeden's mind. He leaned back and closed his eyes. Until Khrazhti spoke.

"I must go to the fortress. There is something there I need to do." She started moving toward the main keep.

❧ 39 ❧

"**W**ait," Aeden said. "Khrazhti, wait. I'm coming with you."

"I do not think that a wise choice, Aeden. Your friends are correct."

"If they're correct, you can't go either."

"I must."

"You just said—"

"It is something that must be done. I have just sensed something...someone. There is no choice for me." Khrazhti strode toward the fortress as if her three companions had ceased to exist.

Aeden stood for a moment, unsure of what was happening, of what Khrazhti was doing, what he was doing. Then he started after her.

"I don't know why you feel you have to go," he said to her, "but if you go, I go, too. I'll not let you face whatever it is alone."

She looked at him, imperious, and then her stern mask cracked into a tiny smile. She turned her head forward and, chin lifted, ate up the distance to the fortress with each determined step.

Aeden kept her pace, though it wore on him. He wanted to ask her what was going on, but honestly, he didn't have the breath for it.

Fahtin and Raki hurried and caught up to him. He knew they would. The time for trying to persuade them to sit this battle out was over. He took simple pleasure in the fact that the four of them would face what was ahead together, though it didn't eliminate his worry over it.

"Uh, Khrazhti," Fahtin said. She watched Aeden breathe. "Could you maybe slow down a little? Aeden isn't really in top condition right now. If we keep this up, he won't be able to fight at all."

Aeden gave her a level look, but she was right. He had just been too stubborn to ask himself.

Khrazhti stopped and allowed the other three to catch up. "Yes, I am sorry. There is no reason to hurry overmuch now, though we cannot delay too long."

They settled into an easier pace for Aeden to maintain. He didn't like the way they all snuck looks at him, almost as if they needed to check on him to see if he would fall. If he was honest with himself, though, he felt as if he could fall on his face just from the act of walking.

The barren stretch of land leading to the fortress had once been a road. It was still fairly level and free from obstructions. Still, he didn't remember it being as long as it now seemed. Would they never get there?

Khrazhti stopped, looking back at Aeden with an inscrutable expression on her face. Or maybe it was a lack of expression. He didn't know.

"I have thought of something," she said. "My spell, Power Drain. It is the one I used to take the energy from the light-ning thrown at me so I could use that energy against our opponents. I think I may be able to use it to give power and not take it."

"Really?" Fahtin said.

"Yes. I am unable to do so with animaru, but the way humans utilize magical energy, it is different. Perhaps I could lend some of my power to another."

Fahtin's eyes went to Aeden.

"Lend some of your power?" Aeden asked.

"Yes. Power Drain allows me to absorb the energy of magic cast at me for use in my own spells. If I am fatigued from combat, some of the magic erases that tiredness. I think perhaps if I change the way I cast the spell, I can release some of my own magical energy into you to remove some of the effects you feel from using too much of your magic."

"You can do that?" Fahtin asked. "Just change around your spells to do other things?"

Khrazhti shook her head. "Not as you seem to think. I have been studying and using magic for thousands of years. Within a narrow boundary of use, I can change a spell slightly. In this case, instead of taking energy, I can give it. I tried similar things in Aruzhelim for some of my lieutenants in battles, but it did not work. I think I will be successful with Aeden."

"Why?" Aeden asked. "Why is it different?"

Khrazhti glanced away, seeming uncomfortable. "It feels right. My...human half, it seems possible to make a magical connection with another human."

Raki spoke up. "What if it doesn't work? Will it make things worse, maybe hurt Aeden? Or you?"

"I do not believe so, but with magic, one is never completely certain."

Aeden caught Khrazhti's glowing eyes as she looked up toward him again. He held them for a moment. It was difficult to read emotion in them because they were so foreign—

all one color and glowing. The lack of a pupil made it awkward because it gave him nothing to focus on. "Let's try. What do I need to do?"

"There is nothing necessary on your part. Sit comfortably and I will prepare and cast the spell."

He settled into a comfortable sitting position and then nodded.

Khrazhti closed her eyes for a brief moment and as she opened them, Aeden felt something stirring in the air around her. She made a flicking motion with her hand and pronounced the word, "*Essendi*." It seemed to echo oddly, as if it had gone straight through his skull and rebounded inside it.

The stirring grew, some power growing near him. He could locate its source now, coming from Khrazhti. When had that happened, that he was able to sense magic? He would have to talk to her about it later. Maybe she could explain to him why he suddenly had that ability.

The power built, like a slow glow that gradually grew brighter, though there wasn't any visible light to her magic. Then she released it and it slammed into him.

The cool energy washed through him, not chilly but definitely not warm either. As it raced through his body, it left in its wake a refreshing feeling of vitality. It only took seconds, but at the end of it, his wide eyes found Khrazhti's and he sucked in air in a gasp.

He felt incredible.

"Wow."

"From your reaction, I assume it has worked," she said. "I am glad."

Aeden clenched his fist and released it, feeling as strong and well-rested as if he had slept a whole night. He was still sore and injured, but his tiredness was a thing of the past.

"Thank you," he said. "All my fatigue is gone."

"It was as I hoped."

"Did you...tire yourself out by doing that?"

"No. It used but a small amount of my magical reservoir. It will replenish very soon. I will be as fit for combat as I was before the spell in no time, definitely before we reach the fortress."

"You're going to have to explain it to me when we're finished here. It might help me make sense of some of my own magic."

She smiled at him, something she was getting more adept at. "Yes, we will discuss many things. For now, though, we must go. Will you be able to travel at a faster pace now?"

"Absolutely. But first, everyone bring out your weapons. I'll imbue them with life energy so they can harm the animaru we're sure to find in there. It won't have any effect on Benzal, but it'll help us with the troops he's bringing over from Aruzhelim."

They did as he asked, and he cast Light to Conquer Darkness on all the weapons. A soft white light settled over all of them and then slowly faded, sinking into the items.

As they made their way toward the fortress, Aeden recalled the last time he had been there, not so long ago. Then, he had all his friends around him; now, he had only his two original travel mates and his newest friend who had been their enemy then. It was strange.

Another thing that was strange was how empty the place seemed. Deserted. Aeden's eyes constantly scanned the surroundings, all barren land with a few low-standing ruins scattered about. There wasn't much to hide behind, but still he looked.

"Where is everyone?" Raki asked, his voice cracking at the end as if his mouth was dried out.

"I was wondering the same thing," Fahtin said. "Are we walking into a trap?"

"I'm sure they're here," Aeden responded. "Keep your guard up."

Their steps echoed on the stones of the walkway as they passed the crumbling walls, sections of it still high enough to intimidate the sternest of attackers. Aeden recalled walking through the same opening in the walls, heading toward the squarish buildings ahead of them. It was only weeks before. They strode straight for the doorway of the main keep of the fortress.

Still there was no sign of anything but themselves.

With a last look around, Aeden led them up the steps into the main entrance. Before stepping in and being swallowed by the keep, he tilted his head upward at the main spire. It seemed to touch the clouds, a high, rugged structure of stone that had weathered hundreds of years. Other towers were scattered around it, but none reached so high as the main part of the fortress.

They crossed the great entrance hall, silent except for their footsteps. Aeden headed toward the rear, straight ahead, intending to make his way upstairs where Khrazhti had been. It was logical that Benzal would do his work in the chambers built for the lord of the fortress. They were large and plentiful, an entire floor reserved for the highest level of occupants.

Khrazhti turned toward the right without looking back.

"Is the portal that way?" Aeden asked.

"The portal is no longer open," she said without slowing.

Aeden shared a confused look with his other two friends, shrugged his shoulders, and followed after the animaru.

They still had not seen anyone or anything other than themselves. If a portal was opened to Aruzhelim, why weren't there animaru flooding the halls? All he could think was that they were going the wrong way.

"Khrazhti," he called to her as she entered a doorway

leading to a set of stairs. "Where are we going? Why haven't we seen any animaru yet?"

She didn't answer and didn't look back. What was the woman thinking?

A crash from inside the doorway pushed the thought out of his head. That sounded like...

"Swords clashing." Fahtin sped up and almost passed Aeden. He poured on the speed, too, and made it through the doorway just ahead of her. Raki was nowhere to be seen.

What he did see was half a dozen animaru swiping at Khrazhti with their claws. All except one, who had a sword.

An animaru with a sword and with at least rudimentary clothes, pants that only went halfway down the leg and a snug shirt with no sleeves. That was something he hadn't seen before.

Aeden watched for a moment, gauging the combat so he didn't rush in and interrupt Khrazhti's flow. It took only seconds to realize she probably didn't need him at all.

He had only ever been able to really watch her when he was on the other side of her blades. Sparring had revealed to him that she was skilled, but it didn't give the truth of just how expertly she handled those swords he had given her. She spun, effortlessly batting away strikes from the other animaru's blade while evading all the claws flying at her. She lashed out with her swords, cutting into her opponents and throwing them back. In between strikes, she pronounced words of spells that brought dark fire into being and slammed it into her opponents. Other gestures brought forth a wall of force that threw several of them away from her as if she had struck them with her fists or feet.

The only thing she didn't seem capable of doing with her magic was to actually kill the animaru. As she had explained, combat between the dark creatures typically ended in the losers being severely damaged, even cut into pieces, but they didn't die. Those with the twinkling would disappear to their places on Aruzhelim. Those without would simply be rendered incapacitated and their bodies would begin the process of regenerating, even if they were dismembered. Of course, with her swords carrying the magic he had placed on them, she could destroy them permanently.

And she did.

Still, Aeden wanted to help. He saw an opening where he could attack without interfering with Khrazhti's movements, and he rushed in.

❧ 40 ❧

Khrazhti cut down another of the seren animaru. This one disappeared as she slashed its throat. Another one with the twinkling. It would appear back in Aruzhelim, but at least it would not be in this world.

The sword-wielding semhominus lunged in, assuming she would be too busy with the others to defend.

He was wrong.

She batted away his sword and kicked him in the abdomen. He grunted and spun away, obviously expecting a follow-up sword strike. She didn't bother, knowing he would be anticipating it. Instead, she cut into two more of the seren coming at her with teeth and claws.

There was a definite place in the army for the seren. They were the shock troops, the fodder commanders threw at the enemy, knowing full well many of them would fall. The sem, though, he was an officer. She knew him; his name was Dashrim. Most of his lord's officers were the same semhominus type of animaru his lord himself was.

Some animaru had biases. She did not, possibly because there was simply no other animaru like her. She was humanoid, as were the semhominus and many of the other types of animaru. By S'ru, even the seren were. The sems, though, were more intelligent, more sophisticated in their fighting. And more arrogant as well. They used weapons, and some even could wield magic. Still, for a commander to limit officer selection to only one type of animaru simply because they appeared similar to himself, that was ridiculous.

"You do fight for the fessani," Dashrim said to her. "It is true."

"I fight for what is right. S'ru has betrayed even his own commands. If you blindly follow, then you are no better."

"Blasphemy." He charged her with a flurry of sword strikes.

Again, his sword clanked off hers harmlessly as she ripped into another seren.

Speaking with him would do no good. She had never met him on the battlefield, but only because he simply wasn't important enough. Her armies and the one he belonged to were enemies, though ones that normally did not pursue contact. She would kill him, though she felt a slight twinge of remorse over destroying her own kind.

Aeden rushed into the room after observing for a few moments. No doubt he was trying not to interfere with her rhythm. She appreciated that. He had a good battle sense, surprisingly good considering he had not even lived a century yet. Not even half that. Actually, he hadn't lived a quarter of that amount of time. Remarkable.

He intercepted another charge from Dashrim. Khrazhti turned toward four more seren coming at her. She would let Aeden handle the sem. There would be plenty of others for her to kill when they were done with this small battle.

Khrazhti didn't need to pay close attention to her fight with the lowly seren. She had been defeating those without a thought since she was very young. Instead, she watched Aeden's fight with Dashrim

The semhominus could not use magic. He was an officer in his lord's forces, but he was relatively low in the overall military structure. He used his weapon well, but not nearly so well as Aeden. The human made quick work of the animaru, disarming him and then literally dis-arming him by removing his right arm at the elbow. He followed up quickly with both of his swords puncturing Dashrim's torso and leaving the other side of his body. As Aeden drew his swords out and let the body fall, Khrazhti finished off the last of her opponents.

The room grew silent, no words from her or the humans, nothing else to break the stillness.

Aeden cleaned his blades on Dashrim's clothing and looked around as Fahtin retrieved the knives she had thrown. Raki appeared in the corner of the room.

"This one used weapons," Aeden said, kicking the corpse. "I haven't met too many that do."

"Semhominus," Khrazhti said. "There were few that came to this world when I arrived. They are more powerful, a higher caste. Is that the correct word? Caste?"

"Yes. So, there are different types of animaru?"

"Of course. Are there not different types of humans?"

Aeden cocked his head at her. "No. I mean, yes, but no. There are different varieties of humans, but just color or small physical difference. We're still the same. I've fought animaru that were like snakes, with scales and everything."

"Colechna," Khrazhti said.

"That goes beyond just different types. It's like they're a whole different species."

"Perhaps. One thing you must understand is that transporting animaru here requires vast magical energy. Of this energy, the more powerful animaru require more to come here. Because of this, we started with bringing over mostly seren, the ones you are familiar with. The few more powerful were brought here to command.

"I believe that Izhrod Benzal has decided to begin bringing more powerful warriors through, even if it means bringing a smaller number overall."

"I understand," Aeden said. "And...that's worse, or is it better than before?"

Khrazhti sniffed. "That depends. Would you rather fight a hundred of these," she pointed to the seren lying on the floor, "or ten like me?"

He gulped audibly. "I see your point."

She was going to tell him more, explain what she suspected they would find above them in the tower, but another group of seren charged them from the hall connecting to the stairwell.

"We will talk later." She turned to meet the new attackers. There was no reason to charge them. Let them come to her.

They made quick work of the group, though it was larger than the one before it. There was no officer with them, and all three of the humans joined Khrazhti in fighting. When the last seren fell, she headed toward the stairs. There would be more, but she might as well fight them on her way up rather than waiting for them.

They had barely gone two dozen steps before the next group came at them. If she had been at the top, she would have rolled rocks down the stairs or done something else to take advantage of the higher ground. But seren, though good enough to use as shock troops, were not suited to thinking or using tools. She had tried for nearly a hundred years to get small groups of them to use weapons, but to no avail. When real conflict came, they dropped the tools she had made them train with and resorted to claws and teeth. She was glad of that trait now.

They made it to the next landing without too much difficulty. She and Aeden took the lead so the other two would not be put at too much risk. Still, they all suffered a few small injuries, inevitable in such a confined space with a large number of attackers.

Their rush up the stairs was punctuated with short, intense battles, most of them with different numbers of the seren animaru.

"We should be getting near the top soon," Aeden said. He was breathing hard, but not panting. Considering what he had been through in the last several days and how drained of life force he had been earlier, Khrazhti was surprised he kept pace with her. All three of them did.

She had hoped they could not.

"Perhaps you and Fahtin and Raki should not continue," she said as they finished off the last two seren in the latest engagement.

Aeden looked at her like she had spoken in another language. She reviewed in her mind what words she had used, since she was still not completely confident in her understanding of this Ruthrin language. No, she believed she had spoken correctly. He must have been questioning her reasons.

"It is...dangerous. Soon, we will encounter more powerful foes. I do not want to see any of you injured further."

"Khrazhti, we would continue even if you didn't. We failed to get to Benzal in time to keep him from opening the portal, but if we can stop him now, there won't be any more portals opened. We'll win eventually, even if it takes a little longer to beat the animaru he brought over today. But we have to stop him."

She wondered if she should tell him that they were likely not going to where Benzal was. She couldn't sense the human, not strongly. Not with the interference from the other one she sensed. Perhaps if she told Aeden, he would grow angry and leave to find Benzal.

That was what she wanted, for him to leave, but still she did not tell him. She did not like the thought of him being angry at her. Why did she feel like that? It made no sense. Still, she held her tongue, put her head down, and ran into the hallway toward the next set of stairs.

Khrazhti reached the penultimate level of the minor tower they were in. She remembered the room she entered, one of the larger chambers in the tower. She had assumed she'd find who she was looking for at the top, but she was disappointed once again.

"Khrazhti," a voice she recognized said.

An animaru slightly taller than her strode into the chamber, two dozen others with him, including two more officers.

"Visgot," she said. "You've changed. You look more like him than before."

"Yes. It has not hurt my elevation in his army. He will be anxious to see you." He spared a glance for Aeden and the other two humans and sneered. "It is too bad all he will be able to see is a corpse."

With a motion of his hand, the other animaru charged her human companions as he drew a long, two-handed sword and stalked toward Khrazhti.

She growled in her throat. Changing one's appearance to gain favor from a superior who was biased toward those looking like himself? It just went to show how different her army had been from the typical animaru forces. Well, the army she used to have, in any case.

She pretended the officer she fought was his lord and launched herself at him.

The clash of metal and the vibration that traveled down her sword as she diverted Visgot's weapons, the whistle of steel as it cut through the air, the grunting breaths coming from her opponent, these things removed her from all other thoughts. She let her instincts, honed through hundreds of years of practice, take over.

It was no contest.

She deflected an overhead diagonal strike with her left sword, pivoted and moved inside to cut at her opponent's arm. He leapt back, earning only a shallow cut instead of one that would have ended the confrontation quickly.

Khrazhti pressed him, lunging in with the sword in her right hand as she brought the left-hand blade to her center to guard herself. It was already in position when Visgot twisted to evade her thrust and lashed out with his own sword.

The surprise on his face at the ring of his blade on hers stayed on his face only momentarily. She had positioned him perfectly, and the subtle twist in her hips not only pushed his sword farther away from her, but allowed her to slice her weapon upward, gashing his throat savagely.

Muddy brown animaru blood poured from Visgot's ruined throat, but Khrazhti knew enough not to assume ultimate defeat until her opponent was completely incapacitated. She rotated her hips again, the opposite way, bringing her left sword down diagonally, cutting into Visgot's neck and cutting almost all the way through before it was stopped by his collar-bone. His head flopped to the side and his body collapsed a moment later.

Khrazhti turned to help with the remaining attackers. Aeden and the others had whittled down their number significantly, but there were still more than a dozen left, including one of the officers.

She targeted that one first—Zhelam was another minor officer without magical ability—impaling him with both her swords as he tried to get around Aeden to attack Fahtin. For some reason, that angered her, so much that she felt joy in destroying these foes permanently. That was odd for her. She was usually completely emotionless when it came to battle.

Fahtin, for her part, was doing admirably. She didn't have as much training and experience as Aeden, but her knives stabbed and slashed, causing serious damage to any of the animaru that came too close. Occasionally, she would throw a knife, but she only had so many blades, so she wisely kept herself from casting away all of them.

Raki appeared behind one of the animaru occasionally, slashing its throat or puncturing its torso, and then he faded off into the shadows again. It was impressive, almost as much so as urtumbrus she had utilized in her army. He definitely had some type of magic, though she couldn't determine how much.

Khrazhti worked her way toward Aeden, coming up alongside him and then maneuvering so that their backs were toward each other, cutting down the attackers in a half circle around each of them.

Aeden used only his physical abilities, as did Khrazhti, neither using precious magic for so common an enemy. There was no telling what they faced at the top of the tower. Even with what Khrazhti did know, it would be better to save her power.

The animaru bodies piled up and then, suddenly it seemed, there were no more to fight.

Aeden nodded to her and flicked his blades, spraying blood and bits of hair and flesh from them. He wiped at his face, smearing a glob of dark animaru blood across his cheek. He looked tired. Almost as drained as he had looked before she gave him some of his magical energy back.

She wanted to beg him to stay here while she went up the stairs, but she knew he wouldn't do it. The other two members of her group wouldn't either. There was no use in insulting them by asking again.

She kept checking back over her shoulder, noting the position of each of her companions. She looked anywhere but forward, toward where she needed to go, but where she did not want to go. It was somehow a surprise when, just before the stairs ended at the rooftop, a figure stepped onto the landing.

"Khrazhti," he said. As if there was nothing to them meeting there.

"Suuksis," she hissed. "I knew you would be here. Visgot and Zhelam wouldn't be here without you. One maybe, but not both."

Suuksis looked at her without emotion. She had grown used to being around humans and the way they expressed the many things in their mind through physical gestures and facial expressions. The animaru were not like that.

"I have been told that in this world, one calls the creature responsible for creating them 'father.' Yet you use my name, as if we were equals."

"You caused me to be, but you are no father of mine."

"I see." He inspected her companions for a moment. "If you kill these now and join me, I am sure S'ru will forgive your blasphemy. I can speak for you. The recommendation of the high priest of S'ru is valuable."

Khrazhti felt her knees go weak. She had known S'ru would replace her, but with him? She wondered if her former god did it specifically to spite her. She sucked in a breath and let it out slowly.

"The high priest of a liar and a betrayer is worthless," she said.

"Then it is true; you have completely forsaken your service to S'ru. Very well. Do you desire combat?"

"I desire your permanent destruction. It is long overdue."

"You may find that to be unattainable."

"I think not."

"Very well." Suuksis swung his head to the left and then to the right. "This place is not suitable. Shall we step out onto the roof where there is more space to allow you to die more slowly?"

Khrazhti almost gave into the urge to charge him. Almost.

"Yes. Let it not be said that I did not accommodate you before I killed you."

His smile, showing many of his sharp teeth, did for a reply. He turned and walked out of the doorway to the roof.

Khrazhti followed.

❧ 41 ❧

What just happened? Aeden thought as he hurried to catch up to Khrazhti. He paid close attention to the conversation—all of it in the animaru dialect of Alaqotim—but they spoke fast and there were some words he didn't know. Something about Khrazhti's father?

Aeden swept his eyes over the animaru. He was the type Khrazhti had called semhominus. He was basically shaped like a human, though he was completely hairless, had sharp features like pointed ears and chin, possessed oversized eyes, and his overlarge mouth was full of dagger-like teeth that looked to be made for ripping flesh. He wore little but a loin cloth, his ash-colored skin looking like a cross between leather and stone covering stringy muscle. He didn't appear to be carrying weapons. Did that mean he fought with magic?

Khrazhti had told Aeden that she was born of a human woman who'd been raped by a powerful animaru. Was this creature, this Suuksis, the one? He wondered how Khrazhti would handle it. She didn't seem to have any affection for the animaru lord, but there was no telling what she would do.

A more important thing to consider was where Benzal was. Was he outside the doorway, on the roof? There was nowhere left in the tower they hadn't been through. If he wasn't on the roof, where was he?

As she followed this Suuksis up the stairs and through the doorway to the roof, Khrazhti held her swords easily, almost casually, as if they were a part of her body. Aeden didn't know if she trusted the semhominus or not, but she hadn't put her weapons away. That was good.

Aeden rushed to get within hearing range of the two.

"Yesss," Suuksis drawled. "This is much better. Are you ready, Khrazhti?"

"One of the first things you told me after you decided I was worth training was that I needed to be ready at all times. In the thousands of years since, I have not forgotten. I am ready. I am always ready."

"Are you?" Suuksis said, hissing in what Aeden thought was maybe a laugh. "Are you ready for this?"

Animaru poured out from behind some heaps of broken materials and the structure holding the landing and the top of the stairs. Dozens of them, three of them carrying weapons. Suuksis produced twin swords from somewhere and advanced on Khrazhti.

"Coward," Khrazhti growled.

"Not at all. It is the wise thing. Would you expect me to fight you *and* your friends by myself? That would be stupidity itself."

Khrazhti and her father clashed, but Aeden focused on the animaru coming at him, especially the higher-level ones with swords. Besides, they all looked to be the same type of animaru as Khrazhti's father. He would need to take them out first in case they could use magic.

Suuksis did have some semblance of honor. None of the others attacked Khrazhti. He fought her alone. Aeden was sure his blue friend could take the other animaru in a fair fight. The idea that it might not be fair weighed on him, but he had no time to worry about it as the first of the seren animaru swiped at him with their claws.

Aeden took out the animaru grunts fairly quickly. Their claws could not compete with his swords and the life magic enchantment he had put upon them. He cut the fourth one down as the three weapon-wielding animaru reached him. One had twin swords, like the one fighting Khrazhti, while the other two had single swords that were longer, one a massive two-handed blade. That one wouldn't be nearly as fast as the others.

He weaved through the attacks, parrying a single sword, evading the large one, and forcefully blocking aside the two swords wielded by the one animaru. As he twisted between attacking blades, he managed to cut the hand of one of the single blade wielders. Not enough to disarm or incapacitate it, but enough to give his opponents notice that he was no easy target.

He spun and launched a flurry of blows at the animaru using the large sword. As expected, the dark creature couldn't move his weapon in time to block both of Aeden's swords. He scored another cut, this one to the animaru's left upper arm. The oversized blade dipped momentarily and then snapped back into a guard position. It did so more slowly than before.

Taking advantage of the hole he had created, Aeden ducked a blade from one of the others, deflected a sword from another, and rammed his shoulder into the opponent he had just cut. The look of surprise on the animaru's face as he was forced off his feet was priceless.

Aeden spun, using the momentum to kick out at the other animaru wielding a single sword. The human's foot sailed above the sword the creature had dipped to block

Aeden's blade and connected with the animaru's head, knocking it back a step and throwing off its balance.

In the fraction of a second it took Aeden to reorient himself, he noticed movement in the edge of his peripheral vision. The enemy he had cut was running. Away from the fight. Good, it would be easier to take out the other two if there wasn't a third to help them. He just...

His thoughts stopped cold as he noticed its direction. It wasn't fleeing, it was charging.

Toward Fahtin.

"*Gealich claidhimh d'araesh slaoch*. No you don't." Aeden drew back and then whipped his arm forward, throwing one of his swords. He could hear the voice of his clan battle trainer, Tuach. *Never throw one of your weapons unless you have several spares. Even if you hit your target, you will put yourself at risk.*

He didn't see that he had any choice. He was too far to chase the animaru down, though he was running full out toward the monster as he threw. Fahtin had been ignored for the most part up until that moment, all the animaru deciding he was the bigger threat and swarming him.

He couldn't let one of these three get to her. She wasn't ready for that. As it was, she was having trouble with the seren, and another had taken an interest and was heading for her. Where was Raki?

Another flash of movement and Aeden caught a glimpse of the young man slashing at the animaru heading for Fahtin. The creature dropped to the ground, hamstrung, and Raki blended into the scenery again. Good, he was looking out for Fahtin also.

Aeden's sword flew true, but at the last moment, his target twisted and almost dodged the weapon. It didn't stick in any part of its body, but as the monster tried to evade it, the blade cut a glancing blow as it passed, slicing open the animaru's shoulder and spinning the dark creature so it stumbled, allowing Aeden to catch up to it.

He scooped up his thrown blade and attacked with both his weapons. A few sword strokes later and the animaru lay dead on the ground, not twenty feet from Fahtin.

Unfortunately, the other two animaru officers—and at least half a dozen of the grunts—chased after Aeden as quickly as he chased after their companion. A line of blazing pain traced its way down the side of Aeden's back, a gift from the first of the creatures to reach him before he could turn.

On instinct, Aeden threw his weight forward to gain some space and rotated his body to strike out at the enemies behind him. One of the weapon-wielding animaru deflected one of Aeden's swords but with the other, he tore into one of the lesser animaru, opening its torso up from collar bone to navel. If animaru had navels.

He regained his balance before most of his opponents did, lashing out to keep them from swarming him and blocking the swords of the weapon-wielders.

Aeden's sword licked out, leaving bloody lines on his opponents, but they were wearing him down. Blood trickled down his back, though thankfully it wasn't rapid. He spun, weaved, cut, and blocked, trying to regain control of the battle, not sure what Fahtin or Raki, or even Khrazhti were doing.

The two sword-wielders began to push him, boxing him in on two sides, using their seren as obstacles to keep him from moving away and evading their blows. It was only a matter of time until one of them snuck in a lucky blow and tipped the battle enough to overwhelm him. His thoughts darted about in his head, searching for an edge, anything to help him.

His magic!

He often forgot about the spells he already knew, not being so used to using them in combat. His mind raced.

Which would he use? The simple spells of the Raibrech he was taught were largely worthless in combat because they were either too weak, the gestures too complex to perform during intense physical combat, or they took too long to be useful.

One of the enhanced spells he had figured out might be more useful, but he could also tire himself using one at the wrong time. If he was a fraction slower, in his current circumstances, he would soon be dead.

As his mind locked onto one suitable spell, the two animaru officers and four seren charged in with frenzied fury. It was all Aeden could do to fend off their attacks, in which he was not completely successful. He sported a few new wounds when their flurries dissolved into normal combat.

The two with weapons showed fatigue. There was no better time for Aeden to try something.

He flipped his left sword around and jammed it into the scabbard on his back to free up his hand. He immediately began rolling his wrist at the proper angle while speaking the words of power he would need, all while parrying incoming strikes with his other blade and keeping a relatively low stance to root himself in the magic of Dizhelim itself.

It seemed an eternity to complete the gestures and the words. Aeden felt the magic building as he progressed until, finally, he was ready. He batted away a sword and two clawed hands and then flicked his hand toward the animaru with double swords as the last word was still in the air.

"*Ushma.*"

The animaru froze in place midswing. Its eyes went wide, obviously not understanding what was happening.

Aeden put an end to its confusion before the effect wore off. Dodging the single blade of the other animaru officer, as well as two more claws swiping at him, he cut into the motionless enemy with a backhand slash of his right sword and followed up by drawing and slicing with his left sword in one continuous motion.

The animaru's insides spilled out of its split torso. As the spell wore off, the body followed, swords dropping from dead hands.

For his victory, Aeden got a wicked slash down his left forearm as he wasn't able to completely dodge the remaining sword. His hand weakened, but he was still able to maintain a grip on his sword. He would need to finish the other officer quickly. He wouldn't last long.

Aeden cut down another seren and pivoted to face the sword-bearer. The creature bared its teeth at him, at the same time too human and also not human enough. The Croagh blew out a breath and prepared to finish.

The animaru officer's eyes went wide as a shadow behind it flickered with motion. The monster fell forward to reveal Raki, his daggers slipping from its lower back and the back of its neck as it fell.

Aeden brought his sword up to his forehead in salute to his friend and then started carving his way through the grunt animaru surrounding him. Raki faded from his view as he cast one final look to his friend.

The remaining creatures were easier to kill, but there were still more than a dozen of them. He snuck a look at Khrazhti's battle in between opponents.

It didn't look good.

❧ 42 ☙

Suuksis was not as good as Khrazhti in physical combat. He barely blocked her strikes and showed several cuts already. But as Aeden watched in the brief snippets of combat he could afford to view, the contest between the father and daughter changed.

Suuksis's shadow projected out from him and seemed to solidify. He stopped relying so much on physical attacks and began shouting words that—even if he was close enough to hear them clearly—didn't make any sense to Aeden. With each word of power, he battered at Khrazhti. One powerful, invisible strike threw her back and tore the sword from her left hand, leaving her only one blade.

Aeden savagely attacked the animaru between him and Khrazhti, trying to reach her before Suuksis destroyed her. He didn't know why he thought it was possible, since animaru had never been able to end one another permanently before, but Khrazhti was half human. He didn't want to take the chance that Suuksis could accomplish the task with that dark magic of his.

Cutting, kicking animaru out of his way, and at times simply slamming into them with his body, Aeden moved inexorably toward the blue woman. In doing so, he became reckless, sacrificing his own flesh for his self-imposed mission. He could feel each scratch and slice, but the pain seemed far off. There was one thing he needed to do.

He would die to accomplish it.

Finally, after an eternity, he slashed the throat of an animaru on his left while ramming his other sword through one on the right. He spun, freeing his blade and taking the lower leg off another animaru. Continuing his spin, he prepared to cut down the next creature, but there were none. There was a clear space between him and the pair fighting just two dozen feet from him.

Ignoring the seren chasing him, he leaned forward and pumped his legs as fast as he could to reach them before it was too late.

Before he had taken two steps, Suuksis did something. A word of power, some arcane gesture, and Khrazhti collapsed to the ground as if all the energy had been sucked out of her and she was too weak to stand.

She looked up at her father, teeth gritted, and spat defiance at him, saying something biting in their variation of Alaqotim.

Suuksis raised his hands to use his magic, fingers curling into claws while his twisted face spat words of power.

Aeden couldn't possibly get to them in time. Even throwing his sword wouldn't save his friend at this point. Heart thumping and eyes wide, he tried to think of how to do what was clearly impossible. How he could close the distance, even if just to intercept the brunt of the magic aimed at Khrazhti.

An overwhelming sense of loss and disappointment grew

in Aeden. What good was it to be some hero out of prophecy if he couldn't even protect his friends? If only he could...

His body stopped, almost as if it didn't need his mind to tell it what to do. His knees bent as he dropped into a low, powerful stance. For a moment, his brain rebelled, afraid it was some spell Suuksis was using, but no, it was something more, something his body was doing on instinct.

A rhythm entered his mind and he, without thinking purposefully, began to chant words he knew very well in a cadence he didn't recognize. Magic built in him. He saw the logical conclusion but fought down the urge to rush. Timing was all, and he would perform his motions and speak the words at their proper time.

Almost as if he was only going along for the ride, his body moved his arms in concert. For this particular purpose, there was no need to drop his weapons; they would not affect the end result. Somehow, he knew that. He motioned, the gathering magic warming him from the inside out.

He had performed these same motions just a few weeks ago, when the assassins had first attacked them in Satta Sarak. He had learned something during that casting, or more correctly, his body seemed to have done so. Letting it flow as it seemed to desire, he repeated the spell, refined it. Improved it.

But he would be too late. Though what was happening was good, it would not coalesce in time.

Aeden forced the thoughts away, concentrating totally on what he was doing. He had to have faith in what he could accomplish. Arms gyrating, gathering magic from his surroundings, he looped them back to harness what he had collected.

"*Chadu, nidar, kavach!*"

The last sound hissed from his lips as he pushed his arms

straight out to his sides and mentally directed the magic he had brought into himself.

A flash of light and a soft whisper of a boom, and the spell took form.

🏵 43 🏵

Dark energies swirled around Suuksis's hands and shot toward Khrazhti.

And bounced off an invisible obstruction there, splitting and dissipating into nothingness.

Suuksis showed the first emotion Aeden had seen on the creature's monstrous face. His wide eyes got even bigger and his mouth dropped open. Aeden was close enough to hear clearly and understand what Khrazhti's father said.

"But...but S'ru promised me power enough to destroy you. He promised." The animaru swiveled his head and caught sight of Aeden. "You! It was you. How did you stop my magic?"

Aeden ignored the question. Though the spell had taken more power than he had to spare, he started his body moving toward his enemy. One way or another, this would end now. He'd worry about Benzal when Suuksis was dead on the surface of the roof.

The animaru growled and darted toward Aeden. The two clashed, the steel of their swords throwing off sparks. It was a frantic exchange of blows, neither clearly winning over the other. After several strikes from each, they spun away from each other to gauge their opponent.

Khrazhti rammed her father from the side, barely missing him with her blade, but physically bumping him out of his stance. He seemed to be starting to cast, muttering words of power in preparation to cast a spell.

Aeden slashed at him from his other side, cutting a long gash down the animaru's leg. Suuksis cursed, ruining the spell he had been trying to cast. He was skilled enough, however, to allow his body to flow with the motion of the strike, mitigating what could have been a crippling blow and allowing him to lash out at Khrazhti with one of his swords.

Khrazhti blocked the strike, pushing it away and moving inside her father's guard to jam a fist into his abdomen, and then danced back out of the way as the second sword came around and missed her by a hair's breadth.

Suuksis's strike continued past Khrazhti, swerving in midair to cut at Aeden, who in turn parried the blow and returned two of his own, one from each sword. The animaru, despite his injury, evaded both.

The creature was skilled, Aeden had to admit, though he was at best Khrazhti's equal. It was the magic that made him so dangerous. Aeden planned to push his opponent hard enough that he didn't have the opportunity to cast another spell. He issued flurry after flurry of blows, though he knew that once he stopped moving, he'd barely have the strength to stand. It was to be all or nothing.

Somehow, Suuksis backed himself out of the position Aeden and Khrazhti had put him in between them. His mouth began to move, though any sound he made was drowned out by the clash of swords.

Aeden wasn't sure if it was possible to push any harder

than he already was. He was so tired. His eyes flashed to Khrazhti; she looked as fatigued and beat up as he did. But she wore a small smile.

The blue woman jerked her head nearly imperceptibly toward her right. Toward Suuksis's left. Aeden understood.

He started to circle Suuksis, as if he was going to try to get around to attack him from behind. The animaru reacted instantly, taking a half step to his right and bringing his left sword around, the sword in his right hand remaining in a guard position against Khrazhti's blade.

He apparently didn't see her foot as it swept around and connected with the leg Aeden had cut. It crumpled and Suuksis began to fall backward. Somehow, he righted himself and kept from toppling, but he was off balance, his hands thrown out to regain stability.

Aeden saw the opening and took advantage of it.

He leapt up, windmilling his body to gain momentum for his strikes. He struck first with a backhanded blow with his left sword, carving a deep gash into Suuksis's neck. The blow was followed quickly with a forehand blow with his right sword in the same place. He utilized his spinning body, gravity, and his strength to slice through where the other sword had started. Suuksis's ugly head spun away from his body as Aeden landed in a roll, coming quickly back up to his feet. He only spoiled the spectacle a little by stumbling slightly when he finally stopped. Gods, but he was tired.

The body of Suuksis the animaru lord settled to the surface of the roof. Most couldn't kill an animaru permanently, no matter how hard they tried.

Aeden could.

A burst of motion caught Aeden's attention. The few remaining animaru saw what he had done. Each of them abandoned the battle and ran through the doorway to the tower to escape.

Fahtin heaved a sigh of relief and slumped. Raki stepped out from behind a stack of deteriorating building materials and put his hand on her shoulder to steady her. Khrazhti put her hands on her knees and breathed rapidly, trying to catch her breath.

Aeden sat down right where he had been standing, waiting for the light-headed feeling to pass.

"Impressive. Very impressive."

Aeden jumped to his feet, swords out. He searched for the source of the voice. It sounded like it was far away from him, with an echoing quality.

There. A group of figures stood on another roof of a nearby tower. It was much larger than the one he was on.

One of the figures stood there looking at Aeden and his friends while the others crowded through some kind of doorway.

Aeden blinked. There was no structure associated with the doorway. Those going through it simply disappeared.

"It is unfortunate that you killed Suuksis," the man said. "He was...useful, at least for the short time he had been in my employ. You will pay for that, but not now. The doorway will not stay open long and I have other business to be about."

"Izhrod Benzal," Khrazhti growled.

The man dipped his head toward the blue woman, an infuriating smirk forming on his lips. He was a tall, slender man with stylish curls in his brown hair. Dressed in what looked to Aeden like a young gentleman or lord would wear, he seemed the image of an arrogant noble. From his leather shoes to his long coat, buttoned over a frilly shirt with a dark scarf and white lace at his neck and wrists, he was meticulously and spotlessly dressed. Even knowing nothing else about the man, Aeden would have hated him on sight.

The distance from the roof Aeden was on to the one Benzal occupied was a bit over twenty feet. Benzal's roof was slightly lower, though. Aeden thought he might be able to jump it, with a running start. If he was rested. And uninjured.

Oh, who was he fooling? In his current condition, he wouldn't be able to jump half that distance, and he would probably injure himself severely trying to do so, even if he did manage to make it to the other roof. The drop to the roof of the building in between the towers was at least sixty feet.

"Ah, Khrazhti. It was such a surprise to hear you had joined these others." Benzal motioned toward Aeden, Fahtin, and Raki. His voice matched his looks, a puffed up nobleman who saw everyone else as being beneath him. "Almost as surprising as seeing you here, even though the Falxen were sent to kill you.

"I told you the last time we met, nothing can stand in my way. I have prophecy on my side. It is not a good wager to bet against the Malatirsay."

Aeden's mouth dropped open. The Malatirsay?

"What is it, boy? Are you surprised? Most people have wrong assumptions about what the Malatirsay will do. If you go back to the Alaqotim wording, it becomes clear that he—that is to say, I—will do what is necessary to preserve as many of the human race as possible. That means helping to bring about what will come to pass in any case. You are foolish to fight against such things.

"But I ramble." He looked to the side of the doorway where some type of glowing contraption sat. "I must be away. We will see each other again, perhaps. If you can continue to avoid the Falxen. It matters little. Your death will be by them or by my own hand, but it will come surely, regardless. You will know what it is like to be drawn into prophecy and destroyed by it. Farewell. For now."

Benzal stepped through the doorway, his body flashing briefly before disappearing completely. Several seconds later, the device near the doorway began to pulse, then flashed brightly as it exploded with a loud boom. The doorway, and the glow, faded away, leaving an empty rooftop and a mangled and twisted heap where the contraption had been.

❧ 44 ❧

Aeden sat, stunned by what had just happened. His head buzzed with fatigue and his body thrummed with each beat of his heart, as if the movement of the blood through his vessels was the most powerful thing he could conjure. He looked to Khrazhti, not quite believing they had come so close to catching Benzal and then let him escape.

"I am sorry, Aeden," she said. For once, her emotions were clearly visible on her face. Her forehead was wrinkled and her eyes downcast, her posture penitent. "It is my fault."

He shook his head to clear the fog from his mind. So tired. "What...what do you mean?"

"If I had not led us to this tower, we would have reached Izhrod Benzal in time to stop him from leaving."

"It's okay. You didn't know." Another thought poked through the blanket covering his thoughts. "Did you?"

"I knew that my father was here. I followed my senses to him, thinking he might be where Izhrod Benzal was, though I recognized he might not be. I led you toward my father and because I did, we allowed the one we hunted to get away. *I allowed him to get away.*"

She did lead us here, Aeden thought, *and we did miss out on getting Benzal. For what? So she could have her vengeance on her father?* He cast the thoughts out as soon as they came into his mind.

"No," he told her. "You were trying to help. Without you, we wouldn't have gotten this far. You're not to blame. We came too late, that's all. Any number of things caused us to delay."

The surprise on her blue face made Aeden want to chuckle. If he weren't too tired to do so. "You do not blame me for our failure?"

"No."

Khrazhti turned to Raki and Fahtin, her forehead crinkling even more.

"We don't blame you either," Fahtin said. "We're all doing the best we can. No one of us can take the blame for not getting the ending we want. The most important thing is that we were here for each other."

"I...I thank you," she said. "Failure is rewarded harshly among animaru."

"Aye," Aeden said tiredly. "Then it's a good thing we're human." He forced a smile. Khrazhti's face lit up with one of her own, causing his to grow larger with no effort at all. "For now, though, let's leave off talk of failure and what we did wrong. We can analyze that later. What I would like to concentrate on is what we're going to do about it."

"Maybe rest for a while and treat our injuries?" Raki said.

"I vote for that," Fahtin answered.

"Yes," Aeden agreed. "But after that, what? Izhrod Benzal is still out there, and with him are who knows how many animaru he just brought to this world. We need to stop him before the next time period when he can open another portal to Aruzhelim. We still have a job to do."

"I think I can help with that," Khrazhti said. "After you destroyed my father, I could sense Izhrod Benzal again. I can feel him, far away toward that direction." She pointed toward the east. "I can lead us there."

"Great," Aeden said. "We'll get started as soon as we're fit. Do you think we're safe here to rest?"

"I will take first watch," Khrazhti said. "You can treat your wounds and sleep while I stand guard. No one will get by me. You have my oath."

Aeden sighed. He would take her up on the offer. Codaghan knew he needed the rest, and for a wonder, he trusted in her word. That in itself was a comfort in a world increasingly perilous and untrustworthy.

"Aye. We'll rest, then we'll set off to find Benzal. It should be months until he can open another portal to Aruzhelim. We'll stop him this time. For good."

WARRIOR'S SONG GLOSSARY

Following is a list of unfamiliar terms. Included are brief descriptions of the words as well as pronunciation. For the most part, pronunciation is depicted using common words or sounds in English, not IPA phonetic characters. Please note that the diphthong *ai* has the sound like the English word *Aye*. The *zh* sound, very common in the language Alaqotim, is listed as being equivalent to *sh*, but in reality, it is spoken with more of a buzz, such as *szh*. Other pronunciations should be intuitive.

Abyssum (*a·BIS·um*) – the world of the dead, Percipius's realm.

Aeden Tannoch (AY·*den* TAN·*ahkh*) – a boy who was trained to be a highland clan warrior but found that life had other things in store for him. The hero of the story.

Aesculus (*AY·skyoo·lus*) – the god of water and the seas.

Agypten (*a·GIP·ten*) – an ancient nation, no longer in existence.

Ahred Chimlain (*AH·red CHIM·lane*) – noted scholar of the first century of the third age

Aila Ven (*AI·la ven*) – a woman of small stature who joins the party and lends her skills in stealth and combat to their cause.

Alain (*a·LAYN*) – the god of language. The ancient language of magic, Alaqotim, is named after him.

Alaqotim (*ah·la·KOTE·eem*) – the ancient language of magic. It is not spoken currently by any but those who practice magic.

Aliten (*AL·it·ten*) – a type of animaru that is humanoid but has wings and can fly.

Animaru (*ah·nee·MAR·oo*) – dark creatures from the world Aruzhelim. The name means "dark creatures" or "dark animals."

Aquilius Gavros (*ah·KWIL·ee·us GAV·roze*) – the Dark Prophet; he lived in the Age of Magic, during the time of the War of Magic.

Arcus (*ARK·us*) – the god of blacksmithing and devices.

Arunai (*ah·ROO·nye*) – a tribal people who lived in the southernmost part of the continent of Promistala.

Aruzhelim (*ah·ROO·shel·eem*) – the world from which the animaru come. The name means "dark world," "dark universe," or "dark dimension." Aruzhelim is a planet physically removed from Dizhelim.

Arxus (*AHR·ksoos*) – a semhominus animaru officer in Suuksis's forces.

Bartle Stouth (*STOOTH*) – the old owner of the Spotted Frog inn; he retired several years before the story.

Bhagant (*bog·AHNT*) – the shortened form of the name for the Song of Prophecy, in the language Dantogyptain.

Bhavisyaganant (*bah·VIS·ya·gahn·ahnt*) – The full name for the Song of Prophecy in Dantogyptain. It means "the song of foretelling of the end," loosely translated.

Braitharlan (*brah·EE·thar·lan*) – the buddy assigned in the clan training to become a warrior. It means "blade brother" in Chorain.

Brausprech (*BROW·sprekh*) – a small town on the north-west edge of the Grundenwald forest, in the nation of Rhaltzheim. It is the hometown of Urun Chinowa.

Broken Reach – a rugged, unforgiving land to the south-east of the Grundenwald. There are ruins of old fortifications there.

Ceti (*SET·ee*) – a higher level animaru, appearing aquatic with small tentacles, even though there is no water in Aruzhelim. They are very intelligent and have magical apti-tude. Some of them are accomplished with weapons as well.

Chorain (*KHAW·rin*) – the ancestral language of the highland clans of the Cridheargla.

Clavian Knights (*CLAY·vee·en*) – the fighting force of the Grand Enclave, the finest heavy cavalry in Dizhelim.

Codaghan (*COD·ah·ghan*) – the god of war.

Colechna (*coe·LECK·nah*) – one of the higher levels of animaru, typically highly intelligent as well as skilled with weapons. They are usually in the upper ranks of the command structure. Their agility and flexibility makes them dangerous enemies in combat. A few can use magic, but most are strictly melee fighters.

Cridheargla (*cree·ARG·la*) – the lands of the highland clans. The word is a contraction of Crionna Crodhearg Fiacla in Chorain.

Crionna Crodhearg Fiacla (*cree·OWN·na CROW·arg FEE·cla*)) – the land of the highland clans. It means "old blood-red teeth" in Chorain, referring to the hills and moun-tains that abound in the area and the warlike nature of its people.

Croagh Aet Brech (*CROWGH ET BREKH*) – the name of the highland clans in Chorain. It means, roughly, "blood warriors." The clans sometimes refer to themselves simply as Croagh, from which their nickname "crows" sprang, foreigners not pronouncing their language correctly.

Dannel Powfrey – a self-proclaimed scholar from the Hero Academy who meets Aeden on his journey.

Danta (*DAHN·ta*) – the goddess of music and song. The language Dantogyptain is named after her.

Dantogyptain (*DAHN·toe·gip·TAY·in*) – the ancestral language of the Gypta people.

Daodh Gnath (*DOWGH GHRAY*) – the Croagh Ritual of Death, the cutting off of someone from the clans. The name means simply "death ceremony."

Dared Moran (*DAR·ed·mo·RAN*) – the "Mayor" of Praesturi. Essentially, he's a crime boss who controls the town.

Darkcaller – one of the Falxen sent to kill Khrazhti and her companions. A former student at Sitor-Kanda, her specialty is dark magic.

Darun Achaya (*dah·ROON ah·CHAI·ah*) – father of Fahtin, head of the family of Gypta that adopts Aeden.

Dashrim (*dawsh·REEM*) – a semhominus animaru officer in Suuksis's forces.

Desid (*DAY·sid*) – a type of animaru. They're nearly mindless, only able to follow simple commands, but they are fairly strong and tireless. They are about five feet tall with thick, clawed fingers useful for digging. They have the mentality of a young child.

Dizhelim (*DEESH·ay·leem*) – the world in which the story happens. The name means "center universe" in the ancient magical language Alaqotim.

Dreigan (*DRAY·gun*) – a mythical beast, a reptile that resembles a monstrous snake with four legs attached to its sides like a lizard. The slightly smaller cousin to the mythical dragons.

Drugancairn (*DROO·gan·cayrn*) – a small town on the southwest edge of the Grundenwald Forest.

Edge – one of the Falxen sent to kill Khrazhti and her companions. A former assassin and bodyguard in Teroshi, he is skilled in the use of the Teroshi long sword and short sword.

Encalo (*en·CAW·lo*) – four-armed, squat, powerful humanoids. There are few in Dizhelim, mostly in the western portion of the continent Promistala.

Erent Caahs (*AIR·ent CAWS*) – the most famous of the contemporary heroes. He disappeared twenty years before the story takes place, and is suspected to be dead, though his body was never found.

Erfinchen (*air·FEEN·chen*) – animaru that are shapeshifters. Though not intelligent and powerful enough to be leaders among the animaru, they are often at higher levels, though not in command of others. They typically perform special missions and are truly the closest thing to assassins the animaru have. A very few can use some magic.

Espirion (*es·PEER·ee·on*) – the god of plans and schemes. From his name comes the terms espionage and spy.

Fahtin Achaya (*FAH·teen ah·CHAI·ah*) – a young Gypta girl in the family that adopted Aeden. She and Aeden grew as close as brother and sister in the four years he spent with the family.

Falxen (*FAL·ksen*) – an assassin organization, twelve of whom go after Aeden and his friends. They are commonly known as "Blades."

Featherblade – one of the Falxen sent to kill Khrazhti and her companions. He is the leader of the brace and his skill with a sword is supreme.

Fireshard – one of the Falxen sent to kill Khrazhti and her companions. She wields fire magic.

Fleshrender – one of the Falxen sent to kill Khrazhti and her companions. She uses weapons not unlike Aila Ven's vinci, blades on long chains. She is also mentally unbalanced.

Forgren (*FORE·gren*) – a type of animaru that is tireless and single-minded. They are able to memorize long messages and repeat them exactly, so they make good messengers. They have no common sense and almost no problem-solving skills

Formivestu (*form·ee·VES·too*) – the insect creatures that attacked Tere's group. They look like giant ants with human faces.

Fyorio (*fee·YORE·ee·oh*) – the god of fire and light, from whose name comes the word fyre, spelled fire in modern times.

Gentason (*jen·TAY·sun*) – an ancient nation, enemy of Salamus. It no longer exists.

Gneisprumay (*gNAYS·proo·may*) – first (or most important) enemy. The name for the Malatirsay in the animaru dialect of Alaqotim.

Great Enclave – a nation to the west of the Kanton Sea and the Hero Academy.

Greimich Tannoch (*GREY·mikh TAN·ahkh*) – Aeden's close friend, his braitharlan, during his training with the clans.

Grundenwald Forest (*GROON·den·vahld*) – the enormous forest in the northeastern part of the main continent of Promistala. It is said to be the home of magic and beasts beyond belief.

Gulra (pl. gulrae) (*GUL·rah*) – an animaru that walks on four legs and resembles a large, twisted dog. These are used for tracking, using their keen sense of smell like a hound.

Gypta (*GIP·tah*) – the traveling people, a nomadic group that lives in wagons, homes on wheels, and move about, never settling down into towns or villages.

Heaven's Teeth – the range of mountains to the east of the Kanton sea, in between that body of water and the Grundenwald Forest.

Ianthra (*ee·ANTH·rah*) – the goddess of love and beauty.

Izhrod Benzal (*EESH·rod ben·ZAHL*) – a powerful magic-user, one who has learned to make portals between

Aruzhelim and Dizhelim. The dark god S'ru has an agreement with him so he is second to none in authority over the animaru on Dizhelim.

Jehira Sinde (*jay·HEER·ah SINDH*) – Raki's grandmother (nani) and soothsayer for the family of Gypta that adopts Aeden.

Jintu Devexo (*JEEN·too day·VEX·oh*) – the high chieftain of the Arunai during the time of the false Malatirsay.

Kanton Sea (*KAN·tahn*) – an inland sea in which the island of Munsahtiz, home of the Hero Academy, sits.

Kebahn Faitar (Kebahn the Wise) (*kay·BAWN FYE·-tahr*) – the advisor and friend to Thomasinus; the one who actually came up with the idea to gather all the scattered people and make a stand at the site of what is now the Great Enclave.

Keenseeker – one of the Falxen sent to kill Khrazhti and her companions. He is a huge, strong warrior who wields a massive battle axe.

Khrazhti (*KHRASH·tee*) – the former High Priestess to the dark god S'ru and former leader of the animaru forces on Dizhelim. At the discovery that her god was untrue, she has become an ally and friend to Aeden.

Kruzekstan (*KROO·zek·stahn*) – a small nation due south of the highland clan lands of Cridheargla.

Kryzt – a type of animaru with spikes all over it, shaped roughly like a wolf but with a longer tail. It has sharp claws and teeth.

Lela Ganeva (*LEE·lah·gahn·AY·vah*) – The woman Erent Caahs fell in love with.

Lesnum (*LESS·num*) – large, hairy, beastlike animaru. These sometimes walk around on two feet, but more commonly use all four limbs. They are strong and fast and intelligent enough to be used as sargeants, commanding groups of seren and other low-level animaru.

Loneblade – one of the Falxen sent to kill Khrazhti and her companions. He wields a very long blade.

Maenat (*MAY·nat*) – an animaru, one of the two assassins utilized by Khrazhti to try to kill the Gneisprumay.

Maggie Stouth (*STOOTH*) – the daughter of Bartle Stouth. She runs the Satta Sarak inn called the Spotted Frog since her father retired.

Malatirsay (*Mahl·ah·TEER·say*) – the hero who will defeat the animaru and save Dizhelim from the darkness, according to prophecy. The name means "chosen warrior" or "special warrior" in Alaqotim.

Manandantan (*mahn·ahn·DAHN·tahn*) – the festival to celebrate the goddess Danta, goddess of song.

Mellaine (*meh·LAYN*) – goddess of nature and growing things.

Miera Tannoch (*MEERA TAN·ahkh*) – Aeden's mother, wife of Sartan.

Migae (*MEE·jay*) – the God of magic.

Moschephis (*mose·CHE·feess*) – the trickster god, from whose name comes the word mischief.

Mudertis (*moo·DARE·teez*) – the god of thievery and assassination

Munsahtiz (*moon·SAW·teez*) – the island in the Kanton sea on which the Hero Academy Sitor-Kanda resides.

Osulin (*AWE·soo·lin*) – goddess of nature. She is the daughter of Mellaine and the human hero Trikus Phen.

Pach (*PAHKH*) – in Dantogyptain, it means five. As a proper noun, it refers to the festival of Manandantan that occurs every fifth year, a special celebration in which the Song of Prophecy is sung in full.

Percipius (*pare·CHIP·ee·us*) – god of the dead and of the underworld.

Phoenixarrow – one of the Falxen sent to kill Khrazhti

and her companions. A statuesque red-haired archer who had a penchant for using fire arrows.

Pilae (*PEEL·lay*) – a type of animaru that looks like a ball of shadow.

Pouran (*PORE·an*) – roundish, heavy humanoids with piggish faces and tusks like a boar.

Preshim (*PRAY·sheem*) – title of the leader of a family of Gypta.

Promistala (*prome·ees·TAHL·ah*) – the main continent in Dizhelim. In Alaqotim, the name means "first (or most important) land."

Raibrech (*RAI·brekh*) – the clan magic of the highland clans. In Chorain, it means "bloodfire."

Raisor Tannoch (*RAI·sore TAN·ahkh*) – a famous warrior of Clan Tannoch, companion of the hero Erent Caahs.

Raki Sinde (*ROCK·ee SINDH*) – grandson of Jehira Sinde, friend and training partner of Aeden.

Repun Chinda (*REP·oon CHEEN·dah*) – leader of the Chinda Family of the Gypta.

Rhaltzheim (*RALTZ·haim*) – the nation to the northeast of the Grundenwald Forest. The people of the land are called Rhaltzen.

Ritma Achaya (*REET·mah ah·CHAI·ah*) – Fahtin's mother, wife of the Gypta family leader Darun.

Ruthrin (*ROOTH·rin*) – the common tongue of Dizhelim, the language virtually everyone in the world speaks in addition to their own national languages.

S'ru (*SROO*) – the dark god of the animaru, supreme power in Aruzhelim.

Salamus (*sah·LAHM·oos*) – an ancient nation in which the legendary hero Trikus Phen resided. It no longer exists.

Sartan Tannoch (*SAR·tan TAN·ahkh*) – Aeden's father, clan chief of the Tannoch clan of Croagh.

Sarya Chinda (*sah·REE·ah CHEEN·dah*) – the young Gypta girl Fahtin saves from being attacked in Satta Sarak.

Semhominus (*sem·HOM·in·us*) – one of the highest level of animaru. They are humanoid, larger than a typical human, and use weapons. Many of them can also use magic. Most animaru lords are of this type.

Seren (*SARE·en*) – the most common type of animaru, with sharp teeth and claws. They are similar in shape and size to humans.

Shadeglide – one of the Falxen sent to kill Khrazhti and her companions. She is small of stature but extremely skilled as a thief and assassin.

Shaku (*SHOCK·oo*) – a class of Teroshimi assassins.

Shinyan (*SHIN·yahn*) – a nation on the northern tip of the western part of Promistala, bordering the Kanton Sea and the Cattilan Sea. Things of Shinyan are referred to as Shinyin, including the people.

Sike (*SEEK·ay*) – a class of Shinyin assassins.

Slizhk (*SLISHK*) – one of Khrazhti's generals.

Solon (*SEW·lahn*) – one of the masters in Clan Tannoch, responsible for training young warriors how to use the clan magic, the Raibrech.

Srantorna (*sran·TORN·ah*) – the abode of the gods, a place where humans cannot go.

Sunot (*SOO·not*) – the mother of the little Pouran Tisig

Surus (*SOO·roos*) – king of the gods.

Suuksis (*SOOK·sis*) – an animaru lord; Khrazhti's father.

Tejin Chinda (*tay·JEEN CHEEN·dah*) – Sarya Chinda's father.

Tere Chizzit (*TEER CHIZ·it*) – a blind archer and tracker with the ability to see despite having no working eyes. He is Aeden's companion in the story.

Teroshi (*tare·OH·shee*) – an island nation in the northern part of Dizhelim. Things of Teroshi, including people, are referred to as Teroshimi.

Thomasinus, son of Daven (*toe·mah·SINE·us*) – the hero who banded the troops together to create the Great Enclave. Once they elected him king, he changed his last name to Davenson.

Tilsin Mont – Izhrod Benzal's spy in Satta Sarak.

Tisig (*TISS·ig*) – the little Pouran the party sees while traveling.

Tollen (*TALL·en*) – a semhominus animaru officer in Suuksis's forces.

Trikus Phen (*TRY·kus FEN*) – a legendary hero who battled Codaghan, the god of war, himself, and sired Osulin by the goddess Mellaine.

Tsosin Ruus (*TSO·sin ROOS*) – the Prophet, the seer and magic-user who penned the Song of Prophecy and founded Sitor-Kanda, the Hero Academy.

Tuach (*TOO·akh*) – one of the masters in Clan Tannoch, responsible for teaching the young warriors the art of physical combat.

Twoblades – one of the Falxen sent to kill Khrazhti and her companions. He uses dual blades and, as all the Falxen, is very skilled.

Urtumbrus (*oor·TOOM·brus*) – a type of animaru that are essentially living shadows.

Urun Chinowa (*OO·run CHIN·oh·wah*) – the High Priest of the goddess Osulin, a nature priest.

Vanda (*VAHN·dah*) – a modern god, claimed by his followers to be the only true god. It is said he is many gods in one, having different manifestations. The Church of Vanda is very large and very powerful in Dizhelim.

Vatheca (*VATH·ay·kuh*) – the headquarters and training center of the Falxen. It is a mixture of two Alaqotim words, both meaning "sheath."

Vincus (pl. vinci) (*VEEN·cuss*; *VEEN·chee*) – Aila's chain blade weapons.

Visgot (*vees·GOTT*) – a semhominus animaru officer in Suuksis's forces.

Voordim (*VOOR·deem*) – the pantheon of gods in Dizhelim. It does not include the modern god Vanda.

Whiteshadow – one of the Falxen sent to kill Khrazhti and her companions. She is a master swordswoman and has no fewer than four swords strapped to her at all times.

Xiphis (*KHY·fiss*) – Suuksis's main administrator in Aruzhelim.

Zhelam (*SHAY·lahm*) – a semhominus animaru officer in Suuksis's forces.

LETTER TO THE READER

Dear Reader,

Thanks for joining Aeden and the group in Dizhelim. The story is well and truly started now, but what will our two groups do next? Tere and his companions are in a dark, dirty jail cell and Izhrod Benzal has slipped through the grasp of Aeden's party. There are still dangers mounting for both groups. We'll find out all about them in the third book in the Song of Prophecy series, Heroes' Song.

I appreciate you reading the series, just as I appreciate any comments you may have. **Please take just a moment to leave a review for the book.** It will not only help me to see what you thought and to improve the next story, but it will help tremendously in indicating to other readers how you feel about the book. As an indie author, there are few things better than word of mouth to spread the news to other readers. Thank you in advance.

So, what's next? Obviously, Aeden and all his friends have more than enough troubles plaguing them. They still need to stop Benzal from bringing more animaru over to their world and Tere, Urun, and Aila need to get out of the jail cell, preferably alive.

Not only that, but there are other things afoot, things that are shaking the very foundation of magic on Dizhelim. Don't miss the third book in the series, Heroes' Song, where you'll not only be treated to more combat and magic action, but also the resolution of some mysteries that you may have been wondering about.

I hope you'll join me for the conclusion of the Song of Prophecy trilogy. There may even be a big surprise at the end regarding where the story might go next.

P.E. Padilla

AUTHOR NOTES

I had always planned on the Song of Prophecy series being a trilogy, but only had a few big ideas about where the story would go. After releasing Wanderer's Song (in the multi-author boxed set and then on its own), I got distracted with several other series. It wasn't until recently that I was finally able to get back to Dizhelim and continue with the story.

Instead of risking being distracted again, I plotted and structured the second and third books together. Then, I wrote most of this book during November along with the National Novel Writing Month (NaNoWriMo) and finished it up in December. I wrote the third book, start to finish, in January.

It took a few months to go through my own edits of both books and then to send them through my editor and proofreader. At the time I'm writing this, both the second and third books in the series are edited and I have just gotten the final cover art for this book, Warrior's Song. I will be launching this book and the third book about a month apart.

That isn't all, though. There is a surprise that I'll keep under my hat for just a little longer. I'll explain it fully in the author's notes for Heroes' Song, the third book in the series. Suffice it to say, I'm excited about it all and I hope you will be, too. Keep an eye out for news about the world of Dizhelim. I hope to see you there again real soon.

P.E. Padilla

ABOUT THE AUTHOR

A chemical engineer by degree and at various times an air quality engineer, a process control engineer, and a regulatory specialist by vocation, USA Today bestselling author P.E. Padilla learned long ago that crunching numbers and designing solutions was not enough to satisfy his creative urges. Weaned on classic science fiction and fantasy stories from authors as diverse as Heinlein, Tolkien, and Jordan, and affected by his love of role playing games such as Dungeons and Dragons (analog) and Final Fantasy (digital), he sometimes has trouble distinguishing reality from fantasy. While not ideal for a person who needs to function in modern society, it's the perfect state of mind for a writer. He is a recent transplant from Southern California to Northern Washington, where he lives surrounded by trees.

pepadilla.com/
pep@pepadilla.com

ALSO BY P.E. PADILLA

Adventures in Gythe:

Vibrations: Harmonic Magic Book 1 (audiobook also)

Harmonics: Harmonic Magic Book 2 (audiobook also)

Resonance: Harmonic Magic Book 3

Tales of Gythe: Gray Man Rising (audiobook also available)

Harmonic Magic Series Boxed Set

The Unlikely Hero Series (under pen name Eric Padilla):

Unfurled: Heroing is a Tough Gig (Unlikely Hero Series Book 1) (also available as an audiobook)

Unmasked (Unlikely Hero Series Book 2)

Undaunted (Unlikely Hero Series Book 3)

The Shadowling Chronicles (under pen name Eric Padilla):

Shadowling (Book 1)

Witches of the Elements Series :

Water & Flame (Book 1)

Song of Prophecy Series :

Wanderer's Song

Warrior's Song (this book)

Order of the Fire Series:

Call of Fire

Hero of Fire

Legacy of Fire

Order of the Fire Boxed Set

Made in the USA
Monee, IL
21 June 2021